THE WORK WIFE

CJ MARTÍN

THE WORK WIFE

We've all been there before: wanting something—or *someone*—we can't have. Whether it's a decadent slice of chocolate cake that will blow a diet, the too expensive yet oh-so-cute shoes that cost more than an entire paycheck, or the drool-worthy barista who whips up this morning's macchiato...the point is, we *can* relate.

Meet Charli. A slightly awkward, forever single twenty-eight-year-old woman who *definitely* wants what she can't have. Enter Oliver. A thirty-eight-year-old executive chef who can't stop thinking about his quirky co-worker, even though he's engaged. Life is about choices, and saying "yes" to one person means saying "no" to another. But what if Charli and Oliver have been saying yes to the wrong people?

The timing isn't right. The place isn't right. *But is it ever?*

They say if you can't take the heat, get out of the kitchen. Charli and Oliver just may set the kitchen on fire.

The Work Wife is a standalone romantic comedy. Equal parts cocky and self-assured, a pinch of awkward sprinkled with a dash of sass, topped with a whole lot of sizzlin' heat, you'll love this laugh-out-loud romance by best-selling author CJ Martín.

ASIN: B07P6DYM42

Cover Design: KassiJean Formatting & Design

Edited By: Bree Scalf, Vivid Words Editing

Proofread By: Elaine York, Allusion Graphics and R.c. Craig

Formatting By: CJ Martín Books, LLC

LETTER TO THE READER

Before you embark on this journey with Charli and Oliver, I'd like to share some important notes with you. To me, beginning a new book is like entering into a contract of sorts. You, the reader, have expectations, and I want to be clear about what this book offers.

Some novels are about finding your path, or falling in love, or good old-fashioned sex. While this story has elements of all these things, this book is primarily about relationships—relationships between family, co-workers, friends, and lovers—and how those bonds affect the decisions and choices we make.

Infidelity is a hard limit for many readers. There is no physical, *sexual* cheating in this book. However, the lines are definitely blurred in regards to emotional infidelity. What defines emotional infidelity is subjective; if this is a trigger for you, please do not read this book.

Still with me? Okay, great.

I read this quote many years ago, and it has profoundly impacted the lens through which I view the world: *You never have enough information to judge somebody*.

Please keep this in mind as you embrace Charli and Oliver's characters. They are real. They are flawed. I hope that as you begin this adventure with them, you can understand their motives, and not necessarily forgive their shortcomings, but empathize with their situation...because in the end, we're all just doing the best we can.

Thanks for reading,
    xoxo, CJ

PLAYLIST

Stone Cold – Demi Lovato
Borrowed – Leann Rimes
Shouldn't Be a Good in Goodbye – Jason Walker
Love on the Brain – Rihana
Before He Cheats – Carrie Underwood
God Bless the U.S.A. – Lee Greenwood
Symphony for Piano, 1st movement - Alkan
Tal Vez – Ricky Martin

This is for all of the people who work hard to achieve their dreams despite the naysayers. Hold your head high and keep fighting the good fight. Don't quit before the miracle.

It's better to cross the line and suffer the consequences than just stare at that line for the rest of your life.

PROLOGUE: CHARLI

One year ago

I'm going to kill him. Sweaty and out of breath, I lie there, splayed flat on my ass, on the corner of Broad and Market streets. Precisely three blocks—three *long* city blocks—from my starting point.

"Winston!" I shout, digging my heels into the pavement to prevent him from dragging me farther along. "Winston!" I yell again, desperation rising in my voice as I wrap the black leash around my wrist so tightly it nearly cuts off the circulation.

People rush by in a hurry. Most walk around me, giving me a wide berth, one distracted woman *almost* steps on my leg, and a few nosier passersby stop and stare with mouths agape. But, mostly, everyone ignores me and Winston's incessant, annoying bark. Save for one person.

Him.

The man who sprinted three blocks from the restaurant and didn't even break a sweat. Not one drop.

The man who watched in half-amusement, half-horror when I collided with the heavy sign as I finally caught up to Winston.

The man who made me gasp—*aloud*—when he pinned me with his intense, cocoa-colored eyes.

"Are you okay?" the man asks, voice laced with concern as he extends his hand toward me.

My hair is wild and messy, ponytail undone. My gym shorts are bunched near the tops of my thighs, and I'm wearing a silly t-shirt that states in big, bold letters "I Like Big Mutts and I Cannot Lie." Definitely not my finest moment.

I want to maintain some semblance of dignity, which is damn hard given my current state. "I'm fine, really, but thanks," I answer and roll onto all fours, practically mounting the wooden sign that boasts "Mecca's Daily Specials."

When I finally get up, I'm colored with vibrant streaks of chalk dust, and the slate menu board has been wiped clean. I quickly scan the length of my body. No obvious scrapes or bruises anywhere. Besides the ones to my ego, that is.

I direct my attention to the dog that prances several feet in front of me, barking and howling as if his life depends on it.

"Come on." I yank the leash with a bit more force than is warranted. If his owner, Mrs. James, finds out about our little "incident," she'll have my head. She's a crazy dog lady if I've ever seen one. Not only does Winston eat a healthier diet than most humans —organic, fowl-free, low allergen, and low glycemic, but he also has standing appointments with his dermatologist, dentist, *and* psychologist. It's a wonder Mrs. James let me within fifty feet of her beloved German shepherd to begin with. My guess is she has no idea how unskilled of a dog walker I actually am. This may be due to the fact that I oversold my dog expertise by, oh, I don't know, a million percent.

But I needed a job, and busy city dwellers like Mrs. James are willing to pay top dollar for their precious pooches to be exercised on daily walks. Never mind that I'm scooping up shit every few feet and stopping to piss on every pole. The dogs, that is, not me.

"You sure you're okay?" the man asks, voice soft. His eyes move over me, slow and lazy. His gaze caresses my skin, heats my flesh, causing me to flush even more. But this time *not* with embarrassment.

"I'm fine." Holding the dog's leash with a firm grip, I lean forward to try to right the fallen sign, but it's too heavy to manage one-handed. *Jesus*, how the hell was Winston able to run three city blocks dragging a fifty-pound sign behind him? I'm properly winded having only carried myself.

The man's fist closes around the other edge of the menu board, and together, we stand it up. His chin tips toward the wooden sign, the corners of his mouth curling into a sexy smirk. *God, he is delicious.* "Care to tell me how this ended up all the way down here, attached to your dog?"

"He's not my dog." I don't know why that's the first thing I choose to divulge. Judging by the circumstances of my current situation, I'd say it's the least relevant piece of information.

His eyes widen. "Okay."

The explanation comes out in a rush. "I'm a dog walker. Or at least I am for a few more days."

His brow quirks as if to say, "I think that's for the best."

"I'm starting a new job." My gaze darts from him to the sign. "At Mecca. Have you heard of it?"

His eyes shine with amusement. "You could say that."

"Well, I was supposed to stop in to drop off my tax forms for the owner. It wouldn't have taken long, ten minutes, tops. Winston"—I jab my thumb in the dog's direction—"had to be walked anyway, so I thought, why not kill two birds with one stone?"

I give in to my desire and permit my eyes to sweep the man's face. It's a nice face. More than a nice face, really. It's a hot face. Clean-shaven, angular jaw, and strong, well-defined brows that frame rich coffee eyes that shine with a trace of humor. Short-ish, slightly wavy dark brown hair that's spiked in the front.

Not that he complains about my ogling. Instead, he uses the opportunity to assess me as well. His eyes skim over my bare legs and continue upward to my waist, ribcage, throat, and face, before his heavy, heated gaze finally returns to my breasts, lingering just a moment too long to be considered polite.

I clear my throat. "Anyway," I carry on, halting my inventory of his handsome face. "I looped his leash around the signpost—I was only going to be a few minutes, after all, and I knew I couldn't bring him inside." A nervous chuckle escapes my mouth. "I'm not a *complete* idiot."

The man doesn't laugh. *Awkward.*

Undeterred, I keep going, "Before I even got the door open, ol' Winny here took off. I tried to stop him, run after him, but..." My eyes find his and hold. "Well, you saw how well that worked out."

His lips twitch, and my guess is he's doing his damnedest not to laugh. Finally, he speaks, "You brought your dog to a job interview?" Those cocoa brown eyes sparkle. "At a Michelin-rated restaurant?"

"He's not my dog." I huff, jolting forward a little as Winston pulls on the leash. Instinctively, the man reaches his hand out to brace me from falling. I jerk back from the contact, from the spark of heat where his palm circles my bicep. "Thanks," I murmur, retreating a few steps. "And it's not an interview," I add, finally processing the rest of his question. "I already have the job."

His lips twitch again, drawing my attention. He has full, pillowy lips. Sensual lips. Lips that look soft and kissable.

"All right." I turn in place, wanting to end this exchange sooner rather than later. "I guess I'm going to go." I pull Winston alongside me and stand next to the sign. Hooking my arm around the top, I do my best to drag it beside me, but it's heavy and cumbersome. At this rate, I'll make it back to the restaurant in *fifteen hours.*

The man watches for what could only be a few seconds yet feels more like minutes. A small smile forming on his face, he finally asks, "Want some help with that?"

"I'm good, thanks," I answer, continuing to struggle. A year from now, I'll look back and still wonder why I refused the help. Maybe it's pride. Perhaps it's determination. More likely it's embarrassment.

Shaking his head, he dismisses my refusal, snatches the sign from my hands, and starts walking faster than I'd think possible with such a hefty load. Winston and I—okay, fine, just I—struggle to keep up. In record time, we're standing in front of the posh double doors of Mecca.

I hesitate outside the restaurant, trying to think of something to say other than a measly *thanks*. Before I can come up with anything witty or cute, he opens the door and begins to walk inside, shocking the hell out of me.

"Where are you going?" I practically shout at his retreating back. He's taking this Good Samaritan thing a bit too far.

He stops and turns to face me, a coy smirk playing on his lips. "Back to work."

I can feel the blood draining from my face, fast and sure, like when you dump a full bucket of water down the drain in one strong rush. "Wait." I hold up my hand. "You work here?" I point at the restaurant in front of me. "*Here* here?"

"Yes and yes."

It's then that my eyes land on the embroidered name printed across the breast pocket of his white coat. A coat that looks danger-ously close to a—"Oh my God." My skin prickles with heat. "Please tell me you're not Oliver Pensen?" My voice rises at the end in ques-tion, even as my addled mind connects the dots. "Holy shit," I mumble, a little breathless, a whole lot embarrassed. "You're the head chef at Mecca."

"Yes again."

"Jesus." I resist the urge to cover what I'm sure is my beet red face. "Why didn't you tell me who you were?"

He looks down at his chef coat. "I didn't exactly hide it."

My eyes narrow in annoyance. "You know what I mean."

He laughs off my accusation. "I was too busy chasing a sign thief."

I scowl again, but he continues to laugh. "It was nice meeting you..." His voice trails off as he waits for me to tell him my name.

Clearing my throat, I say, "Charli."

"Charli," he repeats it back to me, the syllables rolling off his tongue in a smooth yet gravelly tone, and I'm surprised by the effect it has on me.

I want him to say it again. Would it be weird of me to ask? *Probably*.

He offers one last smile. "I have a feeling we'll be seeing a lot of one another."

Charli.

"I'll tell Don you're here."

I nod before he enters the restaurant, leaving me standing on the sidewalk, a goofy, almost shell-shocked grin on my face.

Charli.

They say you only get one chance to make a good first impression. It takes just three short seconds for a stranger to form an opinion about you based on your mannerisms, body language, and appearance.

In that moment, Oliver Pensen made the biggest impression on my mind, my body, and my *heart* of anyone ever before. What I had no way of knowing was that the man who stole my heart already belonged to someone else.

CHARLI

My advice? Never fall in love with a married man. *Don't* spend your days pining away for the most perfect, most handsome, most *infuriating* man you'll ever meet, because his heart belongs to someone else. *Don't* fantasize about his beautiful, full lips pressed against your skin, or the sexy way his brows furrow when he concentrates. And definitely *don't* imagine waking up next to him, naked, wrapped in silky-soft one thousand thread count organic Egyptian cotton sheets that smell like lavender while a gentle summer breeze billows the sheer curtains...

"Earth to Charli." The loud thunk of a cardboard box hitting the wooden bar jolts me from my stupor. Joe, our main bartender, waves a hand in front of my face, and I straighten my spine. "You okay?"

"Yeah." I grab the rag from the countertop, barely resisting the urge to twist it in my hands. "Why wouldn't I be?"

He shrugs. "You looked a little out of it." He hefts another box onto the bar. "Do you think you could cover my shift tonight?"

Internally, I cringe, but outwardly, I fake smile. Sure, as the food and drink manager, I'm knowledgeable about the liquors we stock, the vendors we have contracts with, scheduling conflicts...but bartender extraordinaire I am not. Even if my skills weren't subpar (they *definitely* are), Mecca's fancy drink specials are sophisticated enough to have even the most skilled mixologist scratching his head. Upscale restaurants like Mecca are awash with high-end clientele who consistently order high-priced top-shelf drinks like they're going out of style.

I square my shoulders to disguise my hesitation. "I don't think—"

Joe cuts me off before I have a chance to finish.

"Tonight's drink specials aren't crazy hard." He flings a laminated placard my way, and I scramble to catch it.

Even though I'm the one who printed the menus, I give the list a precursory skim as if seeing it for the first time.

"Please." His eyes droop into the saddest, most pathetic puppy dog eyes I've ever seen. "Xavier cried all night. I'm running on fumes."

"God." I roll my eyes. "Way to play the 'we just had a baby' card."

He chuckles. "I never said I fought fair."

"Ugh. You're the worst," I tease, tossing the rag on the bar before reaching into the box he's just cut open. "You know I'll do it."

He pats my upper arm. "And you, my dear, have a heart of gold."

"It's my gift." I stand on tiptoes to set a bottle of Pernod on the highest shelf, but I lose my grip on the slim neck, and it slides through my fingers. Before I can catch it, the bottle crashes to the floor. Shards of glass splinter in all directions, and sweet, sticky liquid seeps into the tile cracks. The unmistakable heavy scent of anise fills the air.

"Shit." I grab a terry cloth rag from the counter.

Joe bends to help, picking up the tiny slivers of the broken bottle with his bare hands.

"Careful," I warn as he stands and drops several longer shards into the trash. I crouch on all fours, rag in hand, allowing the liquid to penetrate the cloth. An image of Cinderella flashes through my head. Even as a manager, I'm still scrubbing floors. *Where the fuck is my Prince Charming?*

A door slamming startles me from my thoughts, and I look up just as Oliver enters from the kitchen.

Ask and you shall receive.

I busy myself with the task at hand as Oliver approaches and drops his keys onto the counter before looking down at me. I wish I could say my heart doesn't skip a beat. That my face doesn't flush. I wish I could say that I don't notice he's wearing a light cream t-shirt, my absolute favorite color on him because it brings out the caramel flecks of his eyes. But it'd be a lie. All of it.

"Whaddya drop this time, butterfingers?" Oliver chuckles, his heavy gaze lingering on me for just a moment too long.

My eyes narrow. "Shut up."

One time, *one freaking time*, while I was helping in the kitchen because Melbourne, our former prep cook, unexpectedly stormed out (okay, not so unexpectedly since he and Oliver did *not* get along), I dropped Oliver's highly prized *Le Creuset Saucier*. By the way, who calls saucepans by fancy names like *saucier*? Executive chefs, that's who, but I digress...

The saucier didn't break, but the lid bent and now doesn't seal right. According to Oliver, the saucier is useless, a fact that he reminds me of every time he can't use said saucier to prepare his world famous béarnaise.

He laughs again and extends his hand to help me up, and unlike our first encounter all those months ago, I accept the help, doing my absolute best to ignore the catch in my breath and the flutter of nerves in my belly when his skin grazes mine.

I wonder if he struggles the same way I do, but there's no tension in his features. Just a soft, easy smile that belies his age. At first glance, he could pass for a man my age—twenty-eight—even though he's ten years my senior. He's almost forty. That should turn me off. But it doesn't.

As if that weren't enough, there's also the teeny tiny fact that he's engaged—practically married—and not interested in me. Yeah, there's that too.

I wiggle my hand free of his. "What are you doing here?" Turning away, I snatch a utility knife from the shelf. I slice through the lines of cardboard until the box is smooth and flat. "You're not scheduled to come in until five."

I may have his schedule memorized, but it's not because I'm some weird, psycho stalker. I'm in charge of all the staff schedules, so knowing when someone's shift ends or begins is a natural byproduct of the job.

He grabs the bag from the counter. "I have to prep the vegetables for tonight's special."

"That's Jason's job."

"Eh." He shrugs. "Got nothing else to do."

My stomach sours because I know the exact reason why he has lots of free time. "Ainsley's away again?"

"Yeah."

He begins walking toward the kitchen, and I follow with the folded cardboard on my way out to the recycling dumpster. "Where's she off to this time?"

Ainsley, Oliver's fiancée, is a flight attendant. She's abroad more than she's stateside. Supposedly, after the wedding, she plans to switch to domestic routes only so that she'll have more time to spend with her new husband. Yes, I said *husband*. And, yes, I die a little inside every time I say it, even if it is only in my head.

"Copenhagen." His brow furrows. "I think."

"Mmm," I mumble, already halfway out the door, not wanting to hear any more about his perfect fiancée. Most days are good days. I accept the fact that Oliver's engaged to be married. In a different time, in a different life, maybe we could have been something more than what we are: colleagues, friends, and fellow foodies. I accept that he's with Ainsley, and the kicker of all kickers? Ainsley is an awesome girl. *Really awesome*. Like, if I met her under any other circumstance, I'd want to be her friend.

But today's *not* a good day. Just this morning, my ex-boyfriend's engagement photo popped up front and center on my newsfeed. It's not that I want Ryan back. Things didn't work out between us for a reason and I get that, but it's just that everyone—all of my friends —are so happy. At least, it *seems* they are. My social media feed is flooded with proposals, marriages, and baby announcements, while I haven't gone on a "real" date in more than a year. Maybe that's why I pathetically pine after Oliver. Perhaps I just need to get laid.

I heave the cardboard into the dumpster, let the lid slam down behind me, and walk back toward the restaurant. For a moment, I contemplate using the front entrance so I can avoid Oliver, but decide against it. I'd have to walk almost an entire block out of my way, and it's starting to drizzle.

By the time I make it into the kitchen, Oliver's already at his station, head bent down, a mixture of colorful vegetables spread out before him. I attempt to slip by him without saying a word, but his gruff voice stops me halfway through.

"Charli."

My face flushes. It does every damn time he says my name because I imagine him saying it, low and needy while hovering over me. Naked. Skin to skin.

Shit.

Wetness begins to pool in my panties and I shake my head to dismiss the sexy thought. Clearing my throat, I ask, "Yeah?"

"Were you trying to sneak past me?"

I turn and gesture to the workbench. "You're busy."

His eyes snap up, hold mine. "That never stopped you before."

"Okay, fine." I roll my eyes at his teasing, playful tone. "*I'm* busy." I head into my small office situated in the rear corner of the room to grab a new shirt. Calling it *my* office is very generous. Technically, it's a five-by-eight-foot dumping ground for everyone's shit.

When I walk back into the kitchen, Oliver's gaze darts from the black shirt in my hand to my eyes.

I answer his unspoken question, "I'm covering for Joe tonight."

He nods, returning his attention to the cutting board, but I *swear*, as I push through the door, I can feel his eyes on me, right up until the door swings closed.

"I'm exhausted." Meg, one of our servers, plops onto a stool across from where I stand wiping down the bar.

I'm tired too, but more than anything, I'm relieved that I survived the night of fancy cocktails. Still, I agree with her, "Tell me about it. I've been here since eleven this morning."

Her eyes widen. "Damn. That's rough. I take it you're not going out for drinks with us then?"

"That'd be a no." My eyes drift to the middle-aged couple who still occupies the private corner booth. Someone, I can't remember who, nicknamed it the bang booth, or BB for short, because couples always request it.

I look down and notice that their dessert plates are scraped clean, but their glasses are still full. Those drinks cost me fifteen minutes of googling, and God only knows how much data usage on my already-limited plan. I had no other choice, though, because I had no freaking clue which liquors combined to form a Vieux Carré.

What did my Google search uncover? I'll put it this way: the innocent, unassuming middle-aged couple is getting turned up tonight. Vieux Carrés are made with a shit-ton of alcohol.

My gaze snaps to Meg's as I say, "Doesn't look like BB is going anytime soon."

Meg rolls her eyes. "Ugh, I know." She squeezes the back of her neck. "It's their twentieth anniversary. They have a sitter."

"Hmm, that explains the fancy drinks," I say, more to myself than Meg. Internally, I hope Mrs. Middle-Age has purchased equally fancy lingerie for Mr. Middle-Age. Maybe she'll even get a little wild tonight, let him spank her. They *are* celebrating, after all.

Suppressing a smile at my dirty train of thought, I ask, "How do you always manage to get everyone's life story?"

She shrugs. "I have a friendly face, I guess."

"I guess." I throw the rag into the sink. "Well, I think I'm about done here. Rebecca will cash you and the other servers out after closing."

"No problem." She hops off the chair. "Oh, I almost forgot, Oliver wants you to stop and see him before you leave."

Groaning, I ask, "What does he want now?"

"Who knows?" She makes a face. "You know how he needs you for everything." She taps her nails on the bar. "You're the only one who can manage him and his..." She hesitates as she searches for the right word. "*Particular* ways."

She's not wrong. Months of working side by side with a top-rated chef such as Oliver will teach a girl a few things. Oliver is borderline obsessive about which food distributors we use and why. And his kitchen staff? Turnover is rampant. Oliver gives one hundred and ten percent and expects *everyone* on his team to do the same. But after eleven-plus hours on my feet, I don't know if I'm up for his *charming* personality.

To be frank, professionally speaking, Oliver is a huge pain in my ass. His attention to detail is relentless, and I swear, his brain never shuts off. I guess one doesn't get to be a three-star Michelin chef due to cutting corners or laziness. There's no doubt that Oliver has taken Mecca from up-and-coming restaurant to a front page, you need to call six months in advance, top-rated restaurant. Don, the owner, gives Oliver a lot of freedom. A little too much of it, in my humble opinion.

With a reserved sigh, I peer inside the swinging door, and the motion catches Oliver's eye almost instantly. "What's up, Ollie?"

Oliver growls at the nickname, and I have to admit his angry snarl is half the reason why I call him by the moniker more often than not.

"Nothing, Chuck."

I shrug. "You know that doesn't bother me."

A knowing smile creeps across his face. "But Chucky does."

"Fuck you." A shiver passes through me. I'm not a fan of scary movies, at all. Especially ones with grotesque dolls wielding sharp, deadly knives. "That's just cruel." I shake my head and walk farther into the large kitchen. It's loud—pots and pans scrape against the stainless steel grates of the commercial gas stove, and it's at least ten degrees warmer than in the dining room. "You know that movie scares the shit out of me."

"Poor baby." He swats me with a towel.

"You're not the one whose cousin pranked her with an actual Chucky doll and a butcher knife."

His tone turns patronizing. "I'm sure it was all very traumatic." He cocks his head. "How old were you again? Thirteen? Fourteen?"

"I was *nine*." I try to smack him, but he darts out of the way. I roll my eyes and then ask, "What do you need, Chef? Can it wait until tomorrow? I'm beat."

He shakes his head no.

Of course, it can't.

"The delivery from THC Foods is fucked up." He snatches the purchase order pinned to the bulletin board. "I specifically ordered chanterelle mushrooms, not white button."

My nose scrunches as I try to recall the purchase request. I can't remember if I ticked the box to allow for substitutions.

His voice drips with disdain. "They're *unusable*."

"Jesus." I grab the slip from his hands. "You're such a snob."

"Says the girl who *devours* everything I make."

"I devour McDonald's too, so that's not really a compliment."

He places a hand over his heart. "Now that hurts."

Laughing, I grab my purse from the bottom drawer of my desk and begin to fish for my keys. "I'll take care of it tomorrow." I look up to meet his gaze. "Will there be anything else, Master?"

"Master?" His lips tip into a wicked grin. "You trying to tell me something, Charli?" His tone deepens and his eyes glimmer with a hint of mischief. Or at least I think they do.

Maybe I just wish they did.

Ignoring the litany of thoughts flooding my mind, I flip him the bird on the way out the back door, and he calls my name again. Agitated, I spin to face him. "What?"

He holds a long butcher knife in his right hand, poised at his shoulder like some deranged serial killer. "Sweet dreams."

"Asshole," I mutter under my breath.

Too bad he's an asshole who stole my heart.

OLIVER

CHOPPING AND DICING are two of my favorite things to do in the kitchen. I like to lose myself in the monotony of it. The rhythm of the sharp blade slicing through the paper-thin skin of the vegetable, the click-click-click of the wooden handle of the knife as it hits the counter. The perfect linear cuts creating new pieces from a whole. It soothes me. It also gives me a chance to think, which is why, even though we have a prep cook, Jason, and my sous chef, Giancarlo, I still do most of the prep work myself. Some people sit in the dark chanting, "Om." Me? I chop vegetables.

And tonight, more than ever, I need to lose myself because my mind is in fucking overdrive.

It's an irrevocable, undisputable fact that things either happen all at once or not at all. Three hundred eighty-nine days ago, my girlfriend, Ainsley, and I decided to take our relationship to the next level. I popped the question, she said yes, and then she moved into my house the following week. I wish I could tell you that our love is the life-altering, can't-live-without-you, stars-in-our-eyes type of love, but it isn't.

Our love is steady. Calm. *Familiar*.

By the time I finally proposed marriage, we'd been dating for almost two years. Our relationship isn't the stuff of Hallmark movies, but we enjoy each other's company, and give each other space to be our own person. I work a lot, and with Ainsley being out of the country for weeks at a time, the relationship is ideal for us both.

So a little over a year ago, I bought a ring, and over Indian takeout—Ainsley's favorite—I asked her to be my wife. No over-the-top proposal. No confession of "I can't live without you." No talk of finding my soul mate. Looking back, and it embarrasses me even to think this, the whole ordeal seemed rather formal. It was crisp, efficient, business-like, but then, Ainsley isn't a hearts-and-flowers kind of woman.

The crazy thing is, at the time it all seemed so normal. I told myself that if Ainsley was happy with the way things were, so was I.

Then things changed. Three hundred seventy-three days ago, I met Charlotte Ann Truse and my world tipped on its axis. Charlotte crashed into my life, *literally*, with such force that I was drowning in her before my dumbstruck mind thought even to take a breath.

From the day I chased her and that damned dog down the sidewalk, something sparked inside me. It was like a switch had been flipped. Like I had been living in the dark my entire life and she finally brought the light. *My light.*

Too corny? Maybe. But it's the fucking truth.

Everything about her intrigues me. From her round blue eyes, to her pert nose, to the lone beauty mark that sits just above lips so plump and juicy that I don't know *how* I've resisted taking a bite, to the long brown hair she always wears tied up in a loose knot that my fingers itch to run through.

But it's more than just her physical appearance. Even if I weren't attracted to her—and trust me, it's damned near impossible to imagine that—she'd still take my breath away.

A little awkward, a little unsure, a whole lot feisty, she keeps me on my toes. Her take-no-shit attitude keeps me—and my arrogance —in check. I have to fight back a smile every time she scolds me with that smart mouth. A mouth that I ache to have pressed against my lips, my skin, my *dick*.

But what makes her the absolute total package? She's a foodie, just like me. She will try any and everything at least one time. Never turns her nose up, never questions calories or fat content, simply leans in and takes a decadent bite. She enjoys food the way it's meant to be enjoyed. Slowly. Sensually. With all five senses. And it turns me the fuck on.

I probably shouldn't admit this, but sometimes I get a boner watching her eat. Not all the time. Okay, yeah, usually I do. But when these tiny, soft moans of uncontrolled pleasure escape her mouth, or when she tips her head back and smiles in ecstasy, or when she licks her fingers...

A man would have to be made of stone *not* to be affected.

There are so many reasons why I cannot have feelings for Charli. I could write a book about the ways our getting involved is a bad idea. It would probably be a three-part series by the time I finished listing the ways.

For one, I'm engaged. It's my strongest defense against her and probably the reason why I told her almost instantly about Ainsley. You know how sometimes when a guy is trying to pick up a girl at a bar and the girl casually mentions "her boyfriend" to ward him off? I know, *smooth*, right?

But that was me. I was the lame one, spouting nonsense about the significant other to establish clear boundaries. It didn't even make sense, but on Charli's first official day when she was stocking the bar tray, she asked if I liked maraschino cherries. I blurted, "No, but my fiancée does."

I don't know what the hell came over me, but somehow I figured telling her about my relationship right away would draw a line in the sand between us. After a rather long, awkward pause, she smiled and said, "Good to know."

Reason number two: she's my coworker. I'm reasonably certain that Don wouldn't care if we dated. He's very laid back and adores Charli. He likes me too, but that's mostly because I bring prestige to his restaurant in the form of press and Michelin stars, and he *knows* it. I don't think he'd care if I banged the entire staff as long as I kept pumping out top-rated dishes and earning glowing reviews from the food critics. But even if Don were on board and I weren't engaged, things between Charli and me would have the potential to get messy. I'm a huge proponent of the mantra "don't shit where you eat."

Sighing, I grab three fresh, vibrant carrots that will be used in the *mirepoix*.

Peel. Slice. Chop. Repeat.

Now, where was I? Oh yeah, number three: Charli's ten years younger than me. On nights when Charli has me really wound up—nights like tonight when she wears a flimsy floral dress that could easily be undone with a quick pull of the tie around her waist—I cool off by reminding myself that she was eight when I was eighteen. That kills *any* indecent feelings real fast.

Moving on. Number four—

"Oliver." My dark eyes slowly look up, landing on a perfect set of round, full tits leaning toward me. *Why, God? Why do you torture me so?*

"Oliver."

Charli snaps her fingers, and my attention jumps to her face.

"Yeah?" My voice comes out gruff.

Her brow quirks. "You okay?"

"Yeah." I clear my throat. "What do you need?"

"Let Jason finish that." She gestures to the Vidalia onions and stalks of celery that I've yet to touch. "Michael Brown is here."

I sober in an instant, the color draining from my face. According to the insider tip we received, Michael isn't supposed to arrive for his evaluation until tomorrow. I haven't even prepared the salt rub for the bass yet. *Goddammit.*

"From the *Times*?" I wipe my hand on the rag tucked in the front of my apron. "Don told me the tasting was scheduled for tomorrow."

She shakes her head. "Change of plans."

Even though on the outside I appear calm and put together, I'm more than a little anxious. Few things rattle my steel-hard resolve. I've run two full marathons back to back, gone cliff diving in the Maldives, and even competed in the Colorado Trail Race. It's safe to say I'm a bit of an adrenaline junkie.

But no matter how many times food critics have sampled my cuisine, no matter how many rave reviews I've received, no matter how many awards or accolades trail my name, tastings are nerve-wracking as hell. I mean, the person's *entire* job is to criticize, to critique the meal that a chef (a.k.a. *me*) has painstakingly prepared. And the Zagat and Michelin associations are not shy about taking stars away if a restaurant (again, *me*) doesn't meet their stringent requirements.

Reading my hesitation, Charli assures, "You're a rock star." Her eyes shine with pride. "You got this."

A slow smile tips the corners of my lips. "Thanks, Charli girl."

She swats my ass as I walk past, and I'll admit, I like it more than I should. "Now go dazzle Mr. Food Critic with your super sexy..."

I snap my eyes to hers, wanting her to comment on my body—just once.

Arms.

Mouth.

Dick.

I hold her gaze for a moment longer, and her smile widens as though she knows exactly what I'm thinking. "Food, Oliver. Your super sexy *food*."

Chuckling, I push the door open.

I'll take the compliment.

The truth is, I'd take anything from her.

CHARLI

ON MONDAY NIGHTS, Oliver and I have a tradition. He cooks. I eat. We both eat and evaluate the dishes, eventually deciding which entrées would make good additions to our seasonal and specials menu. What started out as a work function quickly turned into a pseudo-date night. Well, for me, anyway.

We update our menu once a month, sometimes twice, depending on the time of year, so it isn't necessary to meet *every* Monday. But neither of us seems to mind our weekly get together. I like spending time with Oliver. Having him cook for me is just icing on an already-delicious cake.

Even still, I can't resist the urge to tease him. "I don't know how I got suckered into this." I dip my finger into the dish of butter-whipped potatoes.

"I know." Oliver's eyes narrow, sarcasm bleeding into his voice. "Having a world-class chef prepare dinner for you is such a hardship."

"World class?" I jibe. "Hardly."

"That's not what Michael Brown said." He deepens his voice. "And I quote, 'Mecca's dishes are inspired and flavorful, leaving the palate well-rounded and satisfied. Chef Pensen is world class and deserves more stars than this organization allows.'"

I stare at him, mouth agape. "Did you memorize the whole article?"

He shrugs, a sly smile on his face. "Not the whole thing. Just the important parts."

I snort. "You mean the parts about your being 'world class'?"

He chuckles. "Charlotte, haven't you ever heard the expression don't bite—or in this case, insult—the hand that feeds you?" He grabs a tall wooden pepper mill and cracks some fresh peppercorns into the glaze simmering in the stockpot.

Laughing, I say, "I'd be worried, but you're all bark and no bite."

A brow quirks. "Is that so?"

"You don't scare me, Oliver," I tease with warmth in my voice.

Heated eyes find mine and hold. "I should."

His words settle around us, and the tension, *the goddamn tension*, is so thick I fear I may suffocate. *What the hell are we doing?*

Because I'm a coward, or maybe because I'm scared that I *haven't* been misreading his signs, I look away, breaking the spell.

After several long seconds, I ask, "How come you never invite Ainsley?" Mentioning his fiancée does the trick. I watch as the heat vanishes from his eyes. "Doesn't she like you cooking for her?"

"Nah." He shrugs. "All she eats is bird food."

It's the closest thing to an insult I've heard him say about Ainsley. And even now, I'm stretching.

He pulls two plates from the shelf. "You're like me." His gaze catches mine, and his expression changes for the briefest moment. "You live to eat. Not the other way around."

My mouth hangs open, and I remind myself to close it. I'm not sure if I should be insulted or flattered. Yes, I enjoy food. Yes, my stomach isn't as flat as it once was or my thighs as slim as I'd like them to be, but I make no apologies. My dad's a cook and raised me with a hearty appetite and an adventurous palate.

Oliver must sense my uneasiness, because he says, "Relax, Charli. It was a compliment." I snort, but he continues, "Seriously? You have no idea how *awesome* it is that I found someone who enjoys food as much as I do. You *get* me."

"Mm-hmm," I mutter in agreement, because even though Oliver enjoys food, but it certainly doesn't show. His body—at least, what I've seen of it—is chiseled perfection.

Have I failed to mention that Oliver is a runner? He doesn't run because it's trendy or to maintain his weight, although I guess that *is* an added benefit. No, he runs because he *enjoys* it. He says it helps him to relieve stress, and even with his busy schedule, he runs religiously three times per week. I know, I don't get it either.

Last year, all the restaurants under the Cal Group, LLC umbrella participated in a 5K to raise awareness about hunger in America. Rather than pay an entry fee, participants were asked to bring non-perishable donations that were dispersed to several local food pantries. Registrants could walk or run—I walked, *obviously*. Oliver not only ran, but also placed number one in his age group. After crossing the finish line, however, he went back to the beginning and ran the same course again. Without a break.

I'd never seen anything more ludicrous in my life. A second loop? For the love of God, *why*?

"What?" He'd dragged a palm across his forehead, but it was unnecessary really, because he hadn't broken a sweat. "It's only six miles total. I usually do eight on my long runs.

I, on the other hand, had been sweating like a pig after completing the measly three miles. And I had walked. Power walked, but still.

"Charli." Oliver's clear voice filters through my thoughts, pulling me back to the present. "Charlotte."

"Yeah?" I jerk forward a little and plant both hands on the counter to brace myself.

"Dinner's ready. Can you grab that dish for me?" He gestures with his chin to the green beans almandine.

Taking the ceramic plate, I follow him into the dining room to the second booth along the back wall. *Our booth*. The same place we sit every Monday evening when I serve as the guinea pig for his new recipes.

Maybe I shouldn't feel special.

But I do.

I absolutely do.

I'm in the beginning stages of a food coma when Oliver's voice bursts the cozy, warm bubble that shrouds my skin, my body, my mind. My senses are dulled, woozy. "Which do you like better, whiskey glaze or spicy balsamic?"

A contented sigh escapes my lips. "I can't choose. They were both good."

"You have to pick." Oliver narrows his eyes. "That's the whole point."

I shift in my seat, belly full. My hands graze my shirt, smoothing the fabric over my midsection. I'm grateful that I decided to wear my looser leggings and a long tunic, even if they are somewhat more casual than what I usually have on for our dates. "I don't know." I exhale. "They're completely different."

"You're not being very helpful," he scolds.

"Then stop making dishes that are so delicious." My brows pinch together. "You know what would help me?" I don't wait for him to answer before I continue, "A scorecard. Like the ones they use in the food competition shows on TV."

He nods as if he's actually taking my suggestion seriously, even though I know he's not. "I'll get right on that. In the meantime, spill. What did you think?"

I eye the near-empty bowl of potatoes. "I *loved* the potatoes."

"I know." He rolls his eyes. "They're your favorite. That's why I made them, despite the fact that a different starch would've paired better."

A genuine smile touches my lips. "Thank you."

He returns my smile and answers, voice sincere, "Of course. Now quit stalling." He drums his fingers on the table. "Which marinade?"

"Hmm." I tap my finger to my chin, truly contemplating my response. "The whiskey one was a bit too sweet for me. It might work if you cut the brown sugar by half?" My voice tips up at the end, asking him if he thinks it's a valid suggestion.

My eyes find his as he says, "I completely agree." He drags his fork through the residual sauce on his dish. "And I don't really think the chives worked well. Leeks would've been better."

I point to the second option. "The spicy beef was more tender."

"That's the vinegar." He nods. "It breaks down the fibers of the meat." He reaches for my plate and stacks it atop his. "So we're going with spicy balsamic, then?"

"I think so," I say, pushing myself to stand. I stretch my arms over my head and sway from side to side. "I'm so stuffed. I swear I'm not gonna eat for a whole week."

He chuckles. "What about your favorite part?" He waggles his eyebrows. "Dessert?" he asks, walking into the kitchen, dishes in hand.

"There's always room for dessert." No truer words have ever been spoken. No matter how full I am, I *always* need something sweet to end my meal.

He winks and then begins to rinse our plates before loading them into the industrial dishwasher. A man who cooks and does dishes? My heart literally swoons inside my chest.

Oliver = dream man.

From experience, I know it's useless to offer to my assistance. Oliver is *very* particular about his kitchen. It's better to stay on the sidelines than to get in his way, because I'd be more of a hindrance than a help.

Hopping onto the counter beside him, I sit and chat and dry the occasional large pot or pan that he's hand washed because it doesn't fit inside the dishwasher.

After everything's cleaned and put away, Oliver locks up, and we walk around the block to Besty's', the little coffee shop we visit every Monday night for dessert.

Oliver grabs an open table while I place our order. Although he's ultra-traditional, he always lets me buy him coffee as a thank you for the meal, probably because he knows I would stop coming altogether if he didn't let me thank him in some way, no matter how small.

After setting our coffees on the table, I unwrap the single gourmet chocolate bar I purchased. This week's choice is Amedei, a high-end confection imported from Italy which boasts seventy-five percent cacao. I break off two squares and hand one to Oliver. We clink the pieces together before popping them into our mouths. The bitter chocolate melts on my tongue, and I sip my coffee, allowing the sweetness of the cream and sugar to balance the flavor. "So good," I murmur and take another sip.

"Mmm," he agrees, setting his cup down.

We're both quiet, each enjoying the other's company, listening to the familiar sounds of the café: the cracking of the coffee grinder, the ticking of the register tape, and the bell above the front door as patrons enter and leave.

It's a perfect night. Mondays always are. The loud buzzing of my phone as it vibrates against the table breaks the spell.

My eyes automatically dart to the screen and I scan the text message that pops up, demanding to be read.

I groan when I read the name: Julia.

"Everything okay?" Oliver asks over the rim of his cup.

"Yeah." I swipe my thumb across the screen. "It's my sister."

His head bobs in acknowledgment. Oliver knows a little bit about the complex relationship between Julia and me. He's been my sounding board on more than one occasion after she's called me with whatever bullshit drama she'd been involved in that day.

His gaze finds mine. "You know, you don't have to answer her the second she texts."

I squeeze my eyes shut. While my relationship with Julia is complicated, and I know Oliver means well—he may even be right to some degree—something niggles at me. As her big sister, I have an uncontrollable desire to answer whenever she calls. Julia is wild and needs protecting. If I don't look out for her and keep her out of danger, who will?

I look at him and ask, "You're telling me you don't always answer when Margot calls?"

"That's different."

I grin. "Why? Because you're twins?"

He smiles back. "Touché." He taps his fingers on the table. "It's just that..." He pauses for a moment before continuing, "Julia always seems to upset you.

My jaw gapes open, and I wonder how he can read me so well, and more importantly, why he genuinely seems to care. But nothing, not even Oliver, can stop my fingers from flying over the keys. It's a twisted addiction, one I wish I could break because, in truth, I answer out of obligation rather than actual desire.

I type a quick reply, and after a one-minute exchange, I set my phone on the table, face down this time.

"Want to talk about it?"

I shake my head. Julia and her drama have a way of sucking the life right out of

me. No need to bring him down too.

His warm chocolate eyes find mine and hold. "You sure you're okay?"

"Yeah." I spin my nearly empty cup in front of me.

"Okay," he says, voice cautious. "Do you wanna head out?"

"Sure," I agree easily. After all, I do have a houseguest coming soon.

CHARLI

JULIA ARRIVES three short days later, toting her craziness behind her like two misbehaving children in full meltdown mode. I love my sister, I really do, but to say our relationship is complicated would be the understatement of the century.

From an outsider's perspective, our bond appears stable, but it's superficial, a patchwork of childhood memories, two common parents, and a few shared laughs. Our personalities couldn't be more different, and I often wonder how we could belong to the same family. Julia is attention-seeking, loud, and often referred to as "the life of the party." And me? I'm *not* any of those things.

After everything that went down with Ryan, Julia has made a strong, genuine effort to be my friend. So I figure if she's willing to try, then so am I because a person can:

1. mature
2. change
3. learn to not hook up with her sister's boyfriend of three years

"You have nothing to eat." Julia slams the last kitchen cupboard door shut and plops onto the stool. "I'm starving."

Dropping my purse on the counter, I suppress my eye roll. "There are plenty of things to eat." *Sorry my food choices aren't up to your standards, Princess Julia.*

I pull the first of three takeout containers from my fridge and crack open the lid. Dipping my head, I sniff the contents to ensure they're still fresh, and luckily, they pass my "it doesn't smell like death" test.

"Here." I slide the container across the countertop. "Eat this."

Her eyes narrow in skepticism and I say half-jokingly, "How long are you here for again?"

"A week."

Great.

"Just until the dorms reopen." She shrugs. "I couldn't take one more day at Mom and Dad's house."

I nod because *I get it.*

She picks up the container and asks, "What is this?"

I grab a plate and fork for her. "Sautéed vegetables."

Julia scrunches her nose as she studies the contents with suspicious eyes. "Are you sure there's no meat in it?"

"Yes, I'm sure," I manage to grind out, even though I'm fairly certain Oliver deglazes the pan with beef stock. But that doesn't count as *meat*, right?

She dumps the veggies onto the plate I pulled from the shelf and pops it into the microwave. While the food heats, Julia pours two glasses of wine, sliding one down to me.

That's the other thing. Julia loves to drink. Okay, that sounds bad. I guess most twenty-two-year-olds do, and I'm not against imbibing in a glass (or two or three), but I'm not a fan of getting piss-ass drunk on a work night.

The microwave beeps, and I hand her the dish. She's silent for a few moments as she takes the first bite. Then she moans loudly with pleasure, "Oh my God. This is so good."

Chuckling, I roll my eyes. "I think you're just really hungry."

"No." She shakes her head. "This is so good that I'd make love to these vegetables. No"—she shakes her head again—"I'd *marry* these vegetables."

"You're nuts," I say, sipping my wine.

"Oliver is an amazing chef."

My eyes narrow. "How do you know he made them?" I mean, he did, of course, but the fact that she immediately discounts my cooking ability pisses me off a little.

Her fork pauses mid-bite and her eyes hold mine for a beat before she breaks into a laugh. She doesn't say anything as she shovels another forkful into her mouth.

"Thanks for the vote of confidence," I gripe.

"Come on, Sis." She reaches for her wine glass. "Even if I didn't already know you sucked at cooking—"

"I don't suck." *My cooking skills have improved. Marginally.*

She makes the OK sign in a way that tells me she doesn't agree. "Even *if* you could cook, the to-go container kind of gives it away."

I snap my fingers. "Dammit."

"Besides, if I had Chef McHottie cooking for me night after night, I'd never cook either."

"He doesn't cook for me *every* night."

She sets her glass on the counter, angles her body to face me, and gives me a look that says, *"Please."*

"He doesn't," I insist, taking another considerable gulp, only to realize I'm out of wine. *Holy shit, I better slow down.*

Julia reaches for the bottle and tries to pour me some more, but I cover the glass with my hand. "No more for me."

She tuts, swatting my hand away, and gives me a refill. "Non-sense. I love Drunk Charlotte."

My eyes narrow. "Not happening. I have work tomorrow."

"I know." She nods. "With Chef McHottie."

"Jules, please stop calling him that." Despite my protests, I take another sip from my now-full glass. "You know he's engaged."

She shrugs as though I've told her something nonessential,

something like "Oliver hates drinking tap water." Yep, he's a total water snob, and it drives me bananas. I mean, seriously, does he not realize how detrimental all those plastic water bottles are to our environment? But I digress.

"You like him." She scrapes the last of the veggies onto her fork.

Now it's my turn to shrug. Jules is the only person whom I confided in about my Oliver crush. This will make me sound like a terrible person, but I'm going to confess it anyway. I've confided in Julia, not because we're close—we've already discussed the fact that we're not—but because Julia has a very lax moral compass, and I knew she wouldn't judge me. If I told Em, my best friend who's married with two kids, she'd click her tongue in reproach. Or if I fangirled to Meg at work about Oliver's hotness, she'd sneak knowing, accusatory glances at me every time he and I were alone together. So I keep my shameful, dirty secret to my guilty self.

It should also be stated that Drunk Charlotte was present during my confession to Julia. Drunk Charlotte is a chatty bitch and apparently has never learned the expression, "Loose lips sink ships."

Julia drops her fork to her plate. "I say bang him."

"Julia!" I gasp in mock horror, because I certainly won't admit that I've thought about just that more often than not.

"What?" She pushes the dish away. "You're already in a relationship with him." One shoulder lifts. "Might as well be having sex. That's the fun part."

"You're right." I nod, and her eyes widen at my easy agreement before I add, "We *are* in a relationship. A *professional* relationship."

"And if you believe that's all it is, I have a bridge to sell you."

Scowling, I ask, "What's that supposed to mean?"

"It means"—she looks directly in my eyes—"you're the work wife."

My nose wrinkles. "The work wife?"

"Yeah." She pours herself a second glass. "You spend all your time together—"

I interrupt, "Because we *work* together."

She continues, unfazed, "He cooks for you all the time."

"He's a chef, Jules."

"You two have all these inside jokes, you talk about him constantly, and you think he's 'the sexiest man alive.'" She makes air quotes around that last part.

Guilty. Guilty. Guilty.

I did say that, didn't I? Well, not me, per se. Drunk Charlotte said it. Remind me to cut a bitch. My face flushes a deep crimson red and gets so hot that I can feel the heat pouring from my skin. And the wine is only making it worse.

Stalling, I lift my glass to my lips and empty the contents in one swig. Then I finally bring my eyes back to Jules. "So what if all those things are true? He's engaged, Jules. *Engaged.*" My tone turns sorrowful. "You saw what Dad's affairs did to Mom. I can't—I *won't* —be the other woman."

Julia sneers. "Monogamy is outdated and unrealistic." She watches as I spin my glass by its stem. "Mom and Dad's marriage sucks. But you know what? Mom chose to stay with him, Charli. She *chose* it." Her eyes find mine. "You can't steal someone who doesn't want to be stolen. You can't *make* a man cheat. Everyone has free will, free choice." Her voice turns a touch colder, and I know her well enough to see that this is a façade, her way of acting tough so she doesn't get hurt, because the truth is, my dad's affairs—yes, plural, he had several, and my mom still stuck by him—affected us. "I'd rather be the cheater than the one being cheated on."

Squeezing her thigh, I smile, trying to communicate that our parents' relationship isn't all bad. When things were good between our parents, they were really good.

Maybe Mom should have left when she found out the first time he was unfaithful. I was six and Jules was just a baby. Every woman likes to think she'd leave, that she'd never tolerate her husband sleeping with a twenty-year-old waitress in the stockroom of the diner where they both worked, but my mom was young, jobless, and loved my dad fiercely. She still does. Who are we to judge?

Jules places her hand on top of mine and squeezes back. The melancholy that flickers behind her eyes is replaced by a mischievous smile as she asks, "Wanna crack open another bottle?"

CHARLI

I HATE DRUNK CHARLOTTE. Drunk Charlotte is the reason I tossed and turned for more than half of the night and woke up with a pounding headache. Drunk Charlotte is the reason for the dark circles under my eyes and the ratty, untamed hair piled in a messy knot atop my head. And she's also to blame for Julia attending Sunday brunch at Mecca this morning.

Sunday brunch is a tradition that began at the restaurant long before I started working there. Don, the owner, is a really nice guy. I know that's an expression that is often overused or undeserved, but he truly is. He takes chances on his employees (I'm a prime example of this) and works hard to foster a sense of community amongst his employees.

The first Sunday of every month, all employees are invited to attend a feast prepared by our kitchen staff. The budget is very generous, and the food is always delicious. Every employee, from dishwasher to manager, is invited along with his or her spouse. Most of us never bring a plus one, but apparently, Drunk Charlotte thought it was an excellent idea to invite Julia along since she's staying with me through next week.

"What happened to you?" Oliver asks as soon as I walk into the kitchen.

"Don't ask." I peer over his shoulder at the creamy gravy he's mixing for his signature chicken fried steak. The smell, thick and buttery, causes my stomach to roll.

"Jesus." He pauses, placing a hand on my shoulder. "Are you okay?" He ushers me toward the empty chair shoved in the back corner of the workspace. It's been broken for almost two weeks but still hasn't found its way to the dumpster.

"Hey, Charli!" Julia's voice booms from the entryway, loud enough to be heard over the clatter of the pots and pans. "You back here?"

"Yeah, Jules," I groan, voice dry. "I'll be right out."

Oliver's eyes find and hold mine. "Julia's visiting?"

"Yeah." I close my eyes and blow out a breath, trying my best to dull the pounding in my head.

"That explains a lot." He turns and begins to walk away.

Although Oliver and Julia have never met in person, he's witnessed several FaceTime calls over the past year. Not to mention the fact that I've talked to him about her—both good and bad. Sure, she's my sister and I love her, but sometimes I can't stand her. On a scale of one to ten, I'd say we'd rank right about an eleven as being polar opposites.

My eyes pull down, and refocus on the rounded black curve of Oliver's shoes. The unmistakable, pungent smell of scrambled eggs floods my nose, and my head snaps up.

"Here." He hands me the plate, along with a glass of fresh cold-pressed apple juice. "Eat and drink this. You'll feel better."

"I'm fine," I say, even as I begin to shove the eggs into my mouth. By the third bite, I realize I'm ravenous and quickly finish the generous portion. The eggs are good. *Really* good. Light and fluffy, seasoned with the perfect amount of salt and pepper, precisely the way I like them. Selfishly, I wish I were in a better state of mind to appreciate their flavor.

He quirks a brow, a smug, knowing smile on his face. "Good?"

Oliver's ego is already huge, and I'm not about to inflate it any more. I have no doubt he could make actual *shit* not only taste good but have a person begging for seconds. What's worse? He knows it. I shrug. "It was all right."

"Oh, Charli." He chuckles, actually chuckles, as he takes the empty plate from my hands. "Some things never change."

I manage to pull myself out of the chair, but it's awkward since the one leg is broken, and it feels like I'm sitting in a lopsided hole. Plus, I also feel like I've been run over by a truck.

"You're right, Chef." My eyes find his. "But someone's gotta keep you in line."

He hands my empty plate to Simon, our newest dishwasher. Oliver's eyes sparkle with mischief as they hold mine. "Well, then, I hope you're up for the task."

I open my mouth, about to protest when he commands, a challenge in his voice, "Now get out of my kitchen."

The morning goes from bad to worse. After leaving *Oliver's* kitchen, I head straight to the "party" room, a small square space that we use for reservations of twenty or more, where brunch is always served. To my surprise, Ainsley is sitting at the table.

Ainsley—Oliver's *fiancée* Ainsley—and she's chatting with Julia.

Dread like I've never felt before coils low in my stomach. Jules would never say anything intentionally to out me or my feelings for Oliver, but she's also a bit dense and a little too forward for her own good.

Ignoring the throbbing pain in my head, I rush over to the table and inject myself into the conversation rather ungracefully. "Ainsley!" I exclaim. "I didn't know you were back."

"Charli!" Ainsley pushes herself to stand and hugs me. "So good to see you."

Here's the thing. Ainsley is a sweetheart. Genuine. Kind. Caring. At least, from what I could ascertain from the handful of times I've met her, and Oliver rarely says a bad word about her. Come to think of it, he doesn't say much about her at all. Apart from the weird exchange my first day, Oliver never talks about his girlfriend—I mean fiancée. Semantics.

"Nice to see you too," I say, pulling away from her to find an open chair next to Julia. "I take it you've already met my sister, Julia."

Ainsley nods as Julia informs me, "Ainsley just got back from Copenhagen."

"Wow." I muster with minimal enthusiasm in my hung-over state. Seriously, I don't know how Julia is so bright-eyed and bushy tailed. Even if she is a few years younger than me, at twenty-two, I was still wrecked the morning after a night of drinking.

Several servers enter the room and set up large silver pans along the side table. Brunches are served buffet style so that everyone can eat and chat. Oliver and Don follow not a minute later, and Don announces to the room, "Bon appétit."

Most rush to the buffet line, but Oliver takes a seat directly across from me.

This morning just keeps getting better and better.

OLIVER

MY EYES LINGER on Charli as she stands in line with her sister and Meg, one of our waitresses and probably Charli's closest friend at the restaurant. Well, besides me, that is. I watch as she bypasses the crystal tray of mimosas and goes straight for the pan of fluffy Belgian waffles. She piles them high on her plate before topping them with fresh cut strawberries and whipped cream. Charli isn't shy about the foods she loves. I gotta say, the chef in me genuinely appreciates her hearty appetite. I've learned in her year tenure at the restaurant, waffles are her favorite, and because of this, I include them on the menu at each of our brunches.

"Ol." Ainsley's voice draws my attention, and I angle my body toward where she sits at my side. "The food's great."

I smile at her compliment, even if it's forced, because her praise is unmerited. Ainsley is the world's pickiest eater, and she rarely, if ever, eats the food I prepare. Case in point: Her plate is comprised of exactly one scoop of fruit salad, a single slice of sourdough bread —no butter, no cream cheese, no nothing—and an assortment of olives. "Thanks, Ains."

Charli, Julia, and Meg return to the long banquet table and sit opposite us.

It's quiet for a few moments as we all dig into our food. I keep stealing glances at Charli while she eats because her face is so expressive. With just a glance, I can tell instantly if she loves or hates something.

When she cuts a piece of sausage and pops it into her mouth, her eyes roll back a little and she moans, "Oh my God. So good." The ecstasy in her voice is almost vulgar, and if we weren't in a restaurant surrounded by thirty other people, if my fiancée wasn't sitting right next to me, I might find it a turn on. Fuck, okay, I do find it a turn on, and it's a problem. A big fucking problem.

"You like it?" I ask, even though it's obvious she does.

"Yeah." She lifts another bite to her mouth. "Andouille?"

"Good girl." My eyes sparkle. "I added a bit of Cajun seasoning this time."

"Yum."

Leaning forward, I snatch a piece off her plate.

"Hey!" She swats me with her fork. "Get your own." Chuckling, I grab another piece, and this time, she *almost* stabs me, but deep down, I know it's an idle threat. We've shared food a million times before. It's one of the things I love about her. If she likes something, she wants everyone else to like it too.

"Aww," Julia quips. "You guys are so cute." The look that Charli gives her sister is murderous. I'm not naïve. Yes, I can be clueless, I can be self-absorbed, I can be an asshole, but I get the idea that Charli has a crush on me. Or, at the very least, is attracted to me.

I truly don't mean this the way it sounds, but a lot of girls are into chefs. I'm not sure if it's the crisp white jacket or that cooking is an aphrodisiac or what it is exactly, but it doesn't make it any less accurate. If I wanted, I could have any number of girls at the ready. The problem is, Charli is the only girl I've ever imagined things going further with. Sure, there's been some innocent, harmless flirting between us, but for the most part, she's rather conservative with me, almost as though she's afraid what could—or would—happen if we both let our guard down.

She's right to be worried.

"I still can't believe how much you and your sister look alike." Ainsley gestures between the two sisters.

Both Julia and Charli scrunch their noses. Julia speaks first, "You think?" She shakes her head. "I don't think we look alike at all."

"Yeah," Ainsley replies. "You both have wide blue eyes. Same oval face, same slim nose." Ainsley turns to me. "Don't you think?"

Suddenly all sets of eyes are on me, awaiting an answer. Truthfully, I don't think Charli and Julia could be more different. Charli is healthy and voluptuous, with full, round breasts and curvy hips. Her hair is a few shades darker than her sister's, and her eyes are a touch bigger, wider, and more mysterious. But the real distinguishing feature is the beauty mark above the right corner of Charli's lip. I've never seen anyone with such a prominent mark. I've thought about pressing my lips to that delicate spot more times than I care to admit.

Julia, in comparison, is waiflike. She's very thin, and if I'm honest, looks almost skeletal, like she could use a good meal. Or twenty. Her eyes are the same color as Charli's, but her hair is lighter, almost a mousy brown. Don't get me wrong, she's pretty, attractive even, but if this were a beauty competition, Charli would win by a landslide.

"Ol?" Ainsley nudges me with her elbow and repeats the question, "Don't you think they could pass for twins?"

Clearing my throat, I give the best answer I know, "I have no idea." I shrug. "What do I know? I'm a *guy*."

Ainsley chuckles, and I say a silent prayer that the conversation drops. But not even five minutes later, I'm hit with another bullet.

"I keep telling her"—Julia leans in toward Ainsley—"she's got to start dating again."

Meg raises her hand. "I agree."

"See, Meg gets it!" Julia smacks her fist on the table before her eyes sweep around the room. "There has got to be at least one hot"—Julia brings her eyes to mine and enunciates the next word —"*single* guy here that we can set her up with."

"Jules!" Charli whisper-hisses. "What are you doing?"

"Getting you laid." Julia reaches for her champagne flute.

"Enough." Charli's hand wraps around her sister's tiny bird arm. "I can't date someone I work with."

"Why not?" Her sister's attention flutters around the room before landing on Simon. The twenty-one-year-old dishwasher. "What about that guy? He's hot."

I can't stop my gaze from sweeping over him. *Kid's a punk.* With his spiky jet black hair, murky green eyes, and tribal snake tattoo— he's not Charlotte's type at all. At least, I *hope* he isn't.

Julia turns in her seat. "Meg, what do you think?"

Meg seesaws her hand back and forth. "Decent."

"No," Charli asserts, barely sparing Simon a glance.

"Again, why not?" her sister repeats.

I force shallow, even breaths, despite the jealousy simmering in my veins. *For fuck's sake, leave it alone, Julia.*

Charli rolls her eyes in exasperation. "Because it's unprofessional."

My mind dissects the reason why Charli disagreed. Not because of Simon, per se, but because they work together.

Maybe she thinks he's attractive.

Maybe she's into younger guys.

Maybe...I'm being a jealous shit.

"Because if it doesn't work out, things could get messy. Because if Don finds out, he'd be pissed—"

"Don loves you," Julia interrupts.

This is true. Don does love Charlotte and regales everyone with the story of how she got her start at Mecca. Apparently, Don's wife, very much pregnant at the time, ordered Chinese food from a local shop. His job was to pick it up before returning home. Unfortunately, the joint only accepted cash as payment, and Don didn't have any on him. Charli was there to get her own order, and seeing Don's crisis, paid for his, ultimately saving him from a very hungry, very hormonal wife. He gave Charlotte his business card and told her if she ever needed a job to give him a call. Six months later, she called, and the rest is history.

"You know Don won't care," Meg chimes in again, nodding her head toward Simon. "I say go for it."

Why the fuck is Meg encouraging this? She just got scratched off of my Christmas list.

My stomach tightens, and I can feel Charli's eyes on me, imploring me for help, but I don't dare look at her, because I'm afraid of what she'll see reflected in my expression. Anger. Protectiveness. Jealousy. I stab the potato on my plate with more force than necessary.

"What about Jim?" Ainsley's suggestion is such a curveball that I choke on the bite I just swallowed. She looks at me expectantly before popping another olive into her mouth.

"Jimbo?" I scrunch my nose. "You want to set Charli up with my best friend?" My eyes widen to match the doubt in my voice. "My recently *divorced* best friend?"

"Sure, why not?" Ainsley shrugs. "I think they'd get along great."

My eyes find Charli's for a brave second before looking away. "Jimbo works all the time." I take a swig of my grapefruit juice, hoping the bitterness will wash away some of my unease. "Besides, he's too old for her."

Charli's face reddens—a mixture of fury and embarrassment—as she holds up her hand. "Guys, enough." She ticks her fingers. "One, stop talking about me like I'm not even here. *Jesus.*" Her eyes cut to Julia, then Meg, and finally, Ainsley. "Two, I don't do blind dates. Sorry. Not sorry."

My muscles, which up until this point I didn't even realize were tight, loosen. I can feel the tension drain from my body, and my chest deflates with a solid puff of air.

Ainsley, however, is undeterred. "It wouldn't be a blind date, silly." She grabs another olive. A black one this time. "We could all go out together. I'm home for the next week. I'm sure we can arrange something." She looks at me, a genuine smile on her face. "What do you think? The four of us? That would be fun, yeah?"

Fun? No way. Hell is a more appropriate word. My teeth grind together in agitation. "Just let it go, Ains."

Confused, Ainsley looks from me to Charli, then to the other girls. Charli shrugs and shakes her head. Meg is busy looking at her phone, but Julia holds my eyes, a mischievous smile stretching across her lips. *She knows.*

There's an awkward pause, a strange moment suspended in time, before Charli reaches for her sister's champagne flute and drains the glass in one single swig. Her voice is confident, assured when she speaks, "All right, I'm in."

"Yeah?" Excited, Ainsley leans forward in her chair.

"Yep." Charli nods, face stoic. "Text Jim." My eyes flash to hers, and I hold her stare as she says, "I'd love to meet him."

CHARLI

HOME. I don't think there's ever been a more glorious word. After the shit show at brunch this morning—seriously, how could I have been so pathetic?—all I wanted to do was go home, curl into a tiny ball, and sleep. The one wrinkle in my beautiful plan is Julia. Having a houseguest is somewhat inconvenient because she'll want to talk and hang out when I all want to do is activate zombie mode.

"For the record, I get it." Julia kicks off her flip flops and collapses onto my couch.

I toe off my own shoes and hang my keys on the hook before sinking into the oversized recliner opposite her. "Get what?"

She eyes me over the top of the pale blue pillow she hugs to her chest. "Your interest in Chef McHottie." I scowl, and she corrects herself, "*Oliver.*" She nods before continuing, "He's hot, kind of has the whole Simon Cowell thing going on. Arrogant and cocky yet insanely likable."

I coach myself to keep my face neutral, even as my stomach sours. Julia doesn't have the greatest track record of behaving around my boyfriends. Or men, in general. Not that Oliver is my boyfriend. Or really, my anything, but still. After the whole Ryan incident, I don't think I'll ever fully trust her again. Even if we both agreed to put the past behind us, it's much easier said than done.

"What?" She snatches the remote off the coffee table.

"Nothing," I say, scooting farther down in my chair. "Throw me that blanket." I tip my head toward the back of the couch, and she tosses the throw that I keep draped over the back cushion at me. We're both quiet as she clicks through the channels, nothing catching our interest.

Finally, she says, "Ainsley seems nice."

"She is," I murmur my agreement. "You two seem to have really hit it off."

My voice is accusatory, bitchy even, and I instantly want to take back the words. I don't want to sound jealous, especially in front of Julia, even though I am. Insanely so.

Julia's hand pauses, the remote suspended in midair as her eyes find mine. "What was I supposed to do? Not talk to the girl?"

I squeeze my eyes shut, frustrated that I'm annoyed that Julia likes Ainsley. Hell, *I* like Ainsley. It's irrational, I know, but part of me wants Julia to hate her on my behalf. Julia is *my* sister. She should be loyal to me. And, yes, I realize I sound all sorts of crazy right now. I'll fly that flag proudly.

I focus my attention on the TV screen as though the program Julia landed on is the most interesting thing I've ever seen. It's not. It's an infomercial for a vacuum cleaner that claims to suck up M&M's whole. Actually, it *is* kind of impressive.

Julia waves the remote to get my attention. "You're really not gonna talk to me?" She pushes herself up to sit. "She's a vegan, so we have a shared interest."

She's a vegan. Like being a vegan is some special privilege. Really? Who willingly wants to deprive themselves of all things good? I think I'd die—literally die—if I could never eat cheese again. "I'm not pissed about Ainsley." *I totally am.* "I'm pissed that you made my dating life—or lack thereof—the topic of our brunch conversation!"

"Give it a rest, Charli." She huffs, flopping back on the couch. "I did you a favor."

I sit up straighter in my chair, voice indignant. "A favor? How so? By embarrassing the shit out of me? By pushing me into a blind date with *Oliver's* best friend?"

"Ainsley did that." My eyes narrow to slits, and if I didn't think it would crack the screen, I'd throw my phone at her.

"At least now you know where you stand." She smiles in victory. "Oliver *likes* you."

"He does not," I say, voice even, but my heart skips a beat.

She scoffs. "He doesn't want you to go out with Jim for a reason."

The small glimmer of hope that began to bubble inside me deflates. Probably for the best, anyway, since there's no use chasing a crush that won't ever happen. "Jules, he's protective of his friends. Jim just went through a nasty divorce."

She quirks a brow for me to continue.

"I don't know all the details." I drop my phone back into my lap. "Just that his wife left him, and he only gets to see his daughter every other weekend."

"Wait." She holds up a hand. "Jim has a kid?"

"Yeah." I nod. "I can't remember her name. She's two or three years old...I don't know. She's in preschool, I think."

"Maybe Jim isn't a good idea." She tugs at a loose thread on the pillow. "Too much baggage."

"Ya think?" I click my tongue. "That's why Oliver didn't want me to get involved with him, not because he..."

Her eyes soften. "Maybe."

"Yeah," I say. "With any luck, he won't be interested or too busy to date, and I won't have to come up with an excuse to back out."

"I'm sorry," she says. Her apologies are so infrequent that her words momentarily take me off guard. "I shouldn't have said anything. I just...you seem so lonely. And I still feel bad after what happened with..." Her voice trails off. She never says his name, and I'm grateful. She clears her throat. "You haven't gone on a date in forever."

"A year and a half isn't that long," I counter. "Besides, it's not like I haven't had the opportunity." Her eyes narrow, but I ignore the unspoken accusation. "I'm focusing on my career. I'm alone because I choose to be. I'm not lonely." *Usually*.

Her eyes find mine and hold. A silent conversation passes between us.

I'm sorry, her eyes say.

You should *be*, mine respond. Kissing my boyfriend was (and still is) fucked up.

But on the other hand, she *shouldn't* be. Who knows if Ryan and I would still be together all these years later had "Kissgate" never happened? Probably not.

I force a smile, telling her that I'm okay and not to worry.

Jules nods and blinks once before breaking eye contact. She picks up the remote again and switches to the Hulu app. "*New Girl?*"

"Sure," I agree, sliding down in the chair, tucking the blanket underneath my chin. Five minutes in, I close my eyes, telling myself I'm only going to rest for a few minutes. Hours later, I wake up, stiff and alone, with the strangest fragments of dreams pulling at my memory.

Oliver.

Ainsley.

A faceless Jim with a deep voice.

Maybe a blind date isn't a bad idea after all.

CHARLI

TWO DAYS LATER AT WORK, Oliver pulls me aside. Well, not exactly. He pulls me into the big walk-in refrigerator at the back end of the kitchen, the only place guaranteed to ensure our privacy. Before the door has even clicked closed, he speaks, "You're not really going to go through with this date, are you?"

My spine straightens. "Why wouldn't I?"

Because he's several inches taller than me, my eyes line up perfectly with his jaw. It's for this reason that I notice the tic, the tight spasm of his muscle before he continues, "I don't think it's a good idea."

My heavy sigh turns to hot steam in the cold air. "Then it's a good thing I don't care what you think."

He tears a hand through his hair. "Don't start."

I square my shoulders to face him. "Start what?"

"Your bullshit." His nostrils flare. "I said no."

I shove his chest, even though I have no right to. When I was a kid, my mom always said: *Hands are not for hitting*. And she was right. But Oliver's condescending preachy-ness drives me fucking bananas. "Who do you think you are?" I make air quotes. "'I said no.' I don't answer to you. I'm not your sous chef or some line cook you can bark orders at."

"I know." Large palms wrap around my shoulders and squeeze. "You *never* give a damn about what I have to say. Never do what you're told."

"What I'm told?" I bark.

He narrows his eyes. "You know what I mean. *Jesus.*"

No, I don't, actually.

I shoot daggers at him. "I'm going out with Jim Thursday night. If you and your *fiancée*"—I enunciate the word to prove even further that he has no control over whom I date, because he's freaking *engaged*—"accompany us, great. If not, well, I really don't give a fuck."

"Nice, Charlotte." He shakes his head. "*Real nice.*"

Clearly, he's pissed. His use of my full name is a dead giveaway that he's angry, but guess what? So am I. I march toward him, stop only when the tips of my leather pumps meet the round curve of his chef clogs. "What's your problem, Oliver? Tell me." I spread my hands wide. "Am I not smart enough? Hot enough? Thin enough for your friend? What the fuck is so wrong with me?"

His scowl drops and he places both his hands on my wrists— even in the cool air, my skin burns from his touch. In one fell swoop, he anchors my arms to my sides. "Is that what you're angry about? You believe that I don't think you're good enough for Jimbo?"

I close my eyes, refusing to look at him.

""Charli." He brings a palm to my cheek and dips down so that his face is level with mine. "Any man would be lucky to have you." His fingers sweep my cheek, delicately, *adoringly*, and my eyes pop open.

He's touching me. Holding *my face with strong, sure hands.*

What. The. Fuck.

The dichotomy of his hot and cold behavior causes my head to spin.

I snort. "Just not your friend, right?"

His voice turns strained, and he squeezes my wrist harder. "*Especially* not Jimbo." His voice breaks on the last word. "*Please.*"

My eyes meet his. "I don't get you, Oliver." I shake my arm free. "We're friends. You should be happy for me to find someone to share my life with. Isn't that the dream? Get married? Buy a house? Have a bunch of kids?" My nostrils flare. "Hell, that's what *you're* doing!"

His irises darken in frustration, or maybe it's anger; I'm not exactly sure. I *am* sure of what I'm doing, however. I'm pushing him, daring him to speak the same words that I hold guarded in my heart. *I think I'm in love with you. I want you. Tell me that these feelings aren't all in my head.*

It's as though time stands still, and we're trapped in this shitty, cold walk-in refrigerator that smells slightly of damp cardboard. After a few long moments when he still hasn't answered, I grow impatient and walk toward the door. "I'll see you Thursday night. Or not. Your call." I walk with my head held high, insides shaking, and I try my best to convince myself that the reason I'm fighting so hard for this date with Jim is that I want to move on. To prove to myself that Oliver is just a schoolgirl crush. A silly girl's infatuation due to boredom and loneliness. And as the door slams shut behind me, I almost believe the lie.

By the time Thursday evening arrives, I'm scrubbed, manicured, and primped to within an inch of my life. I haven't tried this hard to look good in a really long time. It's not that I'm ugly—I'm not. If I had to choose, I'd firmly plant myself in the "average" category. Not too fat, not too thin. Medium height. Smallish nose. Blue eyes that change from a brilliant sky blue to stormy grey, depending on my chosen eye makeup. Round face. Long, wavy brown hair that looks equally nice curly or straight, which is why I usually don't bother to flatiron it because it takes *forever*.

At almost thirty years old, I've grown comfortable enough in my skin to know what works for me, what doesn't, and to appreciate the body I have. A body whose natural state hovers comfortably between a size eight and ten, *not* the size four that I tortured myself to squeeze into in my early twenties.

"How does this look?" I peek my head into my office, otherwise known as the room Julia took over with all of her shit just six short days ago. It feels closer to six months.

She purses her lips as her eyes skim over the paisley print yellow dress. "No." She shakes her head. "Just *no*."

My hands smooth down the front. "What? Why not?"

Julia pushes herself off the inflatable futon. "You're twenty-eight, not sixty-eight!"

I scowl and stalk back into my bedroom, already pulling the fabric over my head. *I thought it was classy. Flirty yet tasteful.*

Julia brushes past me and walks directly into the large walk-in closet, one of the main features that influenced me to rent this apartment in the first place. I have *a lot* of clothes. And purses. And shoes.

She peruses the racks, murmuring to herself before she tosses a few shirts, skirts, and jeans onto my bed. "Try these on."

My mouth hangs open. I'm supposed to meet Jim in forty-five minutes, and even if I take an Uber instead of the train, the commute will take at least twenty. "All of them?"

She nods, adding a pair of skinny jeans to the pile. Jeans that I haven't fit into in more than two years.

"Jules." I exhale, not bothering with the pants. "I'm already running late."

"Then you better hurry up." She clucks her tongue. "You've got a date to impress."

Sighing, I tug the first outfit on, silently repeating Jim's name to myself because, the truth is, the only man I'm thinking about impressing is Oliver.

OLIVER

IT'S FINALLY HERE. Thursday night. The night I've been dreading all week. The night that I've anticipated in much the same way a prisoner on death row awaits his execution. With dread. With fear. With feverish anticipation.

I'm old enough to realize that time passes by in the blink of an eye, and before I've had even the slightest chance to adjust to the idea of Charli going on a date—much less a double date *with me*—the day arrives. Ready and eager. With fucking bells on.

My mind tries to rationalize the situation with no success. Ainsley and I are going to dinner with Charli and Jimbo on a double date. Like we're in fucking junior high.

I *still* can't believe she's actually going through with it. Still can't believe that my Charli agreed to go on a date with my best friend. Though I guess she isn't technically *my* Charli. Even if I've felt that way since the day I chased her and that damn dog down the crowded city sidewalk.

"Why are you in such a mood?" Ainsley saunters into the bedroom, past where I lie on the bed with one arm slung over my eyes in...defeat? Worry? Trepidation?

All of the above.

I bristle at her accusatory tone. "I'm not."

One eyebrow quirks. "You're not?" She marches into the bathroom but leaves the door open as she begins to apply her makeup. "You haven't said two words since you got home from the restaurant, *and* you refused sex."

"I didn't refuse sex." My eyes snap to the mirror, finding hers in the reflection, and I clarify, "You jumped me as soon as I walked in the door. I needed a shower." I rake a hand through my hair, and it stands in all directions. "I reeked of fish."

She nods and her simple agreement causes any irritation to dissolve. *I'm an asshole.*

"Ains, I'm sorry." I scrub a hand over my face. "I don't mean to be a dick. Work

has been crazy and with my sister calling every day about her possible transfer...it's been tough."

"I thought Margot accepted the offer?"

"She did," I confirm. "But now her company is countering and she doesn't know what to do."

"She'll figure it out." She blots her lips with a tissue. "You always help her sort things through."

Of course I do. She's my twin. "Yeah. It's just nerve-wracking, you know? Major life changes shouldn't be snap decisions."

I can *definitely* relate. I struggle with the same every day. On the surface, Ainsley and I are a great match and I'd be lying if I said things *weren't* good between us, because they *are*. They're comfortable. Easy. But still, I can't help but feel something is missing between us. *Should I stay or should I go?*

A huge part of me thinks the fact that I'm even pondering these questions is reason enough to end things.

"Yeah, I know." Ainsley's words pull me back to the present.

I lift myself off the bed and decide to make an effort. "I don't go into work until four tomorrow. Want to go for a bike ride on Slocum Trail?"

She pauses, her mascara wand halfway between the tube and her eye. "We haven't done that in forever."

Smiling, I say, "I know." It's been so long since we actually *connected*. We're more like two passing ships. Spending quality time together, just the two of us, is exactly what we need—what *I* need—to squash this attraction to Charli.

An image of Charli flashes through my mind. *Charli.*

Jesus, Oliver, get it together. You need to Stop—with a capital S—thinking about her. You're engaged. To Ainsley, not Charli.

Ainsley's voice breaks the bubble of my thoughts. "I'd really love to, but I already made plans with Jonas." *Her yoga partner.* "We're going to a reiki class at ten. I'd ask you to come..." Her voice trails off and I know what she's thinking: *I don't fit in with her yoga crew. I'm not bendy or New Age-y or self-aware enough.*

Her refusal is like a swift, hard kick to the balls. I pause and take a deep breath to remind myself that she's not refusing *me*. Even if does feel that way. Even if this is the third time since she's been home that she's made plans without me, without telling me. In fact, tonight is the first night we are actually spending *together*.

Walking into the closet, I say, "I thought our reservations weren't until eight o'clock." I glance at the clock on the night table. It's still early, not even six thirty.

"They're not, but we're meeting at Rouse for drinks first."

Great.

Ainsley's voice carries over my shoulder as I comb through my rack of clothes. "I was thinking you could wear your new shirt." She smiles. "The one I got you."

My jaw tics with a touch of impatience. "Ains, you know I like to pick out my own clothes."

Some men might appreciate help with their wardrobes, but I'm not most men. I can dress myself. In fact, I have great style. Well, my personal shopper at Neiman's does, anyway.

"Please?" She pokes her head in the doorway. "You know I hate those boring solid black shirts you always wear." She shakes her head. "So drab." She grabs her latest purchase. "Here. I picked this up in Denmark and I just know it's going to look *great* on you."

Ainsley's "gifts" range from God-awful Hawaiian print shirts, to over-the-top touristy tees that a middle-aged dad would wear, to the most heinous of all—Speedos. But what more can I do? I've already told her—on more than one occasion—that the gifts are unnecessary. That a simple picture or text would prove she was thinking about me while away. But despite my discouragement, the souvenirs keep on coming. It's not like I can refuse them without looking like an ungrateful asshole.

The only silver lining? She's not home much, so I only have to wear them from time to time. When she's working, it's right back to my signature distressed jeans, fitted black t-shirts, and Ferragamo loafers.

Sighing, I pull my t-shirt over my head and slip into the geometric-print button up she picked up for me on her latest trip. The material is cheap, a scratchy polyester blend with splashes of violet, green, pink, and orange. I'd describe it as very Eastern European—and not my taste at all.

Glancing at myself in the mirror, I button the tiny black buttons, one by one. I'm barely able to contain my groan of displeasure. I feel like I should be dancing to EDM in some discotheque in Germany, complete with strobe lights, while everyone trips on E.

"Oh!" Ainsley dusts her hands over my shoulder and I stand straighter, a little bit shell-shocked. "It looks great on you!" She kisses the side of my face as she passes. "I knew it would."

"Mm-hmm," I murmur, hoping I won't catch too much shit from Jimbo. He knows Ainsley well enough to know her taste is a little eccentric, *and* she'd be hurt if I refused one of her gifts. So I take the path of least resistance and wear the shit. I mean shirt. My bad.

I make quick work of pulling on a pair of black dress pants and slip my feet into my loafers. At least the lower half of me doesn't scream douchebag. I grab my wallet and then my watch off the shelf before walking back into the bedroom.

"Do you like my dress?" Ainsley asks before I've even cleared the doorway. She stands to face me, purse clasped in one hand.

My eyes skim over her as I take in the simple black dress with ruffle sleeves, cinched tight at the waist with an orange silk belt. Our clothes fucking *match*. There's no doubt in my mind she's planned it this way.

Instead of shaking my head at the silliness of our outfits, I plaster on my best smile for her sake. "You look beautiful, Ains."

The compliment, at least, is real. Ainsley's a beautiful girl.

She twirls, her dress catching air as she spins, and it reminds me of when we met at my cousin John's wedding. She and I both attended without dates, but rather than be self-conscious or shy, she danced the entire night, drawing the attention of every guest in attendance.

Ainsley stops after a full revolution and faces me. Her smile is wide, eyes bright, and I feel like such an asshole for all the doubts that occupy my mind more often than not.

Ainsley's a good girl, a *great* girl. I just don't know if she's *my* girl. At least, not anymore. Can you love someone and not be *in* love with them? I don't know...

"You ready?" She reaches for my hand, loops my fingers with hers. I wait for a spark, a tingle, a hint of something to ignite inside me, but it never comes. I try to remember if at one time, back in the beginning, Ainsley's touch felt *half* as exciting as when Charli brushes against me. *By accident.* I can't remember.

Shaking my head clear of thoughts, I squeeze her hand. "Yep, let's do this."

When we get to Rouse, Jimbo and Charli are already cozy at a high-top table in the corner. The lights are dim, but I spot Charli's shiny chestnut hair instantly. She's worn it down—which she never does at work—and it cascades in tight ringlets down her back. Her body is angled toward Jimbo, her hands gesturing in the air as she, no doubt, regales him with one of her (many) over-the-top stories.

I *love* those stories.

"Over there." My hand moves to the small of Ainsley's back as I guide her to where they sit. Even though it's early on a Thursday night, the place is crowded and it takes us several minutes to make our way through the cluster of noisy patrons.

"Hey, guys," Ainsley's bright voice interrupts their conversation, and both Charli and Jimbo's heads snap in our direction at the same time.

"Hey!" Jimbo jumps from his chair and wraps Ainsley in a tight hug. "Long time, no see."

Jimbo releases Ainsley before he clasps his hand with mine and pulls me into a one-armed embrace. "Ol! Good to see you, man." His eyes slide up and down my shirt, a sarcastic smirk on his lips. "Nice shirt."

"Yeah," I murmur half-heartedly, eyes wandering to where Charli sits, back ramrod straight. Her aquamarine top pulls tight across her chest, and the deep V-neckline hints at the treasure below.

Her tits.

Charli has gorgeous tits. Amazing tits. I-want-to-lose-myself-in-them-and-never-be-found tits.

"Over there." Jimbo gestures with his chin to a nearby empty table. "Let's grab two more chairs."

I reach for one while he gets another, and we drag them back to where the girls are sitting, already chatting in the way girls do.

It's a tight fit because the table is only intended for two, but somehow we manage to squeeze in the extra seats. I find myself wedged between Charli and Ainsley. The irony *isn't* lost on me.

Almost immediately, Jimbo starts peppering Ainsley with questions about her latest trip to Denmark. He also loves to travel, but since the birth of his daughter three and a half years ago, he hasn't left the city, let alone the state. Some people read travel blogs; Jimbo talks to Ainsley.

Charli is quiet, listening, I suppose, and I use the opportunity to gauge her mood. We've barely spoken since our *chat* in the refrigerator. "Hi," I whisper, bumping her upper arm with mine.

Her eyes dart to me before sliding away. "Hi." Her voice isn't as bubbly as usual. I'm guessing by her cool demeanor she's still pissed after our tiff. I *was* a bit of an ass.

"So," Ainsley says, glancing between Charli and Jimbo. "You two seem to be hitting it off."

Jimbo's eyes land on Charli, and he smiles. "I think so, yes."

Charli smiles. *Smiles. At Jimbo.*

A sharp stab of jealousy pierces my gut.

"See, I told you." Ainsley swats my chest playfully before explaining to the table, "Oliver was worried."

"I wasn't worried," I counter. Charli rolls her eyes but says nothing.

Feeling antsy, I say, "I'm gonna go get a drink. Be right back." I don't bother asking Ainsley what she'll have, because it's always the same: Perrier with a slice of lime.

"I'll come with." Jimbo pushes himself to stand and grabs his empty beer bottle. He tips his chin toward Charli. "You want another?"

She smiles. "Sure."

We don't talk as we make our way through the tight crowd, but once we're firmly planted in line at the end of the long bar, Jimbo speaks, "Good to see you, man."

"Yeah," I agree. It *is* good to get out. Working most nights and weekends doesn't provide much opportunity for an active social life. I can't remember the last time I went out to dinner or, for that matter, had someone else cook for me.

He shakes his head. "Though with you wearing that shirt, I might have to ask you to back up a bit."

My brow furrows in confusion as he continues, "That shirt screams, 'I don't ever want to get laid again.'"

"Asshole." I chuckle under my breath. "Ainsley picked it up for me."

"Where? Douches-R-Us?"

Resting my palm flat on the bar, I say, "Probably."

"So..." He angles his body toward me. "Charli's hot."

"Mmm," I murmur, because I can't agree. *Can I?*

Of course not, because I'm engaged. *Engaged,* not *dead,* my mind niggles. But still, it wouldn't be right to admit that I want her more than I've ever wanted anyone, *anything,* in my entire goddamn life.

"And those tits?" Jimbo says with a touch of awe in his voice. "I'd love to fuck those tits."

"What the hell?" I snap, leaning back just far enough to see his puzzled expression. *Never mind that I want to do exactly that.* His eyes widen at my outburst, but I continue, undeterred, "She's my coworker *and* friend." I tear a hand through my hair. "Have a little respect."

"Sorry." He raises his hands in defeat. "Sorry, man. It's been so long since Katelyn... I just..." He rests both forearms along the sleek marble top of the bar. "Charli seems like a nice girl."

She is. The best *girl.* I nod, not knowing what to say, because Charli is an amazing woman, and Jimbo would be lucky to have her. But I don't want him to have her. I don't want *anyone* to have her.

Thankfully, the bartender interrupts our conversation when he comes over to take our order. Not even five minutes later, we're heading back to our narrow table, drinks in hand.

The conversation flows, easy and smooth. Typical small talk: the weather, the upcoming Fourth of July holiday, summer vacation plans.

But I can't relax. At least, not fully. Charli's much too close for my liking. Close enough for her to accidentally brush against me as she uncrosses and re-crosses her legs. Close enough for her cotton candy perfume to assault my nostrils. Close enough that when she bends to unhook her purse from the peg beneath the table, her shirt gapes and exposes a lacey black bra that is downright sinful. *Fuck.*

But if my proximity bothers her, she doesn't let on. She devotes her attention to Jimbo. Laughs at his borderline crude jokes. Touches his arm affectionately when he talks about his daughter. Lets him rest his hand on the small of her back as we walk from the bar to the restaurant two blocks away.

The rest of the night passes in a fog. I'm on autopilot. I talk, smile, and laugh when necessary, but even if I were offered one million dollars cash, I wouldn't be able to recall one word from the entire evening. Not. One. Word.

After dinner, we say our goodbyes, and I do my best to downplay my envy as Jimbo climbs into an Uber with Charli. Equal parts of me want to know where they're going, and equal parts don't.

I convince myself they're probably going for an after-dinner drink somewhere. Surely Charli wouldn't sleep with him on the first date. Would she? *No.* My mind answers its own question. Charli is a good girl. Or at least I *think* she is.

When we get back home, I strip off the offending shirt and head toward the bathroom. Ainsley's voice carries over the sound of rushing water as I adjust the taps. "You're showering again?"

"Yeah," I say before adding, "it was a bit smoky in there." I don't even know what the fuck I'm saying and curse myself for not coming up with a better reason for my impromptu second shower.

Her eyes widen in confusion—smoking isn't allowed in bars or restaurants anymore, so it's virtually impossible that I'd smell like smoke—but she accepts my rationale without further question.

Grabbing my clothes from the pile on the floor, I toss them into the hamper before stepping into the spray. I let the fat droplets cascade over my back, willing my thoughts to slide out of my body just as easily as the water slides down the drain.

No such luck.

Charli. With her long brown hair that begs to be wrapped around my fist and pulled.

Charli. With her lacy black bra peeking out from the low neckline of her shirt, tempting me, teasing me with a glimpse of her round, plump tits.

Charli. With those long legs brushing against me every time she moved in her seat, driving me to distraction. Pushing me to the point where it took every ounce of willpower not to slide my hand under the table and caress her smooth thigh. To slip my fingers between her legs to feel if she was as wet as I was hard.

The thrum of the water rushing through the pipes drowns out

my low groans as I fist my cock. I don't let myself think about why I'm in the shower alone, jerking off, when Ainsley—my fiancée—is in our bed, awake and willing.

God, what the fuck is *wrong* with me?

Just one time, my mind bargains.

Allow yourself this one fantasy to get her out of your system.

Then everything can go back to normal.

Twisting my hand back and forth, I close my eyes, imagining Charli's gorgeous tits wrapped in fine, delicate lace. I imagine sliding myself between them, allowing their fullness to swallow me whole. Bracing one arm on the wall for support, I hang my head low, my ab muscles clenching as my hips jut forward. The reality is, I'm fucking my fist, *hard*, but in my mind, I'm fucking Charli's sweet tits. Coming all over them while she smiles, begging me for more.

I shoot all over the stone wall. My eyes squeeze shut as I try to erase the one pure word that slipped from my mouth when I found my release.

Charlotte.

Desperately *wanting* to swallow it back, to rewind time, I suck in a long, slow breath. But I can't change what I said. Can't change what I just did. Can't change the fact that I'm one hundred percent fucked, because I already want to do it again. Only this time *with* her. In my bed—wet, naked, and willing. Night after night.

Charlotte.

She's mine.

All mine.

CHARLI

MORE THAN A WEEK passes until I see Oliver again. He was off for three nights in a row (due to Ainsley being home, I guess) and the nights he did work, I didn't. I'm in the tiny office near the back of the kitchen when he enters. Because I'm on the phone with a client, I hold up one finger to signal for him to give me a minute.

"Yes." I nod. "Yes, Mr. Clack. Everything is all set and ready to go. We look forward to seeing you then." I nod again. "Uh-huh. Thank you. Bye-bye."

As I hang up the phone, Oliver raises his eyebrows. "Pharm Corp?"

"Yep. Their usual." The sound pops in the small space. "Seventy-five of their top execs enjoying an expensive lunch disguised as a business meeting."

Oliver takes a breath, and in true Oliver fashion says exactly what's on his mind, "I acted like an ass."

I'm so thrown by his (sort of) apology, it takes a second for my mouth to catch up with my brain. "What?"

"You can date..." His gaze drifts over my shoulder to a faded food safety poster that looks like it was pinned up on the wall behind me sometime in the seventies. "...Jimbo, or whomever you want."

"Geez, thanks for your permission." My arms cross my chest, even though my tone is playful.

"Look, Charli, I'm trying to apologize here."

"Not very well, I might add."

His eyes hold mine as he faces me dead-on and murmurs two tiny words I desperately long to hear, "I'm sorry."

My voice is whisper soft when I ask, "Why do you even care, Oliver?"

He stares at me for a beat more, and then one hand scrubs over his face as if it pains him to say the words. "I just do."

My eyes hold his. "What do you want from me?"

He exhales a loud breath before speaking again. "I want us to be okay." He leans in a touch more. "Are we good?"

"Sure." I stand, grabbing the stack of purchase orders that still need to be reviewed and paid. Wanting to put some distance between us, I begin to walk toward the door. When I attempt to squeeze past Oliver, he doesn't move, so I'm forced to stop halfway, wedged partly between him and the desk.

We both pause, awkward and unmoving, and his lids flutter closed. We're standing close. Indecently so. My heart knocks a furious pace in my chest, my breathing stilted and choppy.

When he speaks, his voice is layered with emotion, although I can't discern which one exactly: regret, hope, sadness. And I have to wonder if he wants friendship or...something *more*? "Charlotte." He brushes a few stray hairs that have fallen from my ponytail off my forehead. The rough scrape of the pads of his fingers against my sensitive skin causes me to tremble. "I'm sorry."

"You said that already," I whisper in the stillness.

His fingers flex, almost like he's going to touch me, but then he stiffens in place. "I meant it."

My eyes draw to his lips, and I swear, *I swear*, his eyes move to mine as well. Although it's wrong, although he's engaged, although I know his fiancée personally, I lean into him, press against the hard plane of his chest and drink in the warmth of his exhaled breaths.

My body is at war with itself, frozen. I *want* to reach out, to touch him in the ways I've only dreamt about. To press my lips against his, to demand the answer to the questions that have been plaguing me for far too long. *Am I the only one who feels this? Am I going crazy? Am I imagining things that aren't there because I want you so much?*

Meg's voice hits my ears before I actually see her. "Charli, can I—oh."

As Oliver and I pull apart, I stumble back onto the desk. My ass knocks a tray of paperclips to the ground, and they scatter like roaches in the light of day.

Apparently unsure of what she's just seen, Meg stands in the doorway, one eyebrow quirked in suspicion. "Uhh, am I interrupting something?" One foot retreats. "I can come back later."

"No." Oliver scoots to the side, an easy smile stretching across his lips. "I was just helping Charli out." He shrugs, calm and cool. "She had something in her eye."

My eyes dart to him, surprised by his lie, but he merely continues to smile.

Meg's face morphs from one of confusion to understanding. "Oh, that's the worst." She stands in front of the desk, gesturing to her lashes. "I swear, at the rate my eyelashes fall out, I won't have any left by the time I'm thirty."

Oliver chuckles as he walks to the door. He pauses, gives me one last lingering look, the sincere tone of his voice conveying his underlying meaning. "Everything all good now?"

"Yeah." I meet his eyes once more. "It's all good."

I'm dying, *dying* to talk to Meg about what happened. I want to pick apart her brain and analyze, piece by piece, every fraction of every second between Oliver and me. But I can't. I won't...because what will that achieve? Nothing. Besides, I don't want Meg to judge me for lusting after an (almost) married man.

Sure, everyone at Mecca acknowledges Oliver's attractiveness. Describing Oliver as good looking would be like calling Mount Everest a mountain peak. Yes, technically, it is a mountain, but it's so much more. Oliver is exactly the same, just *more*.

He's awe-inspiring. From his chiseled jaw, to his dark eyes that always seem to hold a hint of mischief, to his cocky confidence, to his charismatic personality that I have no doubt could charm the habit off a nun. In one word, he's irresistible. However, he's also unavailable.

Engaged.

Off-limits.

I may be a lot of things, but a home-wrecker isn't one of them. And even if I were, how could I possibly pursue a relationship with him when I'm friends (okay, maybe *friends* is a strong word to describe my relationship with Ainsley, but still) with his fiancée? Ainsley is kind and genuine and *so* doesn't deserve my lusting after her soon-to-be-husband. Is there a home-wreckers' handbook? If there is, I bet rule number one states: Never, *ever*, cheat with your friend's significant other. Or you know, *at all*.

Right now, Oliver's a fantasy. Untouchable and harmless. Even if said fantasy is on its way to becoming a full-blown obsession.

I think about him constantly. I know I shouldn't. But at night when I close my eyes, I imagine us naked, me on top, taking him deep as I ride him slowly. When I'm in the shower, I picture him pinning me to the wall, thrusting into me from behind, our wet bodies pressed skin to skin. When I lie in bed in the morning, I envision waking him up with my lips wrapped around his hard, thick cock.

The fantasies are detailed, explicit, and filthy. This isn't me. I've had tons of crushes before, but never like this. It's lame, but also entirely accurate that I've never had sexual fantasies about real-life crushes. Celebrities? Sure. Book boyfriends? Definitely. But not someone from my *actual* life.

My Oliver fantasies border on depraved. The things I imagine doing, or us doing t*ogether*, make my skin burn with shame. And the worst of it, the thing that makes me think I'm utterly sick in the head is that I've even imagined him fucking Ainsley. Gotten myself off to the image of him pounding her, hands tangled in her hair, sweat dripping, body aching for release, all while I watched.

I'm all kinds of fucked up.

I've never been this sexually attracted to any other man. It has to be chemical, something about the way his pheromones and mine combine, because the pull is *unstoppable*. The desire, the urges are so strong that I'm almost sure he feels them too. Some days, I think we'll both combust if we don't touch. But then other days, days like today, he barely looks at me and mutters a total of five words.

It's driving me insane. *He's* driving me insane. So I do what any (stupid) girl would do. I agree to meet Jim for a second date.

Things between Jim and me ended on an awkward note. During our shared ride, the conversation flowed and when the car pulled up outside my apartment building, Jim walked me to my front door. He was *quite* the gentleman.

But then things got weird. I hesitated before unlocking the door. He leaned in and I *thought* he was going to kiss me, so I readied myself. Pursed my lips. Closed my eyes. But rather than kiss me, he pulled me in for a bear hug and then *patted my head* before he left. #WTF

He texted the next day to explain.

Jim: Sorry I freaked at the end of our date. I'm rusty and haven't been on a date in eight years.

Another bubble pops up, more dots appear as he types another message.

. . .

Jim: Can I get a do over? I promise I won't pat your head. WTF was I thinking?

Charli: Lol. I was a little surprised.

Charli: What did you have in mind?

Jim: Lunch? You pick the place.

We decide to meet at McLaughlin's, a small Irish pub on the outskirts of the city, halfway between my downtown apartment and Jim's suburban rental.

I wait for him outside, near the front entrance, and as he approaches, I feel no flutter of nerves, no rush of excitement. He's handsome enough. Long, square face, strong jaw. His blue eyes are open and honest, and his dirty blond hair is cut short. He wears navy dress pants and a white cotton button-down with thin light blue pinstripes. He's your average Wall Street broker type.

"Hi." This time when he leans in, he *does* kiss my cheek, but I feel nothing. *Shit.*

"Hi."

Jim opens the door and gestures me inside. It's dimly lit, and there's a faint smell of stale beer in the air. He places his hand on my lower back, guiding me toward the hostess stand. It's...*nice*. In a completely non-sexual way.

"Two for lunch, please," he says, not releasing my hand, but my body remains unexcited by his touch.

"Right this way." The hostess gestures toward an oversized booth and we follow her. She gives us each a large menu before dropping two additional menus in the center of the table. "Top one is specials. The bottom one is the wine and beer list."

"Thanks," we say in unison, and she leaves us alone.

As we look over our menus, a server brings us each a glass of water and a breadbasket for the table.

Once I've decided on my order, I lay my menu atop the others on the center pile. Jim's eyes meet mine when he speaks, "I have to say, I'm surprised you agreed to lunch."

"Why's that?" I lift the water glass to my lips.

His voice is calm, matter-of-fact, a direct contrast to the words he says. "Because you're in love with Oliver."

I choke on the drink I've just taken, and water sputters across *all* of the menus. *Nice, Charlotte.* "Wh-what?"

He shrugs. "It was just a hunch." He leans back in the booth. "But your reaction just confirmed it."

Bristling, I reach for my napkin and haphazardly mop up the liquid. "I have no idea what you're talking about."

He knows.

I'm so screwed.

Also, dude, why did you make shit so awkward at the end of the date by trying to not kiss me?

Jim's calm voice invades my mini-attack. "Sure you do." He tears a piece of crust from the bread on his plate and pops it into this mouth.

I don't speak as he chews. I just sit quietly and wait for him to go on, the silence deafening. He swallows and takes a drink before he continues, "I'm a market analyst." He drums his fingers on the table. "I *analyze* people and their behaviors for a living." Still, I say nothing, but he keeps talking. "If it's any consolation, he likes you too."

"He does?" The words spill from my mouth before I can stop them.

"Yeah." He nods. "He almost murdered me when I made a comment about your tits."

"You made a comment about my tits?" Righteous indignation flares. "*When?*"

"Yeah, sorry about that." His smile is boyish and innocent, making it nearly impossible for me to be angry. His eyes drop to my chest before quickly returning to my face. "They're *really nice.*"

"Focus." I snap my fingers to get his attention. "God, guys are such assholes."

He shrugs. "We can be."

"So why invite me on a second date?" I question, because this "date" just turned incredibly awkward, incredibly fast. "What's your game?"

"No game." He extends his hand. "We can be friends, can't we?"

I eye said hand with suspicion, and he continues, "Listen, I have no desire to date someone—no matter how hot she is—when she's in love with someone else." He shakes his head and smiles. "As you know, I just went through a shitty divorce, and it's good to get out. Meet new people. No use sitting at home wallowing by myself."

"I'm sorry," I murmur, but he waves his hand in dismissal before dropping it back to his side.

"Don't be. I don't want to waste time talking about my ex-wife." His tone is light yet sounds forced to my ears, like it's laced with an undercurrent of hurt.

Exhaling a long, loud breath, I meet his eyes and whisper, "I do." One of his brows arches in question at my statement. Taking a deep breath, I flatten my palms against the smooth tablecloth and repeat, "I do like him."

Jim nods, as if this is no surprise at all, as if I didn't just confess the worst possible secret. I'm in love—as wrong as it may be—with someone I have no right loving.

"I wish I didn't." My eyes squeeze shut. "God, I wish I didn't."

He pats my hand across the table, and I peer at him underneath the shadow of my lashes. "For your sake, I wish you didn't either."

Suddenly, the words are rushing out as I confide my secrets to the unlikeliest candidate ever: *Oliver's* best friend. "I don't know what to do. I can't tell him. What could he say? And even if he did reciprocate the feelings, it's not like we'd actually do anything about it. I don't want to hurt anyone." I pause, suck in another breath. "It just feels like...like he's mine." My eyes search Jim's for understanding. For him to see that I'm not a terrible, fiancée-stealing slut. "You don't know how much I wish things were different. That we could have met in another time, another place. Do you believe in fate?"

His sad, open eyes tell me everything his words don't. *No.*

I gasp as I realize I'm rambling, talking nonsense, but I can't quite stop myself. My voice turns sad as I say, "I don't know how to make it go away. It's nearly impossible when I see him every day..."

The ringing of his phone interrupts my diatribe, and he reaches into his pocket, his eyes squinting when he reads the name on the screen, "Speak of the devil."

My eyes widen in panic as Jim accepts the call. "Oliver, what's up?"

Jim offers me a smile, in what I'm guessing is his attempt to ease my nerves. Eyes never leaving mine, he continues to speak into the phone, "No, it's all good. Yeah, I'm out to lunch with Charli." He nods and keep talking, "No, we're not in the city. Yeah, I will. Sounds good. See you then. Later."

He ends the call and rests his cell on the table. I resist the urge to ask what the conversation was about. The questions are there, right on the tip of my tongue. *What will he do? When will he see Oliver? What did Oliver say when he found out we were together?*

Jim's eyes sparkle with playfulness. "I know you're dying to ask."

I shrug, and he chuckles before putting me out of my misery. "We're playing a round of golf tomorrow morning."

"Hmm," I murmur. Golfing. Such a grown-up, manly thing to do. I bet Oliver looks hot in plaid golfing shorts. I'd sure love to handle *his* club. Jesus, I've officially gone crazy.

"Charli." Jim's voice grabs my attention. "Do you want my advice?"

Not at all. "Umm..."

"Well, I'm going to give it to you anyway. Oliver's one of the good ones. He's not going to cheat on Ainsley. Yes, he's a flirt, but that's as far as he'll ever take it. He's not going to leave her." He drums his fingers on the table. "They have a history, *a life*, together. And after the accident—."

I cut him off, my head bobbing, because I *know* what he's saying is true. Oliver is cocky, arrogant, hot as fuck, but he's also honest and decent and *loyal*. To a fault.

"You're young and beautiful. There's a guy out there for you."

A sad smile curves my lips. Jim, Oliver's best friend and my so-called-date, is giving me a pep talk about meeting the right guy. It's pathetic, really, but also, it's the exact dose of reality I need.

"You're right." I nod. "You're so fucking right."

He winks. "Of course I am."

Some of the tension breaks, and a genuine smile spreads over my face. "Thank you for talking sense into me."

"Any time."

I make room on the table as the waitress brings our entrees, and I wait for her to leave before speaking again, already knowing the answer to my next question but still needing verbal confirmation. "You won't say anything to Oliver, will you?"

Jim gives me a perplexed, somewhat hurt look before shaking his head. "Nah. It's a silly crush. Besides, it'll be kinda fun breaking his balls."

"What?" I pause, the bottle of malt vinegar hovering above my fish and chips.

He chuckles. "He thinks we're an item. It's fun knocking him down a peg or two, showing him he can't win *every* girl."

I laugh then, too, because Jim's right. It's easy to get Oliver fired up. My mind is a memory time lapse as it flicks over the many heated blowups we've had. Arguing over how often to change the tasting menu (once a month). Bickering over which decade had the better music (definitely the nineties). Fighting about how many reservations we can comfortably accommodate in the main dining room (one hundred twelve). And most recently, disagreeing about whom I date (not Jim, apparently).

Jim winks. "Let him think what he wants. I got your back, friend."

"Thanks, friend." I smile one last time before digging into the greasy food in front of me, and since this is no longer a date, I eat the whole thing.

It's fucking *delicious*.

OLIVER

"HERE." Jimbo hands me a cup of coffee from the clubhouse. "You look like you could use this."

I nod and take the cup from his hands, ignoring the fact that it's made of Styrofoam and is terrible for the environment. If my sister could see me now, she'd ream me a new one. "Thanks."

"You up for playing the full course?"

"Sure." I take a cautious sip, testing its temperature. The bitterness immediately assaults my tongue. I have no problem admitting I'm a coffee snob. Every morning I drink a rich, smooth blend that needs to be special ordered online because it's imported from Italy and costs a small fortune. Hey, a man has his needs. Mine happen to be high-end, low acidity, smooth-as-a-baby's-ass coffee.

Jim loads his golf bag into the back of the cart before climbing into the driver's seat. I choke back another sip of coffee before stacking my clubs alongside his. "Can I ask you something?"

He pauses then answers, "No, I *didn't* sleep with her."

I don't have to ask whom. I know exactly which her he's referring to. And while I'm grateful for the information, Charlotte is not who I want to talk about. At least, not right now.

I force casualness into my voice. "Who you do or do not sleep with is none of my business, man."

He chuckles as he turns the ignition in the cart before following the path to the first green. "You're right, it's not. But we both know it was only a matter of time before you asked." He shrugs. "I saved you the trouble—and the embarrassment."

"Fuck you." We hop out and I squat down and line up my ball on the tee. "You can bang Charli or a million other chicks. No sweat off my back." *Lies.* The thought of Jimbo and Charli together —naked—makes my skin crawl and my fists clench.

My grasp is tight around the neck of the club as I swing my arms in a wide arc, driving the ball deep across the green.

Jimbo moves behind me, slides his nine iron from his bag. Tees up his shot.

"Okay, then." His arm glides through the air, the ball sailing out of sight. "What did you want to ask me?"

I hesitate because his stupid comments about Charli really pissed me the fuck off. In the end, I shove down my annoyance because I think I'm going through somewhat of an emotional crisis and Jimbo is the only one, besides Margot, that I can talk to.

"Umm." I hesitate as we clamber back into the cart. I clear my throat, not really knowing how to ask the question. Jimbo and I aren't in the habit of having heart to hearts. Sure, there are times when he or I get emotional, like when he was in the thick of his divorce, for example, but more often than not, we just hang out. Do manly things. A total cliché, *I know.*

But I need to talk to *someone.* Normally, I'd go to Margot, but I know she's biased. She doesn't like Ainsley and is very vocal about it. Besides, I'd rather talk to someone who's male *and* who has been married before.

Jimbo's the lucky winner.

The cart jerks to a stop and I speak the words in a long rush before my courage leaves me, "How did…How did you know Katelyn was the one?"

Jimbo's grip tightens around the steering wheel for just a

moment. Then he turns to face me, a sad smile across his face. "Well, she wasn't the one, so..."

I immediately feel like an asshole. "Sorry, I didn't mean to bring up bad memories. It's just that..." My voice trails off as the thoughts that have been plaguing me for *months* start to bubble to the surface. "How do you *know*? How do you pick one person out of millions and decide, yes, this is the girl that I'm going to spend the rest of my life with?"

Jimbo turns in his seat to face me. "Are you having doubts about Ainsley?"

Yes.

No.

I don't know.

My expression must say it all. "Shouldn't you have asked yourself these questions *before* you proposed?"

I exhale a breath. Jimbo's right. These questions would have been better answered before we planned to marry, but we—or at least I—had gotten caught up in the comfort of routine, doing the things that were expected when a couple had been together for so long.

We saw each other very little, and the days when we were together felt magical and precious, like borrowed time. I was thirty-seven, figured it was as good a time as any, and popped the question the night before she left for Tokyo. I didn't see her for nearly two months after that.

Fast forward one full year and we still haven't set a date. Ten months ago, she finally moved her stuff into my house, but we're no closer—intimately—than we were three years ago. Hell, sometimes I feel like I know more stuff about my mailman than I do Ainsley.

But probably the most discouraging of all is when I do learn new things about Ainsley—the more I get to know her, the more I discover what little we have in common.

She's a vegan. I'm a foodie. She's flashy and trendy. I'm classic and elegant. She trusts everyone. I'm a natural born skeptic. While it's true opposite attracts, I'm fearful that we're both fundamentally different people.

Jimbo's concerned voice pulls me out of the clusterfuck that is my mind. "Does this have anything to do with Charli?"

My head hangs and I don't answer his question because I don't know how. Truthfully, I'm not sure if these doubts about Ainsley stem from my attraction to Charli or if my attraction to Charli stems from unhappiness in my relationship.

"All right." Jimbo taps the steering wheel as though coming to a conclusion. "Now's as good a time as any to tell you that I'm *not* dating Charli." My eyes snap to his as he continues, "She's a cool girl, but there's no spark between us."

A heavy weight, one that I didn't even realize was crushing my chest, lightens.

"We decided we're better as friends."

Part of me wants to shout at him for being such a blind fuck. How can he *not* have a spark with Charli? The other part wants to fall to my knees and thank him for sparing me the torture of seeing them together, because I don't think I'd survive it.

"Okay." My throat's so dry that I can barely speak the word.

"All I can tell you is divorce fucking blows." I grunt and he continues, "So I'd be *real* sure. If you're having feelings for Charli, or anyone else, figure that shit out before you tie yourself—legally—to another person." He shakes his head. "I swear I bought my lawyer's vacation house on the Cape with all the money I paid his firm."

It's quiet for a minute as we each reflect on where we are in our lives, me about to begin a marriage, Jimbo ending one. A loud honk interrupts our thoughts as an impatient, grumpy man yells from the cart behind us, "Talk or play!"

We both turn and glance back at the short elderly gentleman with white hair. He looks like he could be someone's grandfather. But at the moment, his downturned eyes and sour expression aren't paternal in the least. The angry slash of his brow lets us know he's infuriated. *Chill out, man, it's golf.*

Jimbo and I jump out of the cart and grab our clubs as Jimbo shouts, "We're playing!"

For the next two hours, I lose myself in the course, thoughts of Charli shoved aside. But once night comes and I'm sitting alone in an empty house, Jimbo's words echo in my head: *I'd be real sure.*

The only problem is, I'm not sure of anything anymore.

CHARLI

IT'S HARD TURNING off your heart. Really fucking hard. After my pep talk with Jim, I dive full force into ridding myself of all my Oliver fantasies. It's easy at first. I'm pumped full of Jim's solid words—Oliver and I haven't worked the same shift in days and I've just spent an enjoyable afternoon with a handsome man who has given me solid advice. But sooner or later, reality rolls in like a foreboding storm cloud. The words fade away, and when Oliver and I come face to face the following week at work, all those same desires come back. Times ten.

I shove those feeling aside and do my best to focus on my main priority, my job. If Oliver notices a difference in my behavior, he doesn't mention it. Not that I suspect he would. I've become a master at hiding my true feelings.

It's not until I'm leaving on Friday night, right after our seven o'clock rush, that he mentions my second date with Jim.

"So..." Oliver looks up from the dish he's just finished plating. "You and Jimbo seem to have hit it off?"

"Yeah." I slip on my jacket. "He's a nice guy."

He barks a laugh. "I can tell you stories that would make you think otherwise."

I level him with a gaze. "I'm sure he'd say the same about you."

He quirks a brow. "Touché."

"So you're here all night?" I ask, even though I know he is. Having a good memory is useful, but also a curse. It's not like I actively try to memorize his schedule. It just happens.

"Yeah." He nods. "You on your way out?"

"Just about." I take down the three notes with my name written across the top that are pinned to the bulletin board. "I think I may get out of here before seven tonight."

"Got a hot date?" His smile is coy. "With Jimbo, I mean."

An odd sensation creeps over me. It's like Oliver's baiting me, trying to draw out some unspoken truth buried deep within my soul. *Did Jim tell him we're better off as friends? Worse still, did Jim out me? Reveal my crush?*

Heat prickles my skin and I fight back of wave of panic. I feign indifference. "Not with Jim." I wink, hoping the (made-up) innuendo is clear.

The smile falls from his lips. "You're seeing someone else?"

One shoulder lifts in a noncommittal shrug.

"Who?" The heat in his voice surprises me, but he's probably just angry on his friend's behalf. He probably thinks I'm playing Jim. "Simon?" he questions.

I can see why he might guess my date is with Simon since he isn't working tonight either. Like I said, I have *everyone's* schedules memorized. Not to mention the fact that Jules made that comment about Simon all those weeks ago...

Spinning on my heels, I stuff the notes into my bag, deciding to read them later when I have a clearer frame of mind.

"Charlotte." The deep sound, the textured rumble stops me dead in my tracks and for just a fraction of a fraction of a second, I imagine the sound of my name leaving his lips while he sinks inside me. Would it sound the same? Deeper? Harder? Rougher?

I blink, my eyes slamming the door shut on the indecent thought.

By the time I refocus my gaze, Oliver stands in front of me, one hand hanging loosely by his side, the other firmly gripping my elbow. "Tell me you're not actually dating Simon?"

I hold his stare for a moment but don't answer. What can I say really? *Nope, no date here. Just super excited to get home early and continue binge-watching my latest Hulu pick.*

His mouth twists. "Isn't he a little young for you?"

Indignation flairs at his accusatory tone. Simon's twenty-one, for Christ's sake. A legal, consenting, full-fledged adult. But if Oliver's narrowed eyes and tight jaw are any indication, he's not happy with the possibility. He might as well come right out with it and call me a pervert.

I match him toe to toe, defending myself. "He's twenty-one." Oliver snorts as I add, "And in college."

"A college boy." He claps his hands together. "Oh goody. You two must have so much to talk about. What, with all the frat parties and keg stands and—"

Part of me wonders how we got here, arguing over my nonexistent romantic relationship with Simon, and I confess as much. "I'm not seeing Simon!" I shout loud enough to be heard over the noisy oven hood, and Giancarlo and Jason pop their heads up, eyes darting between Oliver and me.

His tone softens, but his posture does not. "You're not?"

I shake my head, an angry breath pushing past my lips.

One hand tears through his dark, unruly locks. "Then why did you say you were?"

"I didn't."

"You—"

I hold up my hand, cutting him off. "I didn't, but let's just table this discussion for another night, all right?" My eyes drift to the clock. "It's been a long day and"—I gesture to the counter behind him, piled high with plates of food waiting to be garnished and dressed—"you're busy."

His eyes follow my gaze. "Okay, yeah." His fingers ghost over my forearm. "See you tomorrow?"

"Yep." I nod, my feet taking me toward the door, even though my body demands his touch. His attention. "Good night." I call to everyone over my shoulder, forcing a bright smile.

See? I can totally be his friend. I don't want him to wrap his strong arms around me and fuck me on the counter. I don't want him to demand that I can't see Jim or Simon, or any other man, because I'm *his*. And I definitely don't want him to bury his face between my legs, allow the rough scrape of his five o'clock shadow to scratch my sensitive thighs...because we're friends. And friends don't touch each other. While naked. While screaming in pleasure.

And by the time I crawl into bed nearly four hours later, I'm mostly convinced of the truth in my words.

OLIVER

MOST DAYS I don't feel my age. After all, age is just a number, and if I'm honest, thirty-eight doesn't feel all that much different than twenty-eight. But then again, some days I feel old. Real fucking old. The years creeping in fast and strong, as heavy and ominous as the barrel of a loaded gun.

"Dammit," I hiss as the knife I've been using for chopping crashes to the wooden board.

Charli looks up from where she's crouched down by the back shelves, counting boxes for inventory. "You okay?"

It's Friday morning and we'll be alone until two p.m., when Jason is scheduled to arrive. I shouldn't be as excited as I am to spend time with her, but I am. The only dark spot is that my body aches. And not in a good way.

"Yeah," I grumble, resisting the urge to rub the sore muscle between my neck and shoulder.

I hate that this old baseball injury from high school still plagues me, even after years of physical therapy. Repeated motions—like chopping—and damp weather—like today—exacerbate my *subacromial bursitis*, whatever the fuck that is. All I know is that it makes me feel old and worn out. Especially in front of Charli.

My grip tightens around the smooth handle of the knife as the pain radiates, *pulses* from my neck to my shoulder and down my mid back. I grit my teeth and push on.

Charli eyes me with suspicion. "You sure you're okay?"

"Yeah," I say, abandoning the knife and cutting board. I walk a few paces

away and discreetly try to roll my neck.

"Are you sore?" She pushes herself to stand. "Did you pull something?"

"I'm fine." Turning back to face her, I force a smile. "Really."

She shrugs. "I can help if you want."

One of her brows arches in question, but before I can say anything, she says, "I did go to massage therapy school."

"No shit!" My mouth hangs open in disbelief. *How did I not know this?* "*You're* a masseuse?" I wish my question didn't sound as incredulous as it does, but I'm having difficulty reconciling this new piece of information with the Charli I know.

"Don't sound so surprised." She makes a show of flexing and stretching her fingers, but then her smile falls a bit. "I mean, technically no, I'm not a masseuse." Her shoulders rise and fall. "I never took my boards, but I completed all the training."

"Why not?" Her confused eyes find mine and I clarify, "Why didn't you take your exam?"

"Long story." She sighs. "But I guess it worked out. Not sure if I'd be happy touching naked strangers all day."

When I grunt, it causes my muscles to tighten more and I grimace.

"I could help, you know." She turns back to the stacked sacks of flour, ticking off another column on her clipboard. "My massage partner used to call me 'Magic Hands.'"

I'll bet. Also, her massage partner had better have been a female.

Even though my conscience urges me to immediately decline, my mind whirs to life, assessing the appropriateness of her offer, imagining all of the sexy, *naked* things that can—and do—happen during a massage.

I joke to deflect my refusal. "I don't know if I trust you. With my eyes closed, you're liable to take full advantage of me."

Her eyes hold mine and shine with humor. "I think someone's been watching a little too much porn."

Busted.

Maybe I *am* reading too much into the offer. I mean, we're at work for Christ's sake. We're both fully clothed. It's not like I'll be lying down. And the earliest I was able to get an appointment with my chiro is three days from now. Maybe a massage isn't such a bad idea after all.

"All right," I agree, and her head snaps toward me. "I'm desperate."

Her eyes fall for a split second as she wipes her hands down the front of her pants and I instantly regret making her seem like a last resort. She *is*, but it isn't because I don't think she'll do a good job. It's because I'm scared of *how* good it'll feel.

My cocky confidence wavers a bit as she approaches, but then I ask. "How do you want to do this?"

I walk beside her as she moves into the dining room. She pauses, gestures with her chin to the long bench seat and for a moment I think she'll ask me to lie down, but she says, "Sit."

I do as told and straddle the end of the bench, draping one leg over either side. With my head facing forward, I close my eyes as I feel movement behind me. Soft fingers grip my shoulders and I immediately tense up. "Relax." Her voice is calm, soothing, as she squeezes my flesh.

Exhaling a slow breath, I force my body to relax, but it's damn hard with her pressed against me, her touch heating my skin even through the cotton fabric of my shirt.

She kneads my upper back for a few minutes, and with each second that ticks by, my body relaxes more and more. Her voice is whisper soft when she asks, "Feel good?"

"Mmm," I murmur, voice already getting drowsy.

Slowly, she withdraws her hands and asks, "Which shoulder is it?"

In the moment, I'm so confused, so lost in the euphoria of her touch that I have no idea what she's talking about. "What?"

The pads of her fingertips drag across my upper back. "Which is your bad shoulder?" She touches my right shoulder first. "Right?" Her hand slides across to the opposite side. "Or left?"

"Right," I half-say, half-grunt as her fingers dig into the tight knot of muscle. When I ghost my hand up, it collides with hers, which she quickly pulls away. "Right in here." I massage the crook of my neck, pointing first to my traps and then my deltoids.

"Okay." Her hands resume their position, smoothing over my skin. "Is the pressure okay?"

I pause, wondering if it'd be rude to tell her to press harder. I guess not since she asked, but still, I hesitate. "I like it a bit..." Harder. Rougher. Firmer.

Nope, all those words sound *way* too sexual. Clearing my throat I say, "More pressure is good."

Her hands still. "You sure? I don't want to hurt you. Especially if you have an injury."

"You won't."

I feel her head nod, though I can't see it and she instructs. "Scoot forward some."

Wiggling my ass down the bench, I feel her body slide behind mine, her knees framing either side of my hips.

She explains the new position, "I can use my body weight this way."

Her knees squeeze my ass, her stomach presses into the small of my back, her tits hang heavy against my... "Oh *fuck*," I groan loudly when her fingers dig into a certain patch of tense muscle. My head rolls forward, hanging heavy, my shoulders unable to support its weight. Her touch hurts so fucking good. "Jesus, Charli. Right *there*."

She's silent as she uses one hand to position my head to the side, stretching the muscles taut. The other hand massages the tendons and I lose my breath a little when she pushes on a particularly sensitive pressure point. "God," I moan. "That feels so fucking good."

My voice isn't meant to be sensual or intimate, but it sounds that way, even to my own ears, so I keep talking in an effort to defuse the innuendo. "You really do have magic hands."

She chuckles, her hot breath fluttering across my skin, causing my nerves to tingle and my dick to ache. With my legs spread wide, my already rock-hard cock juts forward, fully displayed, begging to be touched. I have an incredible urge to fist it, stroke myself, as her fingers caress my body. Or better yet, hook the thigh that cradles my side and pull her down to straddle me.

"Your deltoids are really tight. So are your rhom—" She stops abruptly. "Sorry, I guess an anatomy lesson will kill the mood."

I don't add that the only anatomy lesson I need from her is one that I'm certain she can't give me. One that's up close, personal, and *very* naked.

Her fingers begin to slow, the pressure lightening until just a ghost of her touch remains. "Better?"

Please don't stop. "Yeah."

My skin buzzes, I'm hot all over, and I don't want her to see my face. It's probably flushed and my lazy eyes practically drip with desire. She slides off the bench seat, the cool rush of air hitting my skin almost instantly. "I'd make an appointment to see a doctor ASAP."

I grunt. "I go to the chiropractor on Monday."

"That's good." She extends her hand, offering to help me up, and I hesitate but only for a moment. I keep my eyes downcast as she continues to talk, "It'd probably be a good idea to use some topical cream too. Like Bengay or something."

I nod, still unable to meet her eyes. I should have *never* agreed to this massage. I knew it would blur the already messy lines in my head. Knew it would make the fantasies worse, not better. But more importantly, how the hell am I going to hide my boner from her? *There's absolutely no fucking way she'll miss the massive tent in my pants.*

"Thanks," I say, shifting from foot to foot, attempting to

rearrange my dick. I gather my car keys and wallet from the cubby shelf in the back. "I think I'm gonna head out."

"You're leaving?" Her eyes puzzle in confusion. "You didn't even clean up your work station."

My eyes drift to the partially chopped vegetables, dirty cutting board, and knife. "Jason will be in soon. He'll take care of it."

She nods, unsure and I understand her confusion. I never, and I mean *never*, leave my kitchen a mess. But I have to get out of here, create some much-needed distance before I do something stupid. Something life-altering. Something like kiss her. And I'm not talking about on the lips of her mouth.

"See ya tomorrow." I barely speak the words before I brush past her, on a one-way mission out. *Just get the fuck out, Oliver.*

"Bye," she calls, but the door has already slammed shut.

Nights off are rare, but a Friday night off from work? It's a fucking unicorn. Earlier this week, Don and I had a conversation about Giancarlo, our sous chef. He's been with Mecca for just under a year, and although it pains me to admit this, professionally speaking, Giancarlo's as good a chef as...*me*. Which is why Don ordered me, more or less, to start giving him more responsibility.

Of course I protested—Mecca is *my* kitchen—but then Don confided that he's in "talks" to open another high-end restaurant ten miles away on the opposite side of the city. When and *if* this venture comes to fruition, the head chef position is mine, along with a hefty bonus, which isn't as important to me as the promise of full creative license over the menu. I'm talking varied seasonal dishes, organic, locally sourced suppliers, and a finely honed prix fixe menu. All of which makes giving up a minute amount of control at Mecca a touch more bearable.

All day long, I've been dreaming about going home, crashing on the couch with a dozen hot wings, drinking a few cold beers, and watching the Red Sox—my favorite team—on the big screen. That's right ladies and gentlemen, I'm your everyday party animal.

But a man can choose to relax however he wants to. And this man's couch is calling. What can I say? It's been a long ass week.

As soon as I walk through the door, my vision of a perfect evening begins to crumble right before my eyes. Because Ainsley is home. *What the hell?* She isn't supposed to be home for another three days.

"Hey." My voice is louder than warranted, but I'm a little taken off guard. "You're home early?" My voice rises at the end in question.

Really, I should be happier—much happier—to see my fiancée. What I *shouldn't* be is put out. *I used to count the days until she'd be home.*

We've both grown accustomed to our alone time, and part of me wonders if the *only* reason our relationship works so well is because we see each other no more than seven days per month. The nights we sleep in the same bed are even fewer.

"Hey!" Ainsley taps the pantry door closed with her hip, glancing up at me across the counter. "My flight to Austria was bumped for three days."

My eyebrows rise in curiosity. For obvious reasons, it's unusual for commercial airlines to tweak schedules. Changing a flight plan, even just by a few minutes, costs companies tens of thousands of dollars. But Ainsley doesn't elaborate and I'm too tired to press for more information, so instead I ask, "You cooked?"

She gestures to the fry pan still on the stove. "Bean burgers."

So, no wings then. "Great." I glance at the pan, noticing there are six patties

frying. My eyes widen as I gesture to the stove. "Hungry?"

She smiles. "Jonas and Terry are coming over."

I scratch the back of my neck. "Tonight?"

"Yeah." She dumps a bag of pre-washed lettuce into the bowl. "I thought you were working."

And I thought you weren't going to be home.

I grab four plates and line them up on the counter. Ainsley does most of the talking, filling me in on the details of her latest trip. Her schedule rotates every six weeks. During this block, she'll be cycling between the Germanic countries.

Frankly, I think it's a damn shame that she's been to Switzerland eight times and has yet to sample their chocolate. Surely the vegan community could excuse a tiny bit of milk mixed with chocolate, right? It's *Swiss* chocolate, for crying out loud. Some of the best in the world.

Charli would love it. The thought pops into my mind before I can stop it and I fight the urge to smile. If I didn't feel so guilty about my feelings for my feisty coworker, I'd ask Ainsley to bring some back for her. Ainsley definitely would, no questions asked. She's generous and caring.

And fuck, dude, you really need to stop thinking about Charlotte and her damn *magic hands.*

I refocus all of my attention back on Ainsley and the meal she's preparing. I've only ever seen her cook five things, all healthy, of course, but what she does know how to make, she does well.

She slides the burgers onto a serving tray and places them in the oven to keep warm. "I got the mail you left for me on the desk. Thanks." She gestures to the pile of bills and magazines stacked neatly alongside my tube of Bengay. "Your shoulder bothering you again?" she asks.

I nod. "A little."

"Did you see Dr. Cruz?"

"I go on Monday. I thought the cream might help until then." I gesture with my chin toward the medicine. "But it's hard to put on myself."

Ainsley's nose scrunches. "Please don't ask me to do it. You know the smell of that stuff makes me nauseous." She takes a sip from her water bottle. "And it makes my hands all tingly."

"It's fine." I walk toward the sink to wash my hands. "It feels pretty good now." *Charli helped.* "My appointment with Dr. Cruz is soon."

"That's good." She smiles in relief. "Well, I'm going to take a quick shower before my friends get here."

"Okay," I agree, but then ask, "What time are they coming?"

She's halfway up the steps when she answers, "Seven."

"Ains," I call from the foyer. She stops and turns in place. "The Sox are on tonight."

Her nose scrunches. "Can't you DVR it? We planned to binge-watch the new season of *Orange is the New Black.*" Before I can protest, she adds, "We promised that we'd watch it together." She smiles in what I'm sure is an attempt to weaken my resolve. "It's kind of a thing."

What about my *thing?* Sighing, I say, "I really wanted to relax and watch the game tonight."

"Can't you see if Jimbo's around?" she offers. "Or watch it in the basement?"

"Ains." I do my best to tamp down my annoyance, but it's damn hard. "I'm trying to compromise."

"Try harder." She shimmies her hips. "I'm sure there's something I can do to change your mind."

I'm saved from answering when the doorbell rings. "Shit!" She squeals. "They're early."

"Can you let them in?" She strides the rest of the way upstairs. "I'll be down in fifteen."

I grumble under my breath. "Sure."

Ignoring my snippy tone, she pokes her head out of the bedroom door. "See, this is why I love you."

Mind on autopilot, I return the platitude. "You too."

As I make my way to the door, I can't help but question tonight's turn of events. I feel like a stranger in my own house.

Is this what I want for the rest of my life?

Ainsley.

Her friends.

Her schedule.

It's a question that I don't want to think too long or too hard about because I'm afraid I already know the answer: I don't want Ainsley because I'm in love with Charlotte fucking Truse.

OLIVER

MY PHONE LIGHTS up with an incoming FaceTime call. I smile as Margot's name flashes across my screen. Call it sheer dumb luck or an innate twin intuition, but Margot always seems to know when I need her. Whether it's to blow off steam, lend an ear, or simply to make me laugh, she's my go-to. If I were a thug—which I'm *definitely* not—she'd be my ride or die.

"Hey." I rest my phone on the edge of the coffee table. "I was just thinking of you."

On screen, her face freezes for a split second before unfreezing and then a smile stretches across her face. "All good thoughts I hope."

"Always." I chuckle.

Ray, her semi-stray, semi-domesticated cat leaps onto the windowsill behind her.

I arch a brow. "I see he's made his way inside."

A single shoulder lifts. "Sara has a soft spot for him."

"Sara has a soft spot for every animal," I tease.

"Yeah, yeah." She reaches back to run her hand along the cat's back. Ray's purrs of pleasure are loud and obnoxious. He sounds like a car engine that can't quite turn over.

"So what's new?" I prop an arm against the back of my head. "How's work?"

"Same old. Saving the planet one solar panel at a time."

For every single ounce of pride and cockiness I possess, Margot possesses equal amounts in humility and modesty. Although we're both in the service industry, Margot's profession is much more altruistic. My ego and desire for profit, pleasure, and accolades fuel my drive. Margot gets her kicks from preserving wetlands, thwarting deforestation, and sourcing clean water supplies.

She is an unsung environmental champion. Her firm converted over three hundred commercial properties from traditional to alternate energy sources, mostly hydroelectric and solar, last year alone. A campaign that she almost singlehandedly organized. She lectures —for free, mind you—at several local universities regularly about the importance and benefits of recycling. She never uses products that contain BPA, HFCs, sulfates, parabens, and a whole list of other shit, and I have no idea how she can remember it all. And I don't get her started on single use plastic. Let's just say, straws are a *major* hot button topic for her.

"Speaking of work." Her voice pulls me back to the present and I meet her gaze on-screen. "Who's the girl?"

My nose scrunches. "What girl?"

"On Mecca's Facebook page."

Here's the other thing you should know about Margot: she's a social media whore. Sure, she'll tell you she's on Facebook, Instagram, Twitter, Snapchat, and whatever else the latest fad is these days, because she follows "activists" and "bloggers" for work. I call Bull. Shit. If there's juicy gossip to be had, Margot is on top of it. Yesterday.

I, on the other hand, don't do social media. Or texting. Or smart phones at all. Call me old-fashioned, but that shit wastes too much time. I'd rather pick up the phone, make the call, and then get the fuck on with my day. I'm not interested in your cute dog pics. Or inspirational quotes. Or what a terrible day you're having. I have my own life to worry about. Sorry if that makes me a dick, but to be fair, at the end of the day, how much does it really matter? I'd rather connect with people in person. Archaic, I know.

Margot continues to speak, "Curvy, brown wavy hair, blue eyes, I think..." Her voice trails off and I watch as she clicks a few buttons on her tablet. "Yeah, blue eyes. *Big boobs*."

"You mean, Charli?"

Her smile is mischievous. "Recognized her by the boobs, did ya?"

Yes. Maybe. "No."

She turns her tablet to face the phone screen and my greedy eyes dissect the picture. The photo was taken last week when Don suggested we needed to up our online presence. Charli, on a mission to secure the "best candids," snapped photos all night. Much to the chagrin of the staff, myself included. Finally, Meg got fed up and turned the tables, snapping one of Charli by the bar, insisting if our faces had to be posted online, then Charli's did too.

Charli whined, but really, she had nothing to worry about. She looked beautiful, if not a touch nervous. Her wide eyes smiled at the camera, but her teeth trapped her bottom lip. *My* teeth wanted that full, plump lip. And a whole lot more.

"Oliver." Margot shakes the device to get my attention. "This your girl?"

I wish. "Yeah, that's Charli." I clear the lump in my throat, not knowing if what I'm feeling is guilt for wishing Charli could be mine. Or is pure attraction? "She's the manager."

"Huh." Margot's deep gaze penetrates mine as she quietly scrutinizes my oversimplified explanation of who Charli is. Of what she means to me. Margot continues to stare as though reading my internal thoughts and I know if I don't distract her *soon*, I'm screwed. "What's Sara up to?"

"Don't try to change the subject," she scolds.

"What subject?" I raise my eyebrows in mock innocence.

"How you failed to mention how freaking hot Charli is!"

Of course Margot finds Charli attractive. We share the same DNA, after all. And Margot's not blind. Charli *is* hot.

I shrug, schooling my features into a neutral line. "Guess it never came up."

"Never came up?" She scoffs. "Look me in the eye and tell me you don't want to bang her."

"Margot!" I drape my forearm over my eyes. "How do you think my fiancée would feel about you saying things like that?"

She scoffs again. "You mean the ghost?" Her eyes roll so hard and so fast that I'm fearful they'll fall out of her head. She adds, "It's not like she's ever home."

"You never liked Ainsley," I say, rather than argue, because Margot is right. Ainsley is rarely home for more than a few days at a time.

"I don't even know her," she corrects. "Well, I met her once a year and a half ago for like five minutes."

Also true. Margot and Sara had flown up for a rare weeklong vacation and my dad invited us all for dinner. Ainsley committed to attending, knew how excited I was about having her finally meet my family, and then she flaked at the last minute. Ironically, the airline "forced' mandatory overtime that same weekend, but later I found out the "mandate" was a private flight chartered by one of Taiwan's wealthiest couples. Hefty tips were promised to all attendants as well as first class accommodations in one of the power couple's many hotels. Her decision pissed me off, but so much time had passed when I found out that I thought it was useless to argue about water under the bridge.

"I just want you to be happy, Ol." Margot's voice soothes. "Are you happy?"

I purse my lips, poised to answer, but ultimately the question hangs unanswered between us because I don't have a clear answer.

Happy with my career? Yes.

Happy with my health? Sure.

Happy with Ainsley? I don't think so. At least not anymore.

"Are you with her because of...what happened?"

My eyes narrow on Margot's, letting her know she's hit a nerve. "That isn't the reason we're together."

She clearly misses my angry tone or she simply doesn't care. Either way, she continues, "It's been two years already, Ol. You're both okay. It's okay to move—"

"Stop." My hand slices through the air. On a deep, cellular level, I can acknowledge the truth of Margot's words. Part of me wonders if my sense of loyalty toward Ainsley stems from the accident.

We'd been dating a little over a year when it happened. After a long four weeks apart, we were excited to see each other. Because we weren't living together at the time, I picked her up at eleven o'clock, after my shift at Mecca. We hadn't driven more than two minutes when a silver sedan ran a red light, T-boning the front passenger side. Right where Ainsley sat.

Looking back, the night is a blur of memories—loud shrill sirens, Ainsley's moans of pain, the slurred voice of the drunk driver who hit us shouting intelligible words. Much later, we found out his blood alcohol was .287, well above of the legal limit.

The driver and I were fine. Ainsley was not. The impact of the crash broke her right arm and cracked a rib. At the hospital, she was diagnosed with a mild concussion. Thankfully, neither car was traveling at a high speed or the injuries could have been much worse.

Rationally, I know the accident wasn't my fault. There's nothing I could have done to prevent Michael Grover from driving drunk that night. I obeyed all of the traffic signs. Ainsley and I were both wearing our seatbelts. Truly, what occurred was the very definition of the word *accident*. But yet, I harbored an extreme sense of guilt. I was driving. Ainsley got her hurt. I felt responsible.

But still, that's not the reason why I'm with her. *Is it?*

"All I'm saying"—Margot's tone softens—"is that people grow apart, they change, and if you're going to marry her, make sure it's for the right reason, okay?"

I close my eyes, blocking Margot from my vision, wishing I could block her voice from my ears because I don't want to hear the truth in her words.

Somewhere along the way, my love for Ainsley turned to worry then to obligation then to complacency. And right now, I'm not sure if we're going through some sort of phase or if it's time to end things for good.

That's a lie. Deep down in the epicenter of my being, down to the tiniest of molecules that comprise my flesh and blood, my heart beats—screams—for Charli. And it knows that a relationship with her would never turn stale or tired or mundane.

But how, *how*, do you hurt someone you care about? Shatter her hopes and dreams? Break the promise of a marriage and a home?

How?

Sometimes even when you know what the right thing to do is, you procrastinate, drag your feet, hoping for the right moment because it *isn't* easy.

And so I wait. Until you walk a day in my shoes, you shouldn't judge. Sometimes fair doesn't mean equal. Sometimes right doesn't mean *right now*.

So I fucking wait.

CHARLI

TECHNICALLY, Mecca opens at four p.m. but the crowd doesn't usually pick up until closer to six. Sometimes we have the odd early reservation, and for a time, we were booked solid even during the early dinner hours due to our popularity, but things have evened out. Somewhat. Now patrons schedule their reservations *well* in advance—I'm talking three months minimum—to ensure their preferred date and time is available.

It's just after four and apart from the elderly couple at table nineteen and the family of six in the back corner booth, the restaurant is empty. Which is why when Jim texted me after work and asked if he could stop by, I agreed. Oliver isn't scheduled to come in until five tonight but I'm assuming Jim either knows that or specifically wants to talk to me.

We're seated at the small high-top table in the "bang booth". Although it's easy to see why couples request it since it's tucked away in the back corner of the restaurant behind a wall, ensuring *a lot* of privacy, Jim and I need privacy today for a much different reason.

"I'm so sorry." I squeeze his arm in comfort. "That really sucks."

"Yep." Jim takes another sip of the mint tea I brewed for him in the kitchen. "I don't know what's worse, the fact that she's getting remarried only six months after the divorce or the fact that my daughter is going to be her flower girl."

Maddie's her daughter too. It's natural that Katelyn, his ex, would want her to be part of the ceremony but I don't dare say that.

"I don't know how I'm gonna do it, Charli." He leans back against the polished wooden booth and closes his eyes. "How do I accept another man into Maddie's life? I've never even *met* him. All I know is that his name is Ernie and every time Katelyn mentions him, I think of Sesame Street and have an indescribable urge to ask where the fuck Bert is."

"Stop." I lean out of my seat, reaching, reaching, reaching until I swipe a cocktail napkin from the bar. "You're terrible."

His eyes flutter open and he cracks a smile.

"Listen, I'm not going to pretend to know what the right thing to say is or tell you it's going to be okay, because the truth is, it'll be uncomfortable. Messy. Hard." I squeeze his hand that rests on the table between us. "But I do know that you're a *great* dad and you will do whatever you need to do to ensure Maddie's happiness without letting your personal feelings get in the way."

"Thank you." He squeezes back once before releasing my hand.

"You know what you need?" I say, stealing another forkful of the banana crumb cake that we're supposed to be "sharing." I've eaten nearly two thirds of the sweet treat. Jim had *one* bite.

His teacup hovers near his lips. "To bang a hot chick?"

"Close." My smile grows as his eyes widen in disbelief. "Strippers."

He sets his mug on the table. His nose scrunches adorably as he asks,

"Strippers?"

"Yeah." I nod. "What better way to celebrate your ex-wife's engagement than

with strippers?" I raise my eyebrows. "Think of it like the ex-husband's version of the bachelor party."

He chuckles, warming up to the idea. "What?"

"The ex-husband gets a *pussy party*." My hands gesture with enthusiasm as I become more vested in the idea. "It's a rite of passage really. That bitch is someone else's problem now." I smirk at him over my mug of coffee.

A laugh rumbles in his chest. "Jesus, Charli."

My eyes hold his, a hint of a smile still on my lips. "So, you in?"

He folds his arms across his chest. "Do I have a choice?"

I shrug. "Not really."

"Ugh, fine, if I *have* to."

Rolling my eyes, I swat his chest. "I know, right? How terrible of me to take you to a strip club."

He clucks his tongue. "It's always the quiet ones."

"Please. I'm not as sweet and innocent as I look." I tap my phone to pull up my calendar. "Next Thursday work?" I glance across the booth. "I have to work this weekend."

"Sure," he answers quickly.

I pause. "But you didn't even check to see if you're available."

"Charli." He levels me with his gaze. "I'm *always* available for strippers."

I laugh, but after a moment, I tell him, "Invite whomever you want. It's your *pussy party* after all."

His eyes shine with humor. "Please stop calling it that."

"Why? You got a problem with the word pus—"

"Charlotte," he scolds, but I simply laugh. He spins his empty teacup on the

table. "I'll mention it to a few guys at work."

"Great." I nod, but then he asks, "Is it cool if I ask Oliver?"

"Sure." I shrug. "He *is* your best friend."

His brows furrow at my flippant tone. "Help me out here. I don't speak girl.

None of this yes means no and no means yes bullshit. I've had enough of that nonsense to last me a lifetime." He holds up his hand before I can speak. "I don't know what's going on between you and Oliver—"

I interrupt him, "You *know* there's nothing going on."

His brow arches. "If you say so."

Really? Is he deliberately trying to piss me off? After I've offered to take him to see strippers? I push myself to stand, hovering near the end of the booth. "Maybe the party isn't such a good idea after all."

"Dammit!" he curses, standing as well. He reaches for my elbow to stop me from walking away. "I'm sorry. I'm in shitty mood, and I shouldn't take it out on you."

He's right, he shouldn't take it out on me, but I *get* it. I've had my fair share of bad days. "It's fine."

His hand pats my arm. "I'm sorry."

I nod my head, accepting the apology.

He eyes me with caution. "So that's a yes to asking Oliver?"

I dip my head, pick at my fingernails and murmur, "Sure."

Me, Jim, Oliver, and a bunch of beautiful naked women? What on earth could possibly go wrong?

OLIVER

STRIP CLUBS REALLY AREN'T my thing. Don't believe me? It's the truth. I love women. I love sexy women. I love sexy, *naked* women. But not ones who I have to pay for their attention. I prefer women who genuinely want me. And my dick. We're a package deal, after all.

When Jimbo called me last week with the invite, the word "no" was on the tip of my tongue. That was until he told me that Katelyn was getting married to the asshat she'd been dating for less than six months. Because of Maddie, the new guy was essentially marrying Jimbo. Well, not exactly, but this marriage would affect him no matter which way the apple was cut.

But as we stand outside the blacked out doors of the club I'm seriously second-guessing my decision to come.

"She's what?" I shout at Jimbo. I can't believe this fucker left out the fact that Charlotte is joining us this evening. He knows my head is all kinds of messed up over her. I don't doubt for a second that his lack of information was intentional.

"Relax." He squeezes my sore shoulder harder than I expect and I wince. "This was her idea."

Her idea? "Why would she—" The words die on my lips as Charli rounds the corner. My eyes widen as they take in her outfit. It's the most provocative thing I've ever seen her wear. Tight black pants, sky-high black leather heels, and a fitted cream-colored corset type top that nearly doubles the size of her already considerable breasts. *Fuck me.*

"Hey, guys." Charli is pure innocence, completely unaware of the dirty thoughts flooding my mind. Thoughts like unlacing her top slowly. With my teeth. Wrapping my arms around her rib cage, palming her sweet tits from behind while I grind my dick against her plump ass.

"Hey, babe." Jimbo pulls Charli close, wrapping his arms around her as I do my best to gauge how friendly the gesture actually is, but it's damn hard because my mind is still tripping over the fact that he called her *babe*.

Just friends my ass.

Charli returns his hug before pulling away. She turns to me, "Hey, Oliver."

"Hey." My voice comes out gruffer, coarser, than normal given my sour mood.

Her eyes find mine, wide with question. "What's with you?"

I shrug. "What do you mean?"

"You look like you just sucked on a lemon."

"Nah, I'm all good." I tip my head toward the door. "Are we going in or what?"

Jimbo takes a step forward, his hand reaching for the door. "Ladies first."

Charlotte is out of control. Literally out of control. And it's making *me* lose control. Scratch that, she's making me fucking insane. By my count, she's on her third drink and when I suggested she slow down, she tutted me away like I was some goddamn killjoy ruining all of her fun. Which I was—I *am*.

But seriously. Someone has to look out of her. Jimbo certainly

isn't. He may be drunker than Charlotte. A huge part of me sympa-
thizes with his plight. The breakup with Katelyn was tough. Her
engagement even tougher. The threat of losing your child the
toughest. So he's dealing with it the best way he knows how: with
girls and booze. Which is fine—it's his life after all—but he
shouldn't involve Charlotte in his recklessness. She's innocent.
Young and impressionable.

Then again, maybe she's not so innocent. "What the fuck?" I
throw a palm on Jimbo's shoulder, directing his attention to where
Charlotte is getting a *lap dance* from a rather busty stripper. By the
looks of it, they're *both* enjoying it. A little too much.

"Dude!" Jimbo smiles, then yells to Charlotte, "You get it, girl!"

"The fuck?" I growl. "*Don't* encourage her."

"It's harmless. She's having a good time." I tear my eyes away
from Charlotte for just a moment to see Jimbo's smile grow, his eyes
still glued on the duo as he whispers under his breath, "Damn,
that's hot."

My eyes jump back to where Charlotte sits on a low couch, her
long legs spread wide open. The stripper wears a thin pink lace see-
through bra and matching G-string. Her platinum blonde hair
sways with her body left to right as she grinds on Charlotte.

Sure, the stripper is almost naked, sure she's hot in the classic
porn-style way, but she's not the girl who has my attention. The girl
who has my attention—the girl who *always* has my attention—is
Charlotte. Even fully clothed, she makes my dick harder than any
stripper ever could.

Maybe Jimbo's right. Maybe I am overreacting. Maybe I am
being a sexist pig. Fuck, if Jimbo were the one getting a lap dance
I'd buy the lucky son of a bitch another round. Why should Charlotte be any different?

My muscles loosen and I'm about to take another sip of my
water when Jimbo mutters, "Oh shit."

"Wh—" I turn, stopping mid-question as Charlotte climbs up
on stage with her new *friend*. By this point, the girls have gathered
an audience. Slowly, they begin to dance—if you could even call it

that. *Grinding* would be a more appropriate term, the stripper's hands touching places on Charlotte that I've only dreamt about. I force smooth breaths through my nose, ignoring the fact that I wish it were *me* touching Charlotte, *alone*, in my bedroom, but when the stripper begins to unlace the silky tie of Charlotte's corset top, I spring into action.

I plow through the crowd of men, dirty singles being waved around me as I elbow my way to the front of the stage. I shout over the men's cheers, directing my voice at Charlotte, "You're done!"

Her glassy eyes find mine. "Ollliverrrr!" she calls out my name, slurring. "This is Dallas." She smiles as she slaps the stripper's ass. "Dallas Diamonds."

Shaking my head, I reach to pull Charlotte off the stage. "Come on, Charli. You've had your fun."

When her brows pull together and she doesn't immediately take my hand, my temper explodes. "Now, Charlotte!"

"Hey, buddy!" a middle-aged man who looks like he hasn't seen the inside of a gym in more than twenty years yells. "I think she wants to stay." His beady eyes find Charlotte's. "What'd you say your name was, darlin'?"

I direct my hard glare at the man, hoping the look will cause him to back down. "She didn't."

Before he can respond, I reach for Charlotte's ankles and I yank her forward. She falls over my shoulder headfirst. My hand clamps around the back of her thighs as I haul her away from the crowded stage. I'm done playing nice. She thrashes in protest and I do my best to ignore her plump ass that's only inches from my face.

As I hustle through the people, one rowdy patron tries to grab said plump ass. I stop so quickly that Charli jerks forward and I *almost* drop her.

If my arms weren't occupied carrying Charlotte, I'd punch the fucker in the face. I settle for a warning, hoping it will be equally effective. I look the asshole square in the eye. "Don't." My voice, though calm, is laced with a quiet rage. "Don't even *think* about it."

The douche lifts his hands in surrender and backs away mumbling, "I didn't know she was yours."

"Well, she is. So unless you're looking to get coldcocked, I suggest you direct your eyes elsewhere." I stomp back to where Jimbo sits at the table he reserved earlier in the night. My muscles are clenched, my breathing rapid as I drop Charli next to him on an empty stool.

The rage still flows hot so rather than speak to Charli, I direct my anger at Jimbo. "Thanks for your help out there, man." I grab my coat off the back of the chair and throw it over Charlotte's chest. Because Dallas succeeded in loosening the back ties, the material—what little of it there is—gapes in the front, exposing more of her tits than is decent, and quite frankly, a lot more of her skin than I can handle right now. "You're supposed to look out for her." I shake my head in disgust. "Why would you take her here? To a place like this?"

Jimbo pushes himself to stand. "Ol, calm down. Nothing happened. She was just dancing."

"Dancing?" My voice is incredulous. "Did you see the way those guys were looking at her? Do you know what could have happened? She's practically naked!"

With an air of indignation, Charlotte pipes up as if she's just realizing we're talking about her, "I'm not naked."

My eyes slide to hers in challenge. "What the fuck were you thinking dressing like that?"

She doesn't back down at my accusation. In fact, she slides my jacket off her body. "It's called a shirt, asshole."

"A shirt?" My finger slides beneath the loose strap that threatens to slip from her shoulder. "And tell me, do you normally take your shirt off in public?"

She blushes before swatting my hand away. "I'm wearing a bra." She rolls her eyes. "Let me guess, you've never seen one of those before either?"

Goddammit. She's pushing my buttons. Every. Single. One.

I snatch the jacket from the ground where it's fallen. Spinning her away from me, I drape it over her shoulders once more. "Leave it on."

"God, you're bossy." Her tone turns patronizing and she turns to face me again. "Will there be anything else, *Dad?*"

I narrow my eyes at Jimbo. "I'm taking her home."

"I'm staying." Charlotte pushes to her feet, although she wobbles a bit. "I'm

having fun. And this party is for Jim, not you." She waves her hand haphazardly in front of my face. "You're not the boss of me."

You're not the boss of me. What the fuck? Is she twelve?

"Charlotte, I swear to God..." I dig in my pant pocket for my car keys. "You have ten seconds before I carry your crazy, drunk ass out of this club."

She holds my stare, no doubt judging the validity of my threat. I arch my brow. *What's it gonna be, princess?*

After a pausing a few beats, she finally realizes the seriousness of my words and stands. "Fine, *Dad.* Let's go."

Jimbo reaches for his wallet. "Lemme just settle up—"

Charlotte rests her palm on his upper arm affectionately and a surge of jealousy grips my stomach. Jim can do no wrong, apparently. She leans in, nearly falling into his lap as she says, "Stay."

"Nah, babe. I'll go with Ol, make sure you get home safe."

Charlotte shakes her head, her lips turned down in a pout that shouldn't be sexy, but it is. *Fuck*, it is. "Don't let *him*"—she jerks a thumb over her shoulder in my direction—"ruin both our fun. I'll be fine. My apartment's not even fifteen minutes away."

I file that information away. Has Jimbo never been to her apartment?

"Besides." Her smile is mischievous. "I put in a good word for you with Dallas." She winks. "Play your cards right and she'll give you an *extra special* lap dance."

Jimbo's eyes widen with delight. "Babe." He leans in and kisses her cheek. "I think I love you."

Charlotte's face warms in genuine happiness. "Don't mention it." When she turns to face me, all warmth is gone. "Let's go."

CHARLI

OLIVER STANDS next to me on the stoop of my apartment building as I dig through my tiny clutch for the fifth time. My search is useless. The only items inside are my phone, my ID, and a folded up twenty dollar bill. Oh, and a thin tube of lip-gloss. MAC Funtabulous. Because, ya know, that color is my jam.

"They're not here." I complain.

"What do you mean they're not there?" Oliver's strained voice hovers over my shoulder. His warm breath on my cool skin causes a shiver to dance across my spine, and I silently curse myself for shoving his jacket at him the second we were outside of the club.

"They must have fallen out somewhere." I walk back toward the curb, where his Lincoln MKX is double-parked. I pull on the handle impatiently and demand, "Unlock." Realizing how bitchy I sound, I add, "Please."

He clicks the remote and I waste no time in my search. Bending at the waist, I lean over the front passenger seat, fingers dragging across the floor mat (which, by the way, is so clean you could eat off of it), between the console and chair, the door jamb.

"Jesus Christ, Charli," Oliver hisses, moving behind me to shield me from view. "Your ass is on full display."

I don't bother to look up. "My keys are lost, I'm locked out of my house, and you're worried about my ass?"

After another minute of futile searching, I stand up. Not realizing exactly how close Oliver is to me, I bump against him. Directly against his...*oh shit*. What the fuck was *that*?

I should be a good girl. I should move away, pretend that I didn't notice his erection. After all, I'm sure it's involuntary more than anything, maybe even a lingering hard on from the girls at the club, but I'm *not* a good girl. At least, not tonight, with three drinks worth of alcohol flowing through me and my hormones amped up from all that sexy grinding with Dallas Diamonds.

I lean back and slowly sway my ass against him; this time it's deliberate, not accidental, and he groans low in his throat. Goosebumps prickle my skin as his hands move to my waist. He anchors me against him, but rather than encourage my movement, he holds me still, rooting me in place.

After a moment, he releases his hold and steps back, breaking our connection. "Is there someone you can call?" He clears his throat. "Does your sister have a key?"

Not turning to face him, I shake my head. "No. But it wouldn't matter even if she did. She's back in Ohio. Her classes started two weeks ago."

"Fuck," he curses. "How about the management office?"

I turn to face him, a look of impatience marring my face. "It's one o'clock in the morning!" He winces and I wave my hand in dismissal. "Just go. I'll be fine. The office opens in a couple of hours. I can wait here or try to buzz one of my neighbors..." I let my voice trail off with the outlandish possibility. No way am I going to wake someone I barely know out of dead sleep to let me in. Besides, then what? I camp outside my door like a vagrant? Yeah, that's a hard pass.

"I'm not going to leave you here." He splays his palms wide. "*Outside*, dressed like..."

This is the second time he's put down my outfit and I've had enough with the veiled insults. "Dressed like what?" When he doesn't answer, I press again. "Dressed like what? Just say whatever is you've been dying to say all night!"

"Dressed like sin!" His voice explodes. "Like you wanna get fu—"

I stop directly in front of him, my eyes narrowed to slits. "Finish that sentence. I *dare* you."

He pulls his cell phone out and walks a few feet down the block. I have no idea who he's calling, but whoever it is, they don't answer, because I hear him hiss, "Fuck" before shoving the phone back into his pocket. A minute later, he walks back toward his car.

"Get in."

"What?"

"Charlotte." He levels me with a gaze over the hood. "Get. In."

"Where are you taking me?"

"To my house."

"What? Why?"

"Jesus," he snaps. "For once can you just do what you're fucking told?"

Before I can protest, he's in the car, the engine already turned over. I hesitate for a moment longer, and he revs the gas as though to say, "Hurry the fuck up."

I get in, slamming the door shut behind me. Why do I suddenly feel like I've entered the lion's den? And why the hell do I like it so damn much?

The farther we get from the city, the more Oliver's anger seems to fade. We've been on the freeway for more than twenty minutes and I'm beginning to wonder where we're going exactly. I don't know where he lives, and if I didn't trust him as much as I do, I might start to worry for my safety.

With my buzz fading, nerves begin to replace my carefree attitude. With sudden clarity, I realize I'm going to Oliver's house. For a sleepover. Part of me wonders if Ainsley will be there, but I almost immediately discount the idea because I sincerely doubt he'd have agreed to go out tonight—especially to a strip club—if she were home.

To give myself something to do, I fiddle with my phone. I'm not even halfway through my Instagram feed when my phone dies. "Shit!" I curse.

"What?" Oliver glances at me from the driver's seat.

"Phone died." I hold it up to show him the black screen.

"Almost there." He clucks his tongue. "And as luck would have it, this *dad* has a charger you can use."

A nervous chuckle escapes my lips. I did call him *dad*. Several times. "Sorry about calling you that."

He shakes his head. "No, you're not."

He's right. I'm not really sorry, but I feel the need to explain. "I'm not used to people telling me what to do."

My comment is met with silence.

He slows, turns down an unlit, unpaved road. In the distance, I see a white colonial house illuminated by several outside lights.

Rather than pull the car into the garage like I expect, he parks in the circular gravel drive out front.

We sit in a silence for a moment. He doesn't say anything, doesn't make an attempt to get out of the car, but by the way his jaw is clenched tight, I know he's still angry. Whether it's about my dancing, the *dad* comments, or my being at his house in general, I can't be sure. Probably a combination of the three.

His judgment weighs heavy in the car, and the longer the seconds tick by, the madder and more defensive I become. Finally, I blurt, "What do you care what I do, anyway? It's not like I was hurting anyone."

He turns so fast in his seat that the seatbelt that he's yet to unbuckle jerks his body back with force. "How can you even ask me that?"

My eyes widen in confusion, but he continues, "I care about you, Charli." He reaches out to brush a few locks of hair behind my ear. "The way those guys were looking at you, the idea that you'd share *any* part of yourself with them." He closes his eyes, shakes his head. "That would kill me."

Butterflies swarm in my belly because his confession, his concern sounds like *a lot* more than friendship. But then again, maybe he's simply an overprotective person. One time, I saw him kick a customer out of Mecca because he got a little too handsy with Meg. It should be stated that Oliver has no right to throw anyone out of *any* restaurant, including Mecca. The man threatened to call the owner, so Oliver provided him Don's number with a smile on his face. The people Oliver cares about, he protects. Fiercely.

Wanting to extend an olive branch and avoid a—potentially— awkward night, I unbuckle my seatbelt and turn to face him fully. "Hey." When he still hasn't opened his eyes, I rest my hand on his upper thigh and squeeze. Finally, he meets my gaze and I say, "Thanks for having my back."

A warm smile lights up his face. "Always, Charli girl."

I lift my hand and extend it toward him. "We good?"

"Yeah." His large palm encircles mine. "Come on. Let's go inside."

His warm, rich eyes hold mine, and the moment feels signifi- cant, like not only

is he inviting me inside him home, but inside his life, his heart. My brain screams *no*, but my heart squeals in delight *hell yes*. Smil- ing, I take a deep breath and whisper my consent, "Let's go."

CHARLI

WHEN I FANTASIZE ABOUT OLIVER, I never imagine his house. Or his car. Or what

he does on his days off. In fact, I never imagine his personal space, because there, he isn't mine. He belongs to Ainsley. So I limit my fantasies to a tiny bubble of space inside my head.

So far we've had sex at Mecca, my apartment, and once, on a particularly frisky night, in the back row of the movie theater. I think the theater was our best yet. I wonder if Oliver would agree. I mean, if he actually knew about any of these trysts. Moving on...

I've always been insanely curious about where Oliver lives. How he lives. How he relaxes. My greedy eyes dart from side to side, not knowing where to land first. The house is large, two stories, with white siding and dark royal blue shutters. A spacious rectangle porch lines the front with two oversized rocking chairs framing the double front door. The lawn is well manicured and small lights line either side of the sidewalk.

I follow Oliver around to the side entrance, climb the four steps to the landing, and wait as he unlocks the door. We enter a small mudroom where Oliver toes off his shoes and hangs his coat on a hook. Doing the same, I slip off my heels, placing them neatly beside a pair of grey women's moccasins. A not-so-subtle reminder that Oliver doesn't live alone.

Engaged, Charlotte. He's engaged.

He leads me into the kitchen. Centrally located, it's massive and has an open concept. White cabinetry and white subway tiles, paired with sleek stainless Viking appliances give the space a modern feel. And it screams *Oliver*. Expensive, efficient, and pretty to look at.

He walks past the large island that has a small sink, and enters what appears to be a butler's pantry. He returns with an amber-colored glass bottle that I can tell is alcohol, but I'm not sure which type. My eyes squint at the label.

The Macallan. Scotch Whiskey.

His gaze finds mine in question as he lifts the bottle. "Yeah?"

I hesitate. While I'm certainly not one hundred percent sober, my buzz from the club is almost gone. A shot of whiskey, or a *dram,* as they like to call it in Ireland—I read Outlander, okay?—will definitely catapult me into dangerous territory. Drunk Charlotte territory. I don't need that bitch making an appearance tonight. She can't be trusted.

On the other hand, I'm not sure I can handle being around Oliver without something to take the edge off, to calm my jittery nerves.

"Sure." The word slips past my lips. *What the fuck am I doing? Dumb, Charlotte, You are so fucking dumb.*

He inclines his head to the cabinet behind me. "Grab two glasses."

I spin and open the door as the distinct sound of the stopper being pulled from the glass bottle pierces the silence.

I set the glasses on the counter in front of him and he pours without meeting my eyes. I think he's a little heavy-handed on the pour, but what do I know? It's not like I'm in the habit of having a nightcap before bed.

"It was a nice thing you did." My brow arches in question before

Oliver can continue, "For Jimbo. Katelyn really did a number on him."

"Ahh." My expression softens. "Yeah, I'm sure it isn't easy."

"It isn't," he agrees, looking at me but not really looking at me. "Marriage and divorce, it's..."

"Complicated?" I offer.

He nods. "I was gonna say *permanent*."

Now it's my turn to nod. "That's why you have to be sure. Really sure." He nods again and we're quiet for a moment before I say, "Oliver?"

"Yeah?"

"Can I ask you something?"

His eyes find mine. "That depends." I sigh in exasperation and he says, "What?"

"How *do* you know? How can you *really* be sure?"

"I don't know." He spins his glass in his hands. "I don't know if you can ever really be sure. I mean, look at Jimbo. He gave his heart to Katelyn and she stomped all over it. The poor bastard barely gets to see his daughter and now he has to deal with a complete stranger parenting her."

How do you know Ainsley's the one? I wish I had the courage to speak those words aloud, but I'm terrified to learn the answer. Shrugging, I say, "I guess."

"Take it from me." He swirls the liquid in the glass. "Being shuttled between two households, having stepparents, it's not fun."

"I guess," I repeat, yet then add, "But two people staying together for the wrong reasons—for their children—isn't exactly great either."

He gets the meaning of my words without my having to say them aloud. "Are your parents unhappy?"

I snort. "They'd never admit it. Everything is always *fine*." I shrug. "Maybe happily ever after doesn't exist."

"I think we're all just trying to do our best. No one ever wants to intentionally hurt someone they love." Oliver holds my gaze.

"Maybe." After a few moments of silence, I shake my head.

"Geez, I'm sorry. What a buzz kill. How did we even start talking about marriage and divorce, anyway?"

He smirks. "Jimbo."

I crack a smile. "Yeah, Jim." I glance at the clock on the microwave. "He's probably getting a very special lap dance as we speak."

Oliver chuckles. "You're a good friend, Charli."

I smile and raise my glass. "To friends."

I hold his gaze, his eyes seeming to burn with...something I can't quite place. I know what I want to believe it is, but I don't dare allow myself to think he actually feels this crazy attraction too.

He clinks his glass against mine. "To friends."

Bringing the drink to my lips, I toss it into my mouth, downing it as though it were a shot. My eyes pop open, tears stinging them and my throat *burning*.

With a shocked look on his face, Oliver pats me on the back as I choke on air.

"You okay?"

I hold up my finger, indicating I need a moment. I'm sure my face is bright red, and I continue to cough for a few more seconds. "Fuck," I curse, voice hoarse. "That shit's strong."

He chuckles. "You're supposed to sip it."

My eyes narrow. "Now you tell me."

"Here." He brings his glass to his lips, sucks down the contents, wincing slightly before dragging his hand across his mouth. He winks and says, "Now we're even."

I chuckle. "You didn't have to do that."

He shrugs and uncorks the bottle again. "This time, we do it right." He refills both our glasses. "Sip it slowly."

My eyebrows furrow. *Slowly? I'd rather down it and get it over with. It doesn't exactly taste good.*

When he speaks, his tone is deeper, darker, and a whole lot more sensual. "Savor it. Take your time with it. Appreciate its many flavors."

Christ, is he talking about whiskey or sex?

I know which one I'm thinking about. My face flames and I barely resist the urge to fan it.

Oliver grabs his drink and motions for me to follow him into another room. Before he has a chance to turn on the lights, I ask, "Where ya taking me now, *Dad?*"

"Enough with the *dad* talk." He growls, flipping the light switch. "It makes me feel old."

"You *are* old," I jab.

His eyebrows hit his hairline. "I thought we called a truce?"

"We did—oh my God!" I stop short, gasping. "You have a grand piano?" I set my glass on the closed lid of the instrument. "Yours or Ainsley's?" Though it's the first time I've spoken her name aloud, she's crossed my mind more than a dozen times tonight.

He shakes his head in dismissal. "Ainsley hates the piano. She's been hounding me for months to get rid of it."

My mouth drops open. Get rid of this beautiful instrument? Is she freaking insane?

He shrugs. "She says it takes up too much space, and I don't play that often anymore so..." His voice trails off.

I glance around the room. Yes, the piano is large, but it's not like the house is cramped—it's plenty big for two people, no matter what furnishings are in it.

His voice breaks the silence. "What?"

"Nothing." I shake my head. "It figures you'd play." I don't realize I've said that last comment aloud until his eyes cut to me.

"Yes, I play." He sets his glass next to mine. "Since I was five."

I scrunch my nose, pretending to think before asking, "So how many years is that? Fifty?"

"Hardy har har." He comes to stand beside me and asks, "Do you play?"

"I wish." I sigh dreamily. "Playing an instrument is in my top three."

His brow wrinkles. "Top three what?"

Realizing I've said too much, I stall for time by reaching for and gulping the rest of my whiskey. So much for savoring the flavor. To hell with it. I was never—nor will I ever be—the definition of refined. It burns like a motherfucker, *again*, but not quite as badly as the first time. After a moment, I find his eyes and laugh. "It's nothing."

"Charli." His finger dances in front of my face. "I know that look."

I go behind the piano, sit on the bench, and drag my hand across the ivory keys. The sound is jarring in the quiet. "What look?"

"The look that says you're hiding something."

I narrow my eyes. "You think you know me so well."

"I do." He walks over to where I'm sitting and nudges my shoulder, so I scoot over and he sits next to me. Even through my pants, my skin sizzles from where our thighs press together.

"Come on, Charli." We're so close that his breath flutters the wisps of hair along my forehead. "Out with it."

He smirks. It's a slow, lazy smile and I'm not sure if it's him or the whiskey or the fact that my body is buzzing from head to toe, but I relent, "Okaaay. Top three sexiest traits in a significant other."

"You have a list?"

I shrug. "No." But he pins me with his rich cocoa eyes. "Kinda."

"Tell me more about this list. Pianist is one—" My giggle interrupts him and he enunciates the word, "I said *pianist*, not penis." He rolls his eyes in mock reprieve. "Tell me the other two."

He says it so naturally, so confidently, that I blurt out without even thinking, "Knows how to cook and has dark eyes." Then I slap a hand over my mouth, realizing I've described him exactly.

Fuck my life. *Fuck* Drunk Charlotte.

My face flames, and I look down to avoid his gaze.

"Huh." He shrugs, ignoring my confession. "Mine are nice smile, dirty sense of humor, and big tits."

My mouth hangs open. "I was with you until the last one."

"You said we're talking fantasy here." I swear his eyes drop to my chest, although he disguises it by acting as if he's looking at my fingers resting on the keys. Then he shrugs again. "I like tits."

Now it's my turn to roll my eyes. "I never said *fantasy*."

One shoulder lifts. "It could be worse. If I didn't think it'd make me sound like a total pig, I'd swap 'nice smile' for 'ass like J.Lo.'"

My mouth pops opens. "You're right. You *do* sound like a pig." I turn my upper body slightly to face him. "Besides, you have to pick either-or. Everyone knows guys can be classified into two categories: ass men or tit men." His eyes shine with controlled laughter as I continue, "You don't get both."

"Not me." A chuckle rumbles through his chest. "I'm non-discriminating. An equal opportunity admirer." He holds my gaze. "I *want* both."

The tension is so thick around us that it's difficult to breathe. I gasp for more oxygen, my greedy lungs unsatisfied, and my instinct to flee kicks in. "On that note"—I begin to stand—"I should get to bed. Where do you want me? On the couch? In the bedroom?"

His body stiffens, his breath hitching, and I suddenly realize exactly how my inquiry sounded. Hovering awkwardly between the piano and bench, I clear my throat and clarify, "I meant, where do you want me *to sleep?*"

He reaches for my upper arm and attempts to pull me back down next to him. "I want you *here*." His voice is whisper soft. "Let me play something for you." When I don't sit, he bargains, "Just one song."

At his insistence, I drop down beside him, and he inches closer, positioning himself at the center of the keyboard. My heart beats wildly in my chest when his upper arm presses against my bare skin. It damn near explodes when he brushes my chest as he reaches past me to the end of the keyboard. I swear I swoon. Audibly.

He dips his head, his fingers sweeping across the black and white keys, building a beautiful yet melancholy melody that feels like it's voicing my soul's torment. As the tempo increases, so does my desire. I swear this motherfucking song is Oliver's version of foreplay. I shift discreetly and rub my legs together. The music builds, faster and louder, and when the piece reaches its crescendo I half expect to come or combust or see fireworks. *Something.*

But, of course, I don't.

This isn't a fucking movie.

"Jesus," I mutter when he's done, his long fingers still poised over the keys. "That was..." *Explosive. Sexy. Hot as fuck.* "Beautiful."

Oliver's breathing has sped up, his face flushed, as his eyes find mine. I'm positive that I'm not imagining the heat in them, his look confirming I'm not the only one who feels this insane attraction. At least, not tonight.

"Alkan's Symphony for Piano; the first movement," he says, ignoring my compliment.

"You can play from memory? Just like that?"

"Not all songs, but my favorite ones, yeah."

I can understand why the piece is one of his favorites. I've never heard anything so beautiful, and in my alcohol-riddled state, I pray I'll be able to remember the title so that I can download it and listen to it over and over again. Alone. In my bedroom while I indulge in some *sexy* time. With a glass of wine. Hell, I may even smoke a cigarette after.

"Jesus, if I were Ainsley, I'd be having *Pretty Woman* sex all over this piano." Shit. *Did I really just say that out loud?* Attention: drunk Charlotte has

officially arrived.

"What?" His eyes widen, an uneasy smile flitting across his lips.

"*Pretty Woman?*" My voice rises. "You know. When Richard Gere plays the piano in the hotel lounge and Julia Roberts struts in all badass in her bathrobe?"

"Oh, yeah," he says, but it's oh so obvious he doesn't have a clue what I'm talking about.

With great force, I push myself to stand, holding on to the lid for balance because the room is spinning a little bit. Oliver reaches his hand out to steady me, but I swat it away.

He watches me with questioning eyes as I move alongside the piano and align my butt with the closed lid. Bracing my hands behind me I attempt to hoist myself up, but I'm drunk, a little chubby, and out of shape. How did Julia Roberts manage this move so effortlessly? Damn her and her long legs.

By the third try, I manage to get half of my left ass cheek up and I'm able to wiggle backward. Definitely not sexy or graceful. I push my messy hair off my face, gathering it in one hand and twisting it into a bun, but I have no hair tie, so when I pull my hand away, it immediately falls back into place. I cross my legs and lean back slightly on my elbows. "Ta-da." I smile. "Julia Roberts."

Oliver pushes the bench back and comes to stand in front of me. "Does this mean I'm Richard Gere?"

I nod as his hands tap just above my knees, a signal to uncross my legs. I comply and he gets between them.

Clearly, I haven't thought this through. What the fuck was I thinking?

The problem is, I'm *not* thinking. Drunk Charlotte is the one calling the shots and she has only one thing on her mind: sex with Oliver.

Oliver reaches a hand around the back of my neck, his rough fingers kneading, pressing into the delicate flesh. He leans closer and my body tingles with awareness. Is he going to kiss me? Will I respond? Push him away?

Fuck. Fuck. Fuck.

His eyes linger on my lips for just a moment. Then he bends forward, his lips barely grazing the shell of my ear. "Rest assured, this piano is untouched. *A virgin.*"

Every nerve prickles as his hot breath licks my skin. His free hand hooks my thigh, tugging me to the ground. "Come on, Charli. Let's get you to bed. Something tells me you're gonna have one hell of a hangover tomorrow."

I have a hard time sleeping in new places. The unfamiliar night noises, the odd, often too bright lights from the TV and alarm clock, the whirring of the vents—I notice it all. It doesn't matter if it's a hotel room or a lifelong friend's house. I need to break in a new bed. Not in *that* way. Get your head out of the damn gutter.

I was hoping that the alcohol would make me drowsy. And in a way, it *has*. I'm freaking tired, but I'm also restless. Antsy. And my throat is dry as hell.

If I weren't mostly naked—my black undies are the only thing keeping me from being in my birthday suit—I'd go in search of a glass of water. But there's no way I'm going through the effort of getting redressed or fiddling with that corset top. It took me twenty long minutes of twisting and contorting to untie it, and by the time I finally got it off, I was sweating like a hooker in church. So yeah, no glass of water for me.

Curling onto my side I tuck the covers underneath my chin and squeeze my eyes shut. "Time for bed, Charlotte," I whisper into the darkness. "Good night."

But my mind is too wired for sleep. Too busy thinking about Oliver and Ainsley and how big this house seems for just two people. It's a house meant to look lived-in and messy. Filled with children and toys and backpacks, not neat and lacking any personal effects. In fact, besides the moccasins in the entryway, I didn't spot one feminine thing. No makeup. No flowers. No pictures. It's like Oliver lives here alone.

Blowing out a breath, I flip onto my back. I avoid looking at the small alarm clock on the bedside table because seeing the time will make me more anxious.

My mind zeroes in on something else. Oliver's three sexiest traits. Traits that he shared unprompted. Traits that I begin to analyze with painstaking detail.

Trait number one: nice smile. At the risk of sounding conceited, I *do* have a nice smile. Three and a half years of braces, regularly scheduled dental cleanings, and avoiding sugary beverages helps keep my teeth in tip-top shape. Plus, a few years back I splurged on a fancy electric toothbrush that has changed my life—seriously, don't knock it until you've tried it. I floss daily, use mouthwash. Overall, my goal is to die with my natural teeth—no dentures for this girl. All this to say, dental hygiene is a priority of mine. I firmly place a check in box number one. Go me!

What was second? Dirty sense of humor? This one's a *maybe*. I mean, I enjoy a dirty joke as much as the next person, but it's not like I'm a fucking comedienne. I listen, I laugh, and I'm not (usually) offended, because humor is humor. It's not meant to be taken so seriously, and sometimes I think people get their panties in a twist for no reason. It's okay to laugh and still be PC. That's my two cents, anyway. After a minute more of internal debate, I decide to give myself another check. I'm two for two.

And I could never forget number three. *Nice tits.* I lift the sheet to peek at my chest. Is a C-cup considered nice? Big? According to my petite-framed sister who barely fills out an A-cup, she'd say yes. But I tend to disagree. Plenty of girls, girls like Dallas Diamonds, have much bigger boobs than I. Unsure where to put the check-mark, I decide to place it in the yes column. My boobs are decently shaped, still firm, and *big enough*. Besides, it's not like I could ask Oliver what his opinion is. That'd be highly inappropriate, right?

Finally, number four, the bonus trait. *Ass like J-Lo.* Now I'd never be so foolish as to compare myself to the Queen of the booty, but my butt *isn't* small. Apparently, my DNA cocktail was heavy on the big-boned Italian genes (thanks, Mom) and skimpy on the fragile, waiflike French ones (thanks for nothing, Dad.) Seriously, my dad could eat two dozen wings and wash them down with a chocolate milkshake *every day* and still maintain his beanpole figure. I, on the other hand, can merely *look* at the wings and milkshake and gain five pounds. If that's not poetic injustice, I don't know what is. Thankfully, big backsides are the trend. Or at least I think they are —I can name at least a dozen pop or rap songs that glorify the booty. So although my chubbiness is more of an all-over sort of thing, in the words of the almighty Sir Mix-a-Lot, this baby's got back.

Did Oliver confess these traits with me in mind? Is he attracted to me at all? Or worse, did he lie to spare my feelings after I divulged he's the perfect man, my fantasy brought to life?

I turn over again, this time splaying flat on my belly. I nestle my head beneath the pillow trying to shut off my brain, but it's no use. With a sigh, I squeeze my eyes shut and pray that sleep finds me soon.

As I begin to drift off, I remember the feel of Oliver's strong thigh pressed flush against mine on the bench, the burn of the heat pouring from his solid frame, and as my eyes finally fall closed, I swear I can almost feel him lying beside me. *Almost.*

CHARLI

THE KNOCKING at the door accompanied by a loud, deep voice startles me awake. "Knock, knock."

I sit up abruptly, lose my balance and fall back onto my elbows. Streaks of sunlight filter in through the honeycomb blinds as my mind slowly whirs to life. Fragments of last night begin to light up the dark landscape of my brain, much like the way the sun breaks across a black sky at dawn.

Strip club. Missing keys. Oliver's house.

"Just a minute." I croak, voice still hoarse because I never did get that glass of water.

"Take your time." Oliver's voice booms through the door and I wonder how the hell he's so chipper this morning. If I remember correctly, he drank as much whiskey as I did last night. The bastard's room is probably stocked full of water bottles, that's how. He continues to speak, "No rush. Come down when you're ready."

My eyes fall to my clothes scattered on the floor and I groan inwardly. Charli attempts to tie the corset, take two. Slowly, I swing my legs over the side of the bed, and when my feet hit the cool hardwood floor, I gasp a little in surprise.

I pick up the top first, begin to untangle the ribbons and it's

then that I notice the huge tear in the backstitching. "No!" I cry
out quietly, voice etched with panic.

Twisting the blouse in my hands, I spin it back to front, front
to back, hoping that the tear will magically be gone, but, of course,
it's useless. Unless I want to flash Oliver—and anyone else I
encounter along the way—there's absolutely no way I can wear the
top home.

"Jesus!" I curse, throwing it onto the bed in anger. How the hell
do I get myself into these situations? I'm the very definition of a
hot mess.

No keys. No clothes. No *service*.

I swear I could star in my own reality TV show.

I'd call it *Challenged Charli*. It'd be a phenomenal success and
earn millions of dollars in revenue. I'd win an Emmy and get a star
on the Hollywood Walk of Fame...

Okay, exiting fantasyland now.

I snap my bra into place and wiggle into my pants. I know even
before I open the closet door and subsequently the dresser drawers
—all eight of them—I'll find nothing, but the logical part of me has
to at least check.

Pacing in front of the bed, I brainstorm possible solutions, but
there are none. Because I'm locked in an empty room with a torn
shirt. My cell is charging, blissfully unaware, on the kitchen
counter. I've got no other tricks up my sleeve. No sleeve at all, for
that matter. Not to mention, I have to pee like a mother.

How far down the hall is the bathroom?

My hands drag the flat sheet from the bed. Hmm, I wonder if I
can wear it as a pashmina. I wonder if Oliver would notice? Also, I
wonder how the fuck does one wrap a Pashmina...

After pacing a few more minutes, I decide to admit defeat and
call Oliver.

Cracking open the door, I stick my head out just a few inches
and the rich, full aroma of fresh roasted coffee hits my nostrils. I
ignore it in lieu of the more pressing matter at hand. "Oliver!" I
whisper-shout. The only thing that greets me is the slam of a

cupboard door. "Oliver!" I repeat, louder. And then louder still. "Oliver!"

He appears at the bottom of the stairs, his eyes wide with confusion. "Yeah? Do you need something?"

"Yes," I answer, trying my best to tamp down my annoyance. It's not his fault that my stupid top has a stupid tear.

"What's the matter?" He begins to ascend the stairs. "And why are you hiding behind the door?"

Before I can respond, he's standing outside the bedroom, and the only thing separating him from seeing me in my half-naked glory is the thin door. "I have a bit of a problem," I begin.

His brow quirks. "A problem?"

"My top." I clear my throat. "It's ripped. I can't wear it."

"What?" He shakes his head, not following. "How did it rip?"

I was drunk and the tie was stuck because it was double knotted so that I wouldn't have to worry about it falling down, and when I tugged it...you know, one thing kinda led to another and I ended up falling on my ass. It really wasn't a pretty picture.

I keep my voice neutral. "I don't know."

"Okay, I can grab you something of Ainsley's," he offers in way of a solution, already halfway down the hall to what I assume is the master bedroom.

"No!" I shout, and he stops walking but doesn't turn around.

First of all, wearing Ainsley's clothes would be beyond weird. Sisters wear each other's clothes. Friends borrow each other's stuff. But Ainsley and I barely know each other. Besides the weirdness factor, the real problem is her clothes won't fit me. I'm easily more than twice her size.

"Okay," he says again as he turns to face me. "Do you want one of my t-shirts?"

Oddly wearing Oliver's clothes seems more intimate than borrowing something from Ainsley, so I suggest, "Can you just run out and pick me up something?"

"Wait." He holds his hand up as though calling a time out. "You want me to go shopping for you?"

Eyes wide, I nod. "Nothing fancy. Didn't we pass a general store on the way in last night?" *Surely they must sell some type of clothing.*

"I don't shop." He dismisses my idea. "Just let me grab you a t-shirt."

"No," I resist.

"Charli, it's a fucking t-shirt." He drags a hand through his hair. "And it's easier than running out."

"Unless you want me to stay locked in your bedroom forever, *please* go buy me something to wear." My voice rises with each word. It's not like I asked to stay here last night. It's not like I wanted my shirt to rip. It's not like I could go buy one myself at this point.

He pins me with his gaze, stormy chocolate eyes brimming with annoyance.

"You're impossible."

He turns and stomps down the steps as I call out, "Wait, let me give you some money!"

His response? Slamming the front door.

As soon as the door swings closed, I rush to bathroom because I've had to pee for oh, I don't know, about *eight hundred years*. After doing my business, I begin my search of the bathroom. Maybe I should feel funny rifling through the medicine cabinet, but tooth-paste is a necessity at this point, so no guilt here. My shamelessness is probably also due to the fact that I'd just strip-searched his entire spare bedroom.

Unlike my bedroom expedition, the bathroom offers many trea-sures: travel size bottles of shampoo, conditioner, and lotion—all in a variety of scents. Brand new toothbrushes still in the package, tiny tubes of minty fresh toothpaste, and sample size bottles of mouthwash, all within the allotted miniscule three point four ounce travel size restrictions.

I take advantage of it all.

After sniffing all the different scents—there are eleven of them in total, so it takes a while—I grab my favorite one, blueberry lemon, and turn on the shower. When I'm finished washing, I wrap a plush grey towel around my body and head back to my room.

To wait.

For Oliver.

And my clothes.

A laugh escapes my mouth at how ridiculous this situation is. In all of my Oliver-induced fantasies, I never thought I'd be here, in his spare bedroom—wet, stark naked underneath a too-small towel, belly gurgling in hunger as I wait for Oliver to bring me clothes. Somehow I always pictured it the other way. Ya know, him *removing* my clothes.

Shaking my head, I exhale a long breath.

This is my life.

My crazy fucked up life.

Sad but true.

I *can't* make this shit up.

OLIVER

UNLESS YOU WANT me to stay locked in your bedroom forever... Fuck, she has no idea how appealing the notion is. Charlotte, locked in my bedroom. A feisty, topless, at-my-mercy Charlotte. She's making fantasizing about her *way* too easy.

I pace the aisles of the local Jenkins Dollar. Somewhat of a hodgepodge store, a person can find an assortment of products from twine to milk to plastic organizers. What they don't specialize in, however, is fine clothing. Or clothing at all. I've already walked up and down every aisle twice and have yet to find any type of apparel.

Did I mention how much I despise shopping? My wardrobe is simple, consisting of a few timeless, classic pieces that can be worn over and over. Staples that my personal shopper at Neiman Marcus picks out for me twice a year. Shopping, besides for groceries, is my idea of hell on Earth.

Ready to admit defeat, I sigh and turn back toward the entrance. Then I spot an end cap full of Americana attire that's on clearance. My guess is that it's leftover merchandise from the Fourth of July. There's an obnoxious white t-shirt with a giant American flag on the front and "God Bless America" printed in flowing script beneath it. Cheap silver jersey shorts with red, white, and blue stars and "U.S.A." stamped across the ass hang below the shirts, completing the outfit.

I grab a pair of shorts, a t-shirt, and at the last second, I toss in a pair of white rubber flip-flops for good measure.

Charlotte will definitely be representing her country today.

Smiling, I hand over a crisp twenty dollar bill after the clerk rings up the items.

Payback's a bitch.

Should've just borrowed one of my damn shirts, Charli.

———

The door cracks open before I reach the top step. "What took you so long?"

I roll my eyes. Even though she can't see my face, she can definitely *hear* the sarcasm in my tone. "You're welcome." I shove the bag through the tiny sliver of space between the door and frame. As soon as she grabs the package the door slams closed.

I hear the rustle of the plastic bag a moment before she speaks, "Thank—wait, what the hell *is* this?" Her high-pitched voice splinters through the door. "What on Earth did you buy me?"

A grin pulls across my lips. "You don't like it?"

I hear more shuffling and mumbling before she swings the door open. My eyes land on her now-clothed figure. Despite my best attempt not to, a laugh escapes.

She pins me with narrowed eyes. "Don't."

"What?" I follow as she brushes past me to the stairs, her clothes from last night in one hand and her purse in the other. "I think it looks great. But I have to say, Charli, I never knew you were such a patriot," I tell her as I follow her to the kitchen.

"Ugh." Without asking, she grabs a ceramic mug from the tower on the counter and pours herself a cup of coffee from the pot before plopping down on a stool. My eyes watch her for a fraction of a second. *She looks like she belongs here*. At my counter. Early on a Friday morning. Drinking coffee.

Her voice interrupts my thoughts, "I can't believe I have to get in an Uber dressed like this."

I join her after pouring my own mug. "You don't. I'll take you home."

Her eyes dart from her coffee to where I sit next to her. "You've already done more than enough." She drags her finger up and down, indicating the outfit.

"It's working for you," I tease, but really, there's a compliment hiding in my joke. She *does* look good in the cheap t-shirt and shorts. Better than anyone has a right to. She's knotted the oversized t-shirt behind her back, exposing just a hint of her tanned tummy. The shorts sit low on her hips and she's rolled the waistband several times so that the hem hits just above mid-thigh.

Her eyes cross, showing me she thinks I'm crazy. "Thanks." She takes a slow sip of the too hot coffee. "And I'll try not to let the fact that you bought me an extra large top and bottom hurt my self-esteem too much."

"It's all they had." At least, I think it's all they had. I didn't look very hard, because I was grateful I'd found anything at all. But believe me, when it comes to women's clothing, I've always been a fan of *the smaller, the better*.

"Well, I think it's about time to go." She unplugs her phone from the charger and I watch as she pulls up the Uber app.

She presses a few buttons, but before she can complete the request, my hand closes over hers. "Let me take you home."

Her brow furrows. "That's not nec—"

"I know it's not." My eyes hold hers. "I want to."

Shaking her head, she says, "It's out of the way." She draws her hand back and starts pushing more buttons on the phone. "And I'm sure you have more important things to do."

"Actually, yeah," I agree and her eyes widen as though to say *there ya go*.

"I was planning on going to the Crestmont Farmer's Market." Her nose wrinkles as if she's never heard of it. "Wanna come?"

With her free hand, she points to herself. "Dressed like this?"

"Sure, why not?"

"Because I look like a goddam flag."

"Now you're just being dramatic." I swipe her mug from the counter and empty and rinse it before loading it into the dishwasher. "Besides, the market's on the north side, about a forty-five-minute drive from here. I doubt you'll see anyone you know."

"You're serious?" She shakes her head in dismissal, but her eyes tell me that she's considering the idea.

"I asked, didn't I?"

She tugs at the leather strap on her purse. "I *do* love farmer's markets and I haven't been to one in a really long time..." She slips her phone into her purse. A good sign. "I used to go with my dad to Hickory Hills when I was a kid."

I know the one she's referring to. It's a small venue with fresh produce and baked goods. But Crestmont is better. They offer a wider variety of products, better prices, and there are a lot more vendors. Definitely worth the drive.

My brow arches. "Is that a yes?"

She hesitates, unsure, as she glances from me, to her t-shirt, back to me, then to her shorts. "Umm, okay?" she answers, a question still in her voice, and my smile widens.

"All right." I grab her hand to lead her toward the garage but instantly drop it when she tenses. *Shit.* This isn't a date. Hands to yourself, Oliver. Hands to your fucking-self. "This way."

She nods and begins to follow but pauses by the doorway. "Hey, Oliver."

"Yeah?"

"One more thing."

"Yeah?" I repeat, readying myself, convinced she's had a change of heart and doesn't want to go.

But the worry dissolves and I out and out grin when she says, "I'm not paying you back for these clothes."

Winking, I say, "Wasn't even gonna ask."

———

I stumble through the dimly lit garage. It's large, two full stalls, but you wouldn't be able to tell from its current condition. Not a single wall can be seen, hidden behind well-worn cardboard boxes that have sat mostly untouched for months.

Ainsley's stuff.

I squeeze past a row of precariously stacked plastic bins that look like they'll topple over at any second if you exhale too hard.

"I can see why you park outside," Charli says, tipping her head toward the crate tower.

"Yeah." I continue walking. "Ainsley has a lot of..." *Shit.* "Things."

Charli's nose scrunches. "Did she just move in? I thought she moved in—"

"A year and a half ago."

"Oh."

Her *oh* says it all. It says exactly what I think and feel every time I walk through this garage filled with the boxes that contain Ainsley's life.

It's weird.

Our relationship isn't working.

We're barely roommates.

Rather than say any of that, I say, "She works a lot." I shrug my shoulders. "She's used to living out of a suitcase and hasn't gotten around to unpacking the nonessentials."

Charli shrugs. "Yeah, I can see that." Her eyes sweep the space once more. "Your bathroom is chock-full of her travel treasures." She pats her purse as though she's stuffed it with toiletries. Maybe she has. "Thanks, by the way." She winks and then says, "Kidding. Although I did swipe a blueberry-lemon lotion. There were four of them and it smelled really good so..." Her voice trails off.

I laugh. "You stole from me?"

"Is it stealing if I just told you?" she asks, laughing too.

Reaching for the two large canvas tote bags on the peg near the door, I say, "I guess not."

Charli eyes the bags in my hand before bringing her gaze back to me. "Impressive."

My brows rise in question. "You're impressed by the fact that I use reusable grocery bags?" I shake my head. "You better raise your standards, Charli."

"Asshole," she murmurs under her breath. "The environment is important. Recycling is important. Plastic is killing our oceans." Her voice continues to rise with enthusiasm. "Have you seen the documentary on straws?"

I groan. "Now you sound like my sister."

"Margot?"

My nose scrunches. "Do I have another sister I don't know about?"

"I don't know." She hesitates before continuing, "You never really talk about your family."

She's right. I don't talk about my family much—I'm private in that way—and the fact that Charli remembers my sister's name when I've spoken it no more than a handful of times in front of her touches my heart.

Charlotte actually *listens* when I talk.

I shrug as I deflect, "Not much to tell, I guess."

"So Margot's into recycling too?"

I hit the button for the garage door and we both wait as it slowly opens. "You could say that."

As we walk to my SUV, I press the unlock button on the remote and the beep resounds in the quiet. "She's an environmental engineer." I hold up the bags. "These are her influence. She'd have my balls if she knew I used plastic."

Charli smiles. "I think I like her already." She opens the door and slides into the front passenger seat. "Does she live around here?"

Shaking my head I say, "Nope. Lives in Florida with her partner."

Charli turns her head toward me. "Partner? Like a business partner?" I narrow my eyes, return her stare, and understanding dawns on her. "Oh, her *partner.*"

"Yeah. She and Sara have been together for almost seven years."

"That's cool." She glances out the window as I pull onto the road. "Do you have a problem with her being a lesbian or something?"

I bristle at her ludicrous question. "No, not at all. Why?"

She shrugs. "You never really talk about her and she's your twin..."

"Nah." I merge onto the highway easily since there's no traffic at this hour. "It's not like that at all. We're close. We talk at least once a week. And I really love Sara."

She hums her agreement. "I hooked up with a girl once."

Her voice is even, calm, as though she didn't just drop a bomb. An interesting, sexy as fuck bomb. *Charli was intimate with a woman?* Great, now I'm picturing Charli naked, beautiful tits presses against another woman's...

No. Nope. Not going there.

The car jerks forward as my foot slams the brake in surprise. I falter and slide my shoe back over to the gas pedal. Somehow I manage to find my voice. "Hooked up or *hooked up*-hooked up?" *Inquiring minds want to know.*

She shrugs again. "Second base."

My brain trips over the information. Second base is...what? Fingering? Oral? Jesus, I can't remember and I definitely don't want to ask. She already thinks I'm old as it is.

She clarifies, "I was curious. At the time, I was going through an anti-guy phase after my long-term boyfriend..." She pauses as if searching for the right words, "dicked me over. Anyway, it wasn't really my thing. I didn't *enjoy* myself, if you know what I mean."

"Jesus, Charlotte." I adjust the thermostat down a few degrees because suddenly my skin is on fire. "Are you always such an open book?"

"Not really." She smooths her hands over the front of her t-shirt. "You're easy to talk too. Besides, it's not like I'm ashamed of it. Women are beautiful."

I nod, remembering her sexy dance at the club. "Women like Dallas Diamonds?"

She groans, "Oh God, please. Can we not talk about my drunken strip dance last night?"

Chuckling, I ask, "Why not? I thought you were good." My tone teases. "If the whole restaurant manager thing doesn't work out, you always have a backup plan."

"Is that why you stopped me?" Her eyes narrow in skepticism. "Because I'm

so *good?*"

Yes. No. I don't fucking know.

"I stopped you because you were drunk and would regret showing your tits to a club full of perverted, horny men." My eyes find hers, daring her to contradict me, because deep down, she *knows* I'm right. Judging by the way her eyebrows pinch together, I'm guessing she already regrets what little *did* happen.

She sighs. "You're right." She's quiet for a moment, and I think our talk about strippers is over, but she surprises me when she asks, "How awesome a stripper name is Dallas Diamonds, though?"

I grunt because I hadn't really ever thought about stripper's *names*. Honestly, it's never crossed my mind.

Yes, please, or I'd like a lap dance, but before you begin, I must know, what is your name?

"If I'm gonna do it..." She glances at my confused expression before clarifying, "*stripping*, I'd have to have an equally cool name."

"Like what?"

Out of the corner of my eye I see her tap her chin in thought, but her answer is almost instant. "Laney Vine."

My forehead furrows in mock worry. "Should I be concerned

that you've given way more thought to your stripper name than seems appropriate?"

One shoulder lifts. "Ehh, I have an overactive imagination." She looks out the window, then turns her head back toward me. "People would come to see *Laney Vine* dance." She bites her bottom lip. "You'd come to see Laney, right?"

My eyes jerk to hers, wide with question, with heat, with innuendo, and she immediately blushes. "No!" Her hands fumble in her lap. "I didn't mean come see *me* dance. I just meant that..." Her speech falters. "Laney Vine is a cool name. Like people would be curious. You know what? Just forget it. I'm gonna stop talking now." She shifts in her seat, and in a clear attempt to change the subject asks, "Can we listen to music?"

"Sure." I click on the Spotify app synced with my car. "I have just the song for *Laney Vine*."

Her eyes narrow in a scowl, but I laugh. "What? I'm thinking this could be your signature song, like a trademark."

A small smile begins to light her face, but it dies a quick death on her lips as she hears the opening chords filter through the speakers. Sun-kissed arms crisscross against her chest. "'God Bless the U.S.A.?'" She pins me with her steel blue eyes. "*Really?*"

Shrugging, I say, "I thought it was appropriate given your outfit."

She shoots darts at my side profile. "I do *love* my country which is much more than I can say about you." Her eyes shift to the clock. "How much longer am I stuck with you?"

I read the next mile marker as we pass. "A while." Voice light, I tease her. "Come on, *Laney*. There's plenty of time to practice some of your moves." My gaze slides to hers, and I wink before turning back to the road.

To my shock, horror, *delight* she begins to shimmy in her seat. "Is this what you wanna see, big boy?" Her voice lowers, turns sultry as her fingers grip the bottom of her t-shirt before sliding it up her torso, just a touch. "I do *love*..." She arches her back, dipping her head with a dramatic moan. "My country."

Despite it being incredibly dangerous, my eyes veer from the road to hers. Well, not exactly. They dart to her *hands*, which are sliding up her ribcage, skimming the sides of her breasts before she —*Holy fuck.*

The car swerves and hits a pothole, jolting us both. "Eyes on the road," she scolds, back to her normal tone, although it holds a bit more humor than before.

My mouth is so dry that I think my tongue will crumble to dust. Water. Need water. Now.

Her eyes shine with victory. "Still think *Laney Vine* is a bad idea?"

Nope. Not at all. I'd give my left nut to see her dance. For me. Alone. In private. Without the pesky "no touching" restrictions.

Rather than reply, I turn the volume louder, a tightness spreading throughout my body—and my dick.

Charlotte Ann Truse is full of surprises.

And the more I get to know her, the more of her I like, and the deeper I realize how screwed I am.

CHARLI

THE PARKING AREA IS PACKED. This isn't some hillbilly setup in the middle of nowhere. Crestmont is a legitimate open-air market, complete with "You are Here" maps on either end of the lot.

Feeling a little duped, I glare at Oliver. There are hundreds, if not thousands, of people here. And I'm wearing America's finest. *Literally.*

The flag outfit is ridiculous, not to mention that it makes me appear somewhat unhinged. I look as though I'm about to storm Washington, D.C. in protest. All I need is a sign that reads "Not MY President!"

Oliver doesn't share my unease and he begins walking up the main path toward the entrance.

"Wait." My hand reaches for him to halt his progress before he's gotten too far ahead. He stops abruptly, his sneakers kicking up dust as he angles his face toward me. "I don't think I can go in there dressed like this."

"It's a farmer's market." He rolls his eyes in exasperation. "You look fine."

"Fine?" My mouth widens in disbelief. "I look like George Washington and Betsy Ross's love child." He begins to laugh, but I cut him off. "Don't." I narrow my eyes. "Not to mention that I'm not wearing any underwear and you can see the outline of my black bra as clear as day."

What? I wasn't going to put on dirty panties after my shower. #Commando

All playfulness drains from his face. "You're not wearing—" He shakes his head, stops himself from fully asking the question. "You know what? Too much information." He takes a step closer to where I stand rooted in place. He tugs my hands away from my chest, drags them down to my sides. His eyes lower for a fraction of a second before returning to mine. "If the bra is bothering you that much, take it off." He gestures with his chin. "There are bathrooms right over there."

I scoff at the preposterous suggestion. "Take it off? You've seen my boobs, Oliver."

His face flushes a warm red. "I've never see—"

Embarrassed, I hold up my hand to stop him. "All I meant is that I need the...*support*."

We remain in a rather awkward stalemate for a tense thirty seconds. Neither of us moves a muscle. At some point, my brain commands my feet into action and I begin walking the worn path toward the entrance. *I'm already at the party, might as well dance.*

After several moments, and I hear Oliver's heavy, albeit somewhat rushed, footsteps behind me. I can't be sure, but I could swear I hear him mumble, "I'll never understand women."

Inside, the market is controlled chaos. Men and women of all ages amble up and down the cramped, makeshift aisles, some with large tote bags like Oliver's, some with squeaky metal carts on wheels that get stuck on the small stones that line the pathway.

Hideous outfit aside, I'm having fun.

"Try this." Oliver hands me a small cut of an Asian pear from one of the booths. The syrupy juice dribbles down my fingers as I pop the tiny square into my mouth.

My tongue slides over the fruit. It's grainy, almost gritty, but sweet like candy. "Delicious." I grin as I wipe my hands across the legs of my shorts. Poor manners, I know, but it's not like I'm ever going to wear them back up again. God willing, anyway.

"Where to now?" Oliver stops at the intersection of the next two rows.

"Do any vendors sell cheese?"

He nods. "Right this way, baby."

My head snaps up, eyes seeking his, but he's already turned his back and has begun walking toward another building. His body is relaxed. Cool. Calm. Casual.

Meanwhile, I'm freaking the fuck out. *Baby? Did he just call me baby? I can't have heard him right.*

We make our way slowly through the throng of people. In front of one booth, there's a crowd, the line at least twenty deep.

"What's this place?" I glance at Oliver, if doing my best to ignore his hand resting on the small of back connecting us as he guides us through the labyrinth of tables, patrons, and vendors. But I can't ignore it because the contact *sizzles*. And if the market weren't so loud, I promise you'd be able to hear the snap, crackle, pop of his skin on mine. *Fireworks.*

"Paulashinski's." His body slides tight against mine, making room as a woman with three small children under the age of five—God bless her—passes by. "They make homemade kielbasa and other sausage products."

"Oh," I say, my voice and body deflating when Oliver releases me once the crowd thins.

We continue walking until we reach another building. My gaze sweeps the large space. There are at least a dozen vendors, some with deli style showcases, some with food on wooden tables, others with products dangling from wiry ropes secured to the ceiling.

For a cheese lover like me, this is paradise. "Do they *all* offer samples?" I ask, voice eager and excited.

Oliver nods but bypasses all of the stations and heads straight to the back corner. "DelGorgio's is the best."

A man calls to Oliver before we've reached his booth. "Chef Pensen." The use of Oliver's last name catches me off guard as the short older olive-skinned gentleman greets us. "You bring friend today?" The man's warm eyes find mine.

Oliver nods. "Lorenzo, this is Charli. Charli, Lorenzo."

"Nice to meet you." I extend my hand for him to shake, but he surprises me by kissing it.

"*Ciao, bella.*" The man's smile widens. "What can I do for you today?"

Oliver glances from me to the vendor. "We'd like some cheese and yours is the best."

"*Grazie.* You're too kind." Lorenzo beams at Oliver. "What do you like?" Lorenzo turns his attention to me.

A nervous giggle escapes my mouth. "All of it?"

Oliver chuckles. "Let's get a sampler platter." He turns to me. "Does that

sound good?"

It sounds Perfect. With a capital P. And an extra side of 'erfect.' "Yeah."

Lorenzo smiles. "Go now. You bring your girl back here, fifteen minute." He

shoos us with his hands.

Your girl.

Lorenzo called me *Oliver's* girl.

I think I just died a little.

Rather than correct the error like I expect, Oliver glances at me. "We can check out the last building and then come back?"

Oliver's carefree mood is contagious and I reply, "Sure."

For a split second, my body gets ahead of my brain and I reach out to grab his hand. Luckily, my brain aborts the mission before any contact is made. Thank God because that would have been hella awkward.

Because I'm *not* his girl. This isn't a date. Even if I wish it were.

We make our way down the crowded rows and go through a

single narrow corridor into the last building. The space is smaller, but like its predecessors, there are samples aplenty. I say as much, "I know where to come next time I want a free meal."

He nods with enthusiasm. "Yeah, the merchants are very generous, but it's because they love what they do. They care about their customers. Supplying them with the best products creates loyalty. It's good marketing really." He smiles. "You saw the line at Paulashinski's?" I nod. "People travel over five hours every week to buy their kielbasa."

"Can't they order it online?"

He shakes his head. "This is old school, Charli. Few, if any, of these businesses have websites."

"Huh." Part of me likes the idea of local, homegrown products available in limited quantity, but the millennial in me likes the convenient, instantaneous gratification of ordering a product and having it at my door in less than two days.

I stop walking in front of a booth which looks to be selling small, dark onions. Some are cut in half and placed in clear sample cups. I approach the booth, inspecting them further. After a few more seconds of sniffing and poking, I ask, "What are those?"

Oliver leans his head over my shoulder to see what I'm pointing at. "Figs."

"Figs?" My nose scrunches. "I've never had a fig before."

"Really? They're good. Sweet" He moves to stand beside me. "You'll like it."

He takes one out of the cup and holds it to my lips. "Open."

I comply and he sets the fruit on my tongue. I close my eyes as the flavors explode in my mouth. "Oh my God."

He smiles. "Told you."

I pick up my own sample. "Your turn." He hesitates for the briefest of

seconds before he opens his mouth.

With a shaky hand, I raise the sample to his lips, but I overcompensate and end up sticking my fingers in his mouth. Heat floods my face as mortification sweeps through me and I quickly try to pull back, but Oliver surprises me when his tongue sweeps across the pads of my fingers. Then he does something really shocking—he nips them with his teeth.

Before I can even process what's happened, we separate, and I would almost think I imagined it all if it weren't for the sexy wink he gives me as he chews. I stand mute, staring as his throat muscles contract and release when he swallows.

"Come on." He rests his hand on my back once more and leads me in the direction we just came. "Cheese should be ready."

The only thing that could make this more *perfect is if we were sitting on the bank of the Seine with a glass of wine.*

"You think this is perfect?" Oliver's voice drags me from my thoughts and I startle momentarily.

Was I talking aloud?

"I-I umm..." I stutter, already deep into the food coma that threatens all of my (rational) sensibilities. Cheese makes me happy. Cheese is the answer to all of life's problems.

"It is pretty perfect." He muses, "But I'd have to pick Venice not Paris."

I lean back on my elbows, relax into the soft green blanket that serves as a

makeshift tablecloth for our unplanned picnic. "I'll take your word for it."

Oliver leans back as well, turning onto his side to face me. "Never been to Europe?"

I snort. "Never been out of the country." I relax even more until I'm fully on my back, hands splayed across my sated belly. "Well, I've been to Canada, but Niagara Falls doesn't count." I angle my head to face him. "I take it you've been?"

He turns bashful, a look that's incongruous with his usual cocky attitude. "You could say that."

I sign in frustration. Oliver's ten years older than me, more experienced, more cultured. I know he's traveled a lot. His fiancée is a flight attendant, for crying out loud. "You don't have to feel bad for me. I'll get there. Someday."

His eyes hold mine and he nods his head in agreement before saying, "I lived in France for two years."

"Wow." I roll toward him in excitement. *How did I not know this about him?* "While you were studying at the Culinary Institute?"

"Yeah." A smile stretches across his face. "It was part of the CIA's program."

"Where in France?"

"Marseille. But I traveled a lot while I was there."

"That is so awesome." I prop my head in one hand. "What was your favorite city?"

He taps a finger to his lips. "That's a tough question. Can I do top three?" He glances at me and I shake my head no.

He continues, undeterred, "I love London because of the eclectic mix of food. Think New York City, but better. More chic." His sigh is almost whimsical. "But Barcelona has La Boquería, one of the largest open air markets in the world." He pins me with intense eyes. "You'd love it there, Charli. Samples galore."

Before I can respond, he continues, "Paris, in general, is amazing. Their respect for food and meal preparation is awe-inspiring. Sacred. But if you held a gun to my head and made me choose *one* place, I'd have to go with Venice."

"Why Venice?" I ask with genuine interest, more than a little captivated by his travel expertise.

"Venice is unlike any other place in the world. The canals, the architecture, the people. It's a city that is *literally* built on water. St. Mark's Square, the Grand Canal, the Rialto Bridge..." He sighs again. "That's what could make this day more perfect. Sitting along the Grand Canal, near the Rialto Bridge, listening to the serenades of the gondoliers as they pass by. And after, I'd take you to Alaska for dessert."

My nose scrunches in confusion. "Alaska?"

He nods, a faraway look in his eyes. "Only the best *gelatería* in

Italy. They make all their flavors by hand every morning, and they're always unique and different."

My eyes are wide like saucers. "That does sound incredible."

"It is." His finger reaches across the blanket, tentatively strokes my forearm and the contact burns. I wonder how so gentle, so light a touch could ignite such a powerful fire inside my body. His voice is dreamy and wistful when he says, "I'll take you someday."

Mine is equally dreamy when I agree, "I'm ready when you are."

CHARLI

IT'S BEEN five weeks since my and Oliver's...date? Outing? Field trip? Honestly, I don't know what to call it or what to think about that day in general. To me, our time together at the farmer's market was more intimate than any date I'd ever been on. I had his full attention. He had mine. We chatted. We dreamed. We *connected*.

Later, when Oliver drove us back into the city, he walked with me to the management office to make sure I was able to secure a new key. This gesture I could write off—he was being a nice guy. But then he walked me to my door and *hesitated*. Like he was going to kiss me. I would have let him too, but Mrs. Burns, a curmudgeonly widow in the apartment across the hall, chose that exact moment to open her door, killing the mood entirely.

We haven't been alone together since...which brings us to my present situation. I'm alone at Mecca's annual Feed-the-Kids Fundraiser, still holding on to hope, pining for a man who belongs to someone else.

Pitiful. It's a sorrowful word but one that describes my current state perfectly. I shouldn't have said it was okay when Jim backed out last minute. Should have insisted that he attend the back to school event with me because it was going to be awful if last year's experience was anything to go by.

But when Jim's ex-wife called that morning to see if he could take Maddie for the weekend, he obliged. How could he not? More importantly, how could I be upset? Maddie's his daughter. A daughter whom he rarely gets to see. She's much more important than being my pity date for a work function that I didn't want to go to in the first place.

Even so, I'm disappointed. Most of my coworkers are married, or at the very least, in committed relationships. I feel like Bridget Jones, a worthless singleton forced to endure a torturous evening with the "smug marrieds."

The last few beats of "Cha Cha Slide" die out and the DJ switches to a slow ballad. It's like DJ What's-His-Name has just announced that all couples *must* report to the dance floor immediately. It's a miracle no one gets trampled. Seriously, the mass of bodies stampeding is reminiscent of a herd of wild African elephants.

Slowly, I inch toward the corner near the end of the donation table which is already piled high with boxes. I'm hoping no one will catch me hiding out behind the large tower of tuna cans.

Though I remain (somewhat) hidden, I have a clear view of the dance floor, providing me with a crystal clear view of Oliver as he leads Ainsley directly into the center of the crowd. My greedy eyes study their expressions. They couldn't be more different; his face is neutral and reserved, hers soft and playful.

I know I should look away. Why the fuck do I torture myself? But for some reason, I can't stop watching. I'm morbidly curious, like when you drive by a gruesome accident, slowing down to look even as you tell yourself not to. Even as you curse every other person who does the same, causing traffic to bottleneck.

Ainsley's hands loop around Oliver's neck, her body leaning into his, the familiar way a lover does. One of his hand rests at her waist, the other reaches toward her and...

Caresses her cheek.

Intimate.

Caring.

Loving.

The gesture strikes me hard and fast, with equal parts cruel and melancholy. Deep down, I know he's not mine—won't ever be mine —but my heart can't quite comprehend the truth, latches on to the fantasy that I've built in my mind for so long that I can't remember how or when my feelings for him got so out of control.

My heart breaks a little more with each second that passes and I'm forced to face the stone cold reality: Oliver's heart belong to Ainsley. Not me.

I gasp a breath, the realization rushing over me like a strong wave, hitting me slowly and all at once. Biting the inside of my cheek, I will myself not to cry, promising myself that I'm stronger than this silly, stupid crush. I tell myself that fate would never be so vindictive to destine me to love a man who loves someone else.

With shaky hands, I slide my phone from the inside pocket of my purse. I decide to send Meg a quick text that I'm not feeling well and decided to cut out early. Surely she won't miss me with her new boyfriend, Jack, by her side.

Just after I send the message, a shoulder bumps into mine. I look up, startled, and come face to face with Simon. The twenty-one-year-old dishwasher.

"Hey." He stands beside me, beer bottle resting in one hand. "Is this a good hiding place?"

I raise my eyebrows. "Not having fun?"

He chuckles. It's light and carefree and I envy his youthful ease. "Not at all. This party bl—" He stops abruptly.

"Blows?" I finish, a smile stretching across my lips. The first of the night.

"I wasn't going to say that." I arch a brow and he smirks. "Okay, yeah, I was."

I shake my head. "Why are you here?" I don't mean to the question to be rude, but this party is for the full-time employees and management to schmooze the food suppliers into giving more donations to the local food pantries. Really, it's a who's who in the industry and ends up being a major tax write-off for all the companies involved. All this to say, if I were a twenty-something-year-old student, I wouldn't be here.

"I'm a broke college student." He states as though the reason were obvious, but it's not, and he must realize it by my confused expression. "Free. Food."

"Oh," I say, nodding my head like an idiot. When did I become uncool? Twenty-eight sure feels like fifty-eight these days.

He shrugs. "Plus it's for a good cause. They raise a lot of money and donations for the community."

My eyes skim over the full table of non-perishable goods. "Yeah, they do."

"So." He takes a long pull of his beer, finishing the bottle before he rests it on the corner of the table. "How does a beautiful girl like you not have a date?"

I chuckle, amused. "Are you hitting on me?"

"I don't know." He smirks, a lopsided grin that's actually quite endearing. "You tell me. Is it working?"

My eye widen with humor. "How old are you?"

"Twenty-one."

"That's what I thought." My phone buzzes in my purse and my eyes quickly skim the one word text response from Meg: Okay.

"Who's that?" Simon leans into me, peeking over my shoulder. "Boyfriend?"

Shielding the phone from his view, I slide it back into my purse. "I don't have a boyfriend."

"Lucky for me."

I roll my eyes. "I'm too old for you."

"You're *twenty-eight*, Charli." He enunciates the numbers as he inches closer, his strong bicep pushing against my arm. "Besides, haven't you ever heard of cougars?"

Thank God I'm not drinking because I would have spit the liquid from my mouth, the laugh that escapes me is *that* loud and forceful. "Jesus." I gasp, hand clutching my belly.

Simon turns to face me. He's laughing too. "You like me."

"What makes you think that?" Why am I flirting with him? I should just tell him I'm not interested and leave.

He shrugs again. "I have a sixth sense about these things."

"A sixth sense?" I snort. "As in, you see dead people?"

"Nice." He holds up his fist to bump with mine. "I'm digging the Bruce Willis reference."

With wide eyes, I bring my fist to his and tap. *This is so freaking weird.*

His smile lights up his face. "I heard you and Meg talking the other day in the office."

Upon hearing his comment, the smile dies on my lips. "You were eavesdropping?"

"No." He shakes his head, his voice pure innocence. "Oliver ordered me to update the produce logs, but I had no fucking clue where they were because I'm a *dishwasher*."

I snort again. Sounds exactly like something Oliver would do. So bossy and demanding, with no care that Simon was hired to wash dishes, not serve as his personal assistant.

Goddammit. Oliver. I don't want to think about him. Or Ainsley. Or them dancing together. Caressing each other. Doing couple-y things together.

Simon's eyes meet mine. "When I was looking for the logs I heard my name." His grin widens. "And the word *hot*."

Meg's word, not mine. But I don't tell him that.

"Come on." Simon tugs my hand, pulls me farther into the shadows, down a long, narrow corridor that leads to the coat closet. The sensible, rational, *adult* part of my brain knows where this is going. And it's a stupid idea for many reasons. The top three being he's too young for me, I don't have feelings for him, and I'm technically his *boss*.

I follow his lead.

Jesus, apparently I make terrible decisions even, when I'm sober.

Finally, my head catches up to my body. "Where are we going?"

I've barely gotten the words out when his hands band around my waist, pulling me flush against him.

When his lips brush against mine, I pause. They're different than I expected. Softer. Gentler. He pulls back, eyelids half-closed and smiles. "Everyone knows it's not a proper party without a random hookup."

"Really?" I tease. "*Everyone* knows that?" I don't. In fact I haven't made out with anyone at party in more than seven years. Is this what kids are doing these days? Am I'm really *that* old?

"Yeah." He dips his head, slides his nose along mine. "You're sexy as fuck, Charli."

Even though it's probably rude, I giggle. Let it be said that the giggle is partly due to nerves and partly due to his boldness, his perceived swagger. He's twenty-one, practically a baby.

I have to ask, "Are you drunk?"

"Not at all." He's barely finished the words when his mouth closes in on mine again. More insistent this time, a little more forceful. Despite my previous reservations, my body begins to warm up to the idea, begins to wake up in his embrace.

Strong hands slide up my back, fusing our chests together, and my mind starts to question how much longer I'll let this go on. It's been so long since someone has held me, kissed me, *wanted* me.

One more minute of guilty pleasure and I'll stop it.

But that minute never passes.

Loud—no, *thunderous*—footsteps trample down the hall, approaching us at breakneck speed.

At the intrusion Simon pulls away guiltily. My hands draw to my lips, shielding their puffiness. Slowly, I turn my head toward the approaching figure, but I know who it is without even having to look. Know by the sound of the labored, angry breaths. Know by the musky, bitter almond scent. Know by the wild beating of my heart. *Oliver.*

No words are exchanged, just long, snarled breaths on Oliver's part and quiet, submissive confusion on Simon's.

After several *long* seconds, Simon meets my gaze. "I'm

gonna go."

My eyes widen at his cowardice, but I've seen *much* stronger men crumble under Oliver's hard stare. A stare that he turns on me the second Simon rounds the corner.

He *descends*, stalks toward me until we stand toe to toe, each of us breathing hard. Oliver's eyes drill holes through me, but I refuse to show any sign of weakness, because *technically,* I did nothing wrong. Sure, Simon is an employee, but it's not like he's a minor. It's not like Oliver is the boss of me. At work *or* in my personal life.

Finally, *finally*, I break the silence. "What?"

He growls in response. Growls.

"Oh-kay," I begin, voice snippy. "I'm going to go too then."

Rather than respond, he yanks my arm—hard—and pulls me into the adjacent coatroom. A small five-foot-square area, that leaves us much too close for my liking.

"Oliver," I say his name in warning as I back up a few paces to try to put more distance between us. I don't get far due to the large rack of coats that shrinks the room by half.

"Don't." He shakes his head, squeezes his eyes shut. "Don't speak."

I have the sudden, irrational urge to start belting No Doubt's popular hit from the nineties at the top of my lungs, but somehow I don't think he'd appreciate it. I keep my eyes down and wait him out.

"How long have you been fucking him?"

My head snaps up, voice squeaky and proper. "I beg your pardon?" Jesus, who am I, the Queen of England?

"How long?" he repeats, jaw clenched so tight I can see the thick vein pulse along the side of his solid neck.

No way am I answering that question. "Oliver, my love life is none of your business." His chest puffs, and I add, "Just like your love life with Ainsley is none of *my* concern."

His eyes are hard, focused as they hold mine, showing me nothing of what he's feeling. "Like hell it isn't."

My mouth forms a perfect, confused *O*.

"Tell me, Charli." He takes a menacing step closer. And then another. And then another, until I'm out of room to recede, my back pressed against the empty wall. "How long have you been sneaking around with *him?*"

He's acting like I'm cheating on him. This is insane.

I shake my head. "I'm not having this conversation with you right now." *Or ever.* I lean in, sniff his breath, doing my best to ignore the musky scent of his cologne that assaults my nostrils. "On a scale of one to ten, how drunk are you?"

"Zero." His hands reach for my arms, but I quickly turn around in place, refusing to play his game.

"Jesus. What's gotten into you?"

"You." His one word answer causes goose bumps to erupt across my skin. "*You're* what's gotten into me."

"Oliver." His name passes my lips in warning, yet it's also laced with a touch of pleading as I silently beg him not to venture down this road. Not now. Not tonight.

My head is a mess of emotions. For Christ's sake, last time I saw him, he was dancing with his fiancée. Now we're alone in a dimly lit coat closet with what feels dangerously close to a giant erection pressed into my ass.

But he doesn't heed my warning. Instead he circles both my wrists with one large hand, pinning my arms behind my back. He leans forward, speaks directly into my ear, "You're going to deny it?"

My eyes squeeze shut. I don't know what he's accusing me of denying. Sleeping with Simon? Or wanting him? *Oliver.*

"Oliver, please." My breath stutters, body ripples. This side of him—jealous, possessive, angry—is turning me on. I'm so fucked up.

"But this is what you *really* want, right?" Oliver presses his solid chest against my back, pinning me flat against the wall. "Me fucking you so hard you'll feel me for days."

"Oliver." My voice is a breathless whisper as I turn my cheek to one side. My hands wiggle in his grip where he holds them flush against my back.

"Always teasing me. Torturing me with that plump ass and sweet tits and saucy mouth. I wonder how much you'll say when you're choking on my cock."

"Oliver," I moan at his dirty words. I shouldn't be this turned on. My panties shouldn't be wet, nipples shouldn't be hard. I should be fighting this. Fighting *him*.

"You did this, Charlotte. You drove me insane. For months. For *an entire year*. How much can one man take?" One hand holds my wrists as the other wraps around my throat, turns my head to face him. "You wanted to break me? Mission accomplished."

"Oliver." This time my voice is louder as my eyes hold his.

He releases his hold on me for a moment, spins me around. "Tell me you haven't thought about it—haven't thought about *us*. Tell me you haven't imagined me sliding into your tight pussy, stretching you, pounding into you while you beg me for more."

I wish I were stronger, wish I could deny his words, but I can't. *I don't.*

"Yes." My eyes flutter closed. "I have."

A growl escapes his throat and his nostrils flare. He dips his head roughly, but just before his mouth makes contact, I turn my head. My voice is tight, hoarse when I speak, "But not like this."

He ignores my comment. His lips latch onto my throat, sucking hard. So hard in fact that I gasp. But the gasp only encourages him. Next, his teeth nip the tender spot.

A moan bubbles to the surface from deep within my belly. A moan that is anguished yet laced with pleasure and want. A moan that was months in the making.

This.

This is everything I want. He is everything I want. But somehow I need to find the strength to stop him before we go any further.

Because I won't be his fling. His dirty secret.

I'm done being the work wife.

I want every piece of him...

...or I want nothing at all.

OLIVER

MINE. The one word loops through my mind, over and over again. Charlotte is mine.

Mine.

Mine.

Mine.

But the word is a direct contrast to the image seared into my brain: Simon's hands clasped around Charlotte. His thick body pressed against hers. His lips on her skin. *My* skin.

Fury boils in my bones and I growl into the curve of her neck before my teeth sink into her delicate flesh. I bite her, *actually* bite her. Not a soft nibble or nip. No. It's sharp teeth marking, claiming, *owning* her once and for all.

"Oliver," she cries in pleasure. The sound of my name on her lips is like sin, and I curse the layers of fabric between us. If the rational part of my brain were working, I'd actually be scared by how desperate I am. Horrified at the caged animal clawing its way through skin and bones. Terrified of the living, breathing beast that has the power—and is quite capable—of devouring her whole.

I slam my hips against hers, loving the way she spreads her legs wider to accommodate me, allows my rock-hard cock closer to where it aches to be.

Her breath hitches as my hand tracks up her leg, squeezes her ass, kneading the soft flesh beneath her dress. She feels like everything I imagined she would.

Soft. Smooth. *Woman*.

My other hand traces a path, on a one-way mission to her other treasures, but just before my palm can close around her breast, she utters one word that stops me dead in my tracks, "Wait."

No. I don't think I've actually said the word aloud, but when my half-lidded eyes find hers, I know I have. Confused pools of blue with speckles of gunmetal grey stare back at me, a myriad of emotions dancing between us.

Lust. Uncertainty. Desire.

So much fucking desire.

She pushes on my forearm, causing me to release my grip. "We can't do this." She splays her hands flat against my chest. "*I* can't do this."

My head hangs heavy against her shoulder as a loud shuddering breath pushes past my lips. She's right. What's worse, I *know* she is and it pisses me right the fuck off. All of my pent-up desire darkens to anger and my head snaps up so that our gazes meet. "What the fuck kind of game are you playing, Charli?"

Her brow furrows. "What?"

I push away from the wall—away from her—and walk a few paces. Right. Left. "Is this all a joke to you?" I cock my head, pin her with angry eyes.

"What?" she asks again, voice growing louder. "*You* started this."

My mind reels, the fury making my blood run hot. "What the fuck am I doing? What are *we* doing?" My hands clench at my sides. "Why would you be with him *here*? You had to have known I'd see you together."

Her back stiffens, indignant. "I'm not the one who's *engaged*."

"What do you want me from me?" I stop pacing. "It's..." I pause, drag out another slow breath and my eyes hold hers. "Ainsley and I have a long history."

"And what?" She splays her palms wide. "That's supposed to make it all okay?" She's so close that I can see the muscles in her jaw tic. "News flash, Oliver. You came on to me. You started this. Not the other way around."

My hand tears through my hair in frustration. "It's complicated."

"Complicated?" She heaves a deep breath. "Fuck, Oliver. I've wanted you since the day I met you, pined for you, hoping you'd *see* me. *Want* me." Her voice shakes. "Jesus, I think I'm in love with you —how pathetic is that? But none of that matters anymore because I'd rather be your nobody than your sidepiece. I deserve better than that."

Sidepiece? In love with me? My nobody? The words jumble together, my mind unable to process their meanings, their emotions.

"We're done here." She shoves past me, pausing in the doorway to give me one last, hard look. "Figure out what you want, Oliver. For your sake and for Ainsley's and for mine."

Her words cut like a sharp santoku knife to the soft underbelly of a fish. They splay me wide open, exposing my fear, my insecurities, *the truth*. She deserves so much more than I can offer her. She deserves to be the center of someone's universe. The one and only.

But because I'm a coward, I don't say any of what I'm feeling and let my anger fuel my words. And I can be one cruel son of a bitch with the right incentive.

"Have fun tonight with your *boy toy*."

She stops dead in her tracks, body rigid. She spins to face me, the look of hurt quickly replaced by anger. "At least when Simon's inside me tonight, when he's so filling me so *deep*—"

The growl that tears from my throat interrupts her midsentence. I'm like a motherfucking barbarian. Wild. Feral. Volatile.

She catches her breath before delivering her final insult. "I'll know that he's mine and man enough to claim what he wants."

With those final parting words she leaves me panting, burning, undone in the coatroom closet with the worst case of blue balls I've ever experienced.

I know exactly what I have to do. Ultimately there's one goal on my mind: stop Charli from being with Simon. Because Charlotte giving herself to him would absolutely destroy me. But first, *first,* I need to talk to Ainsley and make things right once and for all.

"I've been looking all over for you." Ainsley's voice reaches my ears before she comes into view around the corner and I crash into her, nearly knocking her to the ground. I reach both hands out to steady her.

"Are you all right?" I ask, releasing her from my grip.

She nods once before smoothing her palms down the front of her dress. Her eyes skim over my face, her brows pinching with concern. "Are *you* okay?"

She's right to be concerned. I'm positive my face is red, hot with anger. My shirt is rumpled, tie unknotted and loose around my neck, and my chest heaves forceful, burly breaths.

At least when Simon's inside me tonight...

"Oliver."

...When he's filling me so deep.

"Are you okay?"

I'll know he's mine and man enough to claim what he wants.

Fuck. That.

Fuck Simon touching her. Fuck any other man ever touching her again.

Charlotte's mine.

Small yet firm hands on my bicep shake me, jolting me out of my stupor. "Oliver, what is going on?"

My eyes snap to Ainsley's, searching. For closure. For under-standing. For forgiveness.

"Oliver." Her voice squeaks with nerves. "You're scaring me. What's wrong?"

"We need to talk."

Her eyes widen at my serious tone. "Okay."

I shake my head. "Not here."

"Okay," she whispers. "Just *please* tell me what's going on."

Hand at her waist, I guide her to the rear entrance of the building, not bothering to say goodbye to Don or the other bigwig investors and power couples who sponsor this event. We're both quiet as we snake through the semi-lit parking lot. Ainsley's heels tap against the hard macadam, creating an ominous *tick-tick-tick* sound. To my mind, it's a countdown.

Five. Four. Three. Two. *Boom.*

As my vehicle comes into view, I click the remote and open the door for Ainsley, waiting until she's inside and buckled before rounding the front of the car to the driver side.

"Oliver." She turns to me before I've had a chance to switch on the engine. "What is going on?"

"Let's go home first." I force the words through a clenched jaw. "I'll tell you everything then."

"No." Her steely voice cuts through the silence dismissing my request, my plea. "I need you to tell me what's going on *right now*."

In the three plus years we've been together, Ainsley's never used this tone, never argued, never questioned, but right now, she looks like she's ready to break. Her bottom lip quivers, fingers intertwined in her lap, clasped so tight that the knuckles are white.

I did this to her.

I scrub a hand over my face before exhaling a long breath. Even though it's hard, even though every ounce of me wants to cower, I meet her eyes. "Ains, why are we together?"

She gasps. "What kind of question is that?"

The sick feeling welling inside of me causes my stomach to roll. "Why are we *together*?"

She lets out a long sigh before she speaks, "Because we love each other and we're going to get married." Her eyes hold mine, but her voice shakes. In worry? In confusion? In anger? I don't fucking know.

"But *why* do we love each other?" I turn in my seat to face her, my emotions—anxiety, frustration, sadness—all blending together. "What do you love about me?"

She squeezes her eyes shut. "I don't know."

"You don't know." All of the fight leaves me. Those three small words the assurance I've needed for thirteen goddamn months: this relationship isn't right. It's never going to be more than what it already is: comfortable, easy, *familiar*. Even if there were no Charlotte, Ainsley *isn't* the girl for me.

Ainsley's narrowed, angry eyes snap to mine. "What kind of question is that, Oliver? Where is this coming from?" Her hands splay wide and she shrugs. "Why do you love me?"

I don't. The words are on the tip of my tongue, threatening to spill forward, but I pause to gather my thoughts. "Ains, you're a great girl, you are. You're caring and thoughtful and sweet..." My voice trails off as I dig deep for the words I'm about to speak. "But I'm not in love with you." She reels as if I've hit her. "At least, not the way I should be."

"What?!" she shrieks.

"I'm sorry." I want to reach out to console her. But as *a friend,* not a lover.

"No." Her wild eyes find mine as tears spill down her cheeks. "No. Oliver." She reaches for my hands. "We can fix this."

I lower my eyes. "No, we can't."

"Is there someone else?" She yanks her hands away. "Are you fucking someone else?"

"No."

"I don't understand." She swipes her fingers beneath her eyes, two dark smudges staining her cheeks. "I thought we were happy."

Shaking my head, I exhale deeply. "Ains, if we're honest, we both know things haven't been working for a long time. We've held on because we didn't have a reason to *not* be together. We're familiar, comfortable, but that's not enough to sustain a marriage."

"What are you talking about?" She hiccups. "Our life is perfect."

"Perfect?" My mouth hangs open in disbelief. "We barely see

each other, never have sex, and your stuff is still packed in boxes in the garage. That's not a relationship, Ains."

"We both work a lot." Her voice takes on a defensive tone. "I thought you were happy with the ways things were."

"I'm not." *At least, not anymore.*

"So that's it?" she spits. "We're over? Just like that?"

"I'm sorry."

She inhales a sharp breath, her hand reaching for the door handle. "I can't be around you right now."

"Ains." This time, I don't hesitate to reach for her. "Let me take you home. I'll leave."

Her laugh is bitter. "You mean take me home to *your* house? The house I never really moved into? To a house where I'm no longer wanted?"

With a soft tone I say, "I never said that."

"No thank you." She opens the door. "I'll find my own place to stay." She stands. "I'm not your problem anymore."

"You're not a problem." She gets out of the car, stands in the open doorframe. "Ains, please. I'll take you wherever you want to go. Just get back in the car."

She shakes her head no. "And if you try to make me, I *swear to God,* Oliver, I'll scream and I won't give a shit who hears me." A rumble ripples through the car as the door slams closed.

She takes off down the street, rounds a corner and I throw the car in drive following her until she enters into the lobby of a small boutique hotel. I slam my fist against the steering wheel.

Fuck.

Fuck.

Fuck.

The ride out of the city passes in a blur. Rather than go straight home, I find myself driving, circling the streets, much like the thoughts circling inside my brain.

Ainsley and Charli. Charli and Ainsley. I never meant to hurt either of them and ended up hurting them both.

Sliding my phone out of my pocket, I tap the text-messaging

icon. With careful fingers, I type in Ainsley's name, her number filling the screen after the first three letters. I fire off a quick message.

Oliver: I'm sorry. I never meant for this to happen.

Then I begin a new text to Charli.

Oliver: We need to talk.

This is it. This is where one chapter ends and another begins.

I don't know how long I sit and wait. For a response. A sign. A reckoning.

But nothing comes. It's just me, the quiet car, and the fucking black phone screen to carry me through the long, dismal night.

CHARLI

THE LIGHT from my phone screen illuminates my dark bedroom. Again. This is the third text message from Oliver in one hour's time. Oliver *doesn't* text.

I haven't read any of them.

My thumb stabs the button, submerging the room back into darkness. I flip onto my back, my hands fisting the covers that surround me.

"Dammit," I curse, the sound hissing in the silence. I'm not sure what I'm damning. Oliver for texting me at this hour. For causing my sleeplessness. Or for nearly kissing me.

Oliver.

After storming out of the coatroom with what little dignity I had left, I rushed to the bathroom to splash cool water on my face. Thankfully, all of the stalls were empty, and I took several minutes to calm my shaky nerves because *what the fuck?*

Once my breath had returned to semi-normal, I exited the bathroom and did a quick loop of the perimeter of the party in an attempt to find Simon. At the very least, he was owed an apology. But he was nowhere to be found—not surprising in the least. I found Don chatting with the Fogles, a wealthy husband and wife who patronized all of the Cal Group restaurants frequently. When there was a natural break in the conversation, I interrupted to say my goodbyes, citing a "terrible headache" as an excuse for my early departure.

At this point, the headache is no longer a lie. I've tossed and turned in bed for nearly three hours, vacillating from throwing my phone to clutching it tightly, hoping that *he* would call. Or text, which in and of itself would be a small miracle.

But he *did* text. The messages started a little after eleven p.m., I'm guessing around the time he left the party. Excitement and terror melded together until I convinced myself that whatever he had to say wouldn't matter. Not really.

There was nothing he could say to justify his behavior. Even if he was jealous, which he clearly was, he has no right. And even if I did react to his possessiveness, which I clearly did, I had no right. He's engaged. We both know better than to open Pandora's Box.

The dangerous game we've been playing has finally run its course. He called checkmate and there was no other move but to end this...*flirtation* before a line was crossed that couldn't be uncrossed. Because even though at times I may be foolish, I'm smart enough to know that when you play with fire, you get burned. Allowing myself to give in to my attraction to Oliver would *incinerate* me.

But now it's nearly three a.m., his texts stopped hours ago, and I'm curious. Exhausted but frustrated. Tears prick my eyes because the clock tells me I have to be up in four short hours and I haven't slept a wink. My chest aches and my stomach burns with curiosity.

I slip my hand out from beneath the covers, punching in my code to unlock the phone. My eyes squint at the screen and I immediately adjust the brightness to its lowest setting.

I tap the icon to pull up my text conversations.

Oliver.

Just reading his name causes my heart to beat harder. Faster. More erratic.

I click the thread with his name.

. . .

Oliver: We need to talk. 11: 08 p.m.

Oliver: Charlotte, please. 11:23 p.m.

Oliver: You can't ignore me forever. 11:49 p.m.

My eyes read the three paltry messages a dozen times, but each and every time, I still don't find the words I'd hoped to hear:

I'm sorry.

Please forgive me.

And I'm being completely honest, the words that I most long to read—*It's over between Ainsley and me.*

Dropping the phone next to me, I curl onto my side, hugging my knees close to my chest. So many thoughts run through my mind, most of which are shameful and laced with regret. Tonight I *almost* broke my promise. Tonight I indulged my own selfish desires at the expense of my self-respect, my dignity, and my morals. There's one question that I can't answer, one question that plagues me as I toss and turn in my cold empty bed.

Is Oliver worth the cost?

I'm embarrassed to admit it's not an easy question to answer, and as much as my mind yells *no*, my heart's voice is louder, demanding to be heard in the still of the night. *Yes.*

Jolting awake, I slam my hand down on the small alarm clock on my night table. It's a wonder the clock still functions after all the abuse I've imbued upon it. I despise waking up to alarms and their shrill, blaring beeps. I need to invest in one of those Zen alarm clocks I've read about online that wake you up with the sound of ocean waves or crystal bowls or...something other than a piercing ring.

Stumbling out of bed, I head to the bathroom, completing my routine in my usual order: pee, brush teeth, mouthwash—

"Oh my God." Mouthwash sputters out of my mouth, a few drops landing in the sink but mostly splashing across the mirror. My hand cups the crook of my neck as I lean forward. "What the..."

I lose my breath as my fingers trace the dark, purplish mark that's about the size of a clementine, in the exact spot where Oliver sank his sharp teeth into my skin, taking a big, juicy bite.

It's a hickey. I have a hickey. *Oliver* gave me a hickey.

How am I going to explain this? Everyone will see it. *He* will see it.

Folding to my knees, I dry heave over the toilet, but nothing but spittle comes out. My body twists in place until my back rests flat against the smooth ceramic of the bathtub. I cradle my head with my hands and force shallow breaths.

I can't believe this.

I can't believe what I've become.

The one thing I've always detested: *The other woman.*

I'm not sure how long I sit there, one hand clamped around my neck, shielding the spot that brands me as clearly as Hester Prynne's scarlet *A* marked her.

I have a conversation, albeit an internal one, with myself:

"It's not so bad. People get hickeys all of the time." Sensible Charlotte rationalizes.

"No one knows it was Oliver. Blame Simon." Deceitful Charlotte devises a plan. "No one will be the wiser."

"*Oliver* will know the truth. Come clean, Charli. People make mistakes." Forgiving Charlotte chimes in.

"Are you crazy? She made out with an engaged man. Everyone will judge her for the slut she is." Righteous Charlotte condemns.

"Nonsense," Immature Charlotte interrupts, "Pretend it didn't happen."

"Exactly!" drunk Charlotte yells. "Let's open a bottle of wine and discuss this further."

Enough. I squeeze my eyes shut because I think I've officially gone crazy.

After some time without having reached a conclusive decision, I hobble back into my bedroom and do something I've never done in my entire time working at Mecca—I call in sick.

CHARLI

I CALL in sick the next two days as well. I couldn't have planned it better if I tried. Don remembered me leaving the party early on Saturday night, so my "illness" was one hundred percent believable. To be honest, I panicked when he inquired about my wellbeing. I'm a shit liar, so I said the first thing that popped to mind—a stomach bug—figuring most people are either too grossed out or too polite to ask many questions about intestinal distress.

But I couldn't hide forever. Three days of hiding, three days of sulking, and the damn hickey wasn't fading. I worked with what makeup I had available and even watched some clips on YouTube from beauty gurus, but after two hours of (failed) attempts, I gave up and decided to wear my hair down to detract attention. Because it's late September and still mostly warm, a turtleneck is out of the question.

My nerves rattle as Mecca's large grey façade comes into view. With fingers clutched around the door handle, I take a deep breath and straighten my spine. *You can do this.*

And I do. I push open the door, walk straight by the bar, through the dining room, and power into the kitchen, my legs carrying me dutifully on a one-way track to the tiny office. Once safely inside I resist the urge to lock the door but only because it would raise suspicion. I've never locked the office in the past.

As expected, a tall stack of invoices are piled on my desk, along with five pink "while you were out" notes. I scan them briefly and find that most are from clients wishing to confirm their reservations in our conference room.

I work in silence for the better part of the morning. No one— including Oliver—bothers me, but my nerves are rattled. I keep making silly mistakes. Not even an hour ago I sent an email to an important patron and hit send without proofreading it. Instead of *Thank you, ma'am*, it read *Thank you, mama*. What's worse is that I didn't even realize the autocorrect error until the customer emailed back and signed her reply, *mama* ;).

At least she had a sense of humor about it. I, for one, am not laughing.

The day trudges along slowly until four p.m. when Meg arrives for her shift.

"Hey!" She cautiously pops her head in the door. "Feeling better?" I nod, but

she hesitates on the threshold, asking, "You're not contagious, are you?"

I force a smile. "Nope. All better."

"Thank God." She walks in and plants herself in the single chair across from

my desk. "It's been so crazy without you here."

My brows pinch together. *Crazy? Crazy how?*

Meg continues, "Joe had to leave early on Monday night because the baby

was sick. We had seventy confirmed reservations plus walk-ins and were so short-handed that Simon had to cover the bar."

"Simon?" I try to keep my voice even. He's the other man I've been avoiding since the fundraiser. "Does he know anything about bartending?"

"Nope." She shakes her head. "It was a disaster." She shifts forward in her seat. "And Oliver's been a *bear*."

My face heats as she adds, "We started calling him 'Cactus.'" My brows rise in question and she explains, "Because he's been a *real* prick."

I fumble with some papers on my desk just to give my hands something to do and to avoid her gaze. "He flipped out on Giancarlo. Threw an entire tray of duck breasts because they weren't 'seared' correctly. It's been an absolute shit show." She sighs. "When Simon tried to help clean it up, Oliver—"

"Oliver what?" I incline my head, ears straining, but Meg stops abruptly and stares at me with an open mouth.

"What?" I push the hair behind my ears, a nervous habit.

"Charli?" Meg stands, leans over the desk. "Is that a *hickey?*"

Shit. "Umm." One hands reaches up to cover the spot, heat radiating from my body. My face, my arms, my *toes* are no doubt bright red.

"Holy shit!" Meg grabs at my fingers, tilts my head this way and that. Her voice is loud when she says, "Someone really took a bite out of you."

"Meg!" I hiss. "Quiet."

"Damn." She chuckles. "Haven't had a hickey since ninth grade. This guy must really be feeling you."

I, on the other hand, have had a hickey, precisely *never* times. "It's not like that."

"It's *exactly* like that." She clucks her tongue. "There's only one reason a grown ass man would do that." She points at the offending mark on my neck. "He's peeing on you—"

I interrupt, "What?"

Her smile is huge. "Marking his territory. Letting all the other *dogs*"—she

winks for effect—"know you're his."

My eyes widen, but she continues, "I happen to think it's hot as hell." She takes a step back. "So who's the lucky guy?"

When I don't answer, she quirks a brow. "Lucky girl?" But she dismisses the idea with a laugh.

Words push past my dry lips. "No one you'd know." *Lie.*

"Huh, all right." Her smile is coy. "Don't tell me. I'll eventually get it out of you."

God, I hope not. For both of our sakes.

She turns to leave. "I'm glad you're back and feeling better, wink, wink." Her eyes dance with amusement as though she's discovered the real reason for my absence these last few days.

"Thanks," I mutter.

I'm already turning back to my computer screen when she calls out, "And please, for the love of God, can you see if you can talk some sense into Oliver? I'm not sure how much more any of us can take. I swear you're the only one who can keep him in line."

"Sure," I mumble my second lie in a matter of minutes, because the truth is, my entire to do list today consists of exactly one item. One *very important* item: avoid Oliver at all costs.

By Friday, I'm still walking on eggshells. The past two days, I've successfully avoided Oliver. Let me clarify, I've avoided being *alone* with him. Our eyes collided once on Wednesday just as I left for the evening, but I turned my head quickly and ran—Okay, jogged. Fine, walked *briskly*—to the train station.

Then yesterday, we had a brief, very stilted conversation about the weekend specials and what ingredients needed to be ordered. When he tried to steer the conversation to non-work-related topics I called in backup in the form of Meg. It was a dirty move. Meg is the noisiest and most observant of all the staff. Not to mention she knows both Oliver and me very well. She'd be able to sniff something was up with one wrong word. Pissed, Oliver shook his head and stormed out of the small office.

But today I'm a barrel of nerves because I need to be at the restaurant before opening to receive the weekend's deliveries. Oliver almost always works Friday mornings to prep ingredients and finalize the garnishes for the specials.

Are you sensing the problem? No?

Let me spell it out for you: We will be completely and utterly alone until two p.m. when Sasha, our pastry chef is scheduled to come in, giving us *plenty* of time to talk. And while I'm good with going the "pretend it didn't happen" route, Oliver is not. At least, not by judging the sidelong glances he sneaks me when he thinks no one is looking. Or from the unsigned note left on my desk yesterday telling advising me to "Stop avoiding him."

Truthfully, I don't know what to say. I'm ashamed of my actions. Regardless of what happened in that coat closet, my thoughts have been far from pure for far too long. If I had been stronger, I could have—*should* have—shut this shit down a long time ago.

We've been playing a dangerous game of poker, each of us raising the stakes little by little, and when he finally forced my hand, we both discovered I was bluffing the entire time. I *didn't* have a straight. Hell, I didn't even have a pair. I had zip. Zero. Zilch. Because the reality is, I *am not a cheater*. And deep down, I know (or at least I hope) he isn't either.

Oliver doesn't approach me when he arrives like I expect him to. He's been so adamant that we "talk" that I anticipated an ambush at eleven a.m. at the start of his shift. Instead, he completely ignores me. He doesn't say hi after he enters the kitchen and slips on his chef coat. Doesn't offer to share half of his banana walnut muffin as he always does when we work mornings together. And doesn't bat an eyelash when I march past him five —*five*—times, arms stacked high with boxes from the morning's delivery. Oliver *always* insists on carrying the bigger boxes—*in other words, all the boxes*—for me since our new deliveryman refuses to bring the order into the stock room but rather leaves it at the back door.

A bit sweaty and a whole lot miffed, I venture back into my office to peruse the receipts. Every so often, my hand marks an angry slash next to each item received after I've double-checked the price.

I don't have to look up to know Oliver's standing in front of my desk. I can tell by the way my heart skips a nervous beat and the way the pen slides from my slippery palm. Plus, the obvious: his shadow darkens the room, blocking my light.

"Is now a good time?" The cool tone of his voice prickles my skin.

I don't look up. "Not really." I tick a few more items on the invoice just to give my hands something to do.

Don't look up. Do. Not. Look. Up. Stay calm, Charlotte.

"Too bad." His hands snatch the invoice from my hands before tossing it to the side.

I glare at him. "What do you think you're doing?"

"Talking." He slides into the chair across from me. The sight of his large form squeezed into the small chair is almost comical and if I weren't so pissed off, I'd offer to switch seats. But as it is, let his ass get sore. *I don't care.*

"Oh, now you want to talk?" I snort. "After you ignored me all morning?"

"Frustrating, isn't it?" His smirk is wicked. "Being ignored?"

Son of a bitch! Was he trying to get back at me? My fists clench in agitation and I can feel the angry throb of my pulse in my neck. Oliver notices it too because his eyes zero in on my throat, on the —*fuck.*

Yanking the clip from my hair, I run my hand through the messy waves, trying to conceal the mark. *His mark.* It's mostly faded now and I've gotten marginally better at applying cover-up, but if one looks closely, like Oliver is right now, it's noticeable.

Oliver jumps up and I'm so startled that I jump as well. Before I can process what's happening, he rounds the desk and stands directly in front of me. His fingers reach for me, pushing my hair aside and instinctively, my palm closes over the spot.

"Don't." My voice is a whisper. A plea. A prayer.

His eyes narrow as he pries my fingers away. He stares at my neck with an emotion that I can't decipher.

Pride. Lust. Regret.

When his thumb drags over the spot slowly, *ever so slowly*, my eyes close and my breath hitches. His touch is soft and sensual and causing all sorts of crazy sensations in my body. Flushed skin? Check. Pebbled nipples? Check. Damp panties? Check. Check. Check.

"I did this to you?" His voice is soft, his large brown eyes locked with mine, thumb still caressing the fading outline.

Yes. My eyes cast down, my hand reaches for his and drags it down between us. But as I try to pull mine away, long fingers encircle my wrist and squeeze.

"I'm sorry." His sincere tone causes my eyes to snap to his.

"It's fine." I try to pull my hand away again, but his grip tightens. "It doesn't hurt or anything."

He exhales a long, almost painful breath. "I may be sorry, but..."

"But what?" I swear I hold my breath for an entire minute before he answers.

"But..." He hesitates, unsure, before continuing, "I like it." He brings his eyes back to mine. Holds my gaze boldly. Fiercely. "I *like* my mark on you."

I like it too. My body trembles slightly as my legs turn to jelly. I fall a little forward into him, but he uses his arms to hold me steady. "Oliver," I mutter.

"Charlotte." He drags the rough pad of his thumb against my cheek. "What are you doing to me?" He sounds perplexed, confused, like he's truly seeking an answer. Like he thinks I *know* the answer. But I don't. I don't know anything anymore.

Somehow I find my voice. "What happened in that coatroom was a mistake."

"It *wasn't* a mistake." His fingers squeeze me tighter, pull me a hair's breadth

closer.

We can't keep doing this. This has to end now. I have to protect my heart.

"We both know it was." I twist my hand and this time, he lets me go. I take a baby step backward until my back presses against the metal filing cabinet. "You're with Ainsley."

His next words shock me. "What if I wasn't?"

"I-I don't know."

His jaw flexes in anger, though he does his best to disguise it. "Because of Simon?"

"What? No." I shake my head. "Simon and I aren't...it was a silly kiss. Two lonely people sharing a fleeting moment. That's all."

This time when he speaks, he does nothing to hide his anger or downplay the accusation. "It didn't look silly or fleeting."

My face flames in anger. "Yeah? And it didn't look like you were having that bad of a time either. You know, when you were dancing with your *fiancée* all night."

He tears a hand through his hair. "Is that why you're pissed? Because I was dancing with Ainsley?"

"Yes!" I scream, finally taking the brakes off my anger, and damn, it feels good to vent all this pent-up frustration. "Of course I'm pissed!"

His eyes widen as I approach, not that I blame him. I probably look like a madwoman. Hair flying, face red, eyes wild. "You make me feel things for you that I shouldn't. All sexy and cocky and condescending yet sweet and caring. Cooking me meals, taking me to farmer's markets, giving me my first hickey." I slap a hand over my mouth at the admission but quickly get my bearings. "And every time I've tried to move on, push past this *inconvenient* crush, because hell-fucking-o you're engaged to be *married,* you suck me back in. First it was Jim—"

He holds up a hand. "You said you and Jimbo were nothing more than friends." His chest shakes with jealously. "Did I miss something?"

"Of course we're just friends," I snap. "Jim knows how I feel about you!" My voice explodes, my fists held high in the air.

Shit. Shit. Shit.

More words flow from my mouth like an angry tidal wave. "God forbid I show another man attention! Look what happened with Simon. I think you scared the guy half to death. He won't even look at me now!"

"Good." Oliver stalks toward me. "He has no right looking at you!"

My laugh is humorless as understanding dawns. Sure, it took me about

thirteen months longer to draw the conclusion than your average lovesick fool, but apparently, I'm a slow learner.

"That's what this is about, isn't?" I pin him with my eyes. "What it's always been about."

Oliver grunts his response. "What?"

"You don't want me, but you don't want anyone else to have me."

"That's ridiculous," he snarls.

My brows pinch together. "Is it?"

"So I'm the asshole? This is all on me?" His hands flex at his sides. "You're one hundred percent innocent here?"

My mouth opens, but before I can speak, he does, "The massages? The *Pretty Woman* piano sex? I did that, right?"

"You *are* an asshole." I shove past him.

"That's right," he spits. "Run away and go back to ignoring me. *Solid* plan." I stop in the doorway, spin to face him, chest heaving with each angry, labored breath that tears through my body. "We're done." I point between us. "This"—I make air quotes around the next word because fuck if I know how to define whatever we have together—"'relationship' is over. From now on, we're nothing but colleagues. Unless it's work related, we have no reason to communicate. And even that I'm not happy about."

He shakes his head in disgust. "What do you want from me, huh?" One shoulder rises. "Want me to quit so you'll never have to talk to me again?"

"Actually, yeah, that'd be pretty fantastic."

His mouth drops. "You're serious?"

"Dead."

"You know what? Fuck. This." He stomps by me, and seconds later, the large metal fire door slams shut, leaving me exactly how I always end up. Utterly and completely alone.

CHARLI

THE FOLLOWING WEEK Oliver doesn't show up for work. What's worse, no one seems to have any idea of where he is. Possibilities spin in my mind. Maybe he spoke with Don and requested vacation time—he has *plenty* of PTO. Maybe he's sick. Maybe he quit. Or was fired. *Shit.*

"I think I did something really bad," I say as Julia adjusts her phone so that I can see her entire face. "Really bad."

Her eyes dart over the top of the screen and there's a loud thump as a door slams closed. "Okay, she's gone."

My nose scrunches. "Who?"

"The roommate from hell."

Rather than be a good sister and inquire about Julia's roommate troubles, I dive headfirst into my own problems. "I think I got Oliver fired."

Jules pushes off the bed abruptly. "Why? What happened?"

My eyes squeeze shut, even as my heart pounds in my chest. "I don't know. He either got fired or quit—both of which are my fault."

"Wait. Slow down." Her tone soothes, and I'm actually a little taken aback by the concern I hear in her voice. "Start at the beginning."

I take a deep breath before I spill my guts. Every shameful, inappropriate detail. Jules listens with attention, interrupting every so often to ask a question or demand clarification.

"That was a week ago. And no one has heard from him or seen him since."

"Has he ever done this before?" She gestures with her hands. "Not showing up to work, I mean?"

"No." I chew at my fingernail, a terrible, somewhat disgusting habit that I kicked nearly ten years ago. But I can't stop the impulse to bite. It soothes me.

Christ, I'm spiraling.

"Maybe he's on vacation?" Jules offers. "I'm sure he has time saved up."

"I don't think so. Giancarlo, the sous chef, took over and went so far as to redesign the specials menu."

"So? What does that mean?"

"It means Oliver would *never* let anyone touch one of the menus without his explicit permission."

"And you've talked to Meg and Jim? No one knows anything?"

"Meg is just as in the dark as I am. Jim's away with his daughter and ex-wife at Disney World for five more days."

Her brows pull together. "How does that happen?"

Sighing, I say, "They had the trip planned before the split, and something about being progressive and co-parenting." Honestly, I don't know. It all sounded a bit strange to me when he explained it, but who am I to judge?

Her eyes narrow. "Can you say awkward?"

"Yeah," I agree, buy my mind is a million miles away from Jim and his family. I'm worried about Oliver.

"What about Don? You two are close. Have you talked to him?

I chew a different nail. My pinkie this time. "Don is being very tight-lipped and ambiguous. All he's said is that Oliver moved on to explore other opportunities."

"Oh shit." Julia's pupils dilate, and the action singlehandedly confirms my absolute fear. "He definitely got fired."

"You think?" I'm sweating all over, the panic and regret kicking my nervous system into overdrive. Sure I was angry and said some nasty things—we both did. But I didn't *actually* want him to get fired. This is his livelihood we're talking about. His career. His passion.

With no job and no money, he'll be forced to live on the streets. Ainsley will leave him and he'll take to the bottle to drown his sorrows. He'll become friends with a fellow street dweller and together, late at night over a barrel fire, they'll reminisce about "better" days.

Julia's chuckle pulls me from my thoughts. "*Stop.* You're being so dramatic."

My eyes snap to hers. Did I really just blurt that aloud?

"You're not responsible for his choices." Her words don't make me feel any better. It's a false compliment, like when someone tells you "No, you didn't gain any weight." The words are meant to encourage, to make you feel better, but deep down, you know the truth, that yes, you most certainly did gain weight, because your goddamn jeans don't button.

"Besides." Julia pushes a few strands of hair from her face. "You failed to mention how *you* got him fired. It's not like you reported him to Don or something."

"Of course not."

"Then how is this in any way, shape, or form your fault?"

"I don't know." My hands splay wide. "Maybe he was so pissed at me that he blew off work and Don had to let him go."

"A"—Jules ticks her fingers—"Oliver's a grown man who controls his own emotions, so if he decided to blow off work, that's on him. And B." She pauses, takes a breath. "I highly doubt Don would have fired him after missing one day. Isn't he like one of the most top-rated chefs in the city?"

The top-rated chef. As in, Oliver is the most sought-after chef within a one hundred-mile radius. Maybe more. I'd need way more than my two hands to count all of the competing restaurants that have tried to poach him in the short time I've worked at Mecca. "Yes."

"All right, then. Unless Don is a dumbass, that's not the reason."

"Okay." I bite another nail and draw blood. *Shit.* "What if Oliver took my words to heart? What if he quit because I told him to?"

"Nope." She shakes her head. "Don't buy that either."

"How can you be so sure?"

Julia exhales a loud breath. "I'm not saying this to hurt you, but..." Her voice trails off and I brace myself for the blow. "The man wouldn't leave his fiancée for you. There's no way he'd leave his *job* just because you two had a fight."

Ouch. Her words sting, poke at the scab that barely covers my already bruised heart. But this is the reason I called. I need Julia's words, the brutal, honest truth that she can give in the way only a sister can.

I don't say anything for a long moment because I'm afraid that if I do, I won't be able to control the flood of the tears pricking the backs of my eyes. Finally, drawing in a shaky breath, I whisper, "You're right."

The screen goes black for a minute and I think we've lost our connection. "Jules? You still there?"

"Yeah." Her voice carries through my phone. "I'm just checking my student calendar."

"Oh," I murmur, a little thrown by the turn of the conversation.

"My morning class is canceled Friday. Why don't I skip my afternoon class and come visit? We could have a girls' weekend."

Honestly? Company sounds wonderful, even if it is Jules. Even if she does drive me nuts. Even if we are polar opposites. Her own special brand of crazy would be the perfect distraction to my predicament. But can I let her miss class because of my meltdown? Jesus, how selfish am I? First with Oliver. Now Jules. It has to stop.

The screen is still black and I'm not sure if that means I can't see her or she can't see me, or both? Just in case, I force brightness into my voice and fake smile extra wide, teeth showing. "Thanks, but I'll be okay."

"Too late." I hear some clicking on her end. "I just bought a train ticket."

"Wait," I say, just as her face comes back into view. "What about your class?"

"Ehh." She shrugs. "It's only Intro to Philosophy." I raise my eyebrows. *That sounds like a tough class.* "The professor posts all of the notes in our online classroom. I'll be fine."

"You're sure?" I ask again.

"Yep. Train schedule says I arrive at the station at four thirty-seven p.m."

"Okay," I agree, hesitation laced in my voice. "You're sure?"

She rolls her eyes. "Yes."

I nod. "Okay, see you then."

"Great." She sits up and just as I'm about to disconnect, she calls my name, "And Charli?"

"Yeah?"

"Make sure you stock up on the Chardonnay. I have a feeling we're gonna need it."

OLIVER

It's been eleven days since I left Mecca. Thirteen days since I last saw Charlotte. Sixteen days since I pressed my lips against her soft skin, sank sharp teeth into tender flesh. Seeing my mark on her made me hard as granite. Thinking about it still does.

Just when I was prepared to tell her I'd ended it with Ainsley, to finally put an end to this cat and mouse game, *she* hesitated. Maybe I waited too long. Maybe she was thrilled by the chase, not me. Maybe there was more between her and Simon than she let on. *Fuck*.

"Does Charli know about the new restaurant?" Jimbo asks before taking a long pull of his beer. It's just after nine p.m. and the bar is still (mostly) empty. In truth, I didn't want to go out tonight, but I had some paperwork that I needed him to look over. Jimbo isn't a lawyer, but he *is* a finance guy. Close enough.

A lot is changing in my life. Remember how I said everything happens all at once or not at all? Not only did I end my three-and-a-half-year relationship with my fiancée, but Don *did* acquire the necessary licenses for the new property. As it is, I'm working side by side with him to design and create the space. The budget is *very* generous. Construction starts in a week.

If all that isn't enough, I was also contacted by the Lees Morgan Group, a national multi-million dollar company based in Las Vegas, Nevada. And get this—they want *me* to be the face of their new cookware line. The contract looks pretty sweet; I'll be paid an upfront endorsement fee, royalties in perpetuity, and there's even an option for a book deal.

But fame doesn't appeal to me—okay, maybe it does a little bit —but mostly, I just want to cook. And what the fuck is there for me in Vegas? My life is here. Charli is here. Even if she doesn't want me, I'll do whatever it takes to stay near to her.

"Well," Jimbo repeats his previous question, "does she know?"

"No." My eyes narrow into a scowl. "And you're not going to tell her either."

"It's only a matter of time before she finds out." Jimbo shakes his head. "Didn't Giancarlo already take over at Mecca?"

I grunt. "Yeah, but everyone just assumes I'm using my vacation time."

"Anyone who knows you will know that's not the case."

He's right. During the six years I was employed at Mecca, I never once used a vacation day. I had exactly two hundred forty hours of paid time off. Truthfully, it should have been a lot more, but the company's policy capped out at six weeks. Some might call the accrued vacation days sad. I call it dedication.

Looking back, my unwillingness to take time away from my job was just another fissure cracking the already shaky foundation of my and Ainsley's relationship. Hindsight is twenty-twenty, I guess.

Jim taps his bottle on the table to gain my attention. "How are you feeling?"

My response is immediate and disingenuous. "Fine."

"Fine?" His eyebrows pinch together. "Your three-year relationship just ended and you're fine?"

A frown tugs down the corners of my lips. "What do you want me to say?"

"How about the truth?" Jimbo taps his chest. "If anyone can understand what you're going through, it's me."

I nod but don't elaborate.

Jimbo heaves a heavy breath, concern marring his features as though he's not quite sure he wants to continue to poke the bear (i.e. me) but does so anyway. "Did Charli have something to do with your decision to end things with Ainsley?"

A snarl escapes my throat. I don't want to talk about Charlotte. In fact, I don't want to *think* about Charlotte. Now if I could only get my brain to listen...

Jimbo doesn't let it drop, and I wonder if he's gunning for a punch in the face. "Well?" His eyes harden a bit. "Did she?"

Yes.

No.

I don't know.

My fingers clench and unclench around the bottle of beer that I've yet to take one sip of. I ponder Jimbo's question, weighing my words carefully. "Not really." My voice is a lot gruffer than I intend. "Ainsley and I...we were together because we didn't have a reason *not* to be, if that makes sense. It wasn't bad, but it wasn't great either. We were *comfortable*."

Every word of that is the truth. Our lives were like parallel lines moving forward side by side but never intersecting. Looking back, there were probably a million little signs that I missed along the way telling me that Ainsley wasn't the girl of my dreams. But eventually, you get to a certain age, a certain point in your life when you're ready to take the next step. Sort of a natural progression of things.

The end of our relationship brought on a mixture of emotions and, yes, sadness is one of them. It's sad when any relationship ends, intimate or otherwise. Ainsley was part of my life for three years. But she wasn't *my* life.

The show will go on. I'll continue to cook. I'll continue to live in the same house I did before she "moved in." And one day I'll look back and remember her as "a girl I used to date."

The point is losing Ainsley didn't shatter me. But losing Charlotte? It's damn near suffocating me.

I glance up from my beer bottle. "I love her, you know?" Jimbo's confused eyes hold mine and I clarify. "Ainsley." Jesus, how much of a clusterfuck is my life that I have to clarify *which* woman I love? But clarification is absolutely necessary because I love them both, albeit in very *different* ways.

Jimbo nods for me to keep talking. "Ainsley's a great girl and we shared some good memories. I didn't want to hurt her, I do love her, but it's the sort of love that you feel toward a close friend or relative." I scrub a hand over my face. "Jesus, I don't even know what I'm saying."

"And what you feel for Charli?"

Explosion. Magic. Desire.

Mine.

Mine.

Mine.

My voice is deep and so low that I'm surprised Jimbo hears me. "Something else entirely."

"Have you told Charli how you feel?"

The look I give him is no different than if he'd sprouted another head. "That'd be a hard no."

He slides his empty bottle to the end of the table before signaling to the waitress for another. "I wouldn't wait too long."

I nod, but my mind is whirring. Last time I spoke with Charli, she more or less asked me to quit my job so that she'd never have to see me again. I don't think she'll be welcoming me with open arms anytime soon.

Besides, Ainsley has yet to move her stuff out my garage. If and when Charli and I do decide to try things out, I want us both doing so with a clear head and minimal baggage. The last thing I want Charlotte to think is that she's some rebound or fling.

The waitress sets down two more beers in front of us and my brow tics in annoyance. I didn't order a second round. Hell, I didn't even drink the first round.

Sliding the bottle to the side, I decide we've spent enough time dwelling on my problems, so I ask. "When do you leave for Disney?"

"Tomorrow." Jimbo gulps his beer. "Can't wait."

"Should be interesting to say the least." I chuckle. "Is the new guy going?"

"No." He shakes his head. "Thank God. I keep telling myself this is all for Maddie."

"You're a good man, Jimbo."

He grunts. "You'll see. It all changes when you have kids, man. You'd do anything to make them happy."

Kids. I've never wanted kids. Or more accurately, I've never given them much thought. My focus has always been on my career, and kids seemed like a distraction. I've never found a woman whom I'd actually *want* to create a life with. Ainsley was clear from the start that she never wanted to be a mother, so even if I did want a child, it wasn't going to happen with her.

My mind pops an image so fast I almost miss it. But it's there for a split second. A beautiful summer day. Charlotte nestled on a blanket with a tiny, faceless infant clutched to her chest. Me lying beside her.

My heart stops beating, pinches with joy, with desire. With love. I fucking want that. With her.

But if our last conversation is any indication of her feelings, there's as much chance of that happening as there is of hell freezing over.

CHARLI

THE DAYS SLOGS by and still no sign of Oliver. Giancarlo has seamlessly moved into the head chef position, and for the past week, he's been the one to tell me what products need to be ordered, what wines pair well with featured dishes, and on what color paper to print the menus.

Every ounce of me hates him for the simple fact that he's *not* Oliver. The bratty four-year-old who has taken up residence in my body and refuses to vacate wants to stomp her foot, scream, and shout that Giancarlo's way of doing things is dumb. Even *if* some of his suggestions have merit.

Because I care—or maybe because I'm weak—I *finally* cave and text Oliver. Several times. He never responds, which I can't say surprises me. He was never much of a texter. "If it's more than a simple yes or no, pick up the damn phone." That was always his stance.

So in a rather startling moment of bravery, I do just that. I call him. My fingers squeeze the phone with such force that I'm fearful the screen will crack. My heart gallops so fast and loud, it'd make any horse at the Kentucky Derby jealous. But all the fear and anxiousness is for naught. The phone rings once and then goes straight to voicemail. *He declined my call.*

I listen to his greeting, my heart pinching at the sound of his voice. God, how I've missed his voice.

Hello. This is Oliver. Leave a message and I'll call you back.

No frills. Straightforward. Simple.

The beep comes way too quickly, and for a second, I panic, breathing heavy on the line as my brain tries to string simple words together.

Finally, I begin. "Hey," I croak. My throat feels like the Sahara, so I take a sip of water and begin again, "It's me, Charlotte. Umm. I'm just calling to say hi and umm...see when you're coming back to work?"

This isn't a business call, Charlotte! Tell him you miss him!

"I also wanted to say I'm sorry for what happened between us. In the office, I mean, not in the coatroom...*Jesus*, sorry. This is awkward speaking to your voicemail. I think we should talk, without the fighting this time. So if you feel like talking, you have my number. At least you did. Unless you deleted it? Shit ...do you need my number? I guess I'll leave it just in case. 501-555-8161. Okay, talk to you soon. B—"

A robotic voice cuts off my goodbye: "If you're satisfied with your message, press one. If you would like to review your message, press two. If you want to delete and start over, press three."

Three. Number three. Choose. Number. Three.

My thumb stabs the number one and I gasp in horror.

I stare at the offending digit, betrayal blooming in my eyes. *Et tu, Brute?*

Tossing the phone onto the counter, I run into my bedroom and hide. Silly, I know—it's not like Oliver can see me through the phone. But in the end, my fear is ill placed, because he never does call back.

There are exactly two good things about Julia's visit. One, her general craziness distracts me from thinking about calling Oliver every five minutes.

Two, wine.

Since I picked her up at the train station yesterday, we've drunk an entire box of wine and are well into our second. Day drinking on a Saturday? Never a good look. But desperate times call for desperate measures.

By the time Jim calls later that evening, Drunk Charlotte is making her presence known. I'd say Drunk Julia is too, but Julia's obnoxious even when she's sober, so it's hard to distinguish between the two.

"Heyyy!" I answer, voice a little slurred. "Jim. Jimmy. Jimbo, my man." I hiccup. "You're baaccck!!! How was Disney? Are Mickey and Minnie still sickeningly in love? The bastards."

"Um." His unsure voice carries over the line.

I hiccup again. "I didn't mean that. I'm happy that they each found their soulmate. Their soul-mouse." I crack up at my own joke.

He chuckles. "Everything okay?"

I laugh a bit too loud. "Yeah, everything's great." In the background Jules has the music cranked loud. She's turned on some playlist she found on Spotify called "Love, Baby, Love." She's currently belting out, rather poorly I might add, "Kiss Me" by Sixpence None the Richer.

Jim raises his voice to be heard over the music. "Are you having a party?"

"No." I push myself to stand, but I lose my balance and stumble backward onto the couch. "No party. Julia's in town visiting."

Upon hearing her name, she spins to face me. "Who you talking to?" She narrows her eyes in accusation. "Is that Oliver?"

Shhh. I press my index finger to my lips, but when I do so, the phones slides out of my grip. "I'm on the phone."

Julia grabs my cell before I can snatch it back. Without pause she launches into attack mode. No *hello*. No *who is this*. Just shrill, angry words. One after the other in rapid succession. "Listen here, *asshole*. I'm sorry if you got fired, but my sister had nothing to do with it! And if you think for one second that you can call her now, after..." She turns to face me and asks, "How long has it been?"

I hold up all ten fingers and put my feet in the air so she can count my toes too.

Her nose scrunches in confusion, but she improvises. "After more than two weeks and she'll just welcome you with open arms, you're even dumber than I—Oh. *Jim?*"

Her eyebrows draw together as she mouths, "It's Jim."

No shit, I want to scream but don't have the energy or the mental focus.

"Sorry about that." She chuckles into the receiver. "I thought you were

that asshole, Oliver."

"Jules!" I hiss, head lolling back onto the couch cushion. "Oliver and Jim are friends."

I can't see it, but I'm sure she shrugs as though to say, *oh well.*

I squeeze my eyes shut in an attempt to make the room stop spinning. Julia's voice filters through the fog in my brain.

"Yeah, we'll be here. Come over." A tap on my thigh. "What's your address, Charli?"

"4731 West Sycamore, Apt. 3B."

"Did you get that?" The cushion squishes as Julia sinks down beside me. "Okay, yeah. See you in a bit."

Julia pokes my side and my hand immediately flies to my stomach. "Ouch."

"Wake up, sleepyhead," she chides. "Jim will be here in a half hour."

One of my eyes pops open. "You invited him over?"

"He kinda invited himself."

I groan. Loudly. He probably wants to make sure I'm okay; I can only imagine what I sounded like on the phone. Or worse, he has an ulterior motive. Maybe he's an undercover spy reporting my every move back to Oliver. My throat constricts a little as the (irrational) panic of such a possibility rushes through me. How does one prepare to entertain a covert enemy in her house?

"He's bringing pizza." She shrugs as though pizza makes everything okay. It kinda does.

"You don't eat pizza." I protest.

"He doesn't know that."

"Does this pizza have pepperoni?" I ask, warming to the idea.

Her eyes widen. "Sure does." She pinches my cheek. "It has whatever you want it to have, Charlotte."

A wide smile spans my lips and I murmur my approval before I promptly pass out with visions of pepperoni fairies dancing in my head.

CHARLI

I WAS ROBBED. Okay, not literally robbed, but the anger I feel is no less significant than if I were. Allow me to explain such a strong accusation.

When I finally drag my hung-over as fuck ass out of bed the next morning, I spy the large pizza box on the counter. Cracking open the lid, I'm pleasantly surprised to see more than half a pan of cheesy, thick-crusted goodness staring back at me. What makes me not so happy? The clear lack of pepperoni.

What's in place of the missing salty meat? Vegetables.

The offending pie is littered with broccoli. Smelly, bitter, gas-inducing broccoli. Who on God's green earth would commit such a travesty?

Jim and Julia. That's who.

They did me dirty.

Because I'm desperate, I grab a slice—okay, fine, two slices, but who's counting?—and slide them onto a plate. Water bottle tucked underneath my arm, I make the long ten-foot journey to my couch. With legs splayed wide in a very unladylike manner, especially since I'm wearing only a sleep shirt, I straddle the low coffee table and begin the laborious task of ridding my pizza of the offending green slime. It proves more difficult than I originally thought because the florets are mushy and break apart every time my fingers pinch them. There are green crumbles *everywhere*. After another five minutes, I close my eyes and take a bite.

Hmm. Not good, but not bad either.

Contrary to what you may think based on Operation Pizza Pull-A-Part, I *don't* dislike broccoli. At the moment we, broccoli and I, that is, have a very strained relationship.

Our very first Monday date night, Oliver prepared roasted sage broccoli and I fell in love. With the broccoli. Not him. Okay, fine, maybe him a bit too. To this day, sage broccoli is one of my favorite dishes of all time. I loved it so much that he nicknamed it "Charli's Crack" because I was (still am) as addicted to it as a strung-out junkie is to the blow. Whenever the accompaniment cycled onto our menu Oliver would *always* reserve a huge takeout portion for me.

Now that you know the whole sordid story I'm sure you empathize with my plight. No? It's simple really. Broccoli makes me think of Oliver and, therefore, must die. Moving on...

It isn't until I've polished off the second slice that I notice how quiet it is. Although Julia has the body of a pixie fairy, she's a noisy sleeper, which is a nicer way of saying she snores. Loudly.

My ears strain as I listen for the telltale sound of her guttural breaths, but I don't hear anything. "Jules?" I call her name.

Still nothing.

"Julia?" I shout, louder still.

Silence.

"Julia Marie!" I scream at the top of my lungs, despite it being only ten thirty in the morning. I really should have more consideration for my neighbors, but at this point, I'd be willing to construct a full-on rap if it meant I didn't have to haul my ass off the couch.

Another long minute goes by and I finally heave myself up.

"She better be dead," I mutter, slamming my plate onto the counter, hoping the noise will wake her. Nope.

I don't bother knocking on the partially closed door, but

instead, swing it open, ready to pounce on the air mattress. I freeze mid-jump, though, when I realize the bed is empty.

Where is she?

Storming back out of the bedroom, I creep around my apartment like a ninja, expecting Julia to pop out at any second and yell, "Gotcha!" The search takes me all of five minutes because the space is small and, realistically, there are only a few places she could be hiding.

My closet? Negative.

The shower? Not there either.

The oven? Okay, that was weird and I have no idea why I actually opened the door to check.

Scrambling back to the couch, I try to piece together my memories from last night. I remember bad karaoke singing. A third —or was it a fourth?—glass of wine. A phone call from Jim. Promises of pizza. After that, it's a big, blurry...blur.

Oh my God. Julia's missing. I fucking lost my little sister.

Okay. Don't panic, Charlotte. It's not like she was kidnaped. You're not on the set of *Taken*, for crying out loud. Breathe. Keep a calm head.

First things first. Find your cell phone. My eyes dart to its usual spot, the charger on the kitchen counter, but it's empty. Next, I rush into my bedroom and toss the sheets aside, but the only thing I find is a crumpled up Kit Kat wrapper. I don't know how that got there, but for now, I won't dwell on it.

I place my hands on my hips assuming a "thinking" pose. "If I were a cell phone, where would I be?"

I turn a bit to the right, then left, hands still firmly pressed against my hips. I chuckle. In the moment, I feel like Wonder Woman and have an *almost* irrepressible urge to shout "Aphrodite, aid me!' I say *almost* because I don't actually shout it out loud. But in my head? I totally do.

Okay, forget the Wonder Woman talk. Where the hell is my phone? I need to call Julia. Find out where she is and when she plans on coming back.

Heading back into the kitchen, I redirect my search, pushing the empty wine glasses and dirty plates aside. I lift the pizza box and it's then that I see a scribbled note dotted with a large grease spot near the top. It must have slid off when I opened the box earlier this morning.

I read the two lines of text:

Went to Conch with Jim. Be back soon.

I read the two lines again, just to be sure I didn't miss anything. *I didn't.*

Conch is a trendy bar located about five miles from my building. If Julia

went there with Jim *last* night and she's currently not home...it could only mean one thing...

"Mother fucking son of a bitch!" I scream, grabbing my purse from where it dangles off the back of the kitchen stool. "I'm gonna kill her."

I leave my apartment in such a hurry that I barely manage to throw on a pair of lounge pants underneath my sleep shirt. Thankfully, when I passed out last night, I was still wearing my sports bra, so at least I'm somewhat decent to be seen in public. Because I never found my phone, I can't call or text Julia. But there's no doubt in my mind she's at Jim's house. Keeping him nice and warm. Typical Julia—once you give her an inch, she'll take a fucking mile.

No phone also means no Uber or Lyft, so I head to the train station four blocks from my apartment and board the next train to the suburbs. By the time I walk the one point five miles to Jim's rental, I'm hot, sweaty, and fuming mad.

I raise my fist and bang it against the door. "Jim!" I step back, look around, and bring my hand back up. "Jim!"

There's a lot of noise coming from inside—voices, feet shuffling, locks scraping, and finally, the wooden door opens wide.

Jim stands before me in a plaid pair of boxers and white undershirt. It looks like he's just rolled out of bed. A bed he undoubtedly shared with my sister.

"Charli?" Jim's confused eyes find mine. "What are you doing here? He walks out onto the small stoop where I stand and scans the street. "Did you *walk* here?"

"Where's Julia?"

"Inside?" His voice rises as if he's asking me a question rather than telling me the answer. His brows pinch together. "Do you want to come in?"

"That'd be great." I huff, pushing past him. I've only been to his house once before, but it's not large and the layout is fairly standard. I storm into the kitchen where Julia stands at the counter, a mug of coffee in her hand.

"I can't believe you," I snarl, beyond pissed. "Why do you have to sink your claws into *every* single guy?"

"I'm confused." Jim stands beside me. "Can someone tell me what's going on here?"

Never one to mince words, Julia shrugs and says, "She's pissed because we slept together."

Jim turns to face me, eyes wide and remorseful. "Charli? Is that true?" A gentle hand touches my arm. "I never would..." His speech falters. "But you're in love with Oliver." There's confusion on his face.

I shake free of his grasp. "I'm not upset with you. It's her." I jab my chin in Julia's direction. "My issue is with her and the fact that she fucks every man in my life."

"Umm." Jim retreats a few paces. "I'm just gonna, umm...I'm just gonna run out to the store. I'll leave you two girls to talk."

We're both silent as a car door slams then the roar of a car engine turning over cuts through the air.

"You slept with him?"

Her smug look says it all. "It's not like you're interested in him."

Shaking my head, I spit, "You're still the same selfish, jealous bitch, aren't you?" My words cut deep, but they're meant to. *Some things never change.*

Julia stands there, mouth agape. At least she has the good sense not to defend herself. "Why, Julia?" My hands splay wide and latch onto the counter as I look her square in the face. "Why?"

She shrugs. "I like him."

"You like him?" I repeat. "You don't even know him."

Her eyes narrow as she finds her anger and self-righteousness. "Are you really angry over Jim or is this because of—"

"Don't go there."

"Why not?" She squares her shoulders, holds her head high. "We both know you've never forgiven me for Ryan."

My eyes squeeze shut for a moment. "He was my first boyfriend, my first love, my first *everything* and you"—my expression hardens—"you couldn't stand that. Had to destroy it."

"I was eighteen and drunk. He thought I was *you.*"

"And you had no problem slipping into my boyfriend's bed? Drunk or not, there's no excuse for what you did."

"Christ! That was almost four years ago. When are you going to let it go? How many times can I say I'm sorry? You said you'd forgiven me."

"Forgiven, maybe. But forget? No." My eyes hold hers. "You know what? I've tried to understand. I know you've always wanted all of the attention, even though Mom and Dad gave you plenty, but you're an adult. When the fuck are you going to grow up?"

"And when are you going to drop the holier than thou act?" Julia's eyes narrow. "I'm not the one sleeping with an engaged man."

Heat flares in my chest. "I'm not sleeping with Oliver!"

She shrugs. "Might as well be."

"Get out."

Her voice hardens. "You can't throw me out of Jim's house."

"Fine. *I'll* go." I clutch my purse against my body. "Jim's a nice guy. He doesn't deserve whatever sick game you're playing."

"I'm not playing a game."

"There's always an ulterior motive with you. End it before you hurt him. He's been through enough."

"You're accusing *me* of playing games?" She taps her nails on the counter. "You don't get them both, Charli. You can't keep Jim as a backup."

"Jim's not a fucking backup!" I screech. "He's my friend and I don't want to see him get hurt!"

I don't wait around to hear her response. My feet carry me as fast as possible to the front door, away from her, because a part of me knows she's right. This isn't about Jim. Or Oliver. It's about Ryan. It's about her insinuating herself into my life and ruining relationships I've worked hard to build. It's about her turning everything into *The Julia Show*.

And even though I spoke the truth—I *have* forgiven her—the cut still runs deep and I suspect it always will.

Sisters or not, some things can't be repaired.

CHARLI

MY EYES DRIFT to the silver sedan creeping alongside me at a pace of five miles per hour. I know the car, but at the moment, I'm choosing to ignore it. And its owner.

"Charli."

Keeping my eyes straight ahead, I walk another few feet before Jim tries again, his voice filtering through the open passenger window. "Charli! I know you can hear me." His agitation grows with each word. "Just get in the car already."

I'm not surprised by how easily Jim found me. It's not like I was trying to hide. Besides, I had to stick to the main roads or I would get lost. Especially without my phone and the aid of Google Maps. I am surprised, however, that he tried to find me at all. I thought for sure he'd be back in bed with Julia. She has a way about her that makes men forget, well, just about everything.

"Charlotte Ann Truse!" My footsteps falter at his use of my full name.

Glancing from my already tired feet to Jim's car, I heave a deep sigh and reach for the handle. "Happy now?"

"Very." He waits for me to snap my seatbelt into place before pulling back out on the road.

"I'm not going back to your house." My tone leaves little room for debate.

"Wasn't going to take you there." He merges onto the freeway heading east, back toward the city.

The urge to discuss my sister can't be avoided. "I can't believe you slept with her."

His brows rise like he didn't quite expect me to mention Julia. *Fat chance.* Turning in my seat I say, "You know she uses people, right?"

His face reddens with frustration. "Who says I wasn't using her?"

Most of my frosty attitude evaporates. "I didn't mean it like that." I squeeze the arm closest to me. "My sister can be..." My voice trails off, not knowing how to phrase *self-centered bitch* in nicer way.

"A bit much?" he offers.

"That's one way of putting it." I exhale a breath pinching the bridge of my nose. Knowing I owe Jim an explanation for my batshit crazy behavior, I say, "Four years ago, I caught Julia in bed with my boyfriend."

Eyes wide with shock turn to me.

"They didn't sleep together." I clarify, "They only kissed." *I interrupted them before it could get that far.* "We were all at a friend's party and had been drinking. Ryan swore he thought it was me...." My voice trails off as I remember the panicked look in Ryan's eyes when I flipped on the light switch. Julia's eyes were hazy, almost smug.

"Anyway, I wish I could say it was a long time ago and I've moved on, but the betrayal, the scar it left, runs deep." I clasp and unclasp my hands in my lap. "Julia was always the wild child, always sought attention. I don't think she wanted Ryan. She just couldn't stand that he wanted *me*."

"I'm sorry," he whispers, but I shake my head, dismissing his apology. What happened in the past certainly isn't his fault and if I'm honest, what happened last night wasn't either.

"When I woke this morning and saw her note, all those feelings—the doubt and insecurity, came flooding back." His brows pinch together and I'm quick to explain, "Julia is a force of nature. She takes over *everything* in her presence." My voice is quiet as I admit the last part, "I already lost Oliver. Now I'm going to lose you too."

He pulls onto the shoulder of the road. "You are not going to lose me." He reaches out to squeeze my hand. "What happened with Julia and me was a one-time thing." He continues to hold my eyes. "I'm not looking to put a ring on it. Been there, done that." His smile turns smug. "Sometimes, a guy has needs, and..."

My lips turn down in distaste. "Gross. She's my sister and you're like a brother to me. I don't want to know about *those* type of needs."

He chuckles. "Fair enough." His voice turns serious. "But if I had any idea how much it would bother you, I would have never even thought about fuc—"

I hold up my hand. "Yep, got it."

"You're my friend and Oliver's girl. I'd never screw that up."

My snort is rather unladylike. "I'm not Oliver's girl."

His smile is satisfied as hell. "I wouldn't be so sure of that."

"What?" I nearly jump out of my seat. "Have you talked to him? How is he? Where is he?"

"Whoa." Jim rests his palm on the console. "Slow down."

"Sorry," I mutter, a little breathless, but I've been going crazy with not knowing. "Is he coming back to work?"

He pauses, seeming to weigh his words before answering. "You'll have to talk to him."

"Jim!" I slap my palm down hard, barely missing his hand. "He's not returning my phone calls. I haven't spoken to him in weeks. Tell. Me. What. You. Know."

He retracts his palm, locks both hands around the steering wheel. "I'm pretty sure that'd be breaking bro code."

"Screw bro code!" I shout. "I thought we were friends."

He chuckles, actually chuckles, and it takes every ounce of self-restraint I have to keep from swatting his chest. "All I'm going to say is he misses you as much as you miss him."

Oliver misses me? A flicker of hope awakens deep in the pit of my stomach. "Did he tell you that?"

"Nope." He shifts the car back into drive, waits for two cars to pass before merging back onto the highway. Before I can say anything, he says, "He didn't have to, Charli. He ended it with Ainsley."

What?

When?

Why?

His eyes cut to mine. "He'd cut off my nuts if he knew I told you that."

"What?" I find my voice. "When?"

"I'm not sure exactly. A few weeks ago, maybe?"

A few *weeks?* I try to make sense of Jim's words. The fundraising party was over a month ago. Did he end it then? After the "incident?"

Oliver's words replay in my mind. *And if I wasn't with Ainsley?* Had he been trying to tell me then. And I, what? Told him to quit his job.

Fuck.

"But if it's over with her, why isn't he answering my calls? Or calling me?"

"Tell me this." He glances my way out of the corner of his eye. "Would you answer if he did?"

Absolutely. "Probably."

He hums. "Maybe you should do more than just call."

What does that even mean?

Five minutes later, the car rolls to a stop outside my building. Before I get out, he reaches for my hand. "I'm really sorry about last night. You know I'd never do anything to jeopardize our friendship."

I nod, fingers clutching the door handle, ready to exit when he says, "So I know this isn't the best time to ask this, but what should I do with your sister?"

Rolling my eyes, I say, "Bring her back here. I'll take care of it."

I always do.

Julia shows up three hours later. I feel marginally better having showered

and cleaned up the remnants of our girls' party last night. I'm still tired, still a bit cranky about her banging Jim, but more than anything, I'm hopeful. If what Jim told me is true, Oliver, for the first time since I met him, is *finally* single.

Maybe our time is now.

"Look." Julia walks through the door I hold open, straight to the small office where she sleeps when she visits. "I don't want to fight with you." Her voice lacks vigor. "I'll get my things and be on the first train out."

That sounds wonderful. But it is also the exact opposite of what needs to happen. We need to settle the score and move on. Once and for all.

"Julia, wait." Sighing, I close the apartment door behind me. "I think we should talk."

"Talk?" Her voice is indignant as she throws her brush and phone charger into her still full duffle bag. "What's there to talk about it? I'm a whore who can't keep her legs closed."

My eyes narrow. "I never said that."

"You didn't have to." She slides the zipper across the top of the bag. "I know that's *exactly* what you think."

"That's not fair." The pads of my fingers press into the corners of my eyes. "I overreacted this morning. The whole thing, finding you with Jim, it brought back bad memories."

She shakes her head. "When are you going to get over it, Charli? It was four years ago." She levels me with her eyes, about to say more, but I cut her off.

"Get over it?" My voice breaks on the question. "I don't think I'll ever get over it." Tears sting my eyes, threatening to spill down my cheeks. "I loved Ryan. We were together for four years. I thought I was going to marry him."

"You still don't get it, do you?" She slings the bag over her shoulder. "You choose to remember things the way you imagined, not the way they actually were. That whole relationship was a fantasy."

My eyes narrow. "What does that mean?"

"Nothing." Her eyes drop to her phone, her fingers tapping across the screen. Indignation pumps through my veins. Maybe it's her cryptic, accusatory tone. Or the fact that my emotions are still reeling over the whole Oliver situation. Or that she's blatantly ignoring me. Either way, I grab the phone from her hands.

"What the—" She snatches it back. "You're crazy."

I feel crazy. "I'm crazy?" I splay my hands wide. "My whole life has been dealing with your shit. One mishap after another. I protected you from the mess of mom and dad's relationship, covered for you when you acted up, made excuses for your misbehavior...and where did that get me?" Hard eyes drill into hers and for a moment, I think she might cry, but I continue on, "I'll tell you what I got. A sister who jumped into bed with my boyfriend the *second* my back was turned!"

Something inside of her snaps, and I witness the exact moment it happens. She drops her bag and her fists clench tight. Her face flushes an angry, almost scary, shade of red, and her chest heaves. "Ryan was cheating on you!"

"What?" The wind is knocked from my lungs, like I've been sucker punched in the gut. My knees buckle and I fall to the couch. Shaking my head, I whisper, "I don't believe you."

Her tone softens and she moves to sit next to me. "He'd been hitting on me *for months*. Since the moment I turned eighteen." My stomach churns, the bile crawling up my throat, burning. "I knew you'd never believe me, so I set him up. I *wanted* you to find us."

"What?"

"Do you actually think I'd sleep with my sister's boyfriend?"

Yes.

My face must say it all and her head turns, a slow shake left to right. "I would never do that to you. Diana told me that she heard Gina Prince bragging that she'd been banging Ryan for weeks."

Could it be true? Diana was—is—Julia's best friend from high school. And Ryan had been spending a lot of time with Gina that summer. He told me he was tutoring her, helping her complete credits for her summer classes. Could I really have been that naïve? Could I have been wrong this entire time?

"Why didn't you tell me about Gina?"

Her eyes cast down. "Would you have believed me? I was desperate. I knew I had to convince you that he was cheating on you, even if it wasn't really with me."

She's right. I wouldn't have.

"I don't understand," I say, and I truly don't. All of this time, all of these years wasted, locked in anger...for what? I should have asked her, tried harder. Made more of an effort.

"I'm sorry." She sinks back into the cushions, her emotion—anger, sorrow, and regret—seeping from her like air from an old, deflated balloon. "I never wanted you to find out about Gina."

I turn to her. "Why?"

She clasps and unclasps her hands in her lap. "I know you think you protected me from dad's affairs, but I knew. And I also knew that you wanted to believe in the fairy tale. I knew you saved yourself for years, that Ryan was your first, and I didn't want you to become jaded."

But I did become jaded, just in a completely different way. Four years ago, seeing Julia in bed with Ryan, the image of them in bed together was the lens through which I viewed every single one of her actions for years. How would things be different had I known the truth? Would I have still tried to make it work with Ryan? Found someone new? Made more of an attempt to connect with Julia?

One pebble causes a tiny thousand ripples.

A single tear rolls down my cheek. "I'm so sorry."

"I'm sorry too." She leans forward, squeezes my hand. "I should have told you sooner." Her eyes cast down. "But you were so angry and the more you pushed me away the easier it became to *not* tell you."

"How didn't I see it, Jules?" My eyes hold hers. "How didn't I see him for who he was?"

"The heart sees what it wants to see. You've always believed in Prince Charming, always wanted the happily ever after." She sighs. "But the truth is, the fairytale doesn't exist, because *no one* is perfect. We all make mistakes—say things, do things we aren't proud of. True love is loving *despite* all of the flaws."

It's a light bulb moment. An epiphany. Her words hit me all at once and it's as though years of pent-up frustration, disappoint-ments, and anger dissipate, and a deep sense of peace washes over me. She's right. She's so fucking right.

"Thanks," I murmur before glancing up at her face. "And I'm sorry about what happened with Jim this morning. I'm sorry about *everything*."

She nods her head. "It's okay."

"No, it's not. I acted like a crazy person."

"Well." She chuckles. "I'm not going to disagree."

I narrow my eyes in jest. "I think I scared Jim."

Julia pinches her fingers together. "A little bit."

"I'm glad you're here," I say, my voice genuine.

She gasps a breath, as if taken aback by my confession. A smile touches her lips. "Me too."

"And Jim would be lucky to have someone like you in his life."

She dips her head. "Thanks. We decided to take things slow, get to know one another."

I giggle. "Didn't you get to know each other last night?"

Laughing, she says, "Yeah, we got to know each other all right. The sex was—"

My hands cover my ears. "Don't want to hear it."

She pries my hands away, a smirk tugging the corners of her lips.

"All I'm gonna say is that older men *really* know what they're doing."

My nose scrunches as she continues, "Speaking of older men, word on the street is that Oliver is single." *Jim has a big mouth.* "Whatcha gonna do about it, Charli?"

My teeth capture my bottom lip and I shake my head. *I don't know.*

"I say go over there and jump that fine man's bones. If not, you'll regret for the rest of your life."

"You know what?" My grin is mischievous. "You're right."

Her mouth gapes open. Clearly, she was expecting me to argue, but I'm done wasting time. If I've learned anything from today it's that holding on to the past causes nothing but heartache, missed chances, and grief. What's that quote always circulating on my social media feed?

Holding on to anger is like drinking poison and expecting the other person to die.

I'm done looking in the rearview mirror. I'm done allowing past mistakes, past hurts to color my vision. Today, I choose to live. And I know just the person to help me.

"Julia?" I push myself to stand, already halfway to my bedroom before she follows. "Would you help me pick out a sexy outfit? I want to make an impression."

She smiles as she flips open my closet door. "Girl, I never thought you'd ask."

CHARLI

WE—JULIA and I—decide to text Jim to ask him a favor. We ask that he call Oliver to make sure he'll be home. Thankfully, he is. Also, I need a ride to Oliver's house, and Jim's happy to oblige.

As I slide into his car, Jim doesn't comment on my straightened mane of hair that frames my face, or the skillfully applied eye liner that makes the sapphire color of my eyes pop, or the cherry lip stain that's much bolder than anything I'd ever choose for myself.

Thankfully, Jim can't see the fitted, low cut shirt hiding beneath my jacket. The truth is, the tight fabric makes me more than a little self-conscious, but I decided to embrace it. Take a risk. Dark blue cigarette jeans and toffee nubuck leather boots complete my outfit. I'm Charli 2.0.

We barely talk on the thirty-five-minute ride to Oliver's place. By the time Jim pulls his sedan into his driveway, I fear I may throw up.

Turning in my seat, I ask, "What did you tell him?"

Jim shrugs. "That I was stopping by to discuss the contracts he asked me to review."

His words glide over me, but my brain snags on the word

contract. If I wasn't so focused on the reason why I'm here, I might have thought to question it. But as it is, I'm barely holding myself together.

"He's working on a new recipe." Jim nudges my arm. "Go. You'll be fine."

"If he's busy, maybe I should come back."

"Charlotte." Jim's stern eyes accompany his no nonsense tone.

"All right. All right." I acquiesce and slowly pull myself from the car.

I've barely shut the door when he yells, "Good luck!" and floors the gas, practically peeling out of the driveway. He's left me stranded. I've no choice but to walk up to the front porch and do this. Either that or order an Uber and hope Oliver doesn't catch me skulking around his property in the interim.

With shaky fingers I press the doorbell and listen as the chime sounds through the solid wood door. My heart skips a beat as I hear footsteps approach. My stomach clenches as the lock slides in place.

"Wasn't expecting you this ear—" Oliver's light, carefree voice stops abruptly once he sees me. "You're not Jimbo."

"No." I squeeze my eyes shut for just a moment to gather my inner courage and then ask, "Can we talk?"

He opens the door wider and gestures for me to come in.

Neither of us speaks as we walk into the well-lit kitchen, each of us giving the other a wide berth. It's a careful balancing act. One slight move in either direction could cause it to topple over.

Are we ready?

Yes. Hell fucking yes.

The counter is a mess of utensils, measuring cups, and spices, and there are two large pots bubbling on the stovetop. I have no idea what's inside them, but whatever it is, it smells *delicious.*

He gestures with his head to one of the stools. "Have a seat. I'm just finishing up."

"Okay," I murmur. Ignoring his formal tone and his obvious

attempt to maintain a decent amount of physical space between us, I hop onto the center island. I set my purse beside me and then smooth my palms, which are sweaty from nerves, down the front of my jeans. *Relax*, I try to calm myself, but it's no use because I know what's coming. At least I hope I do.

He quirks a brow but continues to stir whatever is simmering inside the smaller pot.

Since it's clear he isn't going to speak, I ask, "Where have you been?"

Another brow arch, but no response. Fine. I'll keep talking until he cracks. "Did you get another job?"

He grunts. Marginally better. "Giancarlo redesigned the entire winter menu. And his lobster bisque is nowhere as good as yours."

His gaze snaps to mine. His narrowed eyes say, "Of course it isn't."

I nod before asking, "Did you end things with Ainsley?" According to Jim he has, but I want to hear it from Oliver. From the moment I entered his house, my eyes have been greedily assessing every single item, scouring every surface for signs of her. But there's nothing. Not that it necessarily means anything. Last time all I found were grey moccasins in the mudroom. Dammit I should have knocked at the side door.

His jaw clenches, and his words are tight when he finally speaks, "Where did you hear that?"

I hold his gaze even though every ounce of my being wants to cower under its intensity. "Does it matter?"

He looks down, muttering under his breath, "Fucking Jimbo."

"Please," I say, voice softening. "I'm sorry for...everything. For the way I acted. For what I did, for what I didn't do, for what I should've done. I don't want to fight anymore."

He pauses, long wooden spoon poised over the pot. He sounds tired, defeated when he asks, "Why are you here, Charli?"

"Because I like you and I want to know if there's a chance that you like me too. That we have something more."

Eyes, open and honest, he says, "Of course I like you, Charli.

You're beautiful and smart and fun and..."He takes a slow breath. "I feel most myself when I'm around you. You feel like *home*."

"So you and Ainsley?" I wish my voice didn't shake, but I'm terrified of hearing his answer.

"Done." He picks up a large pepper mill and cranks the top a few times over the pot before resuming stirring. "I should have ended it a long time ago, but it's hard hurting someone you care about, and with everything that happened with the accident..." His voice trails off.

"You felt guilty." I finish his thought.

"Yes." He nods his head once. "But I'm not going to lie to you, Charlotte. I love Ainsley." Without thought, my palm covers my heart, shielding it from his words. It hurts to hear him confess his love for another woman. My hand rubs small circles in an effort to dull the sting.

"But"—his wide eyes find mind and hold—"it's nothing like the way I feel for you." It's as if I've entered a vacuum. No air remains in this wide, open room. I can't breathe. My lungs need oxygen stat, or may I pass out. But I can't focus on forcing much-need air into my body when he keeps talking, his words beautiful and true. "I've fought this attraction for too long and I can't anymore. It's you, Charlotte. It's been you for as long as I can remember."

"Oliver." My voice is a breathy whisper. "I never thought I'd hear you say those words. That you'd choose me. That you'd actually be mine."

"I'm yours, Charli." His eyes find mine and hold them. "If you want me."

"I want you." Then blame it on nervousness, pent-up sexual frustration, or plain ol' stupidity, but I blurt exactly what's on my mind. "Can we have sex now?"

Oliver's hand falters, dropping the spoon into the pot completely. He curses as he retrieves the hot handle, and then he sets it aside as he pins me with coffee brown eyes. "Do you *want* to have sex now?"

My bold answer surprises us both. "Yes."

Although his expression darkens with desire, his body tenses in restraint. "I think we should take this slow." He tears a hand through is hair, almost as if it pains him to speak the words.

Slow? Hasn't thirteen months been slow enough? Maybe he's trying to preserve my honor or treat me with respect, but right now, respect and honor are the furthest things from my mind. *I want him to debase me.* "Oliver, I'm going to die if you don't touch me."

His jaw tightens, his hands curling into themselves at his sides. "Charlotte," his voice warns, but I keep pressing.

"I didn't come here for food." I spread my legs a little wider on the counter, inviting his gaze. "I came here for you to fuck me."

"*Christ.*" He abandons the pot, his palms latching on to my legs, widening them even farther so he can slide between them. He drops his forehead to mine. "You're making this hard, Charlotte. So very hard."

My smile is coy. "Isn't that the point?"

He presses his lips to the beauty mark above the corner of mouth, lingers there, his eyes closed in pleasure. After a few long seconds he pulls away. "You have no idea how long I've wanted to do that."

My breath catches.

"You're not a fling or a rebound, Charlotte." He drops his forehead to mine once more, takes a shuddering breath. "I've wanted this, *you*, for so long."

"Me too," I mutter. "Which is why I don't want to wait anymore. Use me, Oliver. Make me *yours*."

A growl tears from his throat as a strong hand wraps around my neck pulling my face toward his. When his soft yet insistent lips meet mine, my body ignites. Heat pulses in my veins in short, sharp bursts, making me burn all over. Wetness pools in my panties. My nails dig into his strong shoulders, pinching fabric and skin in an effort to get closer.

His arms band around my waist, sliding lower, until his palms grip my ass. In one swift movement, he tugs me right to the edge of the counter and I gasp as his hardness aligns with my core. Taking advantage of our closeness, he snakes his tongue inside my mouth.

Sweeping. Sucking. Exploring.

He tastes sweet, like the raw, unfiltered honey. "You taste good," I murmur against his lips, catching my breath.

"Charli," he whispers my name in reverence, almost as though he can't quite believe I'm here, with him. "Charlotte."

Both of his palms begin at my shoulder blades and trace down my arms. He wraps a hand around each wrist and drags my arms above my head. He holds them high for a moment. Even after he releases his hold, I keep my arms extended high above my head. Oliver's smile is filthy and eager as his fingers grip the hem of my shirt. I sit, waiting and willing, mouth open as he divests me of my shirt.

I've worn my best black bra—peek-a-boo lace with an underwire that thrusts my boobs together in the best possible way. Judging by the clench of his jaw, my efforts are appreciated.

"Jesus, Charli. He moves his nose along the delicate skin of my neck. "I want to look at you at all night."

"You can," I say with a moan as his tongue drags along my collarbone.

"You're wrong." The gleam in his eye is wicked. "I can't look and *not* touch. Not anymore." His palms ghost over the sides of my breasts, down my ribcage, and then land on my waist. "Tonight I'm going to explore every inch of your body." My eyes widen to the size of saucers when he says, "With my mouth."

He roughly palms my breasts, their fullness spilling over and making him groan in pleasure. "You have such beautiful tits, Charlotte." One thumb rubs across my nipple. "I'm going to enjoy fucking them."

I swallow a groan as I reach for his shirt and tug, but don't get very far because his hands refuse to leave my breasts. "Off," I demand, agitated, wanting nothing more than to feel his hot skin pressed to mine.

He takes a step back, reaches a hand behind his head and pulls it off in one quick movement. He grins. "Better?"

"Much." I run my fingertips along his chest, trace the smattering of hair that dots his pecs before grazing my fingernails across his nipples. "Fuck," he hisses, one hand squeezing my hip. Hard.

I grin as I move further down to the compact ridges of muscle that comprise his abdomen to the sharp V-cut that disappears below the waist of his pants. I dip my finger inside the band, high on the rush, lost in the thrill of touching him. Manic from the knowledge that I *can* touch him.

His lips are back on mine, the pressure rough, almost bruising. But it could happen no other way. Thirteen months in the making, it will be miracle if either of us survives.

Oliver's hand is on the clasp of my bra, seconds away from freeing their achy fullness, when a loud, shrill beep startles us apart.

"What the—" I slide back knocking my purse onto the ground. "Is that the *fire alarm?*"

I follow Oliver's gaze to the stove where one pot bubbles over furiously, the flames of the burner licking the side of the pan, smoke billowing into the air in tiny wisps.

"Shit." He grabs an over mitt sliding the pot back and cutting the gas. Quickly, he walks to a keypad by the door and punches in a code. The beeping stops almost instantly.

"*That* was a little embarrassing." He's speaking to me, the person, but *his eyes* are speaking to my tits.

I can't control the laugh that pushes past my lips. "Did we almost set the house on fire?"

"*You* almost set the house on fire." He's back between my legs, arms banding around my waist. "I can't think when you're around."

"Thinking is overrated," I say, circling my arms around his neck.

He chuckles, sliding his arm beneath my legs and lifting me off the counter.

"Where are you taking me?" I giggle into his ear.

"To a place where you won't be able to think at all."

I smile, excited for what's to come. I don't want to think. Only feel.

And I know it's a promise that he'll be more than happy to fulfill.

OLIVER

CHARLI'S FINGERS play with the hair at the base of my skull, and her teeth nibble my neck as I carry her up the stairs. It's incredibly distracting, so much so that I nearly drop her. But it's not my fault —she's licking the column of my neck in slow, smooth strokes, and all I can imagine is her doing the same to my dick.

I groan in protest when she pulls back, her rushed words breaking the silence surrounding us, "Not your bedroom." Her voice is hesitant, almost apologetic. "Not in the bed you shared with her."

The sadness in her tone breaks my heart and for a split second, I wish the house *would have* burned and taken the damn bed with it. I nod, walking toward the spare bedroom, and lay her flat on the mattress, where if you try really, *really* hard, you can smell Charli's perfume lingering on the sheets.

Not that I tried.

Much.

Her hair fans around her like a halo, soft brown curls, framing her face and I wish I could take a picture of her just like this. She's here. With *me*. Giving herself to *me*. Nothing can take away this feeling, this moment. I will *always* remember her like this.

Smiling. Beautiful. *Angelic.*

Her hands smooth along the blankets at her side. "I pictured us in here." Her eyes find mine. In them, I read her desire, her guilt, her *truth.* "The night I stayed over, I wanted you to sneak into my room. To find me."

"Charlotte," I murmur crawling on top of her. If she only knew how much I wanted the very same thing. How I tossed and turned, locked my fucking bedroom door so I wouldn't go to her.

"I knew it was wrong." Her eyes, wide and vulnerable, hold mine. "But I wanted it. I still do."

There are no words as I peel the first, then second cup of her bra down, exposing soft, creamy skin that feels like spun silk. "You're gorgeous, Charlotte." Her pupils dilate as I drag a lone fingertip across the swell. "I want you so much it scares me."

My head dips and I draw her pebbled nipple into my mouth. Her hips buck off the bed, all but slamming into my groin. When my hard cock touches her heat for the first time my brain trips. Short circuits. Reboots. She shifts her hips again, this time grinding against me, and I'm painfully aware that the only things separating us are a few thin scraps of fabric.

My teeth latch on to her nipple, biting, and she moans so loudly that I pull back. I watch her lips twist in pleasure and her eyes flutter closed. Her body continues to move against me, her pace faltering as my lips to switch to the other breast and give it the same attention. She's taking, chasing, *owning* her pleasure. It's the hottest damn thing I've ever seen. The quick, fast rush of an orgasm barrels down my spine, my ab muscles bucking, nerves tingling.

No. Not yet. *Holy fuck.*

"Jesus." I pant, head hanging down. "I'm gonna come." Placing both hands on her hips, I halt her grinding. My voice is laced with equal parts wonder and embarrassment when I say, "I'm thirty-eight years old and I'm gonna nut in my pants." I shake my head, bewildered at how worked up she's gotten me. "*Fuck*, Charlotte."

She props herself up on her elbows, a sexy grin tipping the

corners of her lips, tits flushed and full, begging for my mouth. She grabs me over my pants, her grip firm and solid, and my eyes roll back in my head.

With racecar speed, my fingers pull at her jeans, dragging them down her legs. My eyes nearly fall out of their sockets when I realize she's not wearing panties. "You're going to fucking kill me."

My hands drop to her thighs, spreading her wide open.

For my mouth. For my cock. For *me*.

For a moment, all I can do is stare. Soft, pink, glistening skin. She's so fucking wet. Just from me sucking on her tits.

One finger traces her seam, eliciting a faint gasp from her lips. I stroke down and up. Up and down. Teasing. Avoiding the tight bundle of nerves that rests hooded at the top. "Oliver." She begs, voice needy and desperate, but I shake my head.

"Thirteen months, Charlotte." Dark, passion-filled eyes find mine. "Over a *year* I've waited to have you. I will *not* rush."

She arches her back, hips greedy, seeking more of my touch, but I don't give her what she wants. Frustrated, she changes her tack, reaches for me again, but before she can make contact, I stop her, hold her hand captive in mine while my free hand works my pants and boxer briefs down my thighs.

Her eyes, cast low, land on my rock-hard cock that's pointing straight at her. "Oliver," she murmurs, voice awestruck. I bring her palm to my lips and lick a long, messy line from her fingers to her wrist, and then I rest my hand atop hers and slide it down to circle my length. Tugging up, firm and slow, I guide her, throttling her speed to draw out the pleasure.

When our hands get to the wide mushroom tip, her finger drags across the head, spreading the drops of wetness that have already formed there. Without warning—or my control—my hips jut forward. "Fuck, Charli," I groan, squeezing her hand harder around my shaft. "You think this is enough?" Heavy lidded eyes find hers. "You think we'll both be satisfied with just our hands?" I release her and she falls back onto the bed looking a little stunned.

"Get on your hands and knees." Her breath hitches. When she doesn't move, I demand. "It wasn't a question, Charlotte."

Slowly, her body turns away and she draws herself onto her knees, palms planted on the bed. "So beautiful," I whisper, moving behind her, trailing my hand from the curve of her shoulder down the length of her spine. Her body shivers beneath my touch. "I'm going to fuck you like this," I warn, giving her a chance to protest or stop me, but she doesn't. Her head turns and when she looks back at me, I see dark pools of blue fire in her eyes.

My body hovers over her as I bring my lips to her ear, "I'm going to fuck you like an animal, Charli." A tremble ripples through her and I band my arm around her stomach to keep her from falling. When she's secured in place, I continue, "Because that's what I feel like. A wild, feral, unyielding beast that has *finally* captured its prey." My lips trace a line down the soft skin of her spine, continuing on to the curve of her hips, and when I get to the swell of her ass, I take a bite. She yelps in surprise, but my lips are immediately there to soothe the sting.

She groans as one finger dips between her legs. She's drenched. More than ready. I put two fingers inside her, my thumb reaching for her clit, and her hips push back against me. "Oliver, please."

"You want my cock, Charlotte?" My lips graze her ass, nipping the already red mark where my teeth sank into her juicy flesh. "Is that what you want, baby?"

"Yes," she moans, her head hanging down, muscles taut with anticipation.

I slide the tip of my cock against her silky, slippery lips and we both groan. I push a bit farther the next time, allowing my tip to slip inside her tight, wet heat.

"Now, Oliver," she begs. "*Please.*"

Who am I to deny her? I thrust again, my entire length sliding inside the velvet glove of her body. And *shit*. I just died and went straight to heaven.

Her body spasms around my girth and reflexively, my hips pump forward, my hands grabbing onto her ass for balance. I've just begun to find our rhythm when—"Fuck!" I curse and pull out.

I make the mistake of glancing down. I'm long, rock-hard, and slick with her juices. Dropping one hand, I circle the base of my dick and squeeze. Fuck. My. Life.

"What's the matter?" It's hard to believe the breathy voice that flitters across the darkness belongs to Charlotte.

"Condom," I groan. "I forgot the fucking condom."

Her body stiffens and stills against my fingers. I'd swear she stopped breathing. *Say something, Charlotte.*

I don't want to stop, don't want to think about anything but being inside her, but we need to decide this together. One more second of teasing, of playing, of torture, and I'd be fucking her raw whether we both agreed it was the right decision or not.

When she still hasn't said anything, I add, "I'm clean. I haven't been with anyone except..." I can't bring myself to say Ainsley's name, not here, not now. She doesn't belong in this moment. She has no place anywhere near Charli or me. Not anymore. "But I got tested. Right after things ended."

She's silent for a moment and then she speaks, "Do *you* want to wear a condom?"

Fuck no. I want her tight, wet heat, my skin on her skin. I want to feel every pulse, every slide, every inch of her. Bare. "No," I answer honestly. "But it's not my decision. It's yours to make. Just tell me, because if I don't get inside you now, I'm going to die before we even get started."

She turns her torso toward me and as her eyes find mine, I sense the vulnerability there, but she nods her agreement and speaks, "I never have...without one. But I'm tested every year at my annual appointments."

My fingers squeeze her hips. "Are you on birth control?"

"I have an IU—*fuck!*" she curses, head dropping as I slam back into her. "Fuck, Oliver."

"Charlotte," I groan her name, burying myself as far as I can go. I hold her hips still. "Don't move."

"I have to move." She pants, rocking her hips against me and my balls slap the back of her thighs.

My self-control shatters and I know my orgasm will come and go much too soon, but before I indulge my desire, before I give myself over to the pleasure, I have to get her there first.

"Charlotte, baby." I rest my chest against her back, dip my fingers forward to circle her clit. "You've *got* to come for me." My ass muscles clench as I pump, hard and fast, and my leg muscles cramp, but I don't give a fuck. I'm chasing, climbing, ascending a peak so high, so fast and furious that it's dangerous, but I won't stop. Can't stop.

"I'm right there." Her back bows and she takes me even deeper. How the fuck it's even possible I don't know.

One hand buried between her legs, I use my other hand to smooth the hair from her back to expose her creamy skin. Then she surprises me. "Pull my hair."

I wrap the long strands around my fist and tug gently. "God," she moans. "Harder." I pull with a little more force and her hips jerk back. "Oh my God. Yes! Oh my—Oliver!"

She detonates in my arms. Full body tremors, her hands fisting the covers as she bucks through her orgasm. She convulses around me, milks my cock as though begging for my release. The sensation is indescribable. I've had sex a thousand times before, but I've never—*never*—felt this need, this unspoken demand for more. More connection. More passion. Just *more*.

"Fuck, Charli." I pant, letting go of her hair. I slap her ass once before pushing her down flat on her belly. "I'm gonna come."

I pull out just as the first shock ripples through my body. Fisting my cock at the base I shoot hot, silky jets of come all over her ass. I grunt, dick twitching as I empty the last few drops on her pale skin. "*Fuck*."

I collapse beside her, breath heavy, skin flushed. She turns her head toward me and blinks her eyes open. A shy smile lights her face. "Hi."

"Hi." I lean forward, placing a gentle kiss on her beauty mark.

We're both quiet as we gaze at each other. I inventory her face —take notice of her slack jaw, soft cheeks, the small smile still playing on her lips as her eyes flutter closed, lazy and slow. Finally, she speaks, "I should go get cleaned up."

"Mmm," I murmur, energy fully depleted.

She pushes herself up onto one elbow, glances at her backside, where I've marked her not only with my come but also with my teeth. She tips her head toward her ass cheek. "That's gonna leave a mark."

My eyes find hers and hold. "Good."

Desire turns her eyes from light to dark pools in an instant. "Oliver," she whispers my name, and it sounds like more of an invitation than a warning.

I stroke my hand down her back. "Go take a shower, baby." My fingers pause at the slope of her ass and then travel back up to her neck. "I'll see what I can salvage from dinner."

She sighs. "I could eat."

"Good," I repeat before adding, "you're gonna need all the strength you can muster before I'm done with you."

"Is that a threat?" She traces her finger over the slope of my cheek. "Or a promise?"

"Both." My teeth nip her finger. "Now go take a shower."

CHARLI

I MAKE my way back to the bedroom wrapped in only a towel. Grabbing Oliver's t-shirt, I slip it over my head and follow my nose to the kitchen where he stands shirtless over a pot on the stove. Since his back is turned to me, I'm allowed a few unguarded moments to admire his nakedness under the warm, bright lights. My mouth waters as his muscles contract with each flick of his wrist.

"See something you like?" he asks without turning to face me.

"How did you know I was here?"

He glances at me over his shoulder, fork in one hand. "I can feel your eyes on me, Charli." He smirks. "I always could."

Damn. "What did you make me?"

He shuts off the gas. "Frenched rack of lamb and roasted Jersey Royals." He gestures to the lone pot on the stove. "The red wine cherry reduction is ruined."

"What happened?" A coy smile plays across my lips. Oliver *never* messes up a meal.

"You took your tits out."

"*You* took my tits out."

"Did I?" He smirks. "I can't remember." He plates the two

dishes. "Vegetables are still good and I've just finished warming the meat."

"It smells fantastic," I say, leaning down and inhaling the rich garlic and brown butter scent.

He nods. "I thought about serving you dinner in bed but soon realized it was a terrible idea. His heated eyes hold mine. "But I gotta say, if you keep looking at me like that with those silky smooth legs bare, it isn't going to matter where we are."

My skin flushes from the crown of my head all the way to my little toes, but still I say, "Bring it on, Chef." I wink as I grab a clean plate. "You can take a bite out of me any day."

We don't clean up the kitchen. In fact, the second my fork leaves my hand, Oliver drags me back to the bedroom, lays me flat on my back, and demands his dessert. His tongue laps me like I'm the finest, sweetest crème brûlée he's ever tasted and he can't get enough. When my thighs squeeze tight, toes clench, and breath falters, he sucks harder, longer, curling his fingers inside me, demanding every ounce of pleasure I have to give. He leaves me a sweaty, breathless, exhausted mess, and I need another shower.

I want to return the favor, want to draw the same pleasure from him, but my bones are leaden, heavy, and weak. I don't think I can move, let alone give him one hundred percent of my effort. And he deserves everything I have to offer. However, he doesn't seem to mind or even expect me to reciprocate. He slides inside me, slowly, hands cradling my face like I'm precious. I'm all but helpless, lost in the sensual, carnal world of pleasure he's created, spinning around us like a fine web and cocooning our bodies together.

The pace is slow, deliberate, so unlike the first time, and the dichotomy of the two strike my heart. He's like Dr. Jekyll and Mr. Hyde, and I adore both sides of his lovemaking. Appreciate both in their own right.

This time, he comes inside me, shuddering through his release, teeth sinking into the soft divot of my neck and I feel *him*. Not just his body, but his soul, the connection between us a living, breathing entity all its own.

As we lie naked, he cradles me in his arms, creating a place of safety and comfort. It's quiet, save for the chirping of the crickets outside, when I finally speak. "I love your forearms." I drag the tips of my fingers against the thick muscle stretched around bone. "They drive me kinda crazy."

He chuckles softly. "Tell me more."

"It's true." I sigh. "And when you unbutton the cuffs of your shirt and roll up your sleeves before you wash the dishes?" I groan. "It makes my panties wet."

His arms band around me tighter. "Is that why you always run off to the bathroom on Monday nights?"

Squeezing my eyes shut, I admit, "Yeah. I have to splash cold water on my face to avoid mauling you."

He chuckles again. "And here I thought you had the runs."

I freeze. "The runs? Are you kidding me?" My hand stills and my nose scrunches. "Gross." I shake my head.

"What am I supposed to think?" He laughs again and I can't quite tell if he's serious or goading me. "You're always gone for a really long time..."

I look over my shoulder. "So the automatic assumption is that I have explosive diarrhea?"

His laugh flutters my hair. "I never said *explosive*."

"Oh my God." I turn my head back toward the window. "Thank God, I had no idea you thought that or I would have been mortified."

"Everyone poops, Charlotte." He tuts.

Gross.

Gross.

Gross.

"Moving on." I pinch said sexy forearm.

"Your hair," he mutters.

"Huh?" I ask confused.

"Your hair does it for me." He nestles his nose into the crook of my neck. "When you take it out of its ponytail at the end of the night—I *live* for that moment. Charlotte undone. Messy and wild and free."

My heart rate kicks ups as one hand glides through my still-damp strands,

starting at the nape of my neck and stroking all the way down my back.

"I've imagined what it would feel like caught between my fingers, holding you just like this."

"And?" I whisper.

His deep voice rumbles in my ear, "*Silk*."

I wiggle in his arms. "Oliver."

"Your beauty mark." He turns me in his embrace, lays me flat on my back so that he can look in my eyes. His touch is feather light as he follows the outline of the mark with the pad of his finger. "It's like when God made you, he gave you so much beauty that it couldn't be contained and it bubbled out of you." He presses his lips to the spot, sending a shiver down my spine. "Right. Here." He pulls back slightly so that he can look into my eyes. "I don't think I've ever seen such a beautiful woman, Charlotte. A beautiful *person*."

No one has ever spoken to me the way he just has. With such adoration. With such *love*. Embarrassed by the tears forming in my eyes, I blink them closed. My eyelids flutter as he presses gentle, barely-there kisses against the delicate skin.

"Every word, Charlotte." His fingers trace the smooth curves of my cheeks. "I mean Every. Word." He settles onto his back, guiding me with his arms until I'm almost lying completely across his chest. One arm snakes around me and our legs tangle together.

Sleep finds me quickly, and as I sink into oblivion, one thought loops through my mind: *I absolutely believe him.*

CHARLI

COLD. My body shivers as the first conscious thought of the morning flitters through my mind. I reach to my side, but my palm drags across an empty bed. Snuggling deeper into the blankets, I lie nestled in their warmth for several minutes longer.

My body's sore. My muscles are a little tight, like the one time after I took that Pilates class with Meg. Or was it kickboxing? I can't remember it was so long ago. The point is, my muscles ache but in the *best* possible way.

I slip into Oliver's t-shirt for the second time in twenty-four hours and I can't help my smile. *This* feels natural. There's no awkwardness. No stilted conversation and I wonder if it's because we've been friends for over a year. I've never had sex with a friend-turned-lover.

Stretching, I go into the bathroom—thankfully, there are still plenty of toiletries available—and do my business before heading downstairs.

"Oliver?" I call as I walk into the kitchen, yet nothing but silence greets me. Just as I'm about to check the living room, I spot a note on the counter. It's from Oliver.

Gone for my morning run. Coffee's fresh. Be *naked* when I get home.

My cheeks flame at this command as my eyes dart to the clock on the microwave. It's almost nine forty, and I don't know when he left or what time he plans to be back, but there's no way I'll disappoint.

Snatching a mug from the tower that sits on the counter, I pour myself a cup of coffee before adding cream and sugar. Its smooth, rich taste awakens my senses. It really is one of the simple pleasures in life.

After finishing my coffee, I embark on the rather ambitious undertaking of cleaning up the kitchen. Dozens of dishes from last night's feast—pots, plates, bowls, and a large roasting pan—fill the sink. I'm about halfway through the mess when the front door opens.

"*Shit!*" I squeal, the ceramic plate slipping through my soapy fingers into the stainless steel sink. Quickly, I swipe my hands across the tea towel hanging on a hook at the end of the island to dry them off. I grab the hem of my t-shirt, and I'm *seconds* away from exposing my body in all its naked glory when a loud, shrill voice stops me dead in my tracks.

"Charli?" Ainsley's stride is confident, self-assured as she marches into the kitchen as if she owns the place.

She did live here for over a year.

Her suspicious eyes trail the length of my bare legs, stopping where the too-short shirt hits me mid-thigh. "What are you doing here?" I'm surprised I can hear her confused voice over the blood whooshing in my ears. When her eyes drag across the white CIA logo stamped on my chest, the realization that I'm wearing *Oliver's* shirt hits her. "Is that Oliver's shirt?"

Standing like a deer caught in headlights, I stare back at her—deaf, dumb, and mute.

What's she doing here? How did she get in? I thought they broke up.

"Charlotte," she snaps, her voice louder when I still haven't responded. "Where is Oliver?" She stalks toward me, eyes narrowed to slits, and when she's less than a foot away, I finally jolt into action. I retreat a few paces. I don't think she'd hit me, but I can't be sure because she looks *pissed*. Her normally calm demeanor has vanished, and in its place is a fiery, angry woman...scorned? Betrayed? Heartbroken?

It's hard to say for sure.

Steeling my nerves, I clear my throat as I say, "He's out for his run." She glances at the clock as though judging the validity of my claim.

Her breath heaves, and then she asks, "Why are *you* here?"

I'm guessing her question is rhetorical because anyone, and I do mean *anyone*, can figure out exactly why I'm standing half-dressed in his kitchen at ten in the morning.

Thankfully, I'm saved from answering when the door slams open again. Oliver calls my name, the sound booming in the front foyer, "Charlotte!" His voice is light, teasing, sensual. "Did you get my note?"

"In the kitchen!" Ainsley calls out before I can utter a single word.

Oliver enters and despite the awkward situation, my eyes rake over him. He wears tight compression-style pants with a white long-sleeved Under Armour shirt. His chestnut brown hair that's dampened with sweat, curls up at the ends. His face is flushed the same soft shade of pink as last night when he thrusted into me. Over and over again.

His confused eyes dart from Ainsley to me then finally back to Ainsley. It's like a goddamn game of ping pong. "What are you doing here?"

"I came for the rest of my stuff." Her voice is calm, but her fingers curl into fists. "I could ask the same about her." She jerks her head toward me in disgust. "Is this why you ended things?" She approaches where he stands near the doorway.

"Ainsley, please," he placates, palms rising in a calming motion.

She shakes her head. "You're such a fucking liar." Her voice continues to rise with each word. "You said there was no one else, that we grew apart, that we wanted different things."

He tears a hand through his hair. "We did grow apart. We do want different things." I watch as his eyes find hers and hold. "We both know ending it was the right thing to do, that our relationship wasn't working for a long time."

She closes her eyes and exhales a long breath. When she reopens them, they're hard. "How long?" She pushes Oliver's chest once. Twice. Three times. "How long have you been fucking her?

He catches her wrists in his hands, but she thrashes in his grip. Finding Oliver's gaze, I whisper, "I think I should go."

He holds my stare for a beat, and I think he's going to protest my request, but then his eyes droop in resignation. "Take my car."

I shake my head. *I'll order an Uber.*

"Charlotte." His tone holds no room for disagreement. "Take the damn car."

Rather than argue and extend this uncomfortable situation, I nod my head in agreement. A quick survey of the space tells me there's no other way out of the kitchen other than walking right past where Oliver and Ainsley stand. Inhaling a deep breath, I square my shoulders, and with my head held high, I make my way to the staircase.

Ainsley hisses at me under her breath, the lone word discernible in the quiet: *slut*. I don't react. Outwardly, that is. I ignore the comment, feet propelling me forward. But internally? It slices me in two.

Once back in the safety of the bedroom, I slide on my pants and shoes, but leave on Oliver's t-shirt. *My* shirt is still somewhere on the kitchen floor from last night's antics and there's no way in hell I'm going back in there. Thankfully, my purse and cell phone are in the bedroom and Oliver's car keys are tossed on the entryway table at the base of the stairs.

Strained voices come from the kitchen, but I don't dare interrupt. I slip out the door without a word. Unnoticed.

But one thing's for sure: Shit just got complicated.

OLIVER

Fuck. My. Life. Of all the days Ainsley could've come to pick up her shit she chose today. I'm not embarrassed or ashamed that she found Charlotte half-naked in my kitchen. Not at all. I've hidden my feelings for Charli for far too long. I'm *done* hiding. Life is for living and all that other positive pep talk bullshit they say.

But I do regret that Ainsley made Charli feel uncomfortable. Admittedly, the entire situation is awkward. I try to put myself in Charli's shoes, imagine how I would react if *her* ex-fiancé showed up unannounced mid-morning.

It wouldn't be good. Not in the least.

Still, part of me hesitated before telling Charli to take my car and go home. I didn't *want* Charlotte to leave. But the grown up part of me, the emotionally mature man that resided in a far corner of my brain knew I needed to sort things out with Ainsley once and for all. I owed her answers to her questions, or at the very least an explanation.

Once the door clicks closed, Ainsley asks, okay, more like barks, "What the fuck, Ol?"

I exhale long and low before responding. "Can we please talk about this like adults?

She snorts and I beg, "Please, Ains. Just calm down."

"Calm down?" Her voice is shrill. "Calm down? I catch you fucking another woman and you want me to calm down?"

To be precise she didn't "catch" me doing anything. I wasn't even home when she arrived. Besides, we ended things weeks ago.

I mean, did I move on quickly? Yes. To be honest, it probably *would've* been better to sort through Ainsley and my breakup *first*, give us time and space to disentangle our lives. But when Charli showed up last night, one thing led to another...and *fuck*, there's no going back now. Not after I've had her. She hit a vein and I'm positive that I'll never be able to overcome my addiction. *To her.*

"Ainsley." My voice placates. "We both agreed."

"No." She shakes her head. "*You* agreed. I wanted to take a break." She approaches, takes my hands in hers. "We can still make this work. I-I..." she stutters, then takes a deep breath as she straightens her spine and says, "I can forgive you."

My frantic mind trips over our last conversation. The conversation we had in this very kitchen the morning after the fundraiser. I hadn't slept a wink and looked like hell. If possible, Ainsley looked even worse.

Through all of the yelling, begging, and tears, I'm *certain* I made my intentions as clear as day. *How does my saying we're over equate in her mind to taking a break?*

"Ains," I soften my tone and bring my eyes to hers. "I'm sorry. I'm so sorry, but"—my hands break free of her grasp—"I'm not going to change my mind."

Her face hardens in an instant. Dark brows furrow, jaw clenches tight, and eyes narrow to slits. "So that's it?" She shoves my chest once. "Three and a half years over? Just like that?" The sound of her fingers snapping together echoes, bounces around the room. "Tell me something." She takes a few steps back, holds up her left hand. *Holy shit. She's still wearing her engagement ring.* "Why did you let me keep the ring?"

Because I'm not an asshole. My head dips and I scratch the back of my neck. "I don't know, Ains. I bought it for you. It didn't feel right taking it back."

Her sinister voice vibrates the air. "Aren't you Prince Charming?" She yanks the ring from her finger and tosses it at me. Hard. I flinch when the rough edge of the stone grazes my cheek. "I don't want anything from you, you *asshole!*" Her voice rises with each irate word.

Mouth agape, I stare at her. Ainsley is all peace and love and being one with the universe. To see her this distraught is unsettling and a bit concerning. "Ains, please."

"Don't." Her hand slices through the air, effectively silencing me. "I'll get my stuff and go."

"Let me help—"

A growl tears from her throat and she lunges forward, but at the last minute, she stops herself.

"Okay," I say in a voice that's close to a whisper. "I'll leave so that I won't be in your way."

She doesn't respond. She simply turns and walks into the garage. The door slams behind her.

And when I get back home nearly four hours later, all traces of her are gone. The plastic bins have been cleared from the garage, the grey moccasins by the door are missing, and empty hangers line the rack where her clothes used to hang. It's empty, *bare.* In fact, it's like she was never there at all.

It's been a crazy ass day. I'm mentally drained. For hours I've thought about Ainsley—not about getting back together with her, but rather how things ended between us. Could I have been clearer? Did I fill her with false hope? Would she accept our breakup and move on? I hoped so. Not only for my sake but for hers as well. Despite everything, I do want her to find someone who makes her happy. I'm just grateful that I realized that someone *wasn't* me before it was too late.

Even after everything, or maybe in spite of everything that's transpired today, I want to see Charli more than ever. Want to take her on a real date. Prove to her that she isn't a fling or a rebound. That she's special, important. And so much more than I ever dreamt possible.

While Ainsley cleared out her belongings, I went shopping. Just to refresh your memory, I despise shopping. But I wanted to buy Charlotte something that would make her smile, something that would erase some of the uneasiness from this morning.

Roses felt clichéd, but I wasn't sure what her favorite type of flowers were, so I settled on a dozen long-stemmed in her favorite color: deep violet. And the stripper heels? Well, they were a bonus. As much for me as they were her. I anticipated, hoped, *prayed* she would wear them for me later, after dinner, in my own private show.

CHARLI

THE PHONE CALL comes several hours later. Of course, I expect it. Equal parts dread and anticipate hearing his words, his voice. In the end, my fear nearly wins out, my thumb twitching over the button millimeters away from declining the call. This whole ordeal would be so much easier, so much less confrontational if Oliver would text like every other normal human being on the planet.

I slide my finger across the screen, and with a hesitant voice, I answer, "Hello."

"Hey." Oliver's tone is relaxed, casual, like he hasn't spent the whole day analyzing, overthinking, dissecting every single moment that transpired between us in the past twenty-four hours. It irks the shit out of me. Because I have. I've done all of the above.

"So I guess you're calling about your car," I blurt out the first and easiest point of conversation on our list of 'Shit to Discuss.'"

"Huh?" His voice trips up in surprise, but he recovers quickly. "No. I mean, yeah, I'll have to get my car eventually, but that's not why I'm calling."

"Oh." Hours of waiting, preparing to have this very talk and all I got is *oh*.

"Charli." His loud exhales billows across the line. "I'm sorry about this morning."

"It's fine." My answer is bullshit and he knows it.

"It's not fine," he clips, agitation piercing his calm tone, but then he softens. "I had no idea she was going to show up."

I'll bet. He probably never would have asked me to stay had he anticipated her arrival.

Irritation prickles my nerves and because anger is a much easier emotion to feel than the others that compete for space within my heart, I give in to it. "Oliver, I don't want to get between whatever...." I hesitate, searching for the right word. "*Thing* you've got going on with Ainsley."

Anger tempers his voice at my accusation. "There's nothing going on between Ainsley and me."

My eyes narrow in a scowl even though he can't see them. "It sure didn't seem that way this morning."

"You heard what she said. She came to pick up the rest of her stuff, Charlotte. That's all."

The earnest tone of his voice begs me to believe him, but the coward in me, the part that's filled with self-doubt and insecurity, competes for my attention. It's the latter I indulge. I hedge my words. "Maybe we rushed things." I squeeze my eyes tight, clamp my mouth shut in protest, as if my body can't believe it's me actually speaking the words. "You just ended things with Ainsley a few week ago."

"Formally? Yes." His voice deepens. "But you and I both know that it's been over between her and me for much longer. This thing between us—"

I interrupt him, "Is new and exciting. What happens when the thrill of the chase is gone? You'll get bored of me soon enough."

"What the fuck are you talking about?!" he barks. "Bored of you? I just *got* you, Charlotte." His next words are softer, more controlled. "Don't ask me to let you go. *Not now.*" His voice breaks on the last two words and I imagine his cocoa eyes, wide and pleading. "I love you."

"Wh-what?" My phone slips from my sweaty hand and I barely catch it before it clatters to the floor. "What did you just say?" I *can't* have heard him right.

The same loud words assault my ears. "I love you."

Is this some sort of sick joke? Am I a game to him? Is he saying what he thinks I want to hear—what I've wanted to hear for months—only to string me along?

"Oliver." I breathe his name. "I need you to not say things like that to me."

"Why not?" His voice blooms with frustration. "Because they're true? Because you're scared? I won't lie to you about how I feel."

A humorless chuckle presses past my lips. How can I believe him now when for months, I watched as he played house with his fiancée? When I prayed for him to choose me, only to see him with her time and time again?

"After one night together?" I taunt. "One time and now you love me?" The harsh tone is foreign to my ears and my words certainly aren't my own. "Jesus, Oliver. I must have one magical pussy." I wince at my own crassness.

"You know this isn't about sex, Charlotte." His words are hot coals pressed to naked flesh. They heat. They burn. *They ignite.*

"It's not?" The kernel of hope that blooms in my chest catches wind, snakes into my ribs, branches to my collarbone, until it flows freely down my arms. Why am I fighting this? Fighting him? Maybe it *is* that simple.

"How can you even ask me that?" He growls. "If that's all you were—some quick, dirty fuck—I'd have had you *months* ago. We both know that's not what this is. You're something big. Something more. I knew it the day I met you but was too chicken shit to act on it. I pushed my feelings aside, did everything I could to keep my head straight, but you changed the game, started a chain reaction when you kissed Simon."

"Oli—" I try to interrupt, but he speaks over me.

"In some sick way, I'm grateful. I actually want to thank that bastard because it solidified what I already knew in my heart, in my bones, in the very core of my being—you're *mine*, Charlotte."

My heart beats in my chest and I marvel at how the steady thump taps against my fist even as my head spins.

Thump.

Thump.

Thump.

How can the beat be so strong, so unaffected when I'm falling apart?

"And..." Oliver's voice deepens, takes on the same husky tone as it did last night when he moved inside of me. "If we're being technical, it was two times."

Breathless, I murmur, "Huh?"

"Two. Times," he corrects, voice back to his self-assured cockiness. "Two times I was inside your magical pussy."

"Jesus," I whisper, face flushing with the memories. The beautiful, orgasmic memories.

"So..." He pauses, exhales, breathes in again. "Have I made my intentions clear?"

"Yes."

He chuckles. "Good, then be ready by seven."

"Seven?" I ask, pulling my phone away from my ear to check the time. It's ten after six.

"Yes." I can almost see him nodding his head. "I'm taking you on a proper date."

"Okay," I murmur, but internally, I curse my sex-addled brain for reducing me to a pile of mush, barely capable of uttering one-word answers.

"See you soon."

"Okay," I repeat my consent, but the line's already gone dead.

Oliver arrives at exactly seven p.m. He's nothing if not precise. With my belly a flurry of nerves I tug my apartment door open.

Oliver stands hidden behind a massive bouquet of flowers. He shifts them in his grasp, ducking his head to one side. "Hi."

"Hi." I smooth my hands down my blue jersey knit dress. It's one of my favorites because it matches the blue tone of my eyes perfectly. Added bonus: I found it on the clearance rack at Forever 21. It cost a whopping seven dollars, but when accessorized with the right blazer, shoes, and jewelry, it easily looks like it cost ten times that. "Come in." I step back and swing the door open more.

"These are for you." He hands me the arrangement of twelve long-stemmed roses. They're not the typical blood red hue but rather a rich, deep violet. My favorite color. Instinctively, my nose dips to the fragrant buds.

"They're beautiful." I turn my back, already moving toward the kitchen to retrieve a large pitcher from my cabinet to use as a makeshift vase since I don't own a real one.

Once the flowers are situated, I walk back into to the living room. I watch Oliver, his gaze roaming the place I call home. My apartment isn't small, but it's not nearly as big his as house. His eyes leave nothing untouched, from the four rows of neatly stacked DVDs along my TV console, to the small oval table where I've set the flowers, to the open door at the end of the hall where my bed peeks out, barely visible.

He nods his head once and reaches for a rectangular gift-wrapped box that I didn't see him place on the entryway table.

My eyes fall to the box he holds in front of him. "What's that?"

"These." A sly smile tips the corners of his lips. "These are for *Laney Vine*."

My mouth gapes open as he continues, "I'm hoping she'll wear them when she dances for me later tonight."

If I were British, I'd say something cute and fun or sexy and flirty like, "You cheeky, bastard." But I'm not British or cute and fun or sexy and flirty, apparently, because all I manage to mumble is a belated, "Thanks."

His smile says it all. *Don't be nervous. You know I'll make you come so hard you'll forget your name. I know you want it as badly as I do.* "Let's go." He leads me by the elbow to the door. "We don't want to be late for our reservation."

With our hands entwined, Oliver and I walk the two dark city blocks before reaching his parked car.

His eyebrows rise as he asks, "Why so far away?"

I can understand his question. My street isn't very busy *and* we passed at least a dozen empty spaces along the way. I shrug. "Those spots are tight."

"Tight?" His voice rings with incredulity. "You could park a tractor trailer there." He gesture to one of the spaces.

I dip my head, stopping in front of the passenger door. After several moments, when it's clear he's not going to drop it, I admit, "I can't parallel park, okay?"

"What?" He chuckles as he opens the car door for me. "Isn't that something you need to know how to do in order to pass your test?"

My head bobs, eyes wide. "Trust me when I tell you, it's bad. *Very* bad."

"You do realize my car has a backup camera, right?"

"My puzzled eyes find his as I slide into the passenger seat. "So?"

Shutting the door, he jogs around to the driver's side and climbs in. Winking, he says, "In that case, you better leave the driving to me."

CHARLI

My eyes squint at the small sign hung above the door. *Zala's Café.* As we get closer, I read the fine print below: *An Ethiopian Experience.* Even for someone as adventurous (with food) as I am, I've never tried this particular cuisine. In fact, I'm a bit flustered as the hostess seats us at a low table which lacks the traditional Western silverware and place setting.

I lean toward Oliver. "Have you ever eaten here before?"

He shakes his head. "No, but I've always wanted to try it."

A server appears and greets us with a warm smile. "Welcome to Zala's. Is this your first time dining with us?"

We both nod our heads and he continues, "Welcome, welcome. A few things to point out before you order." He hands us one large menu. "The food is served family style, that is, it's meant to be shared." We nod again. "Also, you may have noticed there are no utensils. Everything is eaten with Injera, a flatbread of sorts." He pauses for a moment and then says, "Okay, I'll give you a few minutes to look at the menu and I'll be back to see if you have any questions."

I watch as Oliver's eyes rake over the menu with genuine interest. I skim over a few dishes, but the names mean little to me.

Shiro. Qey Doro Wat. Ye Awaze Tibs. Most items have a brief description in English, but I don't bother, leaving Oliver to decide. "Whatever you pick is good with me."

His eyes widen in surprise. "Really?"

I shrug. "You know I'm not picky."

He smiles. "Yeah, I know."

The waiter returns and Oliver places our order. When the server departs, Oliver explains that he's ordered us two dishes: one beef entrée and one vegetarian.

The conversation flows freely between us and for a moment, I wonder why I allowed my nerves to get away from me all day. Oliver and I have been friends for over a year, so we can essentially skip all the first date small talk. But best of all, I can skip the first date charade of pretending I have a dainty appetite.

Oliver knows better. Much better.

Sooner than expected, two plates are set before us, along with a smaller dish filled with Injera. The waiter points to the flatbread. "Tear a piece of Injera and use it to scoop up the food." He mimes the motion with his hands. "It's kind of like you're using the Injera to pinch up the food."

Oliver and I tear a piece of bread under the waiter's careful observation. I grab a piece of beef and spinach, but the sauce is messy and dribbles down my fingers. The waiter smiles. "It takes a little bit of practice." He turns his attention to Oliver. "You two are a couple, no?"

"Yes," Oliver answers without hesitation.

A warm smile lights up the server's face. "Thought so." The waiter's gaze flits from me back to Oliver as he directs him, "Take a piece of Injera."

Oliver does as told and the waiter continues, "Now scoop some food and see if you can feed her *without* touching her mouth."

"Without touching her mouth?" Oliver repeats.

"Yes. It's a tradition called Gursha." The server and I both watch as Oliver follows his instructions. "Gursha is only done with those you love. Try it out." The waiter adds, "I'll leave you to it." Then he turns and walks away.

Oliver leans across the table, his intense brown eyes locked on mine. Slowly, I open my mouth as he gently places the wrapped morsel on the flat of my tongue. He withdraws his hand and I close my mouth, chewing slowly. Heat pulses in my body and I fight back the soft moan of pleasure as the spicy, tender meat explodes in my mouth. Oliver's eyes never waver from my lips.

This tradition, *Gursha*, is intimate. More intimate than I expected. Feeding someone, fingers to mouth, lips, tongue, teeth—it's sensual and *very* arousing.

Swallowing, I take a sip of my water before saying. "Let me do you now."

Oliver's nostrils flare at my comment, even though it's obvious —at least, in my mind—that I'm talking about our food.

Tearing off a piece of bread, I pinch a small square of meat and some vegetables. I'm not as graceful as he is, however, and as I bring the pocket to his mouth, my fingers bump against his cheek. "Sorry," I whisper, eyes focused on his full, smooth lips and straight white teeth.

He hooks his fingers with mine as he chews and swallows. "Don't ever apologize for touching me, Charli." He brings my fingertips to his lips, dusts a feather light kiss across each pad. "I've wanted your touch for so long. I don't think I'll ever get enough."

He releases my hand and we continue to chat and eat. Eating without a fork and knife are much harder than you'd think. It slower than normal, somewhat frustrating but fun. Slightly messy, a whole lot sexy and satisfying. By the time the server brings our check, there's not a doubt in my mind that Oliver will be spending the night at my apartment, where I plan to make good on the double-entendre of my words, because I definitely want to *do him*.

Now.

CHARLI

I STARE at myself in the full-length mirror affixed to my closet door. The heels Oliver bought for me, I mean for *Laney*, are hot and actually look semi-decent with my navy dress. I've ditched the sweater and unclipped my hair, tossing it a few times to add a touch more volume to the already messy curls.

I'm not embarrassed for Oliver to see me like this or wearing even less. I don't have much (or any) lingerie, but if I did, I'd have no problem donning it for him. No shame in this game.

But what *does* have my head spinning, what has my stomach churning is what comes next. *The striptease*. Can I really do it? *I don't know*. I've certainly talked the talk, but that now it's time to walk the walk, and I'm freaking the fuck out.

"Come on, Charli." Oliver's voice coaxes from the living room. "Don't back out on me now."

Groaning, I peek my head around the archway. "Maybe we should wait to do this when I don't have a food baby growing inside my belly." This is a legitimate excuse because I *did* eat half of my body weight in food not even two hours ago.

"Nope. Not getting out of it that easily." He whistles. "Maybe you just need some music for inspiration?"

I hear a few quick clicks and taps on his cell phone and suddenly, Lee Greenwood's "God Bless the U.S.A." fills the quiet space. The song prompts me into action and I spring from my hiding spot, ready to attack. "Asshole."

But no rebuttal forms on his lips as I approach. In fact, his phone remains suspended awkwardly in one hand, mouth slightly agape as his eyes widen to the size of hockey pucks.

Boom. Mic drop.

I nearly pump my fist in the air in victory.

A million doubts and insecurities race through my mind, but I shove them aside, using his reaction to bolster my inner confidence. Playing up my sex appeal, I sashay my hips, cross one leg seductively over the other the way I've seen supermodels do on the runway. The sky-high peep toe pumps make my legs appear a mile long, make me feel like I'm traipsing in the clouds, weightless.

"What's the matter?" I whisper, purposefully turning my voice sultry. "Cat got your tongue?" I lean into him, dragging my breasts dangerously close to his mouth, but rather than make contact like he expects, I slip the phone from his fingers.

I type my song of choice into the search bar and within seconds, the sexy, slow notes of Bruno Mars' *Versace on the Floor* filter through the tiny speaker. I drop the cell onto the couch.

"I think this is better, no?" I cock an eyebrow and begin to gyrate my hips to the music, skimming my hands down the length of my dress. When I begin to gradually ghost it up my thighs, I watch his eyes. They beg. They plead. They pray for my hands to continue their journey.

Finally, he mouths the word. *Please.*

Effortlessly, I slide the dress over my head before tossing it to the side. My bravado falters when I stand naked in front of him, save for my white bra and panty set. The pairing might scream purity and innocence if not for the tiny red cherries dotted across the fabric that invite his gaze in *all* the right places.

My lids lower, and I avoid eye contact because what in the actual fuck am I doing? I'm not *Laney Vine*. I'm not even Drunk

Charlotte. I'm just plain ol' Charlotte. And plain ol' Charlotte is nervous as hell.

His gaze, darkened with lust, sets my skin ablaze. "Cherries?" he croaks, a lone muscle ticking in his jaw. "Is this my dessert?" His fingers flex. "*Your* cherry pie?"

The nervous energy bubbling inside of me causes me to tumble back onto the ottoman, but I recover at the last second, turning myself on the seat to face him directly. Testing the waters, I arch my back causing my breasts to strain against the thin fabric cups of my bra. Mimicking every stripper I've ever seen—which let's face it, hasn't been many—I spread my legs a bit wider, allow my hands to trace the skin of my inner thighs.

"Is this good?" I wish my voice didn't shake with insecurity.

"Fuck, yes." Oliver's growl of encouragement emboldens me.

My eyes dart to the ceiling as I summon my inner mojo. I'm not Charlotte Truse, restaurant manager. I am *Laney Vine*, bombshell sex goddess.

Pushing myself to stand, I reach for his legs and tug him farther down the cushion. His little grunt of surprise tells me he wasn't expecting the gesture, but also that he's not unhappy with the turn of events.

Sliding my body between his legs, I drag my breasts along his thick, muscular thighs, over his very visible, very hard erection, over the solid cut of his abs, upward to his chiseled chest, and stopping only when I'm inches from his mouth.

When he tilts forward and tries to nip my breast, I lean back.

"No touching the dancers," I scold, dragging a fingertip across his full bottom lip.

He groans when I pull my finger away. "Baby," he pants, head dropping back against the cushion in frustration. "Please. I want to touch you. I *need* to touch you."

I shake my head, a coy smile on my lips. "Do you want to play a game?"

He clamps his jaw tight but nods his agreement. His teeth grind with so much force it's a wonder he can form the words. "What are the rules?"

Straddling him, I clasp his face with both hands and hold it captive. "Just one." My hips gyrate against him, lining his hardness with my heat. "No touching."

His brows pull together, a frown marring his face as I watch the protest form on his lips. "But you can touch me?" The words are stretched thin, his voice taut with tension.

"Yes." I grab the front of his shirt, pulling his chest flush to mine. "You're always so controlled, so reserved, so self-assured. But let's see." I slide my hips up the full length of him before sinking back down. Feather light. Slow. And not nearly enough of what we both want. "Let's see how long it will last."

His hands fist at his sides as my hips trace widening, concentric circles in his lap. Teasing. Taunting. Daring.

I grasp the hem of his shirt and pull it over his head, exposing the smooth, tanned planes of his chest.

His skin is caramel cream. Bronzed. Sun-kissed from miles upon miles of outdoor runs.

Carefully, I drag one fingernail across his nipple, the pressure just enough to elicit a warning hiss, "Charlotte."

I ignore the warning and bring my tongue to one nipple, then the next. I can feel his ab muscles spasm, jerk, and release beneath me. His body is at war with itself. I watch him struggle to maintain calm. Can see it in the tight set of his jaw, the strong, almost angry furrow of his brow, the white knuckles of each clenched fist.

Straightening my legs, I push myself from his lap. He growls in protest. But whatever words he tries to say die on his lips as I spin away from him and bend forward to touch my toes. My ass thrusts high, just below his face.

I arch up halfway, crane my head over one shoulder. "You never did tell me." A smirk tips the corners of my lips. "Are you an ass man?" I slap my one cheek hard. "Or..." I face him once more as I bring my hands to either side of my breasts, squeezing them together. "A tit man?"

"Jesus Christ." One hand scrubs over his face. "Both, Charlotte. With you, I'm fucking *both*."

Chucking, I straighten my spine and tsk. "If I didn't know any better, I'd say that ironclad control of yours is crumbling mighty fast."

His voice is tortured. "You have no idea."

"Hmm," I hum as I reach behind to the clasp of my bra. *Will this be the*

proverbial straw that broke the camel's back?

"Don't." He lunges forward, his hand grabbing my forearm.

My eyes land on the spot where his fingers circle skin and bone. One eyebrow rises in question, but he speaks before I can say anything, "*I* want to be the one to undress you."

His nostrils flare once before a skillful hand slides up my ribcage. Gentle yet urgent fingers tug down the soft cup of my bra, exposing one full breast.

"I think you lost," I say, but it turns into a moan as he traces a circle with his fingertip around my nipple, causing it to stiffen.

He lifts his head, lazy eyes finding mine. "Lost?" A slow shake of his head left to right. "I hit the fucking jackpot."

After that, my mind trips. My breath hitches. My hips thrust. I'm a victim of my own wants and desires. In this moment, I become someone else. A woman who's self-assured. A woman bursting with sexual need. A woman unleashed.

Filthy words pour from my lips, demanding, "Oliver." My back arches like a taut bow, my head lolls to the side. "Suck my tits."

His mouth dips, obliging, and I feel the vibrations, his rumble of pleasure straight between my legs. I'm soaked. Surely he must feel it. Surely he must *smell* it. And if it were any other day, any other man, I'd drop my head, shutter my eyes in embarrassment. But not with him. Not with Oliver.

He growls as my fingers tear through his hair, holding his head in place. But my strength is fading. I'm falling fast. My body collapses against him. Ass bounces, legs lock around his strong thighs, desperately seeking friction, seeking relief. But he takes his time, savoring one breast then the other.

Lick. Suck. Bite.

Repeat.

The throbbing, burning need between my legs answers his siren's call and as he hurtles me toward oblivion, as I hover on the razor's edge of pure ecstasy, I wonder if it's possible for me to come this way. Just from him playing with my breasts.

Seconds later, my unasked question is answered when he sucks one nipple into his mouth and his fingers twist the other.

I come apart in his arms.

Not come.

Come *apart*.

Muscles quivering, eyes clenched tight, wetness flooding my pussy. Tiny spasms, aftershocks wash over me, jerking my body in his arms. He carries me through it. Allows my teeth to sink into the thick bulk of his shoulder, lets sharp nails pierce smooth skin, steadies the uncontrolled rhythm of my hips as they drag against his cock.

"Oliver." His name is a prayer. A dream. *A reality*.

"That was beautiful." His hand straightens the messy curls that obscure my eyes. "*You* are beautiful."

I watch as one hand reaches down between us, hovering at the band of my panties. "We don't have to do any more tonight." His voice is rough, like crushed shells scraping beneath your feet on a rocky beach. "But I *need* to feel you." His rich brown eyes have turned dark, almost obsidian. "I want to feel how wet you are for me."

Breathless, I nod as one long finger slips inside my panties, going down, down, down, until—

"Oh my God." My head hangs as he dips his finger inside my tight heat, collecting the wetness before finally traveling to my swollen clit. A subtle tap of his finger. A gentle nudge of his bent knuckle. A whispered promise in my ear. "Mine."

"Yours." I'm not sure if I actually say the word aloud, but even so, it doesn't make it any less true.

Eyes never leaving mine, he withdraws his hand and brings his finger to his mouth. Even though I know what's coming, I still gasp as he pushes the digit past the swell of his lips sucking, *licking* my juices off him.

After several long seconds I push myself to my feet. Resting my hands atop his belt buckle, I grin. "Your turn." But what I really meant is to say *my turn* because I've been dying to taste him.

He lifts his ass, helping me remove his pants and boxer briefs in one swoop. My eyes drop to his cock. Thick and angry. Purple and veiny. Throbbing, twitching, aching for...me. My hand. My mouth. My pussy.

The edges of my heels dig into my ass I kneel before him. Peering up at him under thick, kohl black lashes, I say, "You said you wondered how smart my mouth would be when my lips were wrapped around your cock?"

No verbal response, just a sharp intake of breath and a proud twitch of his dick.

Wrapping my hand around the base, I make a tight fist. "Make me choke on it."

He pulses in my palm, his voice animalistic. "Charlotte."

"Fuck my mouth, Oliver." I hold his gaze, my breaths labored and fast.

"Charli," he groans as I pump my wrist once.

"It wasn't a question," I repeat his words from last night. "Now, Oliver."

He hisses. His internal struggle playing across his features in slow motion. He's like a tree doing its damnedest to weather, *to resist* the storm.

Sinking to my knees was the first crack.

The slide of my tight fist against solid flesh. Break number two.

The demand for him to fuck my mouth. The final and strongest blow.

And the limb severs, yielding to the power that surrounds it.

Temptation teases the corners of his eyes, veiled only by a thin cloud of restraint. "*Jesus*. I'm yours." He splays his legs open wide. "All yours."

The first lash of my tongue is slow, controlled, a direct contrast to the need humming in my veins. Flavor blooms in my mouth. Oliver tastes like....

Plums. Tart.

Ocean. Salt.

Nature. Grit.

But more than any of that, Oliver tastes like passion. Life. Love. He tastes like he's *mine*.

Hollowing my cheeks, I suck the swollen mushroom head between my lips, tracing a slow circle before dragging my tongue through the slit. His hips jump, thigh muscles squeeze. *He likes that*.

So I do it again.

"Jesus, Charli." His fingers curl into tight fists. "I'm trying to go easy." He puffs a breath. "*Really* trying."

My fingers knead the corded muscle of his thighs, urging him to stand. I pull away, lips barely dusting his cockhead when I speak, "Stop trying."

Finally, with shaky legs, he stands before where I kneel like a willing servant before her master. "Are you sure you want this?"

"Yes." I nod my head.

One hand grips his cock at the base. "Open your mouth for me, baby." He inches closer. "Let me see that pretty pink tongue."

Wordlessly, I comply, unlocking my jaw as I open wide.

Cautious eyes find mine. "If it gets too much for you or if you want to stop..."His voice trails off. "I'm kinda big so I understand if..."

"Oliver." My tone is harsher than I intended, but I'm done waiting.

He hesitates only the briefest of seconds, before his hips thrust forward, filling me full of his velvet, steely skin. He groans, head tossed back in pleasure, one hand still wrapped around the base of his cock.

I lock my eyes in place, blinking once—slowly—as though capturing a snapshot. If I only ever remember one single thing from this night, please God, let it be this. *Oliver*. Muscle stretched tight over solid bone. One strong hand gripping his length. Eyes pressed shut. Mouth twisted in pleasure.

The moment passes and he pushes forward again. I concentrate on relaxing my jaw as I try to find his rhythm, finally syncing with him push for push.

His pace quickens and both hands tangle in my hair, holding my head at the position that satisfies. The angle that tips the back of my throat.

"Oh *fuck*." The rough, almost untethered tone of his voice has me reaching out for him, has me sliding my hands around his waist, has my fingers pinching his ass cheeks.

The sounds of sex surround us. The soft slap of his balls with each powerful thrust. The tiny coughs that escape my throat every time his length grazes the back of my throat. The harsh groans of a man coming undone.

"Charlotte." His fingers tug my hair as he did last night, lighting up every nerve along my scalp. "I'm gonna come," he groans. "I'm gonna fucking come."

Questioning eyes find mine, seeming to ask, *Where?*

But I don't have an answer—at least, not quickly enough—because he pulls out, shuttles a tight fist up his length.

Once.

Twice.

The third pull releases a torrent of hot, silky come. It rains over my lips, my chin, drips onto my chest. A sound that can only be described as guttural pierces the quiet.

Time slows and it seems like it takes forever for Oliver to open his eyes, but in reality, it's probably closer to a minute. A lazy smile tugs the corners of his lips. "*Charlotte*."

"Oliver." I smile back as he reaches his hand out to pull me to stand.

His fingers trace my plump lips, bee-stung, swollen and shiny.

Continue farther down to the column of my throat, to where my pulse tics wildly beneath his touch. To the thick white swirls glistening across my chest. With concentrated focus he drags his finger through the liquid, circling one nipple then the next.

A shiver dances across my spine, turning my skin to gooseflesh.

"Is it wrong that I don't want you to clean up?" Dark eyes find mine. "That I want part of me to stay with you forever?"

My heart trips over the words. Me. Him. *Forever*.

He doesn't know it, but this night *will* stay with me forever.

I don't think he really expects, or even wants, an answer, so instead I say, "How about if *you* clean me up?" I turn, already beginning to walk toward the bathroom, to where my very large oversized shower awaits.

I smile as I hear his heavy footsteps moving toward me. His hands wrap around my waist as he says, "Now *that* is a plan I can get behind."

CHARLI

MEG PICKS up the round tray filled with drinks from the bar top and my eyes jump to her for a moment before finding their way back to Oliver.

"Just *think* about it," he says, but I translate the words to mean: *stop being ridiculous.*

"I can't go to Vegas with you." I sigh as I refill the cocktail straws at the end of the bar. I'm covering for Joe *again*. With the new restaurant, La Conquistadora, opening in a few short weeks, Mecca's staff is threadbare. Don recruited two of our bussers, three servers, Joe, our principal bartender, and a dishwasher—not Simon —to help train the new hires. I agree with Don's logic, but my workload is more than full enough without having to cover a bartending shift.

"Why not?" Oliver's voice catches my attention. Tonight *was* the only night we had scheduled off together, but due to a scheduling mix-up, Joe never showed up for his shift at six. Hence the reason I'm here, at Mecca, banging out drinks when I'd much rather be banging Oliver.

Bummed, I texted Oliver. Yes, he's texting now. Sure, his responses are never more than five words, but it's progress. Baby steps. He surprised me by showing up with my favorite Jamba Juice smoothie: Razzmatazz.

How sweet. I'm beginning to think Oliver is a closet romantic.

I narrow my eyes at him. "We've been over this."

"Explain to me again why you don't want to go on vacation with me." He snatches the smoothie from the bar, holding it hostage just out of my reach. "Or you don't get this."

Holding his gaze, I lunge for the cup and miss. *Dammit.* With a dramatic exhale, I say, "It's not a vacation. It's a business trip."

"Same thing."

My brow arches in disagreement, but I continue, "Don wouldn't go for it. The shifts are barely covered as it is."

"I'll talk to Don." His voice is confident and self-assured, the tone of a man who's used to getting what he wants.

"Even if Don does approve the days off—"

"He will."

My scowls conveys my displeasure at his interruption. "Even if he did, I can't afford the plane ticket. Besides, Jim's going with you. I don't want to be a third wheel."

"First of all, Jim loves you *almost* as much as I do." His warm smile dissolves some (all) of my apprehension. "And don't worry about the ticket. I have a *ton* of airline miles."

"From Ainsley?" I ask, even though I probably shouldn't. It's none of my business.

He hesitates before answering. "Yes and no." I wait for him to elaborate. "The credit card promotion is with her airline, but they're *my* points. I earned them with purchases..." Both shoulders shrug. "And stuff."

And stuff? What kinds of stuff?

Nodding, I glance at the order Meg's just placed on the corner of the bar and grab a bottle of Pinot Noir. I pour two glasses and set them on her tray before directing my attention back at Oliver. "I don't know, Oliver. You leave in two days."

He shakes his head. "No, *we* leave in two days."

His sexy smile penetrates my cold, hard defenses, my heart

melting into a pile of mush beneath his heated gaze. My mind is made up well before I utter the words nearly three hours later: This girl's going to Vegas.

Of course we're on a morning flight. Of course Oliver insisted on arriving at the airport two hours before our departure, despite the fact that I suggested we could save time (and sleep) by checking in online. And of course there's a long line at the coffee shop where I wait to pay almost six dollars for a freaking cup of black coffee.

"I brought a friend." Jim's voice is quiet, almost apologetic as we meet up with him after going through the security checkpoint.

"Yeah?" I ask, adjusting my Longchamp bag on my shoulder. Okay, the bag *was* a splurge and I don't really have a ton of discretionary income, but *seriously*, their tote bags are the best for traveling. "Who?"

Julia steps out from behind where Jim stands. Her smile is hesitant as she says, "Hey, Charli."

My eyes nearly pop out of my head, darting from Julia to Jim to Oliver. Oliver's gaze holds mine for a moment, silently answering my unspoken question: *Did you know she was coming?*

Nope, I knew nothing about it.

After my initial surprise dissipates I find my voice. "Hey." Leaning forward, I hug first Julia, then Jim. "I'm glad you're here." My eyes slide to Jim's. "Although I didn't know you two were an item."

Julia's face flushes. I've never ever seen her flustered and it's kinda, sorta freaking *adorable*.

Jim saves her from responding. "We're taking things slow."

Vacationing together is slow? I nod. "Oh, that's good."

"Yeah." Her eyes cast to the side to where Jim and Oliver are most likely talking about financial contracts. When I hear the words *royalties* and *margins* I know I'm right.

"So what's the deal with school?"

One shoulder lifts. "Technically, I'm only missing two days because of the

weekend. No biggie."

I wonder if our parents would agree, but I don't dare ask. My guess is they have no idea she's flying halfway across the country. Then again, it's not like I phoned to tell them either. Officially, this is a business trip and I'm still available via phone. Perhaps I should have let them know. Yes, I definitely should have. *Shit*, I'm a terrible daughter. I'll send my mom a quick text before the plane takes off.

Julia nudges my shoulder. "Are you sure you're okay with me coming?"

Things between her and me have been much better since she last came to visit. I'm not going to lie—we aren't suddenly BFFs, but ever since we aired our dirty laundry, it's like a weight has been lifted. I don't harbor the resentment and anger. I think I've finally let it go.

"Yeah, actually." My smile is one hundred percent genuine. "We can hang out while the guys have their meetings or whatever they need to do. Maybe catch a show?"

She waggles her eyebrows. "Chippendales?"

"Did someone say Chippendales?" Jim jokes. "Here we are, ladies." He drags a finger between himself and Oliver. "At your service."

"You wish." Julia teases. Jim retaliates by pinching her side.

The normalcy of it strikes me all at once. I'm going on a couples' vacation with my boyfriend, our friend, and my sister. To Sin City.

How is this my life?

They say what happens in Vegas stays in Vegas. Who would have guessed we were about to blow that catchphrase right out of the damn water.

CHARLI

"BABY, I *promise*. You're not going to see her." Oliver's palm rubs my upper arm in an effort to soothe my anxiety.

I had my reservations about flying on Ainsley's airline (Ha! As if she owns the

company.)

Oliver assured me, multiple times, that Ainsley doesn't work domestic fares, but still, I'm uneasy. I don't know what exactly I think will happen if we bump into each other. It's not like we're going to have a shoot-out or something. But after our last (and hopefully, final) interaction at Oliver's house, I'm not pining to see her.

"Baby." Oliver's lips press against the curve of my shoulder. "Relax."

"I am relaxed," I tell him. But the words sound like a lie, even to my own ears.

His hand moves to my leg, fingers skim the inside of my thigh causing me to

shiver. His voice is dark and low when he speaks, "Do you need me to help you?"

His finger inches closer to the juncture between my thighs and I squeeze my legs together, eyes darting around the cabin as I check to see if anyone takes notice. But it's mostly dark. Only a few scattered bulbs of light illuminate the plane. It appears most passengers are sleeping or are tuned out, watching the screens set within the headrests in front of them.

"Oliver." My voice is meant to warn, but when his strong finger traces up my seam I have to fight to suppress my moan.

"Baby." He leans closer, his wet lips press to the soft skin of my neck and suck. "Let me help you relax. I can be *very* distracting."

Leaning forward I dig out the small travel blanket I shoved into my bag at the last minute and drape it across my lap. It's the only green light that Oliver needs, because seconds later, his hand is *inside* the waistband of my leggings, traveling down, down, down.

He doesn't rush, which strikes me as odd because we are not alone. He works me for what seems like *hours*, bringing me to the edge only to back down. Again and again. It's sweet, blissful torture. And when I finally fall, breath caught in my throat, eyes squeezed shut, lip caught between my teeth, it's the singular most powerful orgasm I've experienced.

Years later, I'll look back on this moment, relive the absolute ecstasy of it, still feel the tender, agonizing touch of the man I love. It's an orgasm that will forever be seared into my memory. And not that I'm in the habit of ranking orgasms, but if I were, this would *definitely* make the top three.

Also, does getting fingered at thirty thousand feet qualify you for membership into the Mile High Club? Asking for a friend...

The four of us spend the first day gambling, but I'm not a fan. After losing fifty dollars in a matter of minutes, I decide feeding my hard-earned money into a slot machine while crossing my fingers and toes for good luck isn't my idea of fun. Not to mention, it didn't work. The crossing of the fingers and toes, I mean.

Oliver and Jim, however, like it. They buy in to a high-end poker tournament which costs two hundred dollars a hand. I can't begin to comprehend or rationalize the cost, but when you make as much as Oliver—or as much as Oliver's going to make—I saw the proposed contracts—I guess it doesn't matter.

Julia and I hang around for a little bit, watching, but after the first game, we get antsy. Although it *is* kind of sexy watching Oliver smoke a cigar. The way his lips stretch around the blunt end, his tongue flicking...it makes my panties *wet.*

Halfway through the second hand, Julia and I have had enough. We entertain ourselves by checking out the shops and neighboring hotels along the strip. I buy a magnet of the iconic "Welcome to Fabulous Las Vegas" sign and a quirky t-shirt for Oliver in one of the souvenir shops that reads "Chop it Like it's Hot." Julia returns empty-handed.

In bed the next morning, Oliver holds me close, my back to his front. "I don't want to get up."

I stroke my fingers along the tight band of muscle that runs the length of his forearm. "Me neither. Can you skip your meeting?"

"I wish." His breath ruffles my hair. "I'll be quick."

Rolling my eyes I say, "You're never quick."

He chuckles softly. "And this is a bad thing?" He gathers my hair in one hand and moves it to the side, exposing my neck.

My eyes fall closed because it's incredibly difficult to think when he's touching me, let alone when his tongue is gliding along the column of my throat.

His lips catch my earlobe and nibble before he whispers, "Is it?"

"Oliver." I sigh as he turns me to lie flat on my back. "Your meeting," I protest, but it's weak. I'll give him whatever he wants. We *both* know it.

"Marry me." His words pull me out of my haze, cause my eyes to pop open, wide and unsure. Did he just say *marry me?* I had to have misheard him. Maybe he said carry me? Or ferry free? Hairy bee?

What. The. Fuck.

He braces himself on his elbows, hovers above me. I hold my gaze to his, studying, reading, assessing. His eyes look glassy, as though he's holding back emotion. As though he's holding back *tears*.

He definitely said it. He said *marry me*. Oliver asked me to marry him.

My chest constricts, heart beat spikes, and my breath falters when he says it again, "Marry me, Charlotte."

In typical Oliver fashion, the request isn't a question. No. He simply commands, his voice confident, cocky, and so damn self-assured. With one hand, he brushes a few curls from my face. "I love you." Using his fingertips, his touch feather light, he traces my forehead, over my brow bones, to my eyelids, the slope of my nose, the curve of my cheeks, to the cupid's bow of my mouth. He tugs my bottom lip down slightly, tracing its fullness with both his finger and eyes. "I want you to be mine." His gaze snaps back to me. "I've waited so long to have you. Can you just be *mine?*" His voice cracks on the last word.

Unlike Oliver, I'm not skilled in guarding my emotions. Eyes open and full, a rogue tear slides down my cheek before I can stop it. I give up trying completely when Oliver leans down, brings his lips to my cheek, catching the drop with a kiss.

I'm melting.

"Yes," I mutter at first, and then repeat louder, "Yes."

This is crazy.

"Yes?" He sits up, pulling me into his arms. "Yes?"

But I don't care.

"Let's do it." I nod, smiling through tears. "Let's get married."

"Baby." His mouth touches my skin everywhere. My hair. My forehead. My eyelids. My cheeks. My jaw. My neck. My collarbones. *My heart.* His lips hover there.

"I can't believe this is real. That you agreed to share your life, your body, your soul with me." He places a soft kiss directly over where my heart beats, loud and strong. For him. "Thank you for trusting me with your heart, Charlotte." His eyes meet mine. "I promise I'll take good care of it, *and you*, forever."

"I don't want to wait."

Wait. What am I saying?

I frame his face with my hands, the words slipping out as if beyond my control. "Tomorrow. Let's get married tomorrow."

His eyes narrow on mine gauging the seriousness of my proposition. "You're serious?"

"Dead."

"Okay." The word falls past his lips, but I barely hear it. I'm too focused on his wide smile. A smile I have no doubt could outshine every light on the strip.

"We're getting married!" I whisper-shout as excitement pumps through my veins.

"We're getting married," he repeats. "Now." He pushes me back onto the bed, his smile coy and mischievous. "It's time to celebrate."

"Uh-uh." I shake my head, giving his chest a gentle push. "It's bad luck for the bride to the see groom before the wedding."

His eyes widen in disbelief. "You're joking, right?"

"Nope." I wiggle my body out from beneath his. "I'll stay with Julia tonight. You and Jim can stay in our room."

His smile falls. "Baby, there's only one bed."

My hand skims the width of the king-size mattress. "There's plenty of room for both of you."

"I am *not* snuggling with Jimbo." He shakes his head. "I want to be..." Pools of dark brown rake over me as he chooses his words. "*Snuggling* with you."

Laughing, I say, "It's only one night." Don't get all crazy on me."

"Crazy?" His nose wrinkles. "Maybe I am crazy." The megawatt smile returns. "Fucking crazy about you."

A brow arches and I question, "Crazy about fucking me?"

His smile is wolfish. "That too."

"Just think"—I move around the suite, gathering the few clothes and toiletries I've already unpacked—"next time you fuck me, I'll be your wife."

His eyes hold mine. "You'll be mine."

"I'm already yours," I confess.

The feral look in his eyes tells me he's ready to pounce and neither of us will be leaving this hotel room anytime soon. "Now." I shoo him with my hands. "Out. I need to shower and get dressed. I have a lot of things to do today."

I have an entire wedding to plan in less than twenty-four hours.

No worries, Charli. You got this.

First order of business, call Julia and freak the fuck out.

OLIVER

She said yes.

CHARLI

"HOLY SHIT." Julia lunges at me, wrapping her arms around me in a tight bear hug. "Congratulations."

In this moment I appreciate her for the all the things she *doesn't* say. I know what she must be thinking, because I'm thinking them too.

Things like: *This isn't like you, Charlotte. Aren't you rushing into things? Are you sure? Are you sure you're sure?*

"So what's the plan?" Julia sits on the edge of the bed in her and Jim's suite. It's nearly identical to ours but is one floor up. "Oliver and Jim are meeting the representatives from the Lees Morgan Group at ten o'clock." I join her on the bed. "I figured we could go shopping." My nervous eyes find hers. "I need a dress."

A dress.

Not just any dress, but a wedding dress. A dress I will wear when I pledge my life to Oliver. A dress that will be in pictures we show our children and our grandchildren. Wait, *stop*. I don't even know if Oliver wants children.

The enormity of what I'm about to do hits me all at once.

"Stop." Julia squeezes my arm. "Stop overthinking it. You love Oliver and he loves you."

But is love enough? Do we agree on major life decisions like having children? Money? Religion?

God, maybe we *are* naïve, rushing into things blindly, two fools in love.

I'm lost in my head as Julia pushes herself from the bed and walks toward the small desk nestled in the corner. She grabs a notepad and pen before rejoining me. "Okay, we need a list."

I nod, allowing her take control because right now, my emotions are all over the place.

"First, we need to book a chapel."

"We did already." My voice doesn't match the shaking of my insides and I read it as a good sign. "The ceremony is at seven o'clock tomorrow night at the Chapel of the Flowers."

Her nose scrunches. "The Chapel of the Flowers? Sounds cheesy."

My mouth gapes. "It's rated as the number one chapel on Trip Advisor!"

Her pen falters as she strikes an item from the list. "Okay, then." She taps the pen to her mouth. "We need flowers, a dress, and oh —" She jumps up as though just remembering something important. "Are you going to call Mom and Dad?"

I shake my head. "Oliver and I decided that it would just be us for now. We agreed to wait until after we get back to tell our parents. We'll have some type of party to celebrate then."

Her face falls upon hearing the news. "Oh, okay."

"No, Jules," I say, clearing up any confusion. "I want you there. I want you to be maid of honor."

Her hand flies to her chest. "Really?"

"Yes." I nod, a smile stretching across my lips. "Oliver's asking Jim today. You will be our witnesses."

"Oh my God, *yes!*" She abandons the pen and paper nearly knocking me backward as she hugs me again.

I pat her back and chuckle. "You'd swear you were the one getting married, Jules."

Smiling, she pulls back. "I'm just really happy for you." She wipes a tear from the corner of her eye. "You know what this means, right?"

My head shakes left to right. "No, I don't."

"I get to throw you a bachelorette party!"

"No." I hold my hands up putting the brakes on her plan before it's even fully formed.

"Yes." She tuts. "You only get married once." *Here's to hoping, anyway.* Her smile is wide and excited. "Looks like we'll be attending a Chippendales show after all."

Once she gets started, Julia is like a rolling freight train. She clutches her phone in one hand, tablet in the other. Every once in a while she stops, scribbles something down on her notepad, and then gets back to planning my 'big day' as she's taken to calling it.

"Don't worry," she assures. "I got this."

Smiling, I nod my head in agreement.

That makes one of us.

OLIVER

"So, Mr. Pensen, what do you think?" Joshua Billows from LMG, Inc. asks, looking directly at me.

Huh? Thankfully, I don't mutter the word aloud, but it doesn't change the fact that I haven't a clue what he or his associate has said this entire meeting. Charli occupies every available nook and cranny of my mind. She is going to be my wife in less than twenty-four hours. I wish it were in less than twenty-four *seconds*.

"We're impressed with the investment strategy, and the bonuses are generous," Jimbo answers smoothly, masking my inattention. "But I have to advise Mr. Pensen to consult legal counsel to review the finer details."

Joshua's partner, let's call him Josh #2 since I've already forgotten his name, nods before speaking. "Yes, of course." He closes the thick manila folder on the table in front of him. "But please keep in mind these documents are time sensitive." Josh #1 and Josh #2 pin me with their gazes. "We'll need your decision within the next forty-eight hours."

When I don't immediately respond—I wonder what Charli's doing right this second. Probably picking out her wedding dress—

Jimbo answers again, "That shouldn't be a problem." Jimbo discreetly kicks my foot under the table. "Right, Mr. Pensen?"

I cough once to clear my throat. "You'll have my decision by then." Decision for what, though, I have no idea.

"Great." Josh #1 smiles and extends his hand first to me, then to Jimbo. "Thank you for your time gentlemen. We look forward to a long, prosperous relationship."

Josh #2 follows behind and shakes each of our hands before walking us to the exit.

Once the conference room door closes, Jimbo turns narrowed eyes on me. "What the fuck, Oliver?"

"What?" I shrug.

"You're asking *what*?" Jimbo repeats. "Since when did you decide *not* to show up to business meetings?" *Since Charlotte agreed to marry me.* "Did you prepare at all?" *No.* He fans the papers in his hands. "Look over the contracts?" Again, that'd be a *no*.

"Jesus," he hisses, but his voice loses some of its initial anger. "You're one whipped son of a bitch."

Maybe. But so fucking what?

"Look these over before tonight." He slams the folder into my chest. "I think it's a good opportunity. I'd take the deal, but you need to get an attorney to verify the royalty payment schedule." He shrugs. "I guess you're planning to talk to him anyway to set up the pre-nup."

My nose wrinkles. "Pre-nup?"

The *what the fuck?* look plastered across his face is almost comical. "You're joking right?"

I jerk my chin but say nothing.

"You seriously can't be considering marrying Charli without a prenuptial agreement." He shakes his head. "You *know* what I went through with Katelyn. That bitch got half of my 401k and stock options, plus I'm paying alimony for *seven years*." His voice turns angrier with each second that passes. "You wanted one with Ainsley and that was *before* this deal came along."

Ainsley was different.

He continues, louder, "Do you have any idea how much money you'll be making? The bonuses alone are north of a million dollars. You need to think with your head, not your dick."

"Fuck you!" I spit, grabbing his shirt, my anger flowing red hot. How dare he insinuate Charli is with me for my money? How dare he even suggest that she's anything like his gold-digging ex? "You have some nerve." I shove him hard, releasing my grip. "I thought you liked Charli."

"I *love* Charli." He straightens his tie. "It's not a question of liking her. It's a matter of protecting your assets. I'd suggest the same to her if she were in your position." I narrow my eyes at the role reversal because we both know she's not. "Be pissed at me all you want. I don't fucking care. I'm being a good friend."

I grunt, some of my anger dissipating. "I appreciate it, Jimbo. I honestly do, *but* I trust Charli. She'd never take a dime from me. Hell, she didn't even want me to buy her plane ticket and I used my fucking airline miles. She's independent."

He nods, the fight leaving him because he knows me long enough to know that I won't change my mind. Stubborn is a word used to describe me more often than not.

"All right." He claps my back. "But let the record reflect that I tried to warn you."

"Agreed." I nod my head as we make our way to the elevators.

"Bunny's Club and beer tonight?"

I suppress a groan. Jimbo knows strip clubs aren't my favorite places in the world, but we already blew through two grand last night in the poker tournament. And tonight *is* my bachelor party. Besides, it's not like Charli is available. She's adhering to the silly superstition and refuses to see me until tomorrow. Until the wedding. *Our wedding.*

And I can only imagine what antics Julia has planned for them this evening.

"Sure," I agree just as the elevator doors ping open. "I'm down for whatever."

The music in Bunny's is loud but low enough to carry on a conversation if you really focus. Jimbo and I are on our second beer when I ask, "So what's the deal with you and Julia anyway?"

Jimbo arches a brow. "No deal. We're just having fun."

Fun. Riiiggghttt. Jimbo and I've been friends since we were sixteen years old—fuck, has it really been twenty-two years? #GodDamnWe'reOld—and he's never been one for casual sex. He's a serial monogamist. He's had three girlfriends his entire life. He finds a girl he likes and dates the shit out of her. But maybe his divorce has changed him?

"She's wild as hell." Jimbo tips his beer bottle to his lips and takes a long pull. "She *loves* to fuck, does this thing with her tongue that, holy shit, feels incredible." He chuckles, then asks, "How are things with Charli?"

Translation: How's the sex?

Amazing. Mind-blowing. Hot as fuck. *The best I've ever had.*

"None of your fucking business."

He laughs again. "Sounds about right."

A waitress in a cut out bra saunters over, her tray stacked with two shots. "Compliments of Joshua Billows form LMG."

My eyes scan the room in search of his suit but I come up short. "He's not here." Her voice drips with sex. "But he put in a special call to give you a little extra *attention*." She winks and shimmies her hips. Jimbo whistles. I bristle.

"Not interested," I say, inching back in the low chair.

"Come on." Jimbo's eyes move from the girl's tits to her eyes. "It's this man's bachelor party." He claps a hand on my shoulder, shaking me a bit.

"Oh." The girl giggles, setting the tray on the table behind her. "Even better. She motions with one hand to another girl in an equal state of undress. "Veronica, we have a bachelor on our hands."

The girl—Veronica—approaches and together they tag team me. Veronica's ass is in my lap, the waitress's tits are in my face.

And, yes, if you're wondering, I *am* hard. Because I'm a guy...and it's ass and tits and naked skin.

But it's not what I want. *They're* not who I think about as they bump and grind or lick and kiss each other. As the song fades, their attention turns to Jimbo. Silently, I count the minutes until we can leave this club, until tomorrow night... Because the only stripper I want is *Laney Vine*.

CHARLI

"You look beautiful, Charlotte." Julia fluffs my dress even though it's unnecessary. I chose a simple off-white satin mermaid style gown. It hugs my curves nicely, but the slight flare of the material at the bottom offsets my midsection.

I've been primped and preened to near perfection. I've chosen to wear my hair down because Oliver likes it that way. The stylist painstakingly curled each tendril with precision. My mane is shiny and smells like the fresh grapefruit shampoo used in the salon. My blue eyes sparkle, contrasting with the dark liner rimming them. And although I was extremely reluctant, I'm glad I agreed to wear the false eyelashes. *I look like I could be a make-up model for Revlon.*

My toes and fingernails are shined and polished. And I was even able to get a last minute appointment with the aesthetician. I'm not a fan of waxing—it hurts and it's hella awkward having a complete stranger *that close* to your lady parts—but for my wedding, I made an exception. Let's just say, Oliver is in for a surprise.

A fist raps on the closed door in the small back room of the chapel. It's been not quite fifteen minutes since we were cloistered inside, but in reality, it feels more like fifteen hours. A light, warm voice speaks, "They're ready for you."

I inhale a deep breath. *Here we go.*

Julia opens the door and steps aside allowing me to pass first. We both wait as the coordinator, Martha, explains what happens next. Julia will go to the altar and then move to the left. Once I hear the music—I chose "Here Comes the Bride", clichéd I know, but whatever—I begin my procession. Oliver and Jimbo are already waiting with the officiant. I'm to ignore the photographer and videographer until instructed otherwise. They will take candids and video during the ceremony. We will pose for photos afterward.

Martha speaks again, "Any questions?"

Can you repeat that all one more time? "No."

She smiles. "Good luck and congratulations."

I've barely said thank you before Julia is ushered forward. She looks back at me one last time, smiles, and mouths *good luck.*

Faster than humanly possible, the organ notes begin to filter through the chapel. There's no pause and no shuffle of noise as the congregation rises to their feet, because there are no guests. Just me, walking slowly, praying to God I don't trip in these ridiculously high heels.

My eyes find and lock on Oliver's. Almost instantly, my anxiety calms. This whole idea may be insane, but at least we're in it together.

Oliver is handsome, dapper, in a dark grey suit with a dark purple tie. *My favorite color.* He's clean-shaven and his hair is styled. Not slicked back, per se, but it's more groomed than I've ever seen it.

He smiles, his eyes holding mine as I approach. When I stop at the altar the music fades and I hand my bouquet to Julia. Oliver turns to me, clasping both my hands in his.

He mouths "You look gorgeous."

I smile, then turn toward the officiant as the ceremony begins. It's standard procedure. We didn't pick our verses, write our own vows, or pick our songs. But none of that matters. In fact, I don't hear one word of the ceremony. All I see, all I hear, all I *am* is Oliver. His smile. His eyes that tell me he's as happy as I am. The whispered words of love and praise: *I love you. I'm so lucky. I can't believe you're mine.*

With shaky fingers we exchange our rings. They're simple white gold bands engraved with our initials and dates. They couldn't be more perfect.

"I now pronounce you husband and wife," The officiant's voice booms with cheer. "You may now kiss the bride."

And kiss me he does.

"Where are you taking me?" I tug at the tie Oliver wrapped around my eyes as soon as the limo door closed behind us. *A limo.* I've never ridden in one, not even for prom, and I was more than a little excited. Grew even more excited when Oliver pushed the button to raise the privacy screen. Panties became wet when he slowly unknotted his tie before slipping it from his neck, eyes pinned to mine the entire time.

Where was this going? I didn't care. I freaking liked it. A lot.

"It's a surprise," he scolds, shifting the silky fabric back into place.

"I don't do well with surprises."

He clucks his tongue. "I noticed."

I can feel the car slowing, rolling to a stop, just as Oliver says, "We're here."

I yank at the fabric again. "Can you take this off of me now?"

"Nope." The rush of air hits my bare arms as the car door opens. I sit, blindfolded, as Oliver gets out, wraps a hand around my forearm, and guides me out.

"I got you," he says in my ear, holding me close as we walk slowly. With my vision gone, my other senses are sharpened. Wherever we are, it's noisy. Loud. The sound of heels hitting concrete, voices murmuring, cell phones beeping. A sweet fragrance permeates the air. It smells like street-roasted nuts. Oliver guides me along as we continue walking. And then it's cool and quiet.

Oliver speaks a few hushed words to someone I can't see. I assume the person is a male, because of the pungent cologne that wafts into my nostrils. We begin walking again, but it's not long until we stop once more. He turns me in his arms and I feel his body move in front of me. His hands glide through my hair as he loosens the tie. It falls away slowly and he commands. "Open your eyes."

Even though the light is dim I squint after being submerged in darkness. Slowly, I realize where he's taken me. To the Venetian Hotel. *To Venice.* "Oh my God."

He smiles. "It's not Italy"—he pauses and gestures with his hands—"but it's the best I could do on short notice."

"It's perfect," I mutter, enamored. The Grand Canal, even if fake, is awe-inspiring. From the painted ceiling frescos, to the curved dark wooden gondola, to the black and white striped shirt of the gondolier. I turn to face Oliver, my eyes wide with wonder and awe and *love*. "I can't believe you did this."

He gives my hand a squeeze. "I'd do anything for you."

My lower lip trembles. I. Will. Not. Cry. I will not ruin my beautiful makeup that cost almost as much as my dress. Even if this moment is the happiest I've ever been. Even if I feel like my life is just about to begin. Even if my heart bursts with gratitude that *this* is my real life.

He releases my hand. "After you, Mrs. Pensen."

Mrs. Pensen.

I'm Mrs. Pensen.

I'm Oliver's wife.

Lifting the hem of my dress I slowly get into the boat. Both Oliver and the gondolier—*Giuseppe* his name tag reads, though I doubt it's his *real* name—steady me. Oliver climbs in next, sliding beside me before wrapping me in his arms.

The next half-hour can only be described as whimsical. I feel like Princess Jasmine on Aladdin's magic carpet. My whole world is shrunk to this moment, this place. It's just Oliver and me. And

Giuseppe. But Giuseppe is situated at the back of the boat, sere-
nading us in Italian, so he I'll let him stay.

We pass many shops and storefronts. There's a chilled bottle of
wine, uncorked and ready to be poured, but I don't touch it. I want
to fully be in this moment, to remember everything. Because this
moment, right here right now, is *perfection*.

Oliver doesn't stop touching me. His fingers play with my curls.
"You wore your hair down."

"Mmm," I hum, eyes closing in pleasure as his touch moves
along my neck, becoming more sensual as his fingertip ghosts along
my collarbone.

"You look so beautiful, Charlotte." His lips graze my ear, his hot
breath searing my flesh. "Every night, but *especially* tonight."

"Thank you." I whisper, not only thanking him for the compliment but for everything—the trip to Las Vegas, the gondola ride,
marrying me.

The gondola's pace slows as we round a curve, passing under a
miniature replica of the Rialto Bridge. Oliver grabs me, holds my
face, and kisses me passionately. Slow. Long. Wet. When he pulls
away, I'm breathless.

"Legend says that if you kiss under the Rialto Bridge, your love
will last forever."

My whole body smiles at the sentiment. *Oliver* is *a closet
romantic*. I lean in, my lips a hair's breadth away from his and
murmur, "Well then, we better do it one more time, just to be sure."

OLIVER

CHARLI GASPS as I carry her over the threshold to our suite. It's the most luxurious, most romantic suite the Venetian offers. With Jimbo and Julia's help, our suitcases are waiting for us inside the wide foyer. The Venetian isn't Italy—not even close—but it serves as a promise of what's to come. Our life together. The adventures that await.

"I can't believe this room." Her eyes survey the space as I set her down gently on her feet. She stands still, marveling at the ornate wallpaper, the sleek mahogany furniture, the dish of chocolate-covered strawberries decorated in matching tuxedos and gowns of white and dark chocolate. Vases of fresh cut lilies line the marble counter.

She continues into the bedroom to where the plush, over-sized comforter is turned down. Rose petals form a heart across the width of the mattress. "Wow." Her fingers skim the flowers. She turns in place and it's then that she notices the candle-lit terrace. Her mouth opens and closes, but no sound comes out.

She's in motion within an instant. I follow her onto the balcony, where a large canopy with gauzy sheets that billow in the soft breeze covers an oversized chaise lounge that's adorned with dozens of taupe and light blue pillows in varying shapes and sizes.

This is worth every penny. I'm not talking about the tumbled marble tiles zigzagging across the patio or the wrought iron bistro set with a fresh plate of fruit and chilled bottle of champagne or the dozens of tea candles that cast the space in a warm glow. It *is* beautiful, straight out of a magazine if I'm honest. But what captures my attention, what makes the space really shine is Charli.

Her face lights up like a kid in a candy store. Curious blue eyes draw to the Jacuzzi hot tub. Wisps of hot steam feather the air as the water bubbles to the surface interrupting the quiet night air.

Charli's head turns toward me. "I love hot tubs," she says matter-of-factly.

Good to know. Her hand skims the sleek marble edge of the tub as she continues, "There's something about being naked in water. The heat on my skin, so slippery and smooth, it's just so..."

Christ. Just so...what? I'm dying for her to finish that sentence.

"Sexy."

Fuck yeah, *she* is.

Charlotte stands facing me for a moment longer before she slowly begins to slide the straps of her dress down her shoulders. My eyes, wide with shock, hold her confident yet vulnerable stare.

Is she really undressing? Out here? On the balcony?

It's a penthouse suite, mostly shielded, but still. We aren't ensured complete privacy. But fuck if it isn't kind of hot.

Her sultry tone caresses my skin. "Help me with the zipper?" She gives me her back and it takes a moment too long for my brain to command my feet to move.

One hand grazes her shoulder as the other wraps around the pull of the zipper, tugging it down slowly. Once the back of the dress is all way open, I bring my lips to her nape and plant a kiss there. I feel a rush of satisfaction when a shiver ripples through her. My mouth trails a path of kisses along her spine, stopping only when I reach the curve of her ass.

She drops her hands by her sides and the dress falls away

completely. I reach my hand out to steady her as she steps out of it. Holding her at arm's length, I allow my greedy eyes to assess her, to study every inch of her perfect body.

Starting at toes painted pale pink, to the curve of her toned calf muscles, up silky, strong thighs that I know from experience feel incredible wrapped around my head, to the juncture between her legs. White lace panties, pure as the driven snow, with one word stitched in pale blue across the small triangle of fabric: *bride* make my dick harder than I ever thought possible. I groan loudly, not caring in the slightest if anyone can hear me.

Tearing my eyes away, I force my gaze upward. Over her soft stomach and cute belly button, to the curve below her breasts and finally over the thin white material that encases the world's fullest, roundest, *most perfect* breasts. Her left hand rests flat against her chest, right against her heart, and the reflection of candlelight from the thin band catches my eyes.

She's wearing *my* ring. Charlotte Ann Truse is mine. Forever.

Full, plump lips stained a crimson red draw my attention when she speaks, voice low and husky, "Join me?"

Before I can respond she turns away and begins climbing the three low steps that lead into the tub.

Fuck. Fuck. *Fuck.*

She's wearing a thong. Her round, juicy, meaty ass is on full display.

I'm like a dog in heat, tearing off my clothes, stripping and sprinting to join her all at the same time. Stark naked in less than ten seconds flat I lower myself into the tub, nestling my body next to hers.

The water is hot, hotter than I expected, but I don't hiss my displeasure or complain. No. Because it has turned Charlotte's bra *transparent*. Her nipples, pebbled and hard, push through the fabric, *begging* for my mouth. I happily oblige.

When my lips latch onto one nipple and suck, hard, she throws her head back and moans, "Oliver."

I don't respond, mouth much too busy lavishing her beautiful tits. It's too much and not enough. I want all of her.

Her hands spear my hair, positioning my head exactly where she wants me. And I love it. Love that she gives in to her pleasure. Gets lost in. Revels in it.

Working one hand below the water, I trace my finger along her seam once before flicking her sensitive clit.

"Oh my God," she groans as both my hands latch around her waist before sliding her panties down her legs. As I drag her onto my lap, she bands her legs around me, and I slowly begin to glide her over my cock. The feeling is unreal, soft and so goddam slippery that I think I may come. *This is amazing.* Why the fuck haven't I done it before?

But when I glance down I'm greeted with real reason this feels sublime. She's bare. Smooth as a fucking baby's bottom. And just as soft. Her pussy lips plump and full hug my cock as I glide her up and down. Down and up. The swollen mushroom head of my cock hits her engorged clit. Every. Single. Time.

"Oliver." She bites her bottom lip. "Oh my God. That feels amazing."

Knowing she's close, I pick up the pace and give her more of what she wants. My mouth drops to one breast while the fingers of one hand toy with the other. Her body stiffens, teeth clench, and her fingernails pierce my skin. She shatters a moment later with a long, low scream.

Before she can come down I pull her to stand and bend her over the side of the tub. The cool night air on our heated skin makes every touch, every stroke, every nerve oversensitive. Not able to resist any longer, I lean forward and take a bite of her ass.

She yelps in surprise.

"Goddamn, Charli. I *love* this ass." I slap her once. Testing. She shrieks when I slap her a second time, harder. Pulling her cheeks apart, I bend and bury my face, swirl my tongue in slow circle, tasting her tight bud. She clenches at first, resisting, but when I dip my finger forward, sliding inside her soaked pussy, she softens. Literally. She slides forward, a loose pile of muscle and bone. I have to wrap my forearm around her waist to prevent her from collapsing.

Encouraged, my tongue becomes bolder, darting inside. The moan of pleasure that escapes her can only be described as guttural. *She likes it.* "Fuck, Oliver. Oh my fucking God."

I pull away, bite the other cheek this time before pushing her down to kneel on the bench seat. This height affords me the perfect angle to enter her from behind *as well as* allow the jet to stimulate her clit.

From the moment I enter her in one full, smooth thrust, she spasms. Her pulses, along with the vibrations from the oscillating jets, make my balls ache. Full and heavy, I'm ready to blow. *Now.* But I hold back, wanting to extend the pleasure.

Slowing the pace, I steady myself with my hands on her hips. But Charli is having none of it. She arches her back, takes me deeper still, before reaching her hand between us to cradle my balls. She rolls them once, gently, encouraging them to spill their seed. Steeling my nerves, I grit my teeth, and continue to pump into her not giving in to the temptation.

I lose my mind, however, when her finger slides farther back. Long, firm strokes trace between my sac and ass. *Holy fucking shit.* I'm done. *Done.*

"Charlotte." Her name tears from my lips as a tidal wave of pleasure rips through me. My breath catches, my toes curl, balls swell, and then I'm emptying into her. Everything I am. Everything I have. Everything I will ever be. She owns it. Completely and forever.

As though she were waiting for my release, her body seizes, the tremors gripping and clutching as they move through her. She pulses, clamps my dick with such force, I feel like I'm coming *again*. Her body milks me. Demands more. And I give it to her. Open hearted and willing.

"*Jesus,*" I hiss, gently sliding out. Reaching for her, I turn her and cradle her in my arms. When we're chest to chest, I lift her out of the water, carry her to the chaise, and lay her flat among the bed of pillows.

Sopping wet and naked, I cover her body with mine, press myself to her. Head to head. Heart to heart. Toe to toe. I've never felt more connected to another person in my entire life.

I kiss her eyelids, her cheeks. Then I pause at her beauty mark and whisper, "I love you, Charlotte."

Her voice is dreamy. "I love you too."

My lips explore every inch of her body as I make love to her once more. This time slowly, sensually, offering myself to her. It's vulnerable and raw, but also safe and soothing. The comfort in knowing she's *my* person. And always will be.

We fall asleep bodies woven together like the intricate tapestries that line the walls, a tangle of hair, limbs, and pillows. It couldn't be more perfect.

CHARLI

OUR VACATION, or should I say our honeymoon, is over much too soon. I want

nothing more than to stay locked away in our massive suite gorging ourselves on delicious food, making love, falling asleep, only to do it all over it again.

The one silver lining? As a wedding present Jim upgraded all of our plane tickets to first class so the flight back home wouldn't suck. As much. First class is a privilege I never experienced before. Not only because I couldn't afford the higher fare, but mainly because I didn't travel often.

Jim and Julia take their seats a few aisles back as Oliver and I nestle into ours. The chairs are large and comfy—well, as comfortable as chairs on a plane can be, I guess—and I can fully stretch my legs without my knees bumping the seat in front of me. #Winning

We watch the safety video, taxi the runway, and takeoff. After several minutes the plane must reach cruising altitude because the "fasten seatbelts" sign is no longer illuminated. That, plus the attendants begin to move throughout the cabin.

I hear her voice before I see her face. "Good afternoon, would you like—" Ainsley voice cuts off abruptly as her eyes first collide with mine, then Oliver's.

Shit. I'm certain I have a deer caught in the headlights look. For how much I worried about running into Ainsley on the flight out, seeing her on the way home never even crossed my mind. Blame it on good food, amazing sex, or a combination of the two.

Ainsley's gaze drops, jumps from the thin band on my left hand to Oliver's. Her voice is shrill, unreasonably loud in the relatively quiet cabin. "You're *married?*"

Oliver loops his hand with mine as he brings his eyes to meet hers. "Yes."

"Wh-when?" she stammers, voice confused. She shakes her head once as though to clear it.

His words are soft. "Does it matter?"

Ainsley turns to me, voice dripping with accusation. "Is she pregnant?"

Of course she'd think I was knocked up.

Then to Oliver, "I thought you didn't want kids."

"Ainsley, please." His voice is firmer, warning her to not press further.

She closes her eyes as she gathers her composure. When her eyes open again, she finds mine. "Congratulations." Is she congratulating me on the wedding or the theoretical baby? I can't be sure and I don't want to ask.

"Thank y-you," I stammer, my heart splitting in two. For her. If the roles were reversed, if I lost Oliver to Ainsley, I wouldn't, *I couldn't*, congratulate her. Maybe that says a lot about my character, proves Ainsley is a better person than me. But imagining Ainsley or any other woman married to Oliver? Carrying his child? *I can't.*

Her attention drifts back to Oliver and she adds almost as an afterthought, "I'm seeing someone."

The smile that stretches across Oliver's lips is warm and genuine. "I'm glad, Ains."

"Okay, well." She nods. "I think it's best if I switch sections with another attendant."

I raise both hands in the air and wave them like I just don't care. *Agreed.*

Well, that's what happened in my mind, anyway.

"You don't have to do that." Oliver squeezes my hand once before asking, "We're good, right?"

I murmur my agreement, but Ainsley shakes her head. "It's not a problem." She turns toward her cart before looking back one last time. "Goodbye, Oliver."

And then she's gone.

Even though we don't see Ainsley for the rest of the flight, her words still bounce around in my head. *I thought you didn't want kids.*

"Baby." Oliver's lips brush against my cheek. "What's wrong?"

I shrug, unsure how or if I should bring it up. Thirty thousand feet in the air with a couple hundred strangers doesn't seem like the most appropriate time for such a serious conversation. But then again...I can't let it go.

Turning to face him, I keep my voice low and ask. "You don't want kids?"

His smile fades and he leans back in his chair. "I never said that."

Remaining quiet, I nod. "But Ainsley did." Another long sixty seconds of silence passes before I ask, "Do you?" I clarify, "Want kids?"

One hand tears through his hair. "I did. *I do.*" His eyes find mine. "Ainsley didn't want them and when we were together, when I thought we were..." His voice peters out and I fill in the words that he doesn't say: *when I thought she would be my wife.* He continues, "I wasn't going to waste time hoping, wishing for something that wasn't going to happen."

I nod again, listening to his words, even if they are hard to hear. "And now?"

"And now." He clasps both hands in mine. "Now I want everything. The house. The kids. The dog." His eyes hold mine as he keeps speaking, each word hitting my heart, "But more than anything, I just want you."

"You have me," I whisper. "I'm yours."

"Then I'm happy."

"Me too, Oliver." I press my lips to his. "Me too."

CHARLI - EPILOGUE

The aftermath

Oliver and I settle into a routine. *Our* routine. It's simple, boring really. I love waking up next to him every morning wrapped in his arms almost as much as he loves coming home from work and having me there. On nights when he works late, I curl up on the chaise in the den, reading or more often than not, sleeping. On early nights I join him in the kitchen, perch myself on the counter to chat while he prepares our dinner. He calls me his beautiful, sexy distraction, and if I'm honest, he's burned more dinner in the past twelve weeks than he has his entire life.

I'm *not* complaining.

Exactly eight weeks ago we had our first *big* fight. We'd—or more accurately I—had been hunting for a new house. Once we got back from Vegas I moved into Oliver's place. I liked his house, and given any other circumstance I probably would have *loved* it, but it was the house he shared with Ainsley. I'm not petty or materialistic or territorial, but I wanted a place that felt like *ours*. One we chose *and* bought together.

"I think I found one that you'll love." The excitement bubbled in my voice as I twirled noodles around my fork.

The dinner Oliver prepared that night was quick yet delicious: bucatinni a la Bolognese paired with a fresh garden salad tossed in a homemade raspberry vinaigrette.

"Really?" he asked, but his excitement felt forced.

"Yeah. It was just listed today. And the pictures, Oliver. The kitchen is *huge*.

There's even a wood burning stone fireplace and hearth for cooking." His lack of reaction only further fueled my suspicion: He wasn't listening. "Did you hear what I just said?"

"I'm sorry, baby." He exhaled a loud breath. "I'm exhausted. Don is driving me insane with all of the last minute menu changes."

I knew he was sorry, tired, burnt out, but in the heat of the moment I didn't want to hear his excuses or his apology. I was tired too. Mecca was booked solid, I was saddled with training, Jacob, the new manager at La Conquistadora, all while hunting for houses. Something Oliver and I should be doing *together*.

Not to mention the blowup with my parents happened just three short days prior.

Now that's a moment worth reliving.

Not.

My parents didn't take the news of my marriage well. At all.

Oliver insisted on accompanying me to their house, despite the fact that I encouraged him not to. I wouldn't say my parents and I have a *close* relationship but close or not, their first-born getting married on a whim, without so much as a phone call? Yeah, I had a feeling our announcement would go over about as well as a lead balloon. In other words, I wasn't holding my breath for congratulations.

Julia came along too for moral support.

I drew the line at Jim. The encounter was already bound to be a shit show. The less witnesses there were, the better.

Although my mom's smile was wide and cheerful as she ushered us into the living room, her drawn, furrowed brows belied her confusion. My dad sat in his worn leather recliner, his favorite mug resting on the end table beside him.

Not one to delay the inevitable, I blurted, "So I'm married now." I held up Oliver and my clasped hands.

My mother gasped, her hand flying to cover her mouth as she murmured. "What?"

I softened my tone as I turned to her. "I'm married."

Tears, of what I hope were joy, flooded my mom's eyes. "When?"

"A few days ago. In Vegas."

My mother's eyes darted from me to Oliver before she asked, "I thought you said it was a business trip?"

"It was." *Oliver's business trip.*

My mom shook her head. "I don't understand."

After another awkward moment of silence, my father demanded an answer to the question I knew was coming even before he opened his mouth. "Are you pregnant?"

"No sir," Oliver, thankfully, answered for me, his head shaking with disgust. "This wasn't a shotgun wedding. I love Charlotte."

Ours was the very definition of a shotgun wedding. I kept my mouth shut.

"Then, why?" My dad's voice boomed, eyes narrowed on mine. "Why rush into marriage? I didn't even know you were dating anyone."

"I know it's quick, Dad—"

"Quick?" His voice boomed with so much force I swear the windows rattled.

"Quick? You married a complete stranger, have the nerve to bring him into *my* house, and expect me to welcome him to the family?" His eyes raked over Oliver, condescension etched into every feature as he dismissed him as nothing more than a nuisance before turning to me. "We raised you better than this!"

Finally, my mother found her voice again, soft and forgiving, as she tried to smooth things over. It's what she always did as the resident family peacekeeper. "Your father's right, honey." She patted my arm as she turned to Oliver. "I'm sorry, what did you say your name was again?"

"Oliver," I answered for him, chest puffed with indignation. "Oliver Pensen."

"Pensen," my dad repeated the name as though trying to place it. It took less than a minute for him to make the connection. "You married your boss?" His voice rose at the end, incredulous.

Oliver leaned forward, but my hand on his arm held him back. Keeping my voice as even as I could given the circumstances, I said, "He's not my boss."

My dad snorted and my mom began talking to divert the conversation. "Why rush into things, honey? You're young. You have your whole life ahead of you. You have plenty of time."

"Time for what?" Julia's question surprised me. "What will that prove? You dated dad for over two years before you married and look how that turned out."

My mother reeled as if Julia had slapped her. My father's face turned redder, angrier. My mouth hung open. It's true that we knew about our father's affairs, but never once, in all the years, has anyone ever spoken of or acknowledged them aloud.

Upon seeing the tears form in my mother's eyes, Julia recanted, "I'm sorry. I shouldn't have said that."

My father, red-faced and angry, turned to Oliver. "I give it a year." With that he stormed outside, the screen door slamming.

My mom, open-mouthed and wide eyed, apologized to us both on his behalf. "I'm sorry." She twisted her hands in front of her. "It's a shock, is all. Give him time."

So, yeah, things between my parents and I weren't exactly peachy. Julia assured me they'd come around. Just yesterday she told me that my mom mentioned hosting a party to celebrate our wedding.

Oliver's fork scraping against his plate drew me back to the moment and for some crazy reason that I couldn't explain it annoyed the shit out of me. Maybe it was the fact that I had been working twelve plus hour days or that Oliver and I hadn't seen each other much the past two weeks, but I snapped.

"I'm tired too." I griped. "You're not the only one burning the candle at both ends. *I* work too. I'm the one whose life has been uprooted. I'm looking for a house plus dealing with my family's drama on top of everything." I huffed a breath. "A little help would be nice."

He pushed away from the table and strode toward the sink, before dropping his plate. "You're the one who wants a new house." He opened his arms wide. "We have a house."

It was absolutely the wrong thing to say.

I was on my feet in an instant. "No!" I screamed. "*You* have a house. I don't have anything." It was the truth. I'd terminated my lease almost as soon as we got back from our trip, I didn't own a car, didn't have much furniture to speak of, and had twelve hundred dollars in my checking and savings accounts combined. If I thought about it too long or too hard, it terrified me.

"Charlotte." He groaned, voice agitated. "What do you want from me? You know what's mine is yours."

Easy for him to say. He was the one with multi-million dollar contracts and endorsement deals, was the face of a new restaurant, and a property owner. I felt shitty for resenting his success, and if I'm honest, I didn't. I was *scared*. Afraid this was all a dream. That I'd blink my eyes and everything would be gone. He would be gone. So I lashed out. Tried to ruin things, hurt him, before he could hurt me.

I stormed up beside him, tossing my dish into the sink with so much force the edge chipped. "Maybe this was all a mistake."

A strong arm banded around my waist before I was able to put even two feet of distance between us. "What did you say?" His hot, angry breath raced through my veins. "What. Did. You. Say."

But I wasn't brave—or stupid—enough to repeat the words.

"You think this is a mistake?" His head dipped as sharp teeth pressed along the delicate skin of my neck. "That *we're* a mistake?"

"Oliver." My voice broke as his palms splayed my ribcage,

sealing my back against his front. The hard planes of his body were causing my brain to short circuit.

In an instant I was in the air, carried roughly to the formal living room, and deposited not so gracefully on the closed lid of his beloved baby grand piano.

"Wh-what are you doing?" I asked, voice low, although it was more than obvious based on the sinful look burning his eyes and the tight set of his jaw clenched with anticipation.

"Showing you how much of a mistake I am."

He then proceeded to give me some of the best orgasms of my life. Yes, orgasms. As in more than one, multiple, many, abundant... He didn't stop. Wouldn't stop. He brought me to the edge over and over again, each time begging me to defy him, to utter the words that I threatened earlier in the heat of the moment. But I couldn't, even if I would have had control of my mental faculties. Because the truth is, we were made for each other. Another truth? *Pretty Woman* sex is pretty amazing. That Julia Roberts sure knows what she's doing.

Our bid on the house was accepted. The one with the stone fireplace and fenced-in yard and huge eat-in kitchen. After the amazing *Pretty Woman* makeup sex, Oliver *really* looked at the listing. We made an appointment with our relator for the next morning, submitted our offer that afternoon, and two days later, it was accepted.

Three months after that, we moved in. We're still settling in, still unpacking lesser-used items from boxes that fill one of our three spare bedrooms. The main areas of the house are decorated in a style that fits both of our personalities. The home looks lived in, homey—like a family lives here. Above the fireplace is a framed picture of my favorite shot of Oliver and me from our wedding. It was taken as we walked down the aisle, just after we were officially pronounced man and wife. My eyes face the camera, but his are on me. We're both smiling, drunk on each other. Drunk in love.

"Hey." Oliver's arms wrap around me from behind as I finish loading the last bowl into the dishwasher. "Everything ready?"

"Yeah." I lean against him. "I can't believe I agreed to this."

He chuckles. "It was *your* idea."

"I had to offer to host." I sigh. "It was either that or allow my mom to plan an entire wedding party, complete with cake and dancing, and that would have been disastrous. She can get a little carried away." I turn in his embrace. "We're killing two birds with one stone."

He raises his eyebrows and I continue, "House warming and wedding? Done." I smile. "Genius, right?"

His lips graze mine. "I knew I married you for a reason."

"Just one?" I tease.

"One of many."

Giggling, I say, "That's better."

He silences me with a long, slow kiss that makes my knees weak and my panties damp. When we finally break apart, I say, "I'm excited to finally meet Margot and Sara."

He rolls his eyes in dramatic fashion. "You talk to her enough online." He kisses the tip of my nose. "I'm starting to think she likes you more than me."

"Maybe." I chuckle. "We're both devout pledgees of the 'One Less Straw' Movement after all." I skim my nails down his chest. "What time are your parents getting in?"

"Dad's picking Margot up at the airport at three, and I think my mom said her train arrives at five." He leans away from me, his brow furrowing. "Speaking of parents, are you nervous to see your dad?"

"A little bit." I admit. My mom has visited multiple times and really warmed up to Oliver. They bonded over talk of the best non-cooking sprays and the rest is history. I've even caught them texting a time or two.

My dad is a harder sell. In my gut, I know he likes Oliver. He's just upset—or maybe offended is a better word—that we didn't include him in our wedding. He took it personally, even though I assured him it was unplanned. Our intention wasn't to hurt anyone. But my dad did help us with the move, even offered to drive the rental truck. It was big step, and a really, really good sign that things were moving in the right direction. No pun intended.

"Are you?" I ask, but when he raises his eyebrows in question, I clarify. "Worried about seeing my dad?"

"Not at all." His voice is so cocky, self-assured, that I wonder why I bothered to ask. He exhales, resting his palms along my back, holding me close. "I understand where your dad's coming from."

This is news to me. "You do?"

"Yeah," he says. "You're his daughter. I'm the guy who took you away. I

can't imagine losing you would be easy."

I give him a *you're crazy* look, but he continues, "I couldn't do it." His eyes hold mine as he clarifies, "Lose you."

My breath catches at the intensity of his words, the seriousness laced in his voice. "You couldn't?" I ask, breathless.

"Never." He shakes his head. "I'd die first."

"So you think we'll last more than a year?" I purposefully keep my tone light, but the truth is, my dad's prediction cut deep. What if he's right?

"Add a couple of zeros to that, baby."

"So like ten or a hundred?" I tease.

"At least a hundred." He drags his nose along mine. "I like having you around."

"Good." I smile against his lips. "Because you're stuck with me."

"It's a good thing, then." Right as his lips find mine, just as my mouth parts to invite his tongue inside, the doorbell chimes alerting us to our first guest.

He pulls back. "To be continued?"

"Promise?"

"Always." He takes my hand in his. "Come on, Mrs. Pensen, we've got guests to greet."

"Wait." I tug his hand, halting his footsteps.

He turns to me, eyes wide with question.

I smile, pull him back into my arms, and whisper, "Five more minutes." As I drag him back to the kitchen, a naughty smile lights my face. "They can wait five more minutes."

ALSO BY CJ MARTÍN

Snowbound

A Virgin Romance

Off Key (A Wreckless Abadon Novel)

A Rockstar Romance

Knockout

A Boxing Romance

Forever Hearts

A Friends-to-Lovers Romance

Touching Down

A College Football Romance

Turn the page for an excerpt from *Forever Hearts*, a standalone, coming-of-age, friends to lovers romance.

FOREVER HEARTS: PROLOGUE

NOW...

I shower, get dressed, make it all the way to my car, before I realize that I left my cell phone in my apartment. I pat my pockets, check my purse, and glance at the dashboard to see if the Bluetooth symbol is illuminated—it isn't. I groan audibly as I switch off the ignition and rush back into the cold. It's mid-March, yet the thermometer has barely reached thirty degrees this week, and with the wind whipping through the air, the "real feel" is in the single digits.

Back inside my apartment I locate my phone on the kitchen counter, still plugged into the charger. As I pick it up, my eyes scan over several notifications, one of which is a text message from Bill.

Bill: Hi, Sweetie. Just got back from the airport with my parents. Reservations are at seven. Are you on your way?

I glance at the clock. It's five forty-five. I can make it across town with *plenty* of time to spare—I think. Bill's perpetually early, as in, if we do not arrive twenty minutes prior to the start of any function—and I do mean *any* and *every* function— he panics. He's chronically early; I'm chronically late. We balance each other out...in theory, anyway.

My thumb swipes the screen, but my fingers are too cold to register the touch, so I drop the phone and blow into my hands in an attempt to warm them up. A minute later, I type a quick message to Bill.

Riley: Omw. Left ten minutes ago.

This is an outright lie; I'm still standing in my kitchen *and* I would never text and drive. He *should* know that after nine months of dating, but he simply agrees.

Bill: Ok.

His response is simple. Quick. Efficient. Just like him.

I knock on Bill's front door *thirty* minutes later—traffic was heavier and slower than I anticipated. His mother and father are seated on the sofa. It's not the first time I'm meeting them, but every time they visit I have the feeling I should be walking on eggshells. They're prim and proper, formal, refined—the exact opposite of me.

"Mr. and Mrs. Lewg." I smile as I embrace first his father, then his mother, in the world's most awkward hug. "So good to see you."

"Lovely to see you, dear." Mrs. Lewg—Carole, though she's never told me to call her that—says. "Bill was just telling us he has a special announcement before we leave for dinner."

"Oh?" I raise my eyebrows as I turn toward Bill. My mind quickly scans over our last few conversations. I can't remember him talking about any major deal specifically, apart from the new property, but that deal closed weeks ago. All right, *okay*, I may not pay one hundred percent attention when he blabs on and on about investment properties or the price per square foot of Building A versus Building B, but can you blame me? Commercial real estate is freaking boring. Take it from me, I should know; it's all Bill ever seems to talk about.

"Riley." Bill makes no effort to move from in front of the mantle where he stands, but he extends his hand and pulls me toward him. "Can you come here for one second? There's something I want to ask you. Something I've wanted to ask you for a long time."

The smiling face of my roommate pops to mind and her words bounce around my brain. *You'll be engaged before me.* But surely that's not what this is. We haven't been together that long. I haven't even given him a key to my apartment yet. He *just* met my family.

"Riley Ann Jones." He takes both my hands, and I will myself to close my mouth, which gapes open in the most unflattering way.

Oh, shit. Oh, no. Fuck. Please don't let him be asking what I think he's going to—

"This past year..." —*nine months,* I automatically correct in my head— "has been the happiest year of my life. You're everything that I want in a life partner: smart, beautiful, kind, honest..."

I swallow. *I'm not so honest.*

He drops to one knee, looks up at me with caring brown eyes. "Would you do me the honor of becoming my wife?"

My gaze darts around the room, heart beating wildly in my chest, not from excitement, but from fear.

His mother smiles at me encouragingly, as Bill cracks open a small, velvet jewelry box. "It was my grandmother's. It's been in our family for generations. I asked my mother to bring it in with her." He waves with his free hand to where his parents sit. "It's part of the reason why they flew in early." He smiles again. "So, will you? Will you be my wife?"

Holy fuck. Bill scrunches his nose and I press my lips together, sending another silent prayer heavenward that I didn't just say *fuck* in front of his parents. In front of my (potential) future in-laws.

"Kind of waiting on an answer here, Riley." His voice jokes, but I can see the tension around his eyes.

I squeeze my eyes tight, swallow a deep breath, and nod. "Yes." My voice is the faintest of whispers. "Yes, I'll marry you."

"Wonderful!" his mother exclaims, clapping her hands in front of her chest. Bill pulls himself to his feet and slips the ring onto my left finger. It's delicate, a solitaire, round-cut stone, light and classy, but it feels like a heavy anchor pulling me down. I'm suffocating. Sinking. Drowning.

Mr. Lewg claps Bill on the back. "Congratulations, son." They shake hands as though they're business associates rather than father and son.

Bill locks eyes with me, the megawatt smile that is plastered on every billboard within a thirty-mile radius beams at me. He mouths "I love you," but all I can do is nod, because there's only one thought looping through my mind right now, and if I'm not careful, the words will escape and topple the house of cards that I've struggled to build this entire year.

Those words are on my mind throughout our indulgent, five-course meal.

They're there later that night when Bill makes love to me and tells me how happy he is.

And they're still there long after his breath has slowed and he has fallen asleep. Then, and only then, do I let the devastating truth fall past my lips:

He's not Jesse.

CHAPTER 1: RILEY

THEN...

Two words: Senior year. A tight coil of nerves, equal parts excitement and dread, sits low in my belly. My emotions run the gamut...happiness because I *finally* made it; sadness because it will all be over too soon; anticipation to see all my friends after a long three months. And Jesse.

Especially Jesse.

I run down the stairs and make a quick stop in the kitchen to grab a banana for breakfast. "'Morning, honey," my mom calls from near the sink.

"Good morning," I parrot, voice light and breathless as I glance at the clock on the microwave. *Jesse will be here in two minutes.*

"You all ready for your first day?" my dad asks, as he walks into the room with my little sister, still half asleep, nestled in his arms.

"As ready as I'll ever be." I grab my backpack from the bench alongside the front door and hoist it onto my shoulder.

A car horn blares.

"Jesse's here," my mom states, even though it's unnecessary.

Who else would be in our driveway at 7:15 a.m. on a Monday morning?

My dad sneaks in a quick hug. "Bye, kiddo."

"Good luck, honey." My mom kisses my cheek.

"Bye, Ry-Ry." Mikayla leaps into my arms. "Have fun at the big kids' school."

I squeeze my arms tighter around her. "And you have fun at the little kids' school."

I know that it's practically mandatory to *hate* your little sister—or at the very least, be annoyed by said sister—but Mikayla is twelve years younger than me, so there isn't any of the typical sibling rivalry. And when I do have to babysit her (on the rare occasion), I can't complain, because who doesn't like to watch Disney movies (although she *was* stuck on *Zootopia* for quite a while) and scarf cookie dough ice cream right from the container? Answer: no one.

The sound of the horn pierces the air again, and I rush toward the door. My entire family follows me out as though they're sending me off to boot camp for six weeks rather than sending me to school for six hours.

"Bye." I wave as I toss my bag into the backseat of Jesse's old Honda Civic. "See ya later."

"Riley." Jesse leans over the console and wraps me in his huge arms. The happiness of seeing him is only slightly overshadowed by the fact that my parents and six-year-old sister are watching us. "I've *missed* you."

I pull back and smooth my hands through my hair. "Couldn't have missed me that much." His brows wrinkle in confusion, so I continue. "You got in two days ago?" My voice rises at the end, and he nods in confirmation. "And I'm just seeing you now?" I smile to let him know I'm teasing, although I *am* a little hurt that I didn't warrant more than a quick text message indicating he was home.

Hell, we've been best friends, nearly inseparable, since we were five, and the fact that he was gone for the *entire* summer visiting his dad meant that we had a lot to catch up on.

He dips his head and scratches the back of his neck. "You know how my mom is. She took the whole weekend off work, and then we went to my grandmother's house to visit."

"In West County?" I question, surprised because his grandmother lives almost two hours away from us.

"Yep." He nods, and then smiles his beautiful smile. The one that is special, only for me. "Don't worry. I'm all yours now."

"I sure hope you mean that, because you missed *a lot* over the summer."

He puts the car in reverse, and I wave to my family one last time. "What's your schedule? What period do you have lunch?"

Even though I have my schedule memorized, I still put it up on my phone to double check. "Fifth."

"Sweet." He glances my way. "Me, too."

We pull into the school parking lot not even ten minutes later, and there are people... everywhere. For a moment I'm shocked by how much *hasn't* changed.

Teachers and principals like to babble on at the beginning of a new school year with (corny) inspirational messages such as: *New year! New you! You **can** succeed. Make good choices.* Blah. Blah. Blah. But nothing ever changes. Not really.

My eyes scan the parking lot. Rachael Trunk, Tori Weether, Heather Plum, and Melissa Riche still roll up in Rachel's flashy red Jetta. And Phillip McNorg and Bryan Traitor are still drop-dead gorgeous and two of Adams High's most popular boys. Veronica Tish and Will Feeble are still *Star Wars* obsessed, with their dark black jeans and matching white Storm Troopers t-shirts. Same cliques, different day.

I rub my sweaty palms on my own denim-clad legs and heave a deep breath. Thirteen years of school. Thirteen first days. You would think I'd be a pro by now...but I'm *not*. I'm freaking nervous as hell.

Truth: I'm not what you would consider popular. Not by any means. While the reverse is also true—I'm not *unpopular*—I'm more of a drifter. I earn good grades—it's not that I'm exceptionally smart, it's just that I actually *try* in my classes. A good chunk of my friends are what could be classified as *nerds*. But I also became good friends with several people from my yearbook class, and they'd be grouped with the *artists*.

And then there's Jesse. He's my saving grace because he *is* popular. He's friends with Phillip McNorg and Bryan Traitor. He's considered the third (and quite possibly the most) popular boy at Adams High. They're all starters on the school's varsity basketball team. And just to be clear, basketball is a *huge* deal, as in, the *entire* school attends varsity basketball games. There's a whole student pep squad dubbed "The Pack" that cheers exclusively for Phillip, Bryan, and Jesse, otherwise known as PB & J. The Adams Vikings won the state championship three years in a row. This year will make number four.

"You okay?" Jesse's hand reaches over the center console and grazes my arm.

I glance at him and nod my head. "Yeah."

"Yeah?" he questions one more time, and this time I smile to mask my nerves. "You ready to do this?"

My fingers grip the door handle and I answer the same way I did to my dad not even a half hour before. "As I'll ever be."

CHAPTER 2: RILEY

I still remember the blue T-rex t-shirt Jesse was wearing the first day we met. I was heavy into my princess phase (okay, okay, I still think Disney princesses are cool, but that's beside the point). I was playing in my green turtle sandbox, attempting to replicate Cinderella's castle. My tools were subpar, at best; I had a half-broken plastic bucket, a rake, and one slim shovel that bent every time I tried digging with it. Of course, I didn't realize any of this at the time, but I digress.

Jesse walked up my blacktop driveway, dark hair slightly frizzy, vibrant blue eyes striking against his caramel skin.

Personal note: We live in a very small town, and up until that moment, I had never seen someone with a different skin color than my own which was white, not the beautiful porcelain white of China dolls, but more like the color of dried paste.

Jesse was different. Exotic. *Beautiful.*

Even at my young age, he sparked something inside me, not sexual attraction, of course, but something deeper, as if my spirit sensed a kindred soul, that caused me to want to be near him.

"Hi." He extended his hand rather formally, but his voice was quite direct for a five year old. "I'm Jesse. Can I play with you?"

I'd barely said "Yes" before he sat down and was digging around the moat I'd created near the two lopsided spires of the castle.

He lifted my cracked, pink bucket. "This is broken."

"My daddy stepped on it," I answered, still combing my rake through the sand.

He didn't say anything else, just lifted the bucket and began packing it full with damp dirt. I'm not sure how much time had passed, but before I knew it, we had constructed a complex structure of ten towers, including a fortress to protect against the flying dragons. I was entirely sure that there were no dragons in my kingdom, but Jesse insisted and I only acquiesced after he assured me it was for the princess' safety.

"Jesse!" a woman's voice called. "Jesse!" It was loud and deep, so unlike the thin, high voice of my mother.

He stood, dusted off his hands and turned back toward the small crack in the fence that divided our properties. A short, heavyset woman rounded the corner and walked into my family's yard through the gate.

"Jesse Samuel!" the woman scolded. "What did I tell you about staying in *our* yard?"

"I'm sorry." He bowed his head, but sneaked a quick glance my way.

She placed a hand over her heart. "You scared me half to death!" Then, if only just realizing I was there, her gaze shifted to me. She had the same striking blue eyes as Jesse and the same warm smile, but her skin was milky white. Like snow.

She turned her head back to Jesse, her voice softening. "You made a friend?"

"I'm Riley Ann," I offered. "We built a sandcastle for the princess."

"Wow." She moved closer to the sandbox. "You two did a very good job."

Jesse returned her easy smile, immediately setting me at ease.

"Jesse." She ran her hand over his coarse hair, and my fingers itched to touch it, too. I imagined it would feel grainy, like the sand we'd just been playing in. "Supper is ready. You two can play after dinner if Riley's parents say it's okay."

Jesse's mom had already turned back toward their yard, but Jesse ran toward me and embraced me in a quick hug. "Bye."

"Bye, Jesse," I squeaked, as I watched him slip back through the fence.

That day Jesse Samuel Collins slipped into my yard, but he's been slipping his way into my *heart* ever since.

"Not to sound like a dick, Ry, but did you lose weight?" Jesse asks me, as we eat our lunches at one of the long cafeteria tables. A slice of cheese pizza for him and a low-fat strawberry yogurt for myself.

My cheeks flame as his eyes continue to drag over me. "Maybe." I shrug to downplay how hard I worked at losing those last ten pounds this summer. I was always a bit round. *Baby weight* my mother had called it. And she was right, for the most part. I had thinned as I grew but those last few pounds were a bitch to get off.

I'd gotten up at 7:00 a.m. every morning for the past three months to go for a two-mile run (I couldn't manage more than that) before the sun became too hot, and I counted calories daily. Sometimes I questioned why I cared so much—a huge part of me screamed: *just eat the damn cake*— but then I'd look at girls like Rachel, Heather, Tori, and Melissa, the *popular* girls, and my willpower would quadruple. Because one of my goals this year? Find a damn boyfriend. I didn't want to have to hold Jesse to our secret pact to take me to our senior prom because *I* couldn't find a date. #Pathetic

"Why?" His brows draw together in confusion, as though he couldn't quite possibly understand *why* a seventeen-year-old girl would be worried about her weight. Even though I knew he didn't understand my plight, I *loved* that he liked me just as I was, that I could be myself with him and not worry about what I looked like or what I ate.

"Why what?" Heather sets her lunch tray down across from where I sit. She plants herself right alongside Jesse. He may not be my boyfriend, but he's still *mine,* and the way she tries to stake her claim annoys me. Heather doesn't seem to get the message. Or maybe she just doesn't care.

Jesse's gaze lingers on mine and I implore him with my eyes not to share our conversation with her, Miss-I-Can-Eat-Whatever-I-Want-And-I'm-Still-A-Size-Zero.

Without missing a beat, he says, "*Why* does Prob and Stats suck ass?"

I smile, thankful he steered the attention away from me, even though I know math is his strongest subject.

"I have Miss Stocker, too." Heather touches her fingertips to his arm, and even beneath the fabric of his blue polo, I can see his muscles tense. "Maybe we can study together some time."

"Maybe." He casually brushes her hand away. "Ry, are we riding home together? I have practice after school—"

"Already?" Heather cuts in. "But basketball doesn't start for another...four months?"

Jesse gives me a *What the fuck?* look, but says, "Pre-season. Coach is riding us hard. Practice makes perfect and all that." Jesse's eyes cut to me again. "So, Ry, after school?"

Not giving me a second to answer, Heather continues. Again. "The Varsity Cheer Squad will be at all home basketball games this year. We've been practicing our new routine... I can't wait to show you my new moves."

He cuts his eyes to her, and I see it there, just for a moment, a look of uncontrolled lust as her words sink in, the innuendo clear. Then his voice takes on a harsher tone, a tone I recognize from the many times I've witnessed him giving a girl the brush-off. "Maybe some other time."

Heather, bless her little heart, still doesn't let her smile slip. "Okay."

"So, Ry." He turns back to me as he crumples his plate and gathers my trash. "See you around four?"

I try to convince myself that I'm not pathetic. I try to convince myself that there are *plenty* of teenagers who don't have their own car to drive. Getting a ride with Jesse is a far better option than sitting on a cramped school bus for nearly forty minutes, when the drive to school barely takes ten from my house. I may not be popular, but even I have my standards; taking the school bus is *so* middle school.

But as I amble into the gym nearly an hour after the last bell, I can't help but wonder if things are ever going to change for me. I was really convinced that if I lost those last few pounds, a whole new world of opportunity would open up for me. That I'd be more confident. More comfortable in my own skin. More like Heather "Hoe Bag" Plum.

Okay, okay, I know calling her a hoe bag isn't nice. We women should stick together and all that jazz... But I know for a fact that she blew PB & J (not all at once, *obviously*) within a week of them winning the state championship last year. And really, was it truly an insult if I simply thought it in my head?

I'm pondering all this as she sidles up to Jesse, her short, pleated cheerleading skirt barely covering her Spanx-clad ass. I snort at my assessment. Heather Plum doesn't need Spanx; her body is *flawless*.

"Penny for your thoughts." Tod Daniels' deep voice startles me, and I drop the three library books I'd been clutching at my chest in a death grip.

"Shit," I mumble, as I bend to pick up the books. He bends, too, and our heads nearly collide, but at the last second I amble back, nearly falling on my butt. *Real smooth, Riley.*

He picks up the book nearest his feet. "*Fahrenheit 51.*" He taps the cover. "Good book."

My eyes widen in surprise. "You've read it?"

"Yeah. Hancock's class. Last year."

I nod because I don't know what else to say. I had Mr. Toliver, so I can't even commiserate over the teacher. "That's good."

He smirks at me in a way that makes my stomach tingle. "Can you keep a secret, Riley?"

I nod, dumbfounded as to why he's even talking to me. We had PE together last year for an entire semester, and not once did he acknowledge me. I'm actually surprised he knows my name.

An easy smile stretches across his face, and he leans in close. So close that I think he may kiss me, which is *ridiculous*, but my heart starts beating loudly in my chest anyway. He angles his head slightly as his lips hover over my ear. "I *didn't* read it. But SparkNotes count for something, right?"

A nervous giggle escapes my mouth, but I'm spared from responding when Jesse approaches. He's drenched in sweat, so teenage *boy*, so familiar, that a huge, *genuine* smile lights up my face. "Tod." Jesse pounds Tod's fist. "What's up?" Then to me, "You ready, Ry?"

"Yep." I grab my bag off the bleachers and turn toward the exit. "Bye," I call over my shoulder to Tod.

Tod's voice washes over me. "Hey." Jesse and I both stop walking as Tod jogs toward us. "You forgot this." He hands me the book he picked up.

"Thanks," I mumble, as I add it to my stack.

But before I can turn away, Tod says, "Phillip's having a party this Saturday. You know, a little back-to-school celebration. There's going to be a keg and music and..." His voice trails off. "You're gonna be there, right?"

My mouth gapes open. *Holy shit,* is Tod Daniels inviting me to a party? "Umm..." I hesitate, stalling for time. I answer "Yes" just as Jesse says "No." Jesse and I exchange a look, his eyebrows raised in incredulity, my own eyes round and wide and so fucking nervous.

"Come on, Ry." Jesse loops his arm around my shoulders. "We gotta go."

"Okay." I let him lead me, but my eyes cast back over to where Tod still stands, smiling at us. *At me.* I can't resist calling over my shoulder, "See you Saturday."

CHAPTER 3: JESSE

Out of the corner of my eye, I watch Tod, there's only one fucking D, with Riley. I *still* can't believe she came to this party. With him. I'd known Riley since we were five and although she's all grown up —*fuck*, is she grown up—she's still the same. She's still the same girl who'd rather stay in and watch reruns of *Everybody Loves Raymond*. Still the same girl who claimed she'd never date a jock because she —and I quote—"hates all sports with a *passion*" is here with none other than high school swim star, Tod Daniels.

And can we just take a moment to acknowledge the fact that this dude probably shaves his legs more frequently than Riley?

I rest my case.

He's playing the game right, laughing at her jokes, touching her, but not too often so he doesn't tip his hand. Because you and I both know the end goal: he wants to get fucking laid. Ignoring the pit in my stomach, I make my way over to the keg but don't grab a beer, as usual. Because *my goal* tonight? Make sure Riley gets home safely.

Gets home safely. With. Me.

"Oh, My God! You still have it." Her voice is loud as she continues, "I can't believe..." She walks toward my dresser.

My eyes drift to the baseball-size beach rock she gave me nearly ten years ago. "The brain." She whispers the nickname for the buff-colored, oblong stone with tiny holes. "Did you know—"

I cut her off, knowing exactly what she is going to say, because she'd told me at least a dozen times that summer. "Yes, Ry, I know. The little holes are created by sea creatures. Sea creatures, like burrowing clams." My grin is somewhat sarcastic as I meet her eyes. "And yes, I find it rather fascinating."

"Hey." Her voice squeaks. "Are you mocking me?"

"Who, me?" I joke, but my voice turns serious when she stumbles—loudly—over the Nike duffle bag resting at the foot of my bed. "Quiet." I close the door behind us. "My mom's sleeping, and unless you want her to see you high off your ass, I'd keep your voice down."

"I'm not high." She stumbles again, her body lurches forward and I think she might fall, but she rights herself at the last minute.

I raise my eyebrows. "How many of those brownies did you have?"

She holds up three fingers, but says, "Two."

I shake my head. "Fucking Tod," I grumble as I flip the switch on my lamp. "He knew those brownies were laced with weed."

She doesn't respond, but begins to undress, slipping the tight sweater over her head.

My anxiety level ricochets about ten notches. She cannot undress in front of me. I won't be able to handle it. I *need* to stop her before, before...that. "What are you doing?" I cast my eyes away, willing myself not to look at her firm, round tits wrapped in perfect pink lace.

She shrugs. "It's not like you haven't seen me naked before."

"We were six!" I practically shout, but she just shrugs.

"Besides, it's like I'm wearing a bathing suit."

This is not the same. This is everything I want from you. This is everything I've dreamt about.

"Here." I shove a t-shirt at her with more force than I meant. "Put this on."

I watch open-mouthed as she slips it over her head and shimmies off her jeans. *Fuck, she looks good in my shirt.*

She tucks her arms inside the material, and seconds later, the soft pink bra lands on the floor next to her jeans. *Fuck me.*

I turn away from her, my dick already rock-hard. Glancing down, I check to see if my boner is visible through my joggers, already knowing the answer. *Shit.*

Her voice drifts over my shoulder, and her words hit me one at a time. Four jolts, heavy hits to my already flailing self-control. Boom. Boom. Boom. Boom.

I swear, *nothing* could've prepared me for her question. "Do you watch porn?"

"Wh-what?" I stutter, nearly dropping my cell phone to the floor. I catch it and connect it to the charger.

She shrugs. "Do you?"

"Do you?" I counter, stalling for time, because I can't tell her the truth: *Yes, a shit ton.*

"Occasionally." She peels back the covers. "I don't really see the appeal though."

This conversation is a minefield. Riley and I never talk about sex. At least, not like this. *She's high*, I remind myself, but still, I press on. My voice is deeper, more sensual. "Why's that?"

"It's all so... I don't know. *Fuck my pussy. Oh, baby. Yeah, that's so good. You're so big.* It's all so fake."

Her words wash over me. I'm still stuck on *pussy* and *fuck.* I want to rewind time and hear her say those words again and again.

"Anyway." She curls into bed. *My bed.* "Guys like it." Her voice sounds forlorn.

I walk to my closet, grab my sleeping bag buried on the back shelf, and try to ignore the solid inch of dust lining the black fabric. I unroll it alongside the mattress. Clearing my throat, I finally say, "It's fantasy. Guys know it's not like that in real life."

Her voice is whisper quiet. "Not all guys."

My mind reels. I'm about to ask her what she means, but then she asks, "Do you have any fantasies?"

Holy shit. I suck in a breath, try to keep my voice casual as I respond, "Yeah, I guess." *All of them involve you.*

"Like what?" she questions again, and I swear, I'm *this close* to cracking, ready to tell her every dirty thought that entertains my mind as I sit in boring class after boring class every damn day.

She rambles on. Riley is chatty on a good day, but tonight she's a downright motor mouth. "I thought he might have been different." She sighs and rolls onto her side.

"Who?" I question, my brain volleying back and forth like a ping-pong ball as we make our way through this fucked-up conversation.

"Tod."

Anger cools the heat of my desire. "Did he try something, Ry?" I sit up and look at her through the light filtering in between the slats of the blinds. "I swear to God if he—"

Her sigh is loud in the quiet room. "He was really wasted, but... he asked me to blow him tonight." The words are an ice-cold bucket of water dousing my heated skin. *That son-of-a-bitch, piece of shit, motherfuck—*

She interrupts my internal tirade. "I'm not that naïve. I know a lot of girls do it. What makes me so special? So different? It's just... I freaked a little when he asked, ya know? I don't even *know* him."

What. The. Fuck. I don't trust myself to speak, too afraid that I'll scare her with the words, the anger flowing through my veins. Tod. Is. Fucking. Dead.

"Jesus." My hands clench into tight fists, as I imagine her beautiful soft lips wrapped around... I choke. "Ry, you don't have to do anything you're not ready for. You know that, right?" Because the truth is: she *is* different. She is special. She is not like any of the other girls. "You are special. *So special.*"

"Thanks," she says softly. "And I know I don't have to..." She's quick to agree, but then continues, "I wouldn't... at least, not yet."

"Ry." My voice slices through the silence. I can't hear any more of this. Not right now. "Please tell me you're not actually consider-ing"—my voice chokes on the words—"*being* with him."

She pffts the air with her hand. "He said he always wanted to be with a redhead ever since he saw this one clip on..." Her voice turns pensive. "I don't even think he'll remember, but still. Fucking douchebag." Her eyes find mine. "Thanks for having my back."

I hold her gaze. "I will *always* have your back, Ry. You're my heart."

Her lips tip into a smile, repeating her line. "Forever?"

"Forever and for always," I agree.

She quiets then, and if I didn't know any different, I'd think she was asleep, but I do know different. I know everything about her, and she still hasn't snuggled onto her right side and tucked the covers under her chin—the way she always does when she sleeps.

Despite my gut telling me not to, I ask the question anyway. "Do you like Tod? Do you want to, *you know?*"

Her answer is immediate, a rush of words that spill forth from her mouth without any thought, in typical Riley fashion. "Yes. I mean, no. God, I don't know." She buries her face in the pillow. "I do have hormones, Jesse. I *am* a teenager. I want to have at least kissed a guy before heading off to college."

"You've never kissed someone?" My nose scrunches as I repeat her words. As her best friend, my duties include listening to her talk about her favorite TV shows, her crushes, her feelings, but I draw the line at sex. Listening to her talk about hooking up with other guys will *kill* me. "You never said—"

She cuts me off. "Of course, I didn't say anything. I didn't want you to know how pathetic I am."

"You're not pathetic," I scold, because I hate when she puts herself down.

"Says the guy who hooks up with anything that walks."

"That's not true," I interject and leave out the most crucial part: *I hook up with other girls in an attempt to get over you.*

Riley gives me a look that says, "Please." She's quiet for a minute then, pulls her bottom lip between her teeth the way she always does when she's thinking. "What if...?" Her voice fades out but then gains strength again. "What if...we kissed?"

"What?" I whisper hiss. "Are you still high? Are you sure you only had two of those brownies?

"Shut up." She throws a pillow at me and clips the right side of my jaw. "Forget I asked."

I stuff the pillow behind my head. My voice is cautious and a whole hell of a lot curious when I ask, "Why do you want to kiss me?"

She shrugs. *Not the best response.* But then she adds, "I'm comfortable with you."

I nod my head. "Obviously."

"I was thinking it wouldn't be awkward with you. And then maybe when I get my first real kiss, I won't be so damn nervous." Her palms twist in the navy sheet, and I follow the movement. *Are we really having this conversation?*

My racing thoughts are a mix of elation—she wants to kiss me —and sadness because it's not for real, dude. She wants to use you as a guinea pig. "Ry, I don't know. Won't that be a little weird?"

She narrows her eyes at me. "I'm gonna try to not be offended right now."

I keep my face an expressionless mask to disguise the fact that my brain is re-enacting one of my favorite fantasies despite my adamant order to not even *think* it for one second: Riley's full, soft lips on my mouth, on my skin, on my *cock,* wearing nothing more than my basketball jersey.

"And no," her voice draws me back to the present moment. "I don't think it would be weird. Just two friends sharing a friendly, non-romantic, non-sexual kiss. I mean, come on, Jesse, you're like a brother to me."

Brother. I absolutely *despise* when she says shit like that. It makes me feel like my attraction to her is gross and wrong and like I'm a pervert for even *thinking* of her as anything more than just a friend.

When I still haven't said anything, she huffs. "But clearly I can see the idea repulses you. I guess I'm not up to *your* standards. Just forget the whole idea."

She flips on her side and I catch a glimpse of her matching pink panties from where my t-shirt has ridden up, before she tucks the blanket back around her.

"Ry." I clear my throat and say louder, "Riley."

"What?" Her voice is short and clipped, and she makes no effort to turn to face me.

"Ask me tomorrow." I stand up and circle around to the opposite side of the bed so I can look into her eyes. My eyes burn with so much heat it's a wonder she doesn't ignite. "Ask me tomorrow when you're sober." Her eyes hold mine and widen as my own pierce hers with the fire and intensity that I usually keep hidden away. "If you still want this in the morning, I'm game."

She blinks, breaking the connection and shakes her head. "Good night, Jesse."

"Night, Ry."

Keep reading...CLICK HERE

ABOUT THE AUTHOR

CJ Martín spends the majority of her days daydreaming, procrastinating, and longing for the day when she can quit her day job and write full time.

She loves all things romance and is a sucker for a happily-ever-after. She also loves traveling, yoga, avocados, and music. She has about a million and one playlists on Spotify that are as random as her personality.

She lives in Pennsylvania with her sweet husband (Literally! He owns an ice cream shoppe!) and twelve year-old Jug puppy, Albert, who is more spoiled than most humans.

One day she will move to Paris and eat all of the wine and cheese, but until then...she dreams.

Stay connected with CJ Martín! For the latest updates, teasers, and newest releases, join her Reader's Group at:

Click Here

Sign up for *Martin's Musings,* her free newsletter, to receive exclusive news, excerpts, and giveaways! Please click the following link:

Click Here

ACKNOWLEDGMENTS

BIG love to all my readers—without you *none* of this would be possible. Thank you for allowing me to share my stories and be part of your world for a short while. It's truly an honor <3

To the many people who've helped sculpt and polish this story —thank you. To my incredibly patient and caring editor, Bree Scalf, your unwavering confidence and advice along this journey means so very much to me. Many thanks to my proofers, Elaine York and R.c. Craig who catch all my typos (even when I swear there aren't any!)

To my beta readers—Dee Montoya, Nickiann Holt, Rachel Reads, Kennedy Mitchell, Lilliana Anderson, and Robin Hill. You're honest input and feedback helped mold this story and ensured Charli and Oliver's story rang true to their characters. Thank you, thank you, *thank you*.

This section is always the toughest for me to write because there are so many people who are owed thanks. Just know that I feel truly blessed to have the opportunity to share my writing with the world and send all my love and gratitude to each and every person who has guided me, mentored me, taken a chance on me as a new author, shared and posted about my books, left a review, or sent me an email—I appreciate it more than you will ever know. Your kind words and passion for reading push me to keep writing.

Until we meet again...

XOXO CJ